The Chrysalis

A Novel

By Bindu Adai

For Mom,
For always believing

&

For Ava,
For you will always be my Chrysalis

Acknowledgements

This novel would have remained an unrealized dream if it weren't for the support, faith, and encouragement of amazing family and friends who rallied around me throughout the years. Thank you for I am truly blessed to have had each of you in my life.

Thank you to God for making a way.

Thank you to my mother, Rahelamma Adai, who bought me my first Dr. Seuss books, followed by countless other children's books, as a first-grader that spurred me into a passionate love affair with books. Your unconditional love and unwavering belief in me since childhood has kept me believing that with God, anything and everything is possible.

Thank you to Shelby Mathew. You have always inspired me to dream big and aim high. I truly appreciate your business-minded perspective and advice, along with your never-ending patience to see this novel come to fruition.

Thank you to one of my best and dearest friends, Suja Jacob. Just from one short story, you believed in me and spurred me on with your endless words of encouragement and belief in my writing. You believed in this novel when it was nothing more than an idea floating in my head. Thank you for those countless encouraging words and hours you spent listening to me, cheering me on to the finish line.

Thank you to all the family and friends with whom I've shared my passion of writing and who have encouraged me with their words over the years: Rebekah Adai, Anita Samuel, Mariamma Mathew, Belen Torres, Noemi Dominguez, Sasha Katz, Jenette Mathai, Christy Varghese, Janney Jacob-Cheeran, Krystal Williams, Rakesh Ravikumar, Chris Mathew, Supriya Joshi, and Jocelyn Samuel.

Chapter 1
SATI

*E*VERYONE'S EYES WERE *fixated on me. I felt the intensity of each stare… the disapproving looks… the shaking of my relatives' heads in dismay as Armaan and I walked around the small fire, symbolically solidifying our union as husband and wife in the traditional Hindu wedding fire walk. Though I could not see their faces with my head down in the façade of humility, I felt their stares through my choli, the long matching scarf that covered my head like a veil. Their intense stares burned through the thin, gauzy material as they silently accused me. I could feign humility no longer and raised my head slightly to observe those who watched us. My cousin, Beena, stood staring at us mouth agape, revealing her braces, which momentarily glistened in the light. Her mother, my Aunt Lizzy, also stared at me, her face contorting from anger to disdain, all while retaining that same severe consternation she used when she was superintendent of the Raj Krishna School—a face that undoubtedly had made many a 12-year-old boy wet himself. Her eyes bulged and her lips pursed, but with her head shaking from left to right continuously, she reminded me of a bobble head, looking more like a caricature of herself than the headmistress of an elite boarding school. For once I didn't allow her to intimidate me, and instead, I raised my chin slightly higher in defiance. For once, I didn't care. I felt happy. I felt free… free to pursue my own happiness… my own dreams.*

As we completed our third rotation around the fire, tiny sparks flew out of the flames, grazing the edges of my skirt and choli. The fire then intensified, and I welcomed its warmth, for after observing the icy disapproval from our families, the

1

room felt suddenly chilly to me. And that was when I heard it. Soft and muffled, at first, the sobs intensified like the volume of a radio being ever so slowly turned up. I glanced around, unable to locate the source. I attempted to ignore the sobs, but it was impossible. The sobs provided a cacophonous backdrop to the chanting of the Hindu priest blessing our union.

After completing our fourth and final rotation around the fire, we were directed to sit on plush, red, ornately gilded chairs that stood in the middle of the mandap, a large tent-like structure that also functioned like a make-shift stage. Beautiful blooming marigolds, carnations, and roses decorated the thin metal poles holding up the tented canopy at all four corners. When I sat in the chair again, I was accompanied by my female cousins and aunts. I kept my eyes averted, doing my best to ignore their dour, frowning faces. The happiest day of my life was beginning to feel more like a funeral. But when I glanced at Armaan, at his strong jawline, the soft curve of his lips, and the sensuous curve of his eyes, my resolve strengthened. Yes, this was the man I wanted to be with—not some stranger I hardly knew, not someone I would have to force chemistry with, and not someone I would have to somehow grow to love. Everything I ever wanted and dreamed about in a man was sitting right next to me.

"Sarai!" The voice, shrill but powerful, resonated through my thoughts… my daydreams… the voice of my childhood, forever reminding me of my obligations to family and to our traditions. "Sarai! Sit up straight… keep your eyes low. Do you not remember anything your parents taught you?"

I responded obediently, well aware that everyone's eyes were still on me, "Yes, Aunt Lizzy." I then felt her cold, clammy hands on my back as she pushed my spine into a rod-straight posture. "Sit up properly, I said!" she whispered through her clenched teeth while her face still retained a broad smile for show. As if sensing the tension, the priest momentarily paused, his eyes flitting from her face to mine, but then he sighed heavily and continued the litany.

I quickly peeked at Armaan and saw the sadness in his eyes as he stared straight ahead. I followed his line of vision. His eyes were fixed on his mother who was crying softly against his father's shoulder. His father's eyes were red as if he had shed his tears earlier, but his countenance remained stoic as he watched us. I wanted to reach out and hold Armaan's hand, but I knew that somehow that slight physical gesture would create even more scandal. I could hear the gossip among the aunties now, "First she marries someone outside our community… and then she can't keep her hands off of him… and in public at that! Has she no shame?" So I did nothing and kept my hands in my lap.

I then caught a glimpse of a familiar figure from the corner of my eye and instinctively sought it out. It was my mother. Dressed in a beautiful red brocade silk sari with her hair pulled back in a traditional bun, she managed to be statuesque and regal despite her petite stature. Behind her stood my father, eyebrows furled together, scowling at me. Unlike everyone else, my mother did not look at me accusingly. But what I saw in her eyes hurt far worse because it was something I had never seen before—disappointment.

I breathed in deeply and felt a lump develop in the back of my throat as I fought back tears. I began to feel that familiar tightness in my chest. The guilt had returned. The overwhelming feeling of failing my entire family was beginning to cloud the shining burst of victory I had felt just seconds earlier. I knew the choice I had made had reverberations all the way back to India where the rest of our extended family—cousins, aunts, uncles, even neighbors—had likely all gathered in the main family home, mourning my wedding as if they were at a funeral.

Yellow, orange, and amber… the flames danced in front of me, hypnotizing me with their primal movement. I stared into the fire's depths, and one flame seemed to twist into a crooked finger, inviting me to end the pain and stop those unrelenting, accusing stares. Perhaps it was beckoning me in the same way it had beckoned widows to follow the tradition of sati, an ancient Hindu tradition that obligated women to throw themselves onto the same funeral fire that had consumed their husbands' dead bodies. For then more than today, women were often seen as nothing more than an extension of their husbands, and the very absence of a husband, whether by death or divorce, only managed to extinguish a woman into non-existence.

Without my initially realizing it, our wedding guests were edging closer and closer, encircling the mandap where I sat with Armaan. Beena suddenly screeched as she frantically pointed at my skirt. I looked down at myself, realizing in horror that the edge of my choli had ignited. Like a snake, the flame seemed to slither closer and closer to me. I turned in desperation to Armaan, but he was no longer sitting next to me. I was alone. The mob of people surrounded me, and I stared in shock and did nothing as the flames began to engulf me. Perhaps just like those widows who felt alone, abandoned, and judged, I surrendered myself to it—for like them, in the end, my wedding fire had indeed turned into my funeral pyre.

I woke up gasping, my arms flailing, as I tried to extinguish the flames. Instead, I woke to find that my rosebud print bed sheets had tangled tightly all around me, mummifying me in my own bed. My eyes darted from one corner of the dark room to the other. The nightlight near my dresser provided little illumination, but I was still able to focus on the familiar pictures of my family and friends lining my dresser. Yes, this was my bedroom, I reassured myself as I slowly released a pent-up breath. It had only been a bad dream. I momentarily wondered if I was having another dream, but as I began to disentangle myself from my bed sheets, reality began to seep in and my breathing became more regular, assuring me that I was indeed awake.

I glanced at the clock. Pixilated red dots formed the numbers **3:38**. It was still too early to get up. So I just lay there, arms folded behind my head, as I stared at the ceiling tiles in my room and attempted to drift back to sleep. But as always, my mind evoked an image of Armaan, and I began to reflect on my dream. The initial memory of the wedding made me smile, but as I remembered the expressions on our families' faces, my smile waned. In Indian families, you are not only accountable to your parents, but to all your uncles and aunts who often think that they have the same rights as your parents, including the right to tell you what to study in school, what to wear, and even whom to marry.

As the eldest sibling of my father, Lizzy Auntie thought of herself as the matriarch of the family here in the US. She took it upon herself to repeatedly remind me that I was a disappointment to the family. I was the only one who had not managed to raise our family name into even more prominence in our Indian community. From surgeons to lawyers to engineers, each of my cousins, most of them first generation Indian Americans, had managed to secure successful, lucrative careers in respectable fields. I, on the other hand, was only a teacher. It didn't matter that I had been voted Teacher of the Year by my school district twice in a row or that my remedial fourth grade students had improved to 8th grade reading levels within a year. None of that mattered because in the end, I was making far less than a six figure income.

When I started dating Armaan—someone outside of my Indian Malayalee community and worse, someone outside my Christian religion—my failure was complete. To most Westerners, it would seem that our match could not be more perfect. He was Indian, I was Indian. We both came from traditionally conservative, family-oriented backgrounds. We were both educated. But lift the veil of our nationality, and one would see that the label of "Indian" was only a veneer. Take a closer look, and one would quickly realize a chasm of differences separated us. Religion, caste, language, culture, and family had created a divide that not even love could completely abridge. We were both from different states in India, which meant we also spoke different languages, practiced different customs, ate different foods, and followed different religions. In India as well as in America, Armaan's family was from the upper echelon of wealth while my parents were the embodiment of middle-class America. In America, differences are celebrated. In India, they are what divide us and keep us separated, especially in marriage. In America, opposites attract. In India, often only "like marries like." In the end, I always knew there would never be a way to make all of us happy. Like my dream, someone's eyes would be red-rimmed with tears, whether it was mine or my parents'.

The ceiling tiles somehow finally faded in the midst of those turbulent thoughts, until I was again jerked awake to the sound of my blaring alarm clock as it flashed the numbers **7:30**. I had only 3 hours to get ready for the wedding.

Chapter 2

IKE MOST BRIDES on their wedding day, I had been very selective in the outfit I was going to wear for the wedding. When I made my grand entrance, I wanted to make a statement. Without a doubt, I wanted to leave the groom with his mouth gaping, and I wanted him to be the envy of his childhood and college friends. I wanted him to know my worth. For men, I learned, are like that, often prizing only what other men covet.

Rather than wearing the traditional ornate, heavily beaded bridal *lengha* in the red and gold colors often preferred by many Indian brides, I eschewed tradition and opted to wear the long fitted blouse with the ankle-length skirt in the traditional American bridal white, which was also more in keeping with my Malayalee Christian heritage.

I had actually selected my outfit in India almost six years ago, long before I was even seriously considering marriage. Six years ago, they had taken me to India in hopes of getting me married before it was "too late" since I had been unable to secure a husband on my own. My father reminded me incessantly of the importance of marriage and having a family life. "In India, there is no room for unmarried women," he would tell me. "They are pitied and looked down upon. Don't believe the Americans... they think it is okay for women to be alone... no, it is not good," he would say gravely. With his thick accent, and his narrow-mindedness, one would never know that he had been living in the US for over 20 years. Somehow despite all the exposure to other ideas and customs, he was as rooted in Indian culture and its opinions as the day he arrived at JFK airport with his two suitcases and family in tow.

When I claimed that I still had time to marry, my father retorted that if I waited too long, my only options would be the recycled ones, recycled meaning *divorced*. Yep, that's my dad—you gotta love him— blunt and politically incorrect as they come. In his eyes, marriage, no matter how miserable for either partner, was forever, and he looked down upon anyone who was divorced.

So after a year of endless nagging, I finally acquiesced. Maybe sur- render was a more appropriate word. Nevertheless, I went to India because according to my father, if I had waited even a few months longer, I would no longer be considered a desirable candidate for marriage. I was twenty-two years old.

On the way back from visiting my parents' hometown villages in Kerala in southern India, we stopped in Bombay and visited my mother's sister, Aunt Leena, and her husband, Uncle Sandosh. We stayed there a few days to do some sight-seeing and, of course, some shopping. Bombay is home to "Bollywood," the Hindi film industry and is arguably India's fashion capital. One of my requirements before I agreed to the whole trip was the chance to shop in Bombay. While you can also shop for typical American clothes, I was more interested in buying traditional Indian clothing. I find it ironic that what we so pointedly fight against in childhood, we so willingly embrace as adults. As a child, I grew up in a predominantly Caucasian school that didn't allow me to embrace my culture. My college years, on the other hand, were nothing but an immersion of Indian culture. Music, movies, and especially the traditional Indian clothing, I began a love affair with all things Indian.

During that visit to India, which I later dubbed as "Husband Search #1," we visited a number of the local markets, which seemed to have an infinite number of small crowded stores set up like an outdoor mall. Walking through the marketplace was like walking through Marrakesh. Vendors housed carts of their wares, and while the "old" still seemed dominant, there was no mistaking a schizophrenic time warp. Ripped jeans lay only a booth away from traditional saris, which lay a few booths away from a 80s Madonna Truth-or-Dare leather ensemble.

Shopping for a sari, even in India, was not a simple task. I was initially overwhelmed by the beauty of the infinite number of jewel-like hues of the gorgeous silk and chiffon saris that vendors splayed before me. To the untrained eye, the majority of traditional Indian outfits could be classified as pretty or beautiful, but the search for a beautiful Indian outfit is not the primary criteria when shopping. The key was to find something unique, some color, or design that stood out. To me, everything looked like the typical Indian outfit I had seen a million times at each of the Indian weddings and festivals I had attended. The tops were all short sleeves and came just to the waist or sometimes to the hips and were typically decorated with fancy, gaudy gold embroidery. The skirts were usually full length, A-line styled, and the design often mimicked the embroidery or beadwork of the blouse. I was looking for something unique and exquisite to wear at the next wedding and Indian function—something that would make women stop and ask me where I had bought the sari—something befitting a Bollywood heroine.

Finally after two days of endless, fruitless shopping and worse, endless walking and sweating in the Bombay humidity, I convinced Aunt Leena to take me to an exquisite design house where I knew I would not only find one-of-a-kind Indian outfits but where I could actually experience the modern miracle of central air conditioning.

She took me to Casa de Kasoor. Kasoor was a British-raised Indian whose designs were often seen in Bollywood movies and on actresses themselves. When I opened the heavy, wood carved door and stepped onto the marble floor, I felt as if I had walked into the home of a celebrity. While I gazed in awe at the waterfall fountain that greeted us in the atrium, I basked in the cool breeze of the air conditioning. Beads of sweat evaporated from my temples and the back of my neck.

As the door closed behind us, I discovered another unique trait of Kasoor's. Rather than standard-size mannequins, his mannequins resembled life-size replicas of famous Indian actresses and models that could rival the wax figures at Madame Troussard's Wax Museum. At the entrance itself, we were immediately greeted by a mannequin who bore a striking resemblance to Preity Zinta. Her head was bowed slightly and the palms of her hands clasped together in Namaste, the traditional Indian greeting to guests. She was dressed impeccably in a chiffon jade green sari. "That is, of course, one Kasoor's original designs," said the sales lady, who seemed to pop out of nowhere. "You might have noticed that that Preity wore this in her latest movie," she said smoothing out one of the pleats of the skirt.

My eyes drifted to the other mannequins who wore equally stunning saris. As we walked through the never-ending showrooms, I suddenly felt self-conscious of my simple cotton *salwar kameez*, a long tunic paired with drawstring pajama-like pants.

"The first floor consists of Indian party wear," said the sales woman, "and the floor is divided into three areas: *lenghas, chaniya cholis, saris*, and *salwar kameezes*. The second floor is completely bridal *lenghas* and *saris*. The third floor is Western-style clothing, and the fourth floor is men's wear." She gazed at me quietly, hands clasped together as she waited patiently for me to let her know which floor I was most interested in exploring.

My eyes followed the wrought iron staircase to the second floor where there stood a likeness of Aishwarya Rai. With thousands of web sites devoted solely to worshipping her beauty, she could easily be referred to as India's most popular and beloved actress as well as mine. But this time, my eyes were not on her, but rather the white and silver-beaded *lengha* she was outfitted in. The material was angelic—the softest, dreamiest white, and the beading and embroidery were a delicate intricate silver. It was glamorous, elegant, and magical. Though I was looking for something to wear to someone else's wedding, I knew I had just unintentionally found what I wanted to someday wear to my own wedding. I immediately pointed to it, and the sales lady, smiled, shaking her head slowly from side to side in approval. "We just got that in. I knew it would not last for more than one day in this store."

When I tried the outfit on, I was delighted to find that delicate sheer straps fit over the curve of my shoulder, creating cap-sleeves that seemed to fit me perfectly. Tiny silver crystals outlined the edges of the sleeve and the back of my blouse. The skirt was a little on the long side, but it was nothing a good pair of three-inch heels couldn't take care of. A sheer matching jewel encrusted short sleeve jacket fit like an overlay over the blouse, providing just the right amount of coverage for modesty's sake while still revealing the beauty and intricacies of the blouse beneath. It was so gorgeous I could do nothing but stare at it transfixed as if I had just met my soul mate.

"We just got it in," said the sales lady. "It's one of Kasoor's latest creations."

As I admired myself in the mirror, I couldn't help but splay out the skirt and take a few turns in front of the mirror. I felt like a jewel, sparkling with every movement, as the light bounced off the beading and embroidery. I was suddenly reminded of an Indian princess. I had no plans to marry in the near future and no potential suitors in the horizon, but I knew this was the dress. Ten years of dreaming of walking down the aisle in a ball gown-style Vera Wang dress with a cathedral train was instantaneously replaced with a Kasoor-designed Indian-style white and silver *lengha* with a matching *choli* to cover my head.

✧　✧　✧

THAT WAS SIX long years ago. It had hung at the back of my closet in a white linen garment bag ever since, and I was finally getting my chance to wear it. As I put it on, I realized that like a pair of strappy dress heels, just because it was beautiful to look at, it didn't mean it was the most comfortable thing to wear. The blouse and the skirt, which were once a perfect fit on my twenty-two year old body, were a little snugger on my twenty-eight year old frame. I struggled with the zipper of the skirt, sucked in my breath, and pulled the zipper tightly, praying the seams would stay intact for the whole day. The beads were already making tiny indentations in my skin around my waist.

But it would be worth it, I told myself. I stared at myself in the mirror and soon forgot about the discomfort. Instead, I focused on the jaw-dropping beauty of what I was wearing. I took another turn in front of the mirror and couldn't help but stare at myself in admiration. I may have misjudged its comfort, but it still made me look and feel unbelievably beautiful. I knew then that it didn't matter how many other people noticed me. I only wanted his eyes on me—just like when we first met.

Far better than any of the fairy tales I had read as a child or any of the romance novels I had read as a teenager, the first time I met Armaan was one of those once in a lifetime experiences. Just like the dress made me feel like a princess, so did Armaan. I smiled as I indulged myself once again and traveled back five and a half years to relive the magic of our first encounter.

Chapter 3

September 1996

I GLANCED AT my watch. It was exactly seven o'clock. "Where are they?" I asked in frustration as I scanned the hall for Mani and Rakesh. The talent show was about to start, and there was no sign of either of them. I glanced longingly across the side railings at our seats—front and center. They were the perfect seats with the perfect view. They were still vacant, but once the show started, they would be up for grabs by anyone. We were gathered in Jones Hall, celebrating the 50th anniversary of India's independence with a fashion and talent show. Jones Hall had been converted to a large, makeshift auditorium. The event was sponsored by our university's United Indian Association to broaden Indian culture awareness. I had been an active member throughout my college years and even served as the vice president during my junior year and as president during my senior year. As an alumnus, I had earned the right to sit back and enjoy the show while the underclassmen did all the work.

"You know the guys," said Reena, looking a lot less perturbed than I did. "They are always late. I think even when they were both born, they were running on Indian Standard Time." We were supposed to have met Mani and Rakesh over thirty minutes ago, before the show began, but they were their usual unfashionably late selves. We waited near the front entrance for ten minutes and then walked to the side rails, glancing at the sea of seats below us. The lights flickered momentarily and then dimmed, indicating that the show was about to begin.

"Nope, no sign of either of them. Typical!" said Reena, beginning to feel as perturbed as I was. As we stood near the doors, right before the last row of seats, the MCs began with their opening welcome. We scoured the entire hall for them from our vantage point but nothing. I glanced once again at our reserved, front-row seats, which we would soon lose. I turned back to the main entrance for one last glance for them, but then I saw *him*, standing alongside the entrance towards the side wall.

All my life I'd been searching… I could never explain what for… but searching, searching for that sense of completeness, that sense of purpose, that sense of fulfillment. I didn't get it from school, from work, my personal achievements, and as ashamed as I am to admit it, not even from God.

And it was at that moment, I suddenly knew the answers to questions that I didn't even know I had. In those few seconds of first seeing him, I knew what every person knows when they helplessly, mindlessly fall in love—that despite the fact that not one word had been uttered and that they didn't even know who the other person was… yet they felt a stirring within, almost a knowing, that somehow they had found the one.

As I stared at him, elation, excitement, and lust began exploding within me like a fireworks display, rising within and bursting with a range of exquisite emotion that I had never known existed, let alone experienced, leaving me breathless, nervous, and excited.

Unlike the typical Indian guys in my Malayalee community, he was taller, at least six foot three. He was broad shouldered, wearing a simple open-collared white shirt with a fitted gray jacket, and he seemed to command attention with his confident stance. His hair was the darkest black and his skin, though slightly tanned, was very light by Indian standards. He had a straight nose and defined jawline, and with his dark, roguish good looks, a lesser connoisseur could have easily mistaken him for Italian. But it was his eyes that were the dead giveaway. Curved in the corner and defined by the darkest lashes, I had seen his eyes many times before in the painting of Mughal princes as they lounged in the court with their prince consort. His lips were full and sensuous. As I stared at him, his smile curved into the most knee-weakening smile I had ever seen. He was heart-stopping, breath-stealing beautiful, and I knew on some level, I was undoubtedly responding to just that. But somehow even as he stood there casually, with one hand in his pocket while the other one rested lightly on the lapel of his jacket, he emanated a presence, an aura that drew me in, and I was as helpless and as hapless as a moth to a flame.

As unbelievable and as unrealistic as these feelings may sound to someone else, they were probably more unbelievable to me, the very one who was feeling this chaotic bliss. I was not the type of girl to react to someone so superficially—at least not before. Though I was surprised at this immediate, albeit over-reaction, I did know myself well enough to know that I had never responded to anyone like this before. And somehow I knew I never would again.

As I stared at my newly discovered beloved, my imagination took over, and I began starring in my own Bollywood film. The music began, and like the popular dance numbers for which Indian films are known for, the talent show guests in choreographed unison parted like the Red Sea, creating a distinct path to him. Even the main talent show only served as a backdrop to us. And then on cue, my beloved suddenly turned to me, his arms outstretched as he began singing of his immediate, intense, and never-ending love for me. *"Dil churale... oh chaand se chehre wale..."*

Unlike the Bollywood stars who typically just mime a song, my beloved could actually sing! But in keeping with the Indian film tradition, I acted the shy, innocent ingénue as he boldly walked towards me and pulled me into his embrace. I, after a nervous giggle, side-stepped his advance, just narrowly missing his kiss. Everything was perfect in my Bollywood fantasy until I was rudely interrupted by my best friend, Reena.

"Sarai... *Sarai... Earth to Sarai*!" She called, and then she flashed her hand like a windshield wiper in front of my gaze. Even then, I could not focus on anything but the beautiful specimen who stood just a few feet in front of me. When I continued to ignore her, she followed the trajectory of my stare. I knew the moment her eyes settled on him.

First, she said nothing, but seconds later, she stammered out an "Ohhhh—my—G-O-D... Who *is* that? He has got to be the hottest guy I've ever seen," she whispered loudly to me. I smiled, for Reena was as cynical as they come, especially since just six months before, she herself had gone through a breakup after an intense two-year relationship. This was the first time since the breakup she had looked at another male without rolling her eyes or making a disparaging remark.

For a few seconds, neither of us said anything as we just unabashedly drooled. And at that moment, his eyes moved from the stage and directly to me, as if he knew who I was. Our eyes locked. My knees immediately weakened, and I had to lean back and grab the railing behind me so I wouldn't fall. Like a deer caught in headlights, I was unable to turn away. It was as if he could see right through me, deep into my soul. I, too, became aware of something deeper and even more beautiful inside of him that seemed to emanate through his intense, dark-eyed stare. And then suddenly there it was. The faintest scent of familiarity. Had we somehow met before? A thousand past images, thoughts, crushes, and fantasies all flashed before my eyes, colliding, merging, and culminating into the composite of this person who stood before me. He seemed to be everything I had dreamed but never thought possible. It was as if in that very moment, God breathed my fantasy into life. My body reverberated with recognition. No wonder he had seemed so familiar... I had been dreaming of him my whole life.

The seconds rolled by. We were unable to tear our eyes off each other until a sudden screeching pitch of the sound system startled us both out of our trance. I winced and covered my ears as the MCs apologized for the technical difficulties. The moment was gone, and suddenly I felt like another zealous fan drooling over a celebrity crush. I turned away, embarrassed that he had caught me staring so openly. I looked back at the stage or at least pretended to as I grappled with those seconds of searing intensity. Had he stared back at me or was I still wrapped up in my initial Bollywood fantasy? I, of course, made the mistake of turning around too soon, only to find him still staring straight at me. His lips turned slightly upwards as if he were amused by something. Beet-red, I jerked back around, gripping the railing even tighter. My heart raced. Breathe, breathe. *Get a grip, Sarai*, I told myself. He's a guy... a very good looking guy, yes... but in the end, just a guy. When did I ever get so worked up over a pretty face?

But like a magnet, I was drawn back to him once again. I turned my head ever so slowly... and there he was, looking as gorgeous as he did five seconds ago. His eyes were still focused on mine as if I had never taken my eyes of his. But this time I did something that surprised even me. I smiled at him. And he did something that surprised me more. He smiled back at me.

Reena had been watching this entire exchange without saying a word. To my horror, I realized her whole body, in fact, was still facing directly towards him. Aghast at her lack of subtlety, I said, hiding my clenched teeth beneath a smile, "Turn around, Reena, you're staring! It's so obvious!"

"Yeah, you're right. Because the last two times you turned around to stare at him weren't obvious at all..."

I winced. She was right. I was *so* obvious. But then again, so was he! Unless he was just staring at me because I was staring at him. Was that all it was? Was it all in my head? Oh, God! Maybe he wasn't the least bit interested and just thought I was some obsessive psycho. But Reena's next words dismissed my immediate fears.

"Besides, I don't think he would have noticed me even if I were stark naked. He hasn't taken his eyes off of you."

I smiled at the thought that he was no more immune to me than I was to him.

"So any idea who he is?" I asked.

"Nope."

"Do you know anyone who might know him?" I asked.

"Nope," said Reena.

"Maybe we should just go up to him and introduce ourselves," I suggested. As soon as I said it, I realized how silly that sounded. How could I just go up and introduce myself? It would come across as too eager, even though that's exactly how I felt. I shook my head and immediately took those words back.

"Actually, I think that's a great idea," Reena said. I stared at her expectantly, waiting for the punch line. When I realized she was not joking, I was horrified.

"You can't actually be serious?" I asked.

"Why not? It's obvious how attracted you are to him and he is to you. Why not just go up to him and say hello?" Reena asked.

It sounded so simple, but I just couldn't do it. Something deep in me rebelled against making the first move. I couldn't help feel that as the guy, he should be the one to make the first move. "I can't, Reen. I'm not bold like you."

Reena sighed, shaking her head. "Yeah, don't worry 'bout it. Besides, that would be way too straight-forward and simple. We gotta drag this out for every ounce of melodrama we can squeeze out of it."

"Stop teasing. I'm sure there is a more dignified way of introducing ourselves. Something not so obvious."

"Not so obvious? I think it's a little too late for not so obvious," Reena said. I longed to turn back to stare at Mr. Beautiful, but I resisted the magnetic force that seemed to surround him.

"Maybe Rakesh knows him," Reena suggested. "He somehow manages to know everyone."

That was true. Rakesh did know most people, especially if they were Indian. However, there was a caveat to that, and I reminded Reena of that. "I think he somehow manages to know all the females. The males, he could care less about."

"Very true," she said.

"So what do you think?" I asked.

"What's there to think about? He's not created for deep thought. He's created for our scenic pleasure," she said and then sighed. I just laughed. Well, if that's what he was created for, he was certainly fulfilling his destiny.

Though we were facing the stage, neither of us were paying any attention to Asha Mohan perform a classical Bharatanatyam Indian dance.

"He*looooooo*, ladies!" Two familiar voices crashed our private inter-change, momentarily distracting me from thoughts of Mr. Beautiful. Rakesh and Mani.

"Sorry we're late. But Rakesh here couldn't figure out which color underwear best matches his Nehru suit."

"Shut it, punk!" Rakesh warned, his index finger wagging ever so ominously. "Or I'll tell them how we had to make two pit stops at a gas station and then at a drugstore due to all your *gas*trointestinal issues tonight."

Ewwwwwww. Reena and I exchanged disgusted looks, and before I could respond, Reena spoke for both of us, "I cannot believe you two. First you keep us waiting for 30 minutes, we lose our front-row seats, and then you finally show up and start talking about *gas*trointestinal issues!" Her nose crinkled in disgust.

Rakesh and Mani smiled sheepishly, looking all of five years old as they wavered between embarrassment and pride. Our glares quickly helped them realize the former and not the latter was the mature choice.

"Okay, sorry, *laaaadies,* you're right. Tell us what we can do to make it up to you." Rakesh proceeded to wrap his arms around both of our shoulders and leaned in towards me. "A dinner and a movie, maybe? We'll even take you to see a chick flick… or maybe skinning dipping in the moonlight is what you'd prefer. Anything you like… you choose."

"Anything, huh?" Reena glanced at me, raising an eyebrow. "*Anyyything?*" she asked coquettishly, taking Rakesh by the elbow.

Rakesh narrowed his eyes, realizing that Reena already had some-thing in mind, and it might not be to his liking. "Well, almost anything, but I won't make out with you no matter how much you beg."

"Ha, ha, ha, ha! No! I wouldn't want you to hurt yourself, Rakesh. What I wanted to ask is very simple. Turn around slowly," Reena instructed, but she quickly had to grab him by the shoulders when she realized he was about to jerk his entire body around. "I said *slowly.* There's a guy standing there in a dark suit. All you have to do is go up to him and introduce yourself and then invite him to join us."

Rakesh peered at us skeptically. "That's it?" First, he looked surprised at the simplicity of our request. "But why would you want—" And then it dawned on him. "*Ohhh*, I get it. One of you ladies likes him."

The guys turned in unison, and they gave Mr. Beautiful a not so subtle once-over, looking at him slowly and thoroughly like he was their adversary in battle and they were assessing him for a flaw or weakness. Luckily, he was engaged in a conversation with someone standing next to him and didn't notice that a group of four people (two who were scowling and two who were drooling) were assessing him from head to toe. Rakesh's face retained a frown as he turned back and dismissively said, "Oh, that's Armaan Shah," as if that should be sufficient and I should then drop the matter entirely.

Shah... the name not only confirmed to me that he was Indian, but that he was probably either Gujarati or Punjabi, which also meant he was probably Hindu, making him (as far as my parents were concerned) completely off limits for anything other than friendship. And even a friendship would have to be hidden from my father. As I stood there, silently grappling and justifying what I knew I was going to do, I heard the voice...

Sarai, what are you doing? Mom and Dad are going to KILL you! If God doesn't strike you with lightning first! It was the voice of conscience, of reason, and of obligation. The same voice had held me in check most of my life. It was the voice I had heeded since I was little when I chose homework over watching television or going out or when I had said "no" to a drink offered to me by a good looking stranger at a club or when I volunteered to be the designated driver whenever we went out for a night on the town. But as I stood there with Reena, staring at my dream come true, I ignored the little voice I had listened to all my life. Besides, I reassured that little voice, it's not like I wanted to marry him, maybe just be friends, and a date or two wouldn't hurt, right? *Right*, I assured myself.

But after Rakesh confirmed he knew the handsome stranger, neither Reena nor I were ready to drop the matter. "So how do you know him?" I asked. "And if you know him, how come we don't know him?"

"Okay, what's up with these chicas?" he asked Mani, holding his hands up like he was fending off groupies at a rock concert. "You two don't know everyone I know. You're not around me twenty-four seven. Anyway, what's the big deal?"

I looked at him incredulously. Sometimes he could be so dense. "The big deal is he is the HOTTEST guy on this planet, and we somehow missed being informed of his existence."

"I see… so *you're* the one who likes him!" Rakesh said, cocking his eyebrow as if he were challenging me to deny it.

"We're both admirers," Reena said, quickly coming to my defense. "And I'm very sure we're not the only admirers in this room either. So spill it. What's the 4-1-1 on Mr. Shah?"

"Not much. He's a chill guy, but not *your* type."

"What do you mean *'not my type'*? What makes you think he won't be my type?" I demanded.

"*'Not your type'* unless you're interested in a guy who is already engaged," said Rakesh.

The joy deflated out of me quicker than air out of an overfilled birthday balloon. At first I said nothing and just stared blankly at Rakesh, wondering if he had just made that up. But I could see he was serious. Then the words started sinking in. "Engaged? What? He's engaged?" I said, truly upset. "But he can't be engaged, he's…"

"He's too young to be engaged!" exclaimed Reena, saving me from embarrassing myself.

Rakesh and Mani briefly exchanged knowing glances, no doubt surprised as to how strongly I was reacting. Reena was right. They would never be able to understand how I was feeling and would probably think I was crazy for saying that he was my soul mate. Well, I didn't know for sure if he was my soul mate, but he made me believe, for once, that all my Bollywood daydreams were more than just a silly fantasy.

But Reena didn't miss a beat. "Okay, since we lost our seats, you owe us now. Now you've got to introduce us to him!"

"And what do I get out of this?" asked Rakesh, always the bargainer.

"You'll get my... *our*," I said grabbing Reena by the shoulders and holding her close, "eternal gratitude." We then smiled coyishly, batting our eyelashes.

Rakesh crossed his arms over his chest and looked us over unimpressed. "You're gonna have to do better than that."

When Reena realized the begging technique was not working, she quickly changed tactics and resorted to guilt. "Either way, you guys OWE us for being so late that we lost our seats. Now go chat with that guy and then invite him to join us." Well, guilt, Reena style, was a series of demands overlaid with a veneer of guilt. "Go! Now!" she commanded as she forcefully turned them around and pushed them towards Armaan.

As much as I was grateful for Reena's intervention, I knew it didn't matter. My Mr. Beautiful was engaged and, therefore, as far as I was concerned, he was very off limits.

As I watched the show, I tried to push him out of my mind, but the damage had been done. He had opened the floodgates of what I had systematically damned up since junior high. For so long, I was fine being Ms. Single and Independent, but seeing Armaan stirred up feelings of longing and loneliness that I indulged only in my most vulnerable moments. My attitude had always been that it was better to be single than to settle. But lately that occasional loneliness burned in me. Here I was, my first year out of college, and I still had never had a boyfriend. But now that I finally found someone who piqued my interest, he was unavailable. What made it worse was that he seemed just as interested in me as I was in him. Why did it have to be so magical? Why did it seem God had read my mind and custom-made him just for me? But why would he look at me like that if he were engaged to someone else then? *What was I doing?*

"Are you okay?" Reena asked me, probably surprised at my unusual reticence.

I nodded and focused once again on Asha's dance. Her movements were methodical and precise. It was like watching a one-person opera. I envied her ability. Dance was an opportunity that I never had. Like many overly strict Malayalee Christian parents, mine had been opposed to me studying classical Indian dance. While all I could see was graceful, artistic form, all my parents could see was a form of worship to a Hindu god. Dancing, like many things of my own culture, was forbidden.

Rakesh and Mani returned. I glanced at Rakesh, attempting to give him a half-hearted smile. Rakesh's eyes were on the stage as he said, "So your boy Armaan isn't engaged."

My head whipped around to Rakesh, waiting for him to continue. "He's not? How can you be sure?"

Rakesh's tone was devoid of his usual pep. "Because I asked him how his fiancé was doing. Turns out I was wrong. He was never engaged."

I didn't have time to dwell on Rakesh's glumness or what that meant. All I could think about was that Mr. Armaan Shah aka Mr. Beautiful was available. Maybe there was still hope! Or God forbid, had I only imagined his interest?

Before my mind could run away with that horrible thought, Rakesh continued. "He asked about you, what your name was, who you were, and if you…" he quickly mumbled the rest incoherently.

"And he asked if I what?" My voice was barely a whisper, afraid to assume what I thought I heard.

Rakesh cleared his throat and reluctantly added, "He asked if you were single." He looked me straight in the eye, almost as if he were trying to gauge how I really felt.

"And what did you say?" I hoped he hadn't made one of his typical Rakesh comments and ruined my chances.

"I said you were single," and then he looked away again before somberly adding, "But good luck in trying to date you. Many have tried, and all have failed."

"Ha, ha! Very funny," I said, mockingly. I had no time to decipher what he meant by that. All I could focus on was that Armaan was available and wanted to know if I was available.

Armaan Shah. My parents would kill me if they ever found out I was dating a Hindu. Not just kill me. But skin me alive and then kill me. Well, it was way too soon to worry about anything more than just friendship. I just wanted to hang out with him… as friends… maybe if

I were lucky, just go on a few dates, live out my Bollywood fantasy, and then get over it and him and just move on with my life.

Surely the angels were singing, for my heart was singing. I felt light on my feet. Just like that, with a few simple words, a renewed energy flowed through me. Somehow I knew this would be the beginning of it all. And it was. It was the beginning of my *Once Upon a Time*.

Chapter 4

FTER THE TALENT SHOW, all the audience chairs were swiftly
removed, and within minutes, the 1st level auditorium space
was transformed into a dance floor, complete with a DJ
spinning *Bhangra* music, the latest Bollywood songs, and a couple of
Hip Hop songs remixed with some of the more traditional Indian
tunes.

After forty-five minutes of shaking my hips and attempting to imi-
tate some of the dance moves I had seen in my favorite movies, I
decided I needed a bathroom break. I yelled into Reena's ear, but rather
than taking my cue and joining me, she just nodded and kept on
laughing and dancing. I glanced at Armaan, but he looked concerned.
He leaned closer, his breath minty fresh. "You're leaving?" His voice
hinted at disappointment. His voice had the faint clip of a British
accent. A hot Indian guy with a British accent and fresh breath. God
was certainly shining down on me.

"No, just to the bathroom."

"Oh, okay, I thought my dancing had made you decide to call it a
night."

I laughed, and shook my head. "No, I'll be back."

"Good, because I'll be waiting." His response made me smile one
of those smiles that revealed every tooth in my mouth.

Afterward, we left the dance and raided a late night diner. We
gorged ourselves on pancakes, waffles, and eggs. Normally it would
have been another night out with my friends, but because Armaan had

been there, that evening was, instead, the most amazing night of my twenty-something life. I was walking on air. After twenty-three years of the mundane, my life finally seemed to be taking a turn for the exciting. I silently said a prayer of thanks.

When the clock struck two, my night as Cinderella ended. As we parted ways, him into his car, and me into Reena's car, I found a last smidgen of boldness and extended my hand out to him. "It was nice to meet you, Armaan." As soon as I said it, a thousand doubts sprung into my mind. Was that too formal? Was I being too aggressive or too forward? He took my hand and shook it gently. "It was nice to meet you, too, Sarai." He said my name almost melodically, stretching it out like the Starship song, "Sarah." And then he gazed deep into my eyes, and asked, "So… can I call you?"

"I'd like that," I said, with a calm, even steadiness to my voice, which was surprising, considering my heart was beating uncontrollably and all I wanted to do was grab Reena's hands and do one of our victory "*I can't believe this is happening*" dances.

Life was good. Life was perfect. This was why I had waited all this time to date. He was my reward for never having had a boyfriend or even a Valentine. He was my prize for not being asked to prom or, for that matter, to *any* high school dance. I once again ignored the small voice that reminded me despite his "perfection," my parents would probably still kill me.

Our first meeting could not have been more perfect. Our first date, on the other hand, could not have been more disastrous, not because anything went wrong, but because it almost never happened.

Chapter 5

B Y THE TIME Reena dropped me off, it was close to two-thirty. By the time I got ready for bed and relived my Cinderella fairytale before finally falling asleep, it was somewhere around four-thirty. At precisely eight thirty-three, my body jerked awake with the faint feeling that something was wrong. Not wrong really, but maybe something that I missed or overlooked. I relived the night again in my head. That initial feeling of falling in love is one of the most powerful amphetamines, and despite getting only four hours of sleep, I felt fully rested and re-energized. I smiled and hugged my pillow. Life was amazing. He was my dream guy come to life, my very own Prince Charming! If I had made a list of everything I wanted in a guy, he undoubtedly would fulfill each wish.

Wait! I told myself as a faint memory came back to me. *The List!* Oh my gosh, where was that thing? Back in my sophomore year in college, our church youth leader had challenged us to write down the qualities we were looking for in a spouse. Eager to no longer be single, I had taken the assignment very seriously, and in precise details, I listed the qualities I was looking for in my ideal mate.

I shuffled through some boxes in the back of my closet and finally found the one that stored all of my old journals. They were stacked chronologically, and I finally pulled out a maroon journal with a small broken lock on it. Sure enough, tucked in its pages, I found two creased sheets of white notebook paper. One was mine, and one was Reena's. Reena had listed about five qualities: *cute, smart, tall, funny, and not a wuss.*

Reena's list may have been short and sweet, but mine was the very opposite. I had titled it, *My Prince Charming*. My list was organized into sections: Personality, Spirituality, Physical Appearance, and even a Miscellaneous section for silly things, such as "likes Thai food." If our youth leader was right and God's desire was to give us the desires of our heart, I didn't want God mistaking what I wanted on my wish list, so I was as specific as I could be.

Under each section, I had written at least seven to ten detailed attributes. For *Personality*, based on what I could observe and based on the comments he made throughout the night, Armaan seemed to fit many of the qualities I had listed: an outgoing introvert, patient, open-minded, family-oriented, and adventurous. At a closer glance, I decided, he actually fit my entire Prince Charming list with only three important exceptions:

1. *He wasn't Malayalee.*

2. *He wasn't a Christian* (an attribute that I had underlined multiple times).

3. *He didn't have light-colored hazel eyes.*

Granted, even I had to admit that the light-colored eyes criterion on my list was a stretch, especially if I expected him to be Indian and even more so if I expected him to be Malayalee.

Soon enough the typical post-date questions began plaguing me. When would he call? When would I see him again? What would we do for our first real date? And then it finally came to me, what had been bothering just earlier, something I had completely missed the night before, something that should have been very obvious at the time.

I dialed Reena's number frantically, and I was greeted by her groggy, scratchy voice. "Heellooo?" She croaked out, her voice invariably hoarse from the night before.

"Reena!" I said breathlessly, "He doesn't have my number! How is he going to call me?" I expected her to be as devastated as I was. Well, maybe not devastated but at least upset on my behalf that somehow we had overlooked this major detail. No answer. "Reena?" I asked, prompting her to say something, anything. "Reena! Wake up! This is serious!"

"I'm awake. I was just thinking." A second passed. Then another. Then another.

"Okay, think faster," I urged her. "What am I going to do?"

"I'm thinking... okay, um, he doesn't have your number? Then you call him," she said, her voice falling into that lull right before sleep.

"Reena! Wake up!" I cried out. "I don't have his number either! Don't you think if I did, I would have thought of that myself?"

"Okay, okay! I got it! You don't have his number, and he doesn't have your number."

"EXACTLY!" I said, shaking my head at how obtuse she was being.

"That sucks!"

"Yes, it does. So what do we do?"

"Hmmm. Look him up in the yellow pages. Or white pages. Or whatever it's called these days!"

Of course! Why didn't I think of that?! "Hold on! I think there's a book in one of the kitchen cabinets here." I grabbed the thickest phone book and began thumbing through the white pages. S...Sh...Sha...Shabraugh and Shazim. There was no Shah! "Reena! It's unlisted! *Aaaargh*!"

"Hmmm. Well, call Rakesh. He might have it." But before I could say bye or hang up to call Rakesh, Reena added, "But wait to call him. He's not going to be happy about being woken up this early just because you want another guy's number." Then she chuckled and added, "Yeah, *especially* if you're calling to get another guy's number."

True, I thought. But based on the occasional glowering looks he shot Armaan's way, I didn't think Rakesh would have even bothered to get his number.

I called Rakesh two hours later when I thought it was safe, and sure enough, I got the irritated, "Why the hell would I have it?" response. To my annoyance, I could have sworn I heard a smile in his voice when I told him of my predicament.

I moped around the house for the rest of the afternoon. Why hadn't I asked for his number? But then again, he was the guy; why hadn't *he* asked for *my* number? For the next few days, I was tortured about how to get ahold of him and how I would ever manage to see him again.

Three days later, I still hadn't thought of a way to find my mysterious Prince Charming. It was, I realized to my dismay, the story of my life. Why couldn't I be like Cinderella and just go back to my normal life and believe if it was meant to be, it would happen?

After wallowing in a deep pool of self-pity that afternoon, I joined Reena, Rakesh, Mani, and Anjuli at the new indoor outlet mall that boasted of haute couture designers one would only find in Manhattan or on Rodeo Drive. However, despite the store displays featuring Roberto Cavalli, Versace, and Prada at discount prices, my mind was not on shopping. I couldn't get Armaan out of my mind. I relived the night I met him over and over and over again. As we walked through the mall, Reena nudged me, noting my mopey attitude. "Cheer up. You guys will get in touch again."

"Really? And just how is that going to happen?"

"I don't know," she said as she shrugged. Then she smiled. "Maybe he'll misdial a number, and somehow it'll be your number, and then—" I glowered at her.

She chuckled. "Okay, you're right! That was a little far-fetched. I haven't the faintest idea how you guys will get in touch with each other," she said throwing her arm around my shoulders. "But it'll happen. Most definitely," she said it so confidently that even I began to believe it. But as we began walking again, I also heard her mumble, "Hopefully."

"Well, that's encouraging," I retorted.

"Maybe you'll be driving somewhere, and he'll be in the next lane, or maybe you'll run into him at the gas station, or maybe at the grocery store, or for that matter," she said as she glanced around. "Who knows? Maybe right here in the mall." She wiggled her eyebrows and looked so silly I had to laugh. I sighed dramatically, reprimanding myself for acting like a love-sick teenager. As much as I wanted to cling onto the ray of hope that Reena was right, I was very well aware of the fact that after living in the same town most of our lives, we had only recently managed to run into each other. And now that I was aware of his existence, I knew with my luck, my chances of running into him now were even slimmer.

We spent about thirty minutes in the Gucci store and made our way towards Nordstrom's jewelry department. Reena and Anjuli were trying on earrings while I browsed the small display racks. Reena was looking at her reflection when something in the reflection of the mirror caught her eye, and she turned around, her eyes wide like a child on Christmas morning. She reached for my arm, nudging me to look. I figured she must have seen a great pair of earrings on sale, but in the reflection of the mirror there he was—the object of my ever-increasing obsession—Armaan! I whipped around, not quite believing the reflection, and blinked several times, praying he was not a mirage or a figment of my desperate imagination. He was standing near the men's jewelry display, being helped by an admiring sales associate who was openly ogling him as she navigated him through the endless assortment of men's sunglasses. Yes, it was definitely him, standing there looking just as beautiful as I remembered. He wore faded distressed jeans and a fitted plain black t-shirt that hugged him like second skin. It was a casual outfit, but the dark colors brought out the darkness of his eyes and hair. I momentarily closed my eyes, trying to take it all in, and not quite believing my luck. I had pined for him for three days, almost fearful I might never see him again. I then took a moment to pause and look upward as I whispered a very sincere and joyous, "Thank you!"

Reena leaned in and whispered an excited, "Did I predict this or what?!"

I'm not sure if Armaan had already seen us and was just trying not to be obvious, but at that moment, his eyes glanced from the sales associate, who was leaning over the counter, openly flirting with him, to us. From across the aisle and a few counters over, he smiled and casually waved. I returned a very feeble and trembling smile, my hand arrested in mid-air as I still tried to digest the fact that out of all places, out of all the times, he was here. Not only had I dreamed him into existence the first time, but after all my pining, wishing, and whining, it was like I had invoked him into being right here.

He mumbled something quick to the sales associate whose smile quickly disappeared as she nodded and began putting some of the sunglasses back into the display. He then made his way towards us. His eyes focused on me as he addressed the group, "Hey! So what are you guys up to?" Though I had every intention of answering, I opened my mouth, and nothing came out. Luckily, Reena must have sensed my nervousness and responded, "We're just, you know, having a girls' shopping day." Rakesh was busy contemplating a solo stud earring to add to his already expansive collection of jewelry. He paused to say hello, but realizing it was Armaan, he mumbled a half-hearted, "Hey, what's up?" and continued his shopping.

Armaan nodded in return, and Reena glanced at Rakesh and then winked at Armaan and replied, "Like I said, we're having an ALL girls' shopping day."

Armaan chuckled in response.

"So what are *you* shopping for?" Anjuli interjected.

He inclined his head towards the watch and men's jewelry section. "It's my dad's birthday tomorrow, so I was just looking around."

I so desperately wanted to ask him to join us, but I knew I wouldn't be able to pull it off without sounding over-eager. Reena, to my delight, stepped up and asked him in the most casual tone, "So why don't you join us while you look around? The more the merrier."

His eyes were on me when he replied, "Okay, sure." His smile widened to reveal even, perfect teeth. "I think I will."

My heart raced erratically while my stomach began flipping. I was still trying to wrap my mind around that fact that he was here... *with me*! Though I typically walk at a brisk pace, I began walking slowly, and to my delight, he slowed his stride to match mine. We soon lagged behind everyone else, but even with that additional privacy, I was so nervous I could not even look at him.

He cleared his throat, as if trying to fill in the silence between us. I finally glanced at him shyly. He smiled at me and then kept his eyes forward. "So I realized something yesterday," he began.

"What's that?" I asked, willing myself to look at him as he talked.

He seemed to be the one to avoid eye contact with me, preferring to look straight ahead as we walked.

"I realized yesterday when I picked up the phone to call you that I didn't know your number."

So he had tried to call me! I toyed with the idea of pretending that I hadn't been waiting for his phone call, but I felt his honesty deserved me being honest with him. "Yes, I actually realized that, too." I almost mentioned the fact that I had looked up his number but couldn't find it listed anywhere, but decided against it. Letting him know I was interested was okay, but letting him know just *how* interested I was would probably not be a good thing.

"So that's why I didn't call," he said, stopping in mid-stride to face me. He almost looked a little vulnerable as he added, "In case you were wondering."

I smile broadly and happily nodded my head like a tongue-tied, lovesick teenager.

He laughed and quipped, "You don't talk much, do you?" Still tongue-tied, I shrugged my shoulders in response.

✧   ✧   ✧

THEY SAY CHEMISTRY fades. But for me and Armaan, it only grew. After the initial months, the butterflies eventually fade, and you're left with the core of the person. So after a couple of dates, I slowly overcame my nervousness and, unfortunately for Armaan, I became quite the chatty talker.

While we were both Indian and had come from relatively conservative families, we were different in so many ways. He was the engineering/math genius. I was the literature-loving liberal arts child. He loved to watch documentaries and world news. I loved watching foreign films, chick flicks, and entertainment news. He loved watching and playing sports while I preferred to read a book or go shopping. Despite our differences, our personalities complemented each other. The only difference that truly did divide us was the fact that he came from a very devout Hindu family while I came from a very strict, Orthodox Christian family. I never would have described myself as overtly religious, and it wasn't until I started dating Armaan that I realized how adamant I was about what I believed and how much my Christian upbringing had influenced my choices and preferences. After the one time our discussion on religion resulted in a huge fight and a three-day standoff, it was a topic of conversation that we both avoided since then. We would deal with it when we needed to, I decided. Until then, there was no point in creating friction in an otherwise, very harmonious relationship.

People would always comment on what a striking pair we were. Back then I wore my hair long, past my waist, and super straight. Armaan was tall, but I was only inches shorter than him when I wore heels. I had been teased in school for being tall, skinny, and gawky, but I knew I'd come a long way since then even though the feeling of being the ugly, awkward duckling somehow never quite leaves you.

Yet, being with Armaan made up for all that. He made me feel like the wait and the rejections had all been worth it. I may have been ignored by all my childhood crushes and gone to my own senior prom without a date, but in the end, none of that mattered anymore. Being with Armaan made me feel as if I ended up with the prom king.

Chapter 6

FROM OUR FIRST MEETING to our first date, to our first kiss, to when he first introduced me to his family, to the day I almost introduced him to mine. The next five and a half years of our life together played out right in front of me like a film reel.

It was the chiming of the doorbell that sucked me out of my mental time machine back to the present. I glanced out my bedroom window. In the driveway was Reena's forest green Ford Explorer. I heard muffled greetings from downstairs when my mom opened the door, and I saw the tops of three heads before they disappeared through the front door. My entourage had arrived.

"Sarai-moooo*ooooo!* Reena, Anjuli, and Maya are here!"

I glanced at my reflection. My curls were pinned up, and they cascaded perfectly down my back. My skin looked luminescent and flawless, and the white and silver *chaniya choli* shimmered with every slight movement I made. I took a deep breath, smoothed one defiant curl into submission, and turned off my bedroom light before starting down the stairs.

I heard simultaneous gasps from each of my friends. Then there was a brief period of stunned silence followed by simultaneous *oohs* and *ahhhs* as they clamored to meet me at the foot of the stairs.

"Sarai! You look so beautiful!" exclaimed Anjuli, as she reached out to touch my skirt. "That is the most beautiful *chaniya choli* I've ever seen!"

I smiled, momentarily enjoying the adulation, drawing on it to give me the confidence to ease my nervousness. My mom said nothing. She only sipped her morning coffee as she watched the girls fawn over me. She still had not changed out of her red and white gingham housecoat. She then made her way towards me, her gaze gliding over my outfit. With one hand still holding her coffee, she cupped my chin with her free hand as she smiled encouragingly. "You look beautiful, Sarai-mol."

Despite her sweet words, her forehead was lined with worry and concern. "Must you still go through with this?" she asked.

I said nothing, but nodded my head adamantly as my eyes pleaded with her to understand. I had made up my mind, she realized, and there was no turning back for me. She leaned forward and lightly kissed me on the forehead, giving me her blessing. Then she held the front door for us. We each walked through the door, and as I made my way to the car, I paused, glancing at my mom whose petite frame seemed so small against the tall wooden door frame. As we drove away, my eyes were still glued to her red-and-white checkered figure as she stood, arms raised partially in mid-air as she waved good-bye. Her smile had faded and her eyebrows were once again wrinkled with worry.

✧　✧　✧

THE WEDDING WAS to be held at Armaan's family estate, which sat on top of Cypress Hill, surrounded by two acres of impeccably manicured landscaping. We made our way up the hill, arrived at the wrought iron gates, and were greeted by the valet. He took Reena's keys and ushered us to a golf cart that took us up the remainder of the long, winding driveway lined with willow trees, the branches of which combined, creating a natural and breathtaking canopy. Soon the path widened to the main entrance and there, in all its majestic, Mughal glory, stood Armaan's family home. Anjuli and Maya gasped simultaneously, reminding me of my own astonished reaction many years ago. Armaan's mom had always been in love with the Taj Mahal as a child and their home was undoubtedly an homage to the beloved Taj. From the long, narrow pool, flanked by perfectly manicured topiaries to curved archways and domed turrets, the outer exterior of the home was modeled in a very similar Mughal architecture. Rather than smooth priceless marble, their home was made of stucco, giving it the appearance of being a Moroccan-Indian fusion style of architecture. And rather than the etched, intricate floral Arabic designs, their home was accented with black wrought iron. The result was something out of an Indian fairytale and nothing short of breathtaking. I smiled realizing that the girls hadn't even seen the inside of their home or the breathtaking view of the hillside from the living room.

But it was truly the main entry doors that made one of the most impressive statements. Standing fourteen feet tall, the heavy, espresso-colored wooden doors were carved with reliefs of Hindu deities, reminding guests of the doors to the Hindu temples that could be seen all over India. But as I walked through those large wooden doors, I was transported to a modern Maharaja palace. Sheer, georgette sheets of jewel-colored fabric lined the entryway, creating a canopy from the entryway to the expansive foyer to the four oversized French doors. Waiters, dressed in seventeenth century Indian outfits, touted appetizers of *samosas* and glasses of *mango lassi* on large silver serving trays. I stood there for a moment in silence, taking it all in, knowing I would never forget this day.

From the main foyer, we were ushered through the expansive living room. All the furniture had been removed with only a few seats lining the walls. I was surprised with the sheer number of guests who had already arrived before I had. Indians were notoriously late for events.

As we made our way through the home, I had to agree it was one of the most beautifully decorated wedding venues I had ever attended. Armaan's family had modeled their home like an Indian palace, and it seemed befitting that the wedding would be held here as well. Their home was more dramatic and more beautiful than any hotel, and there could not have been a more perfect backdrop for a wedding.

We made our way through the French doors to a spacious terrace that overlooked their expansive lawn. As I knew they would, Armaan's family would spare no expense in decorating their massive estate for their one and only son. The two-acre landscaped garden and lawn was dotted with colorful tents in the colors of marigold, tangerine, and ruby red. Then my eyes finally caught what I was really looking for.

Across the lawn, dressed in a black and gold Nehru suit, stood Armaan, looking as resplendent as any maharaja would have. I momentarily paused, breathing in the sight of him. Even at a distance, he still managed to exude confidence. Despite all our years together, he still had the ability to make my knees buckle.

As I was drinking in the sight of him, the sudden movement of a slender, graceful hand moved to rest lightly against his forearm. Wearing a heavily gold-beaded orange-red *lengha* in a mermaid-style sheath, she stood graceful and regal next to Armaan. Her hair was swept up and tied into a sophisticated up-do and intertwined in gold and jasmine flowers. She was, I realized as my stomach and heart churned in protest, the woman who had haunted my dreams for the past eight months. The woman whom I had lost him to—his bride.

Chapter 7

Eight months before

"I HAVEN'T SEEN Armaan for three months, three days…" I paused to glance at my watch to do some quick calculations, "four hours, and twenty-two minutes." Sighing, I took another long, slow sip of my Sprite as Reena stuffed a couple of more French fries into her mouth. Reena and I were at the mall eating burgers and fries at the food court after spending an entire day of summer clearance shopping. "Will you quit looking at your watch? I'm sure he'll page you as soon as he arrives."

After finishing his residency, Armaan had taken a trip to India with his parents and had been due back earlier that morning, but I had already paged him twice with no response. I had already called the airline, too, and they confirmed the flight already arrived, but due to security precautions, they were unable to verify if Armaan had been on the flight.

I pulled out my beeper to see if there were any messages and winced when I saw nothing but two old pages from my mom. "I know. It's just that I haven't seen or talked to him in so long! He was supposed to write me at least one letter every two weeks, but all I got was a postcard from him the first week he left. I'm so used to talking to him every day," I said, sighing as I dipped the same French fry into the ketchup for the third time.

"I'm sure he misses you, too, Sarai. He probably just has jet lag or he probably just hasn't had a free moment to call you. I'm sure he'll call you by evening or by tomorrow at the latest."

"Yeah, I hope so. I just hope he made the flight and that nothing is wrong," I said. "He warned me that he might not be able to call, but I figured he'd find a way to contact me. I know calling by phone can be hard, but he could have at least written me an email or at least one letter."

"Well, you know, you guys have been dating for like a couple of years—"

"Five years and a half years," I readily supplied.

"Wow," she said surprised, "It's already been that long?! And this is like the first time you guys have gone more than a week without talking? Maybe some time apart would do you some good," she said, her eyes twinkling mischievously. "You know what they say… *absence makes the heart grow fonder.*"

"Well, it's definitely made my heart grow fonder. I feel like a little kid the night before Christmas!"

Reena was leaning back in her chair and looking at me oddly.

"What?" I asked, knowing that those wheels were turning in her head.

"So you guys have been dating for over five years now?" she asked somberly. I nodded as I noisily slurped the last few sips of my soda. "*Hmmm.* So have you guys talked about getting married?"

"Not really. I mean, sort of. But not officially. But yeah, that is the idea… eventually. Why do you ask?" I got up and started gathering all our shopping bags.

"Oh, nothing…" she said, her voice trailing off. "I was just wondering that's all."

We then walked to the Macy's Junior's department and picked out some clothes to try. We were in the dressing room, and I was in the process of putting on a pull-over sweater when my beeper went off. My hair had somehow tangled with the price tag that hung from the neck label, but I immediately stopped struggling with it, lunged for my purse, and frantically searched for my beeper.

Jet lag. Sorry for not calling earlier. Meet me tonight
at 7pm on the bridge. I have something important to ask
you. Armaan.

Yes! It was Armaan! I was so blissfully happy that I ran out of my dressing room stall, almost knocked down a shocked woman walking by, and ran into Reena's stall.

"It's him, it's him!" I said, showing her his number on my beeper as if I had expected her not to believe me.

Reena laughed and said, "I heard the beeper, and then I heard you squeal, so I figured it had to be..." She eyed me up and down and shook her head. "But don't you think you should have finished getting dressed first before confirming what I already knew?" I glanced at the mirror. I was in my jeans and bra, and the sweater was bunched up around my neck like a muffler. No wonder the woman outside my stall was horrified. But I didn't care. Armaan was back, and he had called! And he had something important to discuss. I grabbed Reena's hands and proceeded to jump up and down, doing my happy dance, and twirling around as the arms of the sweater swung around me like the blades of a ceiling fan.

✧　✧　✧

REENA CAME HOME with me to help me pick out what to wear. We mulled over the cryptic "important thing to ask you" that Armaan had texted me through his pager. "What could it mean?" I asked as I shoved my arms through a t-shirt and fitted vest.

"I have no idea," she said, wrinkling her nose at my outfit. "It's too casual. You should look at little more dressed up when you see him."

Selecting the right outfit was very crucial, even if it was for my long-time boyfriend. It set the tone for the evening, and after not seeing him for three months, I felt almost as nervous as I did before our first date. I browsed my closet, trying to find the right outfit, and I heard Reena gasp. "Sarai, you don't think..."

I turned around quickly with my head cocked to the side, waiting for her to finish.

She looked at me wide-eyed and then shook her head, "Never mind. I was just being silly." Under her breath, I heard her mumble, "I think."

"What were you going to say?" I asked, crossing my arms and leaning against my closet door.

"I was going to ask you if you thought…" As she looked at me, the corners of her mouth were slightly upturned in a smile. Then she shook her head again. "Forget it. I'm just being presumptuous."

I ignored her dismissing comment. "Okay, just say it. You were saying, 'I think…'" I asked, prodding her along.

She paused at first, like she was still undecided herself, but then she finally said what she was thinking. "I thought that what if, *just what if*, he was going to propose to you tonight?" She looked at me, waiting for my reaction.

I blinked twice in response.

"P-p-propose? Tonight?" I asked, not sure how to react. It wasn't even something that had crossed my mind! Turning back to the closet, I focused my attention on looking for the right outfit. "Don't be silly." But just as I reached for one of my favorite sweaters, I turned around slowly and looked at her quizzically. "Propose? Really? What makes you think he is going to propose?"

Reena shoved her hands into her jean pockets and shrugged her shoulders. "Well, you guys have been dating long enough. He is finished with his residency now, so he's at that perfect age where he is probably getting pressure from his parents about marriage. And you guys haven't seen each other in three months, so I figure he's probably really missing you. Remember what happened last year when he was gone less than a week?"

I blushed at the memory and turned away. There were times when I wished I hadn't told Reena everything that happened in my life.

Reena smiled, wagging her index finger at me, "*Yeaaah, exactly*! So imagine what's going to happen since he hasn't seen you in three months! And he wrote that he has something *very important* to discuss with you. What could be more important than your future together?"

It made sense. I figured he would propose eventually. After all, that was the goal. We had never really discussed the details, but by going along with our relationship, we were silently committing to each other, right? But still... propose?! And tonight?! I shook my head, wanting to believe it but afraid to be disappointed if it didn't happen. "Maybe."

Reena's eyes brightened. "And..."

"There's an '*and*'?" I asked, wide-eyed and blinking uncontrollably.

"*And* he asked you to meet him on the bridge. *The bridge*. That's your spot! Every key step of your relationship has been on that bridge. Your first real date, your first kiss, the first time he told you he loved you..."

"True," I whispered. I couldn't breathe. He was going to propose. Tonight.

Chapter 8

I T WAS A beautiful evening as I began the trek to Central, a park located just a half-mile from my house. If ever there was an evening for a proposal, this was it. It was one of those magical nights where the sun, moon, and stars all seemed to be in alignment. Though it was almost dusk and the sun had settled, it was still eerily bright outside, reminding me of one of those Winnie the Pooh viewfinder scenes I used to stare at for hours on end when I was a kid. The sting of the summer heat had already subsided, and a fresh breeze had cooled off the evening, giving it a light balmy feel. The grass smelled fresh and crisp, reminding me of summer rain. I glanced quickly at the sky and noticed dark, menacing clouds in the distance. They were headed the other direction, I determined. Nothing was going to ruin tonight because whether Armaan proposed or not, I knew it was going to be a special evening. Besides, even if it rained, the night might be even more romantic. Many a Bollywood love story had blossomed under the nurture of a summer shower. As I made my way to the bridge, I could see the faint outline of a full moon. Yes, it was most certainly a perfect night!

The entrance of the park was the children's play area, complete with a swing set, jungle gym, monkey bars, slides, and a merry-go-round. The rest of the park was modeled after Central Park in New York City, and the outer back edge of the park was twenty miles of undisturbed nature. In high school, I had ventured beyond the playground and discovered that if you followed the hiking trail for a quarter of a mile and then veered off to the right, you'd find yourself in an empty meadow that in the summertime would bloom beautiful wildflowers. To the right of that was our signature spot, an abandoned wooden bridge that overlooked the most picturesque little creek. It was a place I had only shown to Reena and Armaan.

All my most significant moments with Armaan took place in this park, right here at the bridge. It's where we had our first date and shared our first kiss. And if Reena's hunch was right, it might also be where he was going to propose.

By the time I arrived, dusk had settled in. Tall black cast-iron lamp-posts were already lit throughout the park, making the evening even more magical. I glanced at the sky again and saw that the clouds seemed to be shifting towards us, rather than away. The sky had darkened a bit more, making me wonder if it weren't going to rain after all. But I wasn't made of sugar, and I certainly wouldn't melt. I buttoned the last three buttons on my cardigan and straightened the skirt of the dress, wondering again if the outfit wasn't overkill. Reena was still convinced Armaan was going to propose, but to avoid being too disappointed if he didn't, I was being cynical and trying to have low expectations. I was trying my best to look casual but still dressed up, just in case our reunion date was more than just that. I pulled out my compact mirror to do a final check. Lipstick and base were still in place. Eyeliner and mascara were intact. *Perfect,* I said to myself with a smile as I recalled one of the many times he had told me that my eyes reminded him of Jasmine from the Disney movie *Aladdin* and how they were his undoing.

I arrived at the park, quickly walking towards our favorite spot just in front of the bridge, and to my surprise, Armaan was already there. He was leaning against the railing of the bridge, with his hands clasped behind him, deep in thought. He was wearing his Stanford polo shirt and jeans. His hair was cut shorter than usual but his bangs had grown, and he wore them neatly combed to the side. It was a simple haircut, making him appear more traditional than I knew he was.

I tried to sneak up on him and catch him off guard, but he heard my footsteps in the grass and immediately turned around, looking slightly startled. When he saw that it was me, he broke into one of his signature heart-melting smiles. I lunged into his arms, and his arms pulled me tight as my feet dangled just inches off the ground.

"Hello, stranger!" I said, squeezing him and breathing in his deep musky scent that mingled with his after-shave.

"Hello yourself!" he said. He then loosened his own tight embrace, and once he placed me firmly back on my feet, he leaned back to look me over. He had a way of looking at me that made me feel as if I were the most beautiful girl he had ever seen. "You look cute. You cut your hair," he said smoothing an unruly curl. "I like it. It suits you."

"Thank you!" I said, as I lightly touched his hair and affectionately squeezed his cheek. "You look cute, too. Just like a good Indian boy who listens to his mommy and daddy." I said the latter part of that in a thick Indian accent. He laughed.

"So how are you?" I asked, looking up at him, the adoration evident in my eyes.

"Good. I'm good," he said, smiling into my eyes. He was still holding me loosely as his eyes dropped to my lips. Armaan was a very good looking man, but even I forgot what a strong effect he could have on me. I closed my eyes and leaned in for the kiss that I was sure would follow, but he abruptly pulled away from our embrace, held my hands loosely for a few seconds and then dropped them altogether. He then shoved his hands into his pockets and began pacing back and forth in front of me, occasionally raking his hands through his hair.

I had expected him to ravish me in an unforgettable kiss, so I was a little thrown-off when he pulled away so abruptly. It wasn't like Armaan to act this way. But then again, this wasn't just a regular night. I could only assume that he was feeling nervous. We hadn't seen each other in three months, so even I felt a little nervous to be around him.

"So how was your trip? Tell me everything!" I begged, eager to get past the awkwardness.

"Everything, huh? Well, there's a lot to tell." He walked over to the bridge, stared at the water, and then gazed back at me with a wistful look in his eyes. I waited for him to say something, but he just stood there, staring at me oddly and then turned back to stare quietly into the waters of the lake. I joined him, standing close to him, expecting him to put his arms around me, but he didn't.

Even a small brook could be so magical at night. The moonlight shimmered on the still water, and the brook hummed gently as it trickled down the rocks before it eventually joined the bottomless waters of the lake. The smell of fresh cut grass was getting stronger, and I knew it wouldn't be long before the rain started. He was once again looking at me, and my heart quickened in nervousness, but luckily the night shadows hid my blushing. Not wanting to break the magical moment, I remained silent even though every part of me wanted to know why he was being so aloof. He could be so enigmatic at times, but I was sure it was the jet-lag that made him seem even more so... or maybe it was being in India for three months. Our motherland had a way of changing you, of seeping in your bones and making you, for a brief time, into the person you would have become had you never left her shores.

The moon was full and round tonight. It was a true Harvest Moon and for a few moments we just continued to stand on the bridge watching the moonlight play against the soft current of the creek.

Finally he spoke.

"Sarai, there is something I have to tell you," he said. My eyes widened, and my throat constricted as I nodded in reply. I inhaled deeply as I tried to steady my nerves. This was it.

He cleared his throat and then rephrased his statement. "Actually, there is something I have to ask you."

I know, you do, I thought silently to myself. *Reena had been right. He was going to propose.*

He reached for my hands and held them. "You know how much I care for you, right? And you know I want you to be happy, right?"

My heart thudded louder against my chest, almost drowning out his words, which were undoubtedly a preamble to his proposal. Did he realize I knew what he was going to do? I still couldn't believe he was going to propose. Maybe it was being away from me for three months that made him realize that he wanted to be with me forever and that we did, indeed, belong together.

"Yes," I whispered. I was partially expecting him to get on one knee, but the poor boy was probably so nervous that he had forgotten about that one tradition.

"Okay, what is it?" I asked, smiling, suddenly feeling very giddy. I reached out to smooth a non-existent wrinkle in his shirt. I just wanted to touch him. He had gotten a little leaner, I realized. He glanced down at my fingers, and then with his left hand, he clasped it over mine. "Sarai…"

"Yes?" I asked gently, my voice tender, almost like a whisper. His face was so beautifully lit in the moonlight. It was so good to see him. I thought of him every day, every hour, and at times, every minute when he was gone. Knowing he would be coming back to me is what kept me from missing him too much. But being around him again made me realize how much he had become a part of my life and a part of me.

He was quiet again and said nothing for a few seconds. I could hear the hesitation in his voice. "Sarai," he began again. But then he paused and looked away. I noticed the reluctance to speak. I looked at him questioningly, wondering why he was struggling so much with the words. Was he that nervous? Although I had expected him to be a little nervous, I hadn't expected him to be so hesitant and unsure of himself. He had to know how crazy I was about him! He cleared his throat a couple of more times, and I held my breath, waiting in anticipation for him to say the words.

The night sky stood in the backdrop, providing the most unbelievable ambiance. It was dusk, and between the smell of rain and the light fog that covered the ground like a sheer blanket, there was an undoubtedly a dream-like quality to the evening.

"Sarai, when I was in India, something happened."

You realized how much you missed me and needed me, I thought.

"My father had a heart attack, and he was in a coma for a few days."

And you realized the importance of not waiting… but seizing the moment.

"And I vowed to Vishnu that if he brought my father back, then I would do anything required of me."

And Vishnu told you it was time to marry the Christian girl you were dating.

"And a few hours later my father woke up from his coma, and I made the same promise to him that I made to Vishnu."

And you told him about me and how much we were in love.

"And he told me how his wish was always to follow in his footsteps and become a doctor and someday take over his cardiology practice."

And you're on your way to fulfilling that wish, I thought, proudly.

"And then he said there were only two more things he wanted."

A wife and kids.

"He said his last wish was to see me married to the daughter of his childhood best friend, Sumas, and to give him grandchildren."

My heart quickened. What an odd thing to say, I thought. *But then you told him about me and how much you loved me and could only be with me.*

But then he looked at me, and I saw his eyes, filled not with anticipation but apology.

"And things happened so quickly. The family came to our house, and I met Sandiya and…" His voice trailed off, and he finally raised his eyes to me. They were sad. Those weren't the eyes of someone who was about to propose. I began to brace myself as I tried to follow what he was trying to tell me. Somehow I knew that whatever it was he had to tell me also was not something I would want to hear.

And you told her how you could never consider her because you were already with someone else.

"Sarai…"

My heart must have stopped beating.

"I'm engaged."

And then silence.

He was engaged.

For a moment, my mind reeled. Had he misspoken? Surely, he meant to say, *I want to be engaged to you.* I waited for him to correct what he said, but he didn't. He looked at me, waiting for the words to sink in. But I just stared at him and repeated his words, "You're engaged?"

"Sarai, I'm engaged… to Sandiya."

Just like that. It was that simple. No, *Sarai, I'm engaged, and I'm sorry.* No, *Sarai, I'm engaged, but I still love you.* No, nothing but a simple, "I'm engaged." As if he were asking me, *and how was your summer?*

I looked at him incredulously, the words taking only seconds to sink in. Now I may have had my tendencies to live in denial, but when the truth is front of me, staring me straight in the eyes, telling me that he now belongs to another, that tendency to be in denial is no longer an option.

"Engaged?" I asked. My voice belied of a calm that I did not feel. It was someone else's voice, for my voice wanted to scream that this was not possible. That we were the ones who were supposed to get married. That I had known it from the first time we met. I had fallen in love with him, hopelessly, deeply, forever, once upon a time, happily ever after. That was supposed to be our story.

"I got engaged in India," he said.

"Engaged?" I croaked out again. This time my voice was raspy, almost hoarse, as I asked, "How is that possible?" My eyes settled on my hand that still lay on his shirt, against his heart. His hand still covered my hand and tightened.

"It wasn't planned. I swear… it was… well, you know they've been pressuring me for a while. And I made them promise to leave me alone about it while we were in India. And then we were there. And my father got sick, very sick. Sarai, we all thought he was going to die. He thought he was going to die. And he had one dying wish…"

"To see you married," I said as I fought waves of nausea.

"Yes, to see me married."

Unbelievable. I wondered if his family had even staged it. I had seen that in an Indian movie once. The family was so desperate to force a marriage that the father had faked a heart attack. But wait! They weren't married. They were engaged. He could break off the engagement. That didn't sound so bad. It was fixable. A hurried promise made in a time of duress. It was excusable, right?

"Take it back," I said, simply. The solution was evident. Just say no, like to drugs, don't fight it, don't justify it, just say no. They couldn't force him to get married like that.

"Sarai, I can't take it back. Our whole family was there at the ceremony. I think my getting engaged helped my father to recover."

"You *can* take it back. You were basically forced," I said emphatically. Why wasn't he cooperating? Why wasn't he thinking of solutions to get out of this? He couldn't be with this girl. Whoever she was. That was NOT an option.

"Tell the girl you can't marry her. Tell her about me. She'll understand. She wouldn't want you if you were in love with someone else."

"Sandiya," he supplied.

"Tell the *girl*," I repeated. I refused to say her name. I couldn't say it.

"They'd understand. You don't love her. You love me... *right? Right?*! You just have to tell them. They can't force you. This isn't the Middle Ages. This isn't India fifty years ago. This is America. You have rights! You have the right to fall in love with whomever you want. The right to chose whomever you want."

But he just shook his head. "Sarai, I can't."

What did he mean he can't? He was shooting down every suggestion she made! He wasn't even trying to get out of out it. *He didn't want out of it*, I realized. Did he want to be with this girl?

"Do you love her?" I asked, hating myself for even voicing that. I didn't think I could bear it if he said yes.

"No! No—how could I love her? I don't even know her." I was relieved to hear that because that meant he would never marry her. But the next words killed that momentary victory. "But I could grow to love her."

"I don't understand," I said, shaking my head, mumbling it over and over. Tears were streaming down my face, and a raw lump developed in my throat. I sat down on the picnic table and then looked up at this person I loved and who I thought loved me back. "What changed? This was just supposed to be a vacation. You promised me that you had no intention of giving into your parents' pressures for marriage!"

He said nothing and just looked at me apologetically again. Was he feeling sorry for me, I wondered? Where were his tears? Why wasn't he torn up about this? My heart and stomach ached, and I was fighting a losing battle with the hysteria building up within me. My life was over.

And there he was, just giving me his sad, apologetic puppy dog eyes. Pitying me. I didn't want his pity. I wanted his love. How could things have changed so quickly? What happened in India? How had they brainwashed him? Where did the love go? How could three months have changed five years of what we had built? I shook my head. I just didn't get it.

"What changed, Armaan? Really, I need to know. What changed?"

"I don't know, Sarai. I don't know." He shook his head and then looked at me helplessly. "It just got too hard, Sarai. It just got too hard."

"That's it?!" I asked hysterically, my arms flailing like a madwoman. "I gave you 5 years of my life, and all I get is a 'it got too hard'? I'd like to know when it all got too hard. I thought we were happy, that everything was fine."

"It was. We were, but, Sarai, when I was in India I realized... I have a huge family. They would never accept you, not completely. And your family would never accept me. And you know family is everything to me. What about our kids? How would we raise them? Hindu or Christian?"

"We'd figure it out because that's what people do when they love each other. They figure it out. They don't just find someone else to marry just because it's easier. They stick it out with the one they love. And they *figure it out*," I said, almost biting the words out. But inside, I knew the answer. He knew the answer. I would have raised them Christian.

"Sarai, I want to raise my kids as Hindu. I love my religion. It's a part of who I am. It's a part of my family. And they are a part of me. You'd never allow it. For you, it would only be them going to *your* church, believing only in *your* god."

I resented him implying that I was close-minded. "You don't even practice your faith! I truly believe mine. For me, faith isn't my prefer-ence, nor is it tradition. It isn't even culture. It's what I truly believe to be the truth. I can't change that as much as I can change the fact that gravity exists or that the sky is blue."

We'd had this argument before. In fact, it was truly the only time we ever did fight about anything. It was the one thing I was unwilling to compromise on, and he seemed to acquiesce. Apparently, I was wrong. He had never given in. And now he had just given up.

Having him break up with me was devastating, but having him break up with me while also telling me he was engaged to another woman was almost more than I could bear. There would be no chance of reconciliation. No breaking up and then getting back together. It was over. Just like that. That simple. For him. But for me, I would be recovering from him for the rest of my life. How could I have loved someone so blindly? I felt abandoned and betrayed. And worse, I just felt empty. Empty with the void that he once filled.

"Sarai," he said, pleading with me to understand. "You don't know how hard it was for me there. My father was sick. I thought he was on his deathbed. I thought I could do something to save him, and I did. If I told him about you, he would have died right there. I would have killed him. And then I could never forgive myself, and my mother would hate me for the rest of her life as well."

"But your father is fine now. Just tell him about us, and they'll understand."

He shook his head, "It's not that simple. Promises were made. My family is obligated to keep them. Our family name and reputation are at stake."

"What are they going to do? Arrest you?" I realized I was fighting a losing battle. God! What was I hearing? I couldn't believe he was seriously considering this. I wanted to shake the sense back into him. How could he let go of our love like this? I could *never, ever* consider anyone else. I looked at him, standing there on the bridge, and just shook my head.

"Things happened so fast..." he said, pacing back and forth again, running his fingers through his hair. He stopped and looked at me desperately, "Sarai, please believe me. I never meant to hurt you."

I didn't understand what the confusion was. "Just get out of it, Armaan," I said matter-of-factly.

"I can't, Sarai."

"Just tell them you can't go through with it!"

He said it again, this time more slowly, "I can't, Sarai."

"So you really are going to go through with it?"

"It's done. I can't go back on it. My family would be shamed. And I can't do that to them. Sandiya deserves better."

Sandiya deserves better? *Sandiya deserves better?* "Oh, you can't hurt someone you barely know, but you can do it to me, the very woman you professed to have loved for the last five and a half years?"

"I know you don't understand now, but one day you'll thank me. I've thought a lot about it, and I think this is for the best."

I looked at him like he was crazy. "For the best? How is this for the best? We date for several years, and you break up with me out of nowhere, and somehow that's for the best? Why didn't you realize this wasn't for the best when you first asked me out? In fact, why the heck did you stay with me for so long anyway?"

His eyes were filled with apology, but I saw nothing that indicated he was in agony like I was over his decision. I continued trying to convince him. "Why should you have to grow to love anyone? Can't it just be there from the beginning, like it was for us?"

"It would never work, Sarai. Who are we kidding? You would never go to temple with me. Neither of our parents would ever really accept it. My parents like you, but they'd never accept you as my wife. And your parents would never accept me. Hell, you haven't even introduced me to them!" he said, looking at me like I was the one who had hurt him.

"How could you say that? I told you I just needed the right time to tell them," I said, my voice no more than a whisper.

"In five years you haven't found the 'right' time!" he said accusingly. He then softened his voice. "Don't you see, Sarai, if you can't even tell them about us dating, then maybe this is just wrong."

I looked at him. His beautiful face. The face I thought I would look at for the rest of my life. The one that made me believe that anything was possible. In our Indian culture, an engagement was almost as official as a wedding. Though it could technically be broken, I knew by looking at him that somehow, between the time he had left for India and returned, something had changed. I had lost him. He had made his decision to follow his family's wishes, and no matter what I said, he would not break his engagement. He wanted to be with this girl, and now he no longer wanted to be with me.

Almost on cue, the sky crackled and rumbled, echoing the turmoil I felt. Huge droplets of rain started falling at first, and then a deluge of rain followed. My soft, flowing, perfectly blow dried hair was a matted, tangled mess in seconds. I hadn't expected the slight scent of summer rain to turn into a torrent of lashing wind and pouring rain, but I didn't care that my hair and my dress were plastered to me and that I probably looked as attractive as a wet, drowning rat. I stared at him through the rain, endlessly hurt and shocked as I tried my best to digest the moment. I stared at his face, begging him to change with every fiber of my being, but he just looked at me with apology and pity in his eyes. I shook my head again, feeling utterly defeated.

It was over.

It could have been such a romantic night like in the movie, *Kaho Naa... Pyaar Hai,* about love birds caught in a beautiful summer storm, but our Bollywood story had reached its abrupt, tragic, and very unfair ending. The playful prancing of innocent lovers in the rain was over. Every true love story had an untimely tragic element, and unfortunately, even though I thought I was the star, destined to live happily ever after, I ended up being the casualty. It was like the movie *Kuch Kuch Hota Hai* where the romantic heroine dies, and by the end of the movie, the "hero" ends up with someone else.

"Come on, I'll take you home," he said, reaching for my arm.

I shirked away from his touch as if he had just burned me. "No!" I yelled out, my voice drowning against the loud sound of falling rain. "Just leave me alone. I'll walk," I said as I started following the path out of the park towards the main entrance.

"Quit being stubborn, Sarai! I'll take you home. You'll get sick out here like this. It's getting cold, and you're going to end up with bronchitis or pneumonia!" He reached out for my hand, but I once again pushed his hands away and stepped out of his reach.

As I walked away, I paused and looked back at him. He was a stranger to me. I didn't know this person. He couldn't be the same guy with whom I had just spent the past five and a half years. With my teeth chattering due to the cold rain, I said, "Y-y-y-you have no r-r-r-rights over me! Y-y-y-you gave away that right when you became engaged to another w-w-w-woman-n-n."

He wanted to argue with me, but he knew I was right, just as I knew it was over between us.

Sometime later I would look back at this moment, wondering if there was something I could have said… something I could have done that would have changed his mind. But at that moment, I knew what it took me weeks, months, and even years to realize over and over again—that our relationship was truly and irrevocably over.

So Armaan followed me in his car while I walked. A gentleman to the end. No, not a gentleman, because a gentleman would never break the heart of a woman he purported to love. A gentleman would never get engaged to another woman while still dating someone else.

But I didn't go home. In the cold rain, with teeth chattering and in a drenched sundress and cardigan, I walked the half mile back to my subdivision, past my house and two streets down and took another right, a left, and another left, straight to Reena's home. I walked past her shocked mother who answered the door, right up the stairs to Reena's bedroom and collapsed on her bed like a rag doll while she tried to comfort me. But how do you comfort someone who's inconsolable?

Chapter 9

B RIGHT, BLINDING SUNLIGHT streamed through my bedroom window the next morning. I raised my arms to shield myself from the searing rays of light as my eyes adjusted. I blinked several times as the hazy images of my room came into focus. My first instinct was to close the curtains, but when I tried to rise from my bed, I was overcome with nausea and collapsed back into my comforter. My arms and legs felt like leaden blocks so I lay there as images of the prior night came crashing back to me in vivid detail, assaulting me with a fresh pain, rather than the vague shadows of dreams. *Meeting Armaan at the park and seeing him in his Stanford polo, sporting a shorter, more preppy haircut. Armaan telling me he was engaged. Armaan adamantly refusing to break his engagement.* Each painful moment came rushing back to me in an excruciatingly detailed flashback.

I recalled walking to Reena's house in the rain and hysterically telling her as much as I could. But how did I get home? Thank God my parents were still in India for another 2 months! My mom knew about Armaan, but my father had no idea, and I'm not sure how I or she could have explained my state of distress to him.

I lay there motionless. What do I do now? I hadn't the faintest idea. This was more than a setback. This was a total collapse. My whole future had been planned around him and now I had no idea what to do next. I thought the worst had come, but the worst had just started. For the minutes, hours, days, and months that followed were sometimes more difficult to get through than that first night. Feeling hopeless was one thing, but realizing how truly I had come to depend on Armaan added a new depth of pain to the loss I was already feeling.

The door to my bedroom abruptly swung open. Reena walked in and sat next to me on my bed. *Reena.* So that's how I got home.

"How do you feel?" she asked, placing the back of her hand on my head to check my temperature. "You were shivering so hard after getting drenched in the rain, that I was sure you were going to catch a cold. I brought you home so I could get you changed into dry clothes. Plus, I knew you'd want some privacy." She looked at me intently, waiting for me to respond, but I said nothing. I don't know why I didn't say anything. I just looked at her helplessly. I knew if I talked about it, I would start tearing up. And if I started tearing up, I would start crying, and once I started crying, I was sure that I would never be able to stop. Reena had gone through a terrible breakup a few years ago, so I knew she could relate to some of my pain.

"Are you up for eating breakfast?" she asked. "I know eating is the last thing you want to do, but you have to. You need food." I had no appetite, and the thought of food was the last thing I had on my mind. I shook my head. Reena's eyebrows curled up like a caterpillar. "You are going to eat, young lady! I don't care that you don't feel hungry or that you have no interest in food."

"You sound like my mom!" I croaked out, my voice raspy, undoubtedly from all the uncontrollable crying.

"Ah, she speaks!" she said. "But crying, screaming, and flailing your fists at Fate takes a lot of energy that you're going to need. Come on," she coaxed. "Besides, I make a delicious toast!"

I managed a weak smile. "I appreciate it, Reen, but I honestly don't..." I struggled to get the words out.

She arched her eyebrow at me. I knew then there was no point in arguing. She wouldn't stop until I had eaten, and I was too weak to fight her.

So I ate her burned toast, her slightly underdone scrambled eggs, and drank her watery chai, all the while images and thoughts of Armaan continuously battled for center stage in my mind.

Reena left me to go to work that morning, leaving me to my tumultuous thoughts. In what only seemed like minutes later, the door had opened again, and she stood at my doorway.

"I thought you were going to work."

"What are you talking about? I did go to work."

Well maybe she had been gone more than a few minutes. "What time is it?"

"Six-thirty in the evening. What time did you think it was?" she asked suspiciously, the back of her hand resting against my forehead.

I fought the urge to push her hands away. I still didn't want to be touched... by anyone. "I thought you had just left," I said vaguely.

"I did. Nine hours ago. So what did you eat for lunch?"

I hadn't eat anything, but I wasn't about to admit that to her. "I ate a sandwich," I replied.

"Oh, really? What kind?"

"Turkey."

"Turkey sandwich, huh?" she asked with a ladle in one hand and the other hand on her hips. All she needed was an apron, and she was set to star in *Mommie Dearest*. "If you had a turkey sandwich, I'm curious to know how you made it since there is no sandwich meat in the fridge, and I used the last of the bread to make your toast this morning."

"Reen, you don't have to do all this," I said, but she walked out of my bedroom. Before long, I could hear her clanging some pots and pans in the kitchen. In about thirty minutes, the delicious smell of pasta and sauce filled the air. Reena returned with a tray that held a plate of lasagna and garlic bread. I didn't recall hearing the sound of the microwave in the time she had been there.

"Lean Cuisine or Stouffers?" I asked, fully aware of my friend's lack of culinary skills.

"Neither," she said with a smile.

"Your mom made it?" I asked suspiciously. I pulled myself up into a sitting position, and straightened my sheets and bedspread so she could set the tray evenly in my lap.

"Nope!" she said with the look of triumph as she watched my reaction.

"You made it?!" It smelled delicious and looked nothing like the soggy, gooey, charred pasta and burnt cheese concoction she had tried to feed me in college when we were roommates. I was impressed.

"Yes, while you have been pining away for Armaan, I have turned into a gourmet chef," she said as she rested the tray on my lap. But I eyed the Andes breath mints sitting on the edge of the tray in their signature green Olive Garden foil.

She saw me staring at them and sighed dramatically. "All right, you've found me out. It's take-out. I just heated the lasagna a bit more in the oven so it would be warm and toasty for you."

I instinctively smiled back and shook my head in amusement. "Well, you heat food up quite well," I said, not quite sure on how to thank her while not insulting her at the same time.

"Ah ha! I got you to talk and to smile all in one sitting! I am a miracle worker!" she said taking a dramatic bow. Then she pulled out her own fork and sat on the edge of my bed. Glancing up at me, she noted my raised eyebrow. "What? I'm a growing girl! I need food, too."

I answered by moving closer to the edge of my bed to make more room for her. We sat there quietly for some time, just eating the lasagna and tearing off pieces of garlic bread.

I paused between bites and realized how lucky I was to have such a good friend. As much as I wanted to be left alone, I also didn't want to be alone. "Reen..." I said.

"Yeah?" she asked, pausing before she took another bite.

"Thanks. For everything," I said, and then looked down, knowing that I would start crying again.

Reena put down her fork and looked at me for a few moments before she spoke. "Do you remember when I broke up with Liju? You insisted I stay with you for two weeks and you made sure I ate every day and that I got out of my bed." She tucked a strand of loose hair behind my ears and then squeezed my hands. "I'm not doing anything that you haven't already done for me. And I would do it all again if I ever felt you needed it. I just don't want you to feel alone, especially with your family still on vacation in India."

My eyes felt prickly. I tried with all my might not to cry. I absently started moving the lasagna with my fork. "I am alone, Reena. I am alone."

"You're without Armaan, but you're not alone. Single, maybe, but never alone, and I'm going to tell you what you told me when I was feeling this way. It's going to be okay." I looked up at her quizzically. How annoying and presumptuous I must have sounded to her back then!

"You were probably tempted to say, '*Shut the hell up, you don't know what you're talking about!*'"

Reena looked thoughtful for a moment and then smiled and shook her head. She lifted the sheets and joined me in bed. It felt like we did when we were kids spending the night at each other's homes. "Actually, no. I think your words gave me hope. You sounded so confident, *so* sure of yourself, that I somehow believed that despite the incredible pain and hole in my heart, I would somehow, someday be okay again."

A hole in my heart. That was exactly how I felt. I also felt like my insides had been gutted and left strung out on a clothesline.

"You will be okay, maybe not today, but someday." While she was trying to be reassuring, in her own eyes I could see both doubt and worry.

I smiled back, suddenly feeling she needed to be reassured more than I did. "I guess I just need to wallow in it, at least for a little bit. Then I'll be fine." *Someday*, I thought to myself. People had prosthetic limbs. If only there was a prosthetic heart.

Reena and Liju had dated for two years, and I could still recall how upset she had been. But they were freshmen in college. I didn't meet Armaan until after we had graduated college. My entire future had been planned around Armaan, and without him, I felt like I had nothing. All my previous accolades and accomplishments meant nothing. I felt like a house whose foundation had crumbled. And for the first time, I truly wanted to die.

Where had I gone wrong? When I first met Armaan, I felt like he had walked out of a Bollywood movie set and into my life. He had been so perfect. Too perfect. Understanding, cultured, gorgeous, and successful. And although my life had been good, I should have known it would have never been that good. Shah... as soon as I heard the name, *I knew*. He was Hindu. I knew I would never be able to introduce him to my parents. I knew if I ever did, I would be risking everything I held close to my heart. I knew it was a relationship that I would have to keep hidden. I had seen it too many times in college—seen it in reverse. Malayalee guys dating a Gujarati Hindu or Pakistani Muslim girl for a year or two, only to break up with them in the end. Our families are all from the same country, but we couldn't be more different. It was a difference that went beyond state lines. It went beyond language. It even went beyond caste. But I thought we would have been different. I thought we would have been the ones to make it. But, in the end, we were another statistic.

Because in the end, the family usually wins. No, I corrected myself, the family *always* seems to win. In fact, I could only recall one example from college where a relationship lasted despite parental objections. And in all the other cases, why did it seem that it was always the guys who are okay with leaving the relationship while the girls seem ready to fight family and tradition. It's the mothers, I realized. You lose because they never leave their mothers.

He had been a dream, a fantasy. I knew a future would have been difficult, if not impossible. I could still recall that small voice I pointedly ignored. I chose to believe what I wanted instead. Was this a lesson then? A test from God? Maybe Armaan had been the forbidden fruit that I was supposed to have resisted. But like Eve, I had been vulnerable, weak, and greedy. So if he had been my test, then I had failed, and I was now serving my punishment. Yes, that must be it. Because that's what it felt like. Only punishment from God could be so brutal, so severe, and so final.

What is it about us women that we perversely enhance our pain? Men typically live in denial about pain and loss while we, instead, choose to wallow in it. We listen to the sad love songs. We relive every moment of our relationship but somehow omit memories of the very issues that resulted in the breakup. My saving grace was that it was summer vacation, and I had an entire two months to sober up and get myself together before I started the new school year. For the first few weeks, I spoke to almost no one with the exception of Reena. I closed my blinds and lived in physical and emotional darkness as I tortured myself with every memory we had shared. It was similar to what I imagined rehab to be like. The hysterics, the gut-wrenching physical pain that wracked my body and made me cry out, the physical convulsions, the irregular heartbeat, and panic attacks, the inability to sleep, and even the desire to not exist just so I could escape the pain I felt. I didn't leave my bedroom except to go the bathroom. I medicated myself with television, allowing the mindless soap opera plotlines to help me forget my own *telenovela*.

Then when I was finally ready to start talking to my other friends again, all I could talk about was Armaan. Talking about him was like a drug. In the midst of describing all these wonderful memories I had with him, I experienced a soaring elation and giddiness that was later followed by a deep hollow abyss in the pit of my stomach. I was then left with an emptiness that screamed to be filled with talk of him again as I relived our early, happy days together. I would talk of him to anyone who would listen, mostly to Reena, of course. But eventually I was forced to move on to Anjuli and Maya. It was ridiculous to be so consumed by one human being. But at that time, it was a compulsion that I could not control and thinking of him was an addiction I thoroughly enjoyed.

My parents returned from their trip a few weeks later, and I finally told my mom about the breakup. While she didn't approve of me dating someone from another religion, she empathized with my pain.

"I don't get it, Mom!" I said in between sobs as she held me.

"Pray to God, Sarai-mol. Only He can help you," she advised as she stroked my hair. Maybe because my mom's advice to "just pray about it" sounded so cliché at the time or maybe part of me felt let down by God, but somehow, something in me snapped.

"God?!" I bit out and jerked my head away from her embrace. "God has done nothing for me but dangle a carrot in front of me... a perfectly shaped, inviting, irresistible carrot, and as soon as I lunged for a nibble, it was jerked away from me." My mom looked horrified at my bitter words, which I knew for her bordered on blasphemy. She let go of me as if I had burned her. Then shook her head in astonishment and disappointment and left me alone. I felt like utter crap and wondered how long it would be before I was struck down by lightning.

Chapter 10

A FEW WEEKS LATER, I caved in and called Armaan. "What did you want to ask me?" I blurted out.

This was the first time I had spoken to him since our breakup. I had picked up the phone several times to call him since we had seen each other at the park, but each time I put the phone back down. Then I waited and waited for days and then weeks for him to call me. I waited for him to tell me that he had made a mistake and that he couldn't live without me. I waited for him to call and apologize. But no call came. Not even a, *"Are you okay? I was just checking up on you,"* phone call. I finally got sick of waiting and called him.

Without a hello or an introduction, I immediately spouted out my question.

"Excuse me? Sarai, I'm sorry, but I'm not sure I follow," he said, his voice somber.

At least he still recognized my voice, I thought sarcastically. So he hadn't forgotten everything about me.

"You said you wanted to tell me something and then you wanted to ask me something. You obviously told me what you needed to tell me. Now what was it that you wanted to ask me?"

"When?" he asked.

I rolled my eyes. How could he forget? "On the bridge, on the night you broke my heart and screwed up my life," I said as coldly as I could.

He sighed and was about to say something, but then mumbled a *never mind* under his breath. "I don't remember what I was going to ask… *Oh, wait!* I do." He hesitated, and finally blurted it out, "I wanted to ask you if we could somehow still be friends."

"Oh," I mumbled. Well, at least I had gotten the first letter right. It wasn't *fo*rgiveness he was seeking, but *f*riendship. I couldn't help but wonder how he could think we could just be friends. Was he naïve? Or was he just being cliché? I wondered if he would have felt the same way if I had broken up with him.

"Friends, huh? *That's* what you wanted to ask me?" I spat.

I sounded like a bitter woman, and I didn't like it. I liked it even less knowing that he knew how bitter I was, especially since he didn't seem all cut up about it. This wasn't the lasting impression I wanted to leave Armaan with. Maybe I was bitter. Maybe I would be bitter and pine for him for the rest of my life. But I didn't want him to know that, and I hated the fact that just like I wore my heart on my sleeve, I now wore my bitterness there, too.

"Friends, huh… *hmmm*…" I said, like I was mulling it over (as if I even needed to mull it over). So I said the only thing I could say at the time even though I had no prior intention of saying it. "So am I invited to your wedding then?" I asked combatively, partly wanting to shock him and partly just wanting to make him squirm.

"Huh?!" he asked, taken aback. Then he was completely silent, no doubt trying to digest my question as well as come up with a very diplomatic response. "Y-y-y-you want to come to the wedding?" he asked, his voice still thick with disbelief. "*Seriously?*"

I tried to sound nonchalant, even though I, too, was in shock that I had actually said it, much less thought it. "Well, that's what friends do, right? They go to each other's weddings."

As I knew he would, he had no answer for that and remained quiet. I broke the silence with a strained laugh, "I didn't think so. No worries. I wasn't looking for an invite, just trying to prove a point. I don't think we qualify as real friends anyway." And without a good-bye, I hung up the phone, hoping I had made my point.

Two weeks later, an oversized silk cream envelope embossed with red and gold gilded lettering arrived at my house. It was Armaan's wedding invitation.

✧   ✧   ✧

I COULD HAVE easily spent the rest of the summer underneath the covers in mourning if it weren't for the intervention of Reena. She surprised me by showing up one Saturday. She barged in, throwing open the door, and shoved aside the curtains. She was done feeling sorry for me, she said, and now she expected me to start acting like a friend to her and start doing things we used to do together.

When I emerged from the house that morning, I flinched under the searing rays of the sun like a vampire. I obediently got into the car with Reena, and we did something we hadn't done in a while together. We went to Barnes and Noble, ordered our venti caramel macchiato, and with a couple of our favorite fashion magazines in tow, we found our favorite spot on the second floor. It was in the back, right next to all the books and manuals on sex. It was a spot we had found years ago, a place where most people were too embarrassed to be around. The chairs were extra cushiony (probably because no one wanted to sit there) and anytime anyone came around to browse through the sex manuals, they immediately left when they saw that they were in direct view of two giggling 20-somethings.

I leaned back into the cozy sofa-chair with the summer issue of *InStyle* magazine and began flipping through the pages as I sipped my coffee. I could see Reena's concerned eyes, checking up on me every few pages, so I would look up and smile to let her know that I was fine and take another sip of my coffee. Soon the pages began to blur, and my thoughts once again drifted to Armaan. I seemed to have passed the anger stage, and now I just felt profoundly sad and empty. I absent-mindedly flipped to the center spread of the magazine to find the glowing face of Jessica Alba in a white strapless lace sheath smiling up at me. The entire middle section of the magazine, I noticed with a grimace, was devoted to summer celebrity wedding fashions. I glanced at Reena who was immersing herself on the latest Brangelina gossip and voiced something I had been pondering since Armaan's wedding invitation had arrived, "I'm going to Armaan's wedding, and I want you to come with me."

Reena paused in a mid-page turn, and her other hand looked like it was going to drop her coffee. "*You're what?!*" she bit out.

"I don't expect you to understand, but Reen, I have to go."

"What is wrong with you? Why would you want to do that to yourself?" she asked, gesturing her hands like an Italian godfather. My eyes were on her coffee, and I began wondering if she was going to drop it or fling it at me.

"Reen—"

"No, Sarai, you listen to me. I've stood by you through everything, but I am NOT going to stand by and watch you torture yourself while you watch him marry someone else. What is wrong with you?"

I was too tired to argue with her. I just looked at her helplessly. The magazine slipped from my lap and landed softly on the floor. "I have to, Reen. I have to be there."

Chapter 11

At the wedding

FOR THE LAST 8 months I had wondered what she would look like. I tortured myself as I concocted a flawless, goddess, superwoman image in my mind. Someone who had the beauty of Bollywood actresses Aishwarya Rai and Priyanka Chopra combined with the creative talent of Pulitzer Prize winning writer, Jhumpa Lahiri, and the intellectual prowess of former Prime Minister of India, Indira Gandhi. Somehow from the time he mentioned her name to the months that I spent pining for him, I pictured the woman whom he had chosen over me to be someone who was nothing short of an UberGoddess. But what we concoct in our heads is often a lot less impressive in person. To both my relief and my disappointment, she fell short of my expectations.

She looked to be less than average height, easily no taller than five-two. The top of her head barely reached his shoulder. Her face was oval, but still retained that childlike plumpness and smoothness that reminded me of a Raphael cherub even though she was probably well into her mid to late 20s. Her skin was very light by Indian standards, contrasting with the darkness of her hair. Her features were soft, no striking cheekbones, no supermodel features. And while she was undoubtedly attractive, I would honestly categorize her as being more cute and pretty than striking or beautiful, though I'll be the first to admit I don't qualify as the most objective observer. Although I felt relieved when comparing myself to her, I also felt disappointed.

Because she wasn't the UberGoddess I had imagined, I couldn't help but wonder what about her had let him choose her over me. Who was this pretty but less than spectacular girl who managed to steal the heart of my Prince Charming? Surely she wasn't just barely above average in all aspects. Part of me needed her to have the looks of a supermodel, someone I couldn't compete with, someone whom I was destined to play second fiddle to. But part of me also needed for her to be exactly who she was—someone who must have had attributes other than just physical beauty. I would have respected Armaan less if all he did was fall for a beautiful face. After eight months of looking for reasons, justifications, and excuses, I concluded it had less to do with her and more to do with his family. He hadn't chosen her over me. He had chosen his family, his religion, his culture over me. But I wasn't sure whether that knowledge comforted me or tortured me even more.

When had marriage gotten so complicated? Why couldn't it just be about two people in love who wanted to be together? Why couldn't it be about being with someone who inspired your soul, about being with someone you couldn't live without? Was he settling for her or did they, too, have that magic connection we shared? When he had agreed to marry her, they were no more than strangers. Even now she couldn't know him as well as I did. She hadn't spent the last five years with him. She didn't know his different sides, his moods, his likes and dislikes. She knew nothing. But she would come to know everything, my traitorous, practical side reminded me. She would soon know him more intimately than I had, I realized with sickening realization.

I knew Armaan needed more than just physical attractiveness. He needed fire, wit, and humor. He needed someone who could challenge him, keep him on his toes. But after observing her on stage with her cherub face, her hands tightly clasped, shifting from one foot to another, I didn't get the impression of a vivacious, challenging femme. She was more an ingénue—young, impressionable, and shy. I couldn't help but feel that she was completely out of her league and that she shouldn't be up there on the makeshift stage with him. I didn't get the feeling she was someone who could put him in his place while at the same time knowing exactly how to inspire the fire that lay dormant within him, just below the surface. She didn't strike me as someone who was tuned in to every gesture, every movement; someone who could read him like a well-loved book; or someone who seemed to instinctively understand him from the beginning without requiring any explanation.

She wasn't... *me.*

Chapter 12

THOUGH I WAS dressed to the nines, I wasn't the only one. Indian weddings were not just about the bride and groom. The older I got, the more they turned into fashion shows with each girl trying to eclipse the other. Even aunties got in on the act, vying to surpass each other in the latest sari fashion.

Weddings were also about reconnecting with distant relatives, old friends, friends of friends, and neighbors. They all came out of the woodwork in their best outfits to attend weddings. With everyone looking their best and with marriage on the mind, it was *the* place for others to find their own potential future spouse. If they weren't looking for a potential spouse for themselves, they were looking for someone they knew, either a daughter or son, a sibling, a niece, a cousin, or a close family friend. With all the restrictions that come with finding one's future spouse, a wedding of a close friend or a relative was like shooting fish in a barrel.

But trying to find a good guy, the right guy, THE guy… now that was like everywhere else. It was still like trying to find that needle in a haystack. Second to college and before the Internet dating sites took off, weddings were one of the best ways to meet marriage potentials.

Dressed in bridal white and silver, I knew I made a sharp contrast to the kaleidoscope of richly colored *saris* and *chaniya cholis* that surrounded me at every turn. I also knew I might be raising a few eyebrows with my outfit choice.

As I stood there, observing the third of seven wedding rituals, I could overhear the remarks of two middle-aged aunties in front of me, one of whom filled out her green and gold sari like a miniature, overstuffed potato sack while the other had a figure that resembled a tall, thin lamppost. Both wore make-up as colorful and as garish as their saris.

"Their fathers are childhood friends, no?" asked the skinnier of the two as she sipped a glass of champagne.

The shorter one was busy biting into a samosa. "Yes. They went to medical school together, too. The girl's father is a cardiologist, like the boy's father." She paused momentarily to take another bite. No sooner had she bitten into it, she began talking again. "And the girl's mother is an anesthesiologist. The girl has followed in her mother's footsteps and is in her final year of residency. A very smart girl."

"Yes, it's a perfect match!" said the tall one. She clasped her hands in delight as if one of them were her own child. "Both are from a family of doctors, and they, too, are both doctors! And they both descend from old, well-respected families. Did you know the boy's grandfather was a personal friend of Mahatma Gandhi and fought during the British Raj?"

"Really?" asked the shorter of the two, her eyes widening in admiration. As she spoke, a small piece of potato fell out of her mouth. Before I could turn away, I heard her exclaim, "Well, I heard the girl's great-grandfather started one of the first colleges in Gujarat!"

"Oh, really?! I hadn't heard that!"

The shorter one began fanning herself with the program as her admiration for the families continued to grow. "And they are so beautiful together, no?"

"Yes! Their children will be like fashion models!"

Her face formed a momentary frown as she said, "But she shouldn't have worn that orange-red color. Deep red is more becoming, no?"

The skinner one shook her head in dismay as her face contorted into a sneer. "These girls these days! They are always trying to break from tradition. She could eat some *gulab jamun* and some *ladoo*... she could use with some more weight. She is too skinny, no?!"

"Oh, don't worry. Did you see her mother? She will no doubt gain weight once she has children," said the other, snorting, and like a duo of conniving tweens, the comment sent them both into a fit of muffled giggles.

"Sarai!" exclaimed a familiar voice that I couldn't quite place. I whipped around to find Tejal, one of my old college suitemates, looking me over. "Wow! I thought that was you! You look gorgeous!!" she said as she pulled me into a hug. Then with a twinkle in her eye she added, "But I hate to tell you that white is worn to funerals, not weddings!"

"Tejal! It's been so long! How are you?!" I asked. "Actually, I did know that, but I thought with all the silver embroidery and beading, this outfit could be an exception!"

"True, true. Well, it is undoubtedly an exceptional outfit. And wow, you really do look *beau-ti-ful*!" she said, enunciating each syllable as she looked me over again. "Did you get this outfit in Bombay?"

"Yes, I did! How did you know?" Tejal had an eye for fashion, and she always seemed to have the most beautiful outfits. When we were in college, she graciously loaned her clothes to our college Indian fashion and talent shows, and she always let her less fashion-forward Indian friends, like me, borrow from her closet when we had an Indian function that required something really nice.

"Because you could only find something that exquisite in India. Plus, if it had been in one of our local Indian shops, I undoubtedly would have grabbed it myself! I frequent the sari shops at least once a week, and the owners are all under strict orders to call me when they have a new shipment!"

"Well, you don't look too shabby yourself," I said, admiring her sheer, peacock blue sari that she paired with a matching halter top. The edge of her *pallu* as well as the *sari* blouse was made of real peacock feathers. "You always manage to find the most unique outfits and you always have the best blouses!"

Her smile deepened at my compliment. "Well, thank you, but I would kill to have your outfit in my collection. So be careful, Sarai," she warned, shaking her index finger at me. "Don't be surprised if your house gets broken into and the only thing missing is this outfit."

I laughed. "So what have you been up to? It's been what, two years?"

"Yeah, I think we last saw each other at Renni's wedding, remember? And where is your other half?" I was taken aback by her comment because as far as I was concerned my other half was no longer my other half.

From the look on my face, she realized her blunder and immediately corrected herself. "I mean Reena."

I smiled and replied, "Reena, Anjuli, and Maya are all at the appetizer table. I think they're afraid that dinner won't be served or something so they're getting their meal in now."

"Oh my gosh, Anjuli and Maya are here, too?! I haven't seen either of them in a while. I feel like we're having a dorm reunion!" She said excitedly as she scanned the appetizer tables. "Oh, there they are!" she exclaimed, waving excitedly. Reena must have been watching us, and soon everyone was waving at each other.

As we made our way toward the girls, Tejal tried to ask me in the most diplomatic way, "So how are you holding up?"

I put on a smile and tried to muster up a convincing, sincere voice. "I'm good. Really good... considering."

Perhaps it was too convincing because Tejal then surprised me with her next question. "So what *are* you doing here? Honestly, you're the last person I expected to see!"

What was I doing here? It was a question I wasn't entirely sure how to answer. Perhaps for no other reason than I just knew I couldn't *not* be here.

Luckily, she didn't wait for an answer. "When I heard you and Armaan had broken up a few months ago, I was in shock. If anyone would have made it, my bet would have been on you guys."

"You and me both," I said wryly with a half-smile.

"Honestly, if my parents didn't force me, I wouldn't have come, but I have to admit that I was curious to see the wedding and how elaborate it would be. And so far, it hasn't disappointed. Were you here during the *baraat?*" When I shook my head, she said, "He arrived on an elephant! Can you believe that? An elephant. And they carried her in one of those palanquins held by poles. It was something out of a Bollywood movie!"

We had reached Reena, Maya, and Anjuli. After the squeals and hugs, the three of them started playing catch-up.

In the meantime, my attention returned to Armaan. After eight months of not seeing him, being confronted with his beauty was almost like seeing him again for the first time.

Most of the time his attention was focused on what the priest was saying, but occasionally his eyes would scan the lawn, probably surprised at the sheer amount of guests, or maybe looking for one particular guest? Did he think I would come? Did he ever wonder about me?

I recognized that look that told me he had just seen something humorous that he wanted to mimic. He leaned over and whispered something in Sandiya's ear. She laughed back. My chest tightened as I watched them share what was possibly their first inside joke. I bitterly swallowed the sweet mango *lassi* that I had been holding and lowered my eyes. I tried to gather my composure before the tears that were welling became a floodgate that I would not be able stop. Deciding that I just needed something else to eat, I turned on my heels, ready to do some damage at the appetizer bar but nearly collided into Rakesh.

"Sarai!" he said, sincerely shocked, his arms on my shoulders, bracing us for our near collision. His hair was slicked back, albeit with a little too much gel. He wore a black Nehru-style blazer and matching pants, but I had to admit, he looked handsome and, daresay, even more mature... or so I thought until he opened his mouth.

"What are you doing here?" he asked immediately. But before I could reply, he looked me over from head to toe, his eyes ever so slowly and appreciatively assessing me—exactly the way I had pictured Armaan looking at me. "Wow... you look beautiful! If I didn't know better, I'd think *you* were the bride!"

"She does look beautiful, doesn't she?" asked Reena, appearing out of nowhere, acting like a gushing mom. Wishing they were both Armaan saying that, I took another sip of my mango *lassi* as I hoped neither of them could see the tears in my eyes.

Rakesh was still admiring my outfit, but as always, he added his own one cent's worth. "Of course, you do know that we Hindus wear white to our funerals and not to our weddings."

"Oh, yeah, that's right," I said, shooting Reena an annoyed look. "But I'm not Hindu."

"Yeah, that always seemed to be the problem." Realizing what he just said, Rakesh immediately looked sincerely contrite as Reena shot him the look of death.

And then Rakesh committed a common male folly. Rather than leaving things be and changing the subject, he felt the need to "make up" for his comment and create an even bigger grave to bury himself in.

"But white or not, that outfit is beautiful, Sarai, and you look gorgeous in it." It was a very sweet, generous comment, which would have been nice if he stopped there. But no, he continued. "Actually, I wasn't joking. You do kinda look like a bride. So why are you wasting it on Armaan's wedding? You should have saved it for your own wedding!" Reena immediately elbowed him. He winced, covering his stomach protectively, and said, "What did I say now? You Malu Christians wear white to your weddings, right? She could have worn this to her wedding."

"*Rakeeeesh…*" Reena began, ready to lecture him on etiquette, but then she looked at his bewildered expression and decided he was a lost cause. "Never mind. Just stand there, be quiet, and look cute."

"*Sooo…* you think I look cute, huh?" asked Rakesh, smoothing back his hair, clearly pleased with the compliment from Reena who never doled out compliments to him.

"Yeah, and I also think pugs and miniature boxers are cute," she said, glaring at him.

Rather than admitting defeat, Rakesh decided to turn his attention to me again. "So what *are* you doing here? I can't believe you're crashing Armaan's wedding, especially after all those times you lectured me about doing stuff like that!"

"I'm not crashing his wedding. I received an invitation!"

He looked from me to Reena, who was nodding in agreement, to me again. "He sent you an invitation?" he asked, covering his mouth with a clenched fist, trying unsuccessfully to hold back his shock and a chuckle. "Ooh! Dang that boy has balls! He breaks up with you and then invites you to *his* wedding with the girl he broke up with you for?"

"We're friends, Rakesh," I said defensively. "I'm here supporting his decision as a friend."

"Does his wife know you guys are *friends*?" At that, Tejal came to the rescue. She interlinked her arms with his and dragged him away. "So Rakesh, it's been a looong time! What have you been up to? And tell me where you got this beautiful Nehru suit," she asked, softly touching the black silk material. Rakesh smiled, immediately distracted and intrigued with the sudden attention. As they walked away, she turned around briefly back at us and winked. I mouthed a very generous and relieved "Thank you!"

Not knowing what to say to everyone else, I smiled weakly and sipped on my mango *lassi*, which I now wished was spiked with some vodka. As I looked away, Maya and Anjuli gave me the supportive rub on the back.

Soon we were joined by other members of our old college crew, but Reena kept them busy until I could regain my composure. As expected, all of them were shocked to see me there. But with the skill of a true diplomat, Reena had them all forgetting the fact that I was Armaan's ex-girlfriend, and soon they were all gushing over my silver and white outfit. After mingling with everyone, I once again slipped away to the outside terrace where I watched the rest of the wedding ceremony. I glanced down at the wedding program as I attempted to figure out what stage of the ceremony they were in.

I sighed, realizing there were only three additional major rituals left to observe, and Armaan still had no idea that I was even there. I wasn't quite sure what I had expected, but when I had initially imagined attending the wedding, I figured I would have somehow invariably crossed paths with Armaan. Something meaningful and long enough to give me that closure I needed. Maybe a passing glance as he mingled with guests or even a passing encounter in the buffet line. But some-how the moment never came. He and his bride remained under the stage of the *mandap* throughout the entire afternoon, almost oblivious to individual guests. As guests, we were all mere observers. As the afternoon wore on, I realized my chance meeting with Armaan may never be.

To my surprise, the MC announced that guests could approach the *mandap* and take official pictures with the bride and groom. Typically that wasn't done until the entire wedding ceremony was over. I assumed it was due to the large number of guests that they tried to break up the time in the receiving line so no one would be waiting too long. While Armaan and his wife remained seated on stage, a line of people had formed. Family by family, they joined them on stage to congratulate them and take the official wedding picture with the almost wedded couple. I watched him interact with each guest, most of whom I'm sure he didn't even know. As I realized my own window of opportunity to talk to him was growing smaller, I found myself actually contemplating joining the line of guests. At no time when I had imagined this moment of crossing paths with Armaan had I thought of actually meeting his new wife.

"Does she know about me?" I had asked him during one of our last phone conversations. "No," he had said, "I didn't think it was wise to tell her about you. If I did, I doubt she would approve of you being invited to our wedding."

How would he introduce me to her if I were to meet them in the greeting line? Would he keep it simple, like "Sandiya, this is my friend." Forget what he would say, what would *I* say? I began imagining the various types of introductions that could be made: "Hi, I'm Sarai, Armaan's girlfriend." Her eyes would undoubtedly widen in shock. And then I would laugh and apologize and say, "Oh, I'm sorry, forgive me. I meant to say that I'm his ex-girlfriend now. He broke up with me after he got engaged to you. It only took him three months to tell me. But don't worry. He told me as soon as he came back to America that we could no longer be together." She would momentarily be taken aback. I would then stop there, smile my most dazzling smile, and say something dramatic, maybe even shocking and scandalous, something to make her wonder, like "a word of advice, in the morning he prefers to eat a light breakfast; just toast, jam, and he prefers his coffee like his women—dark, sweet, with just a hint of bitterness." Then I would smile my most innocent and sincere smile and walk away. It would almost be worth it to see the shocked look on Armaan's face.

But Armaan only invited me to his wedding because he knew without a doubt that I was too mature to resort to such childish antics. I would be lying if I didn't admit that I wanted to punish him and watch him squirm as he explained himself to his wife. But Armaan was right to assume that I would never disgrace him, or myself, like that. And Sandiya... she herself was innocent in a sense. She did not know of his ties to me. If it wasn't her, there would undoubtedly have been another female his parents would have forced upon him, and more than likely, he would have succumbed regardless. As I watched her shake hands with the various guests, most of whom were strangers to her, I noted the warm smile, the sincere handshake. I wanted to hate her, but I couldn't. She seemed nice. Perhaps in another situation, in another lifetime, if she hadn't just married the love of my life, I may have been friends with her.

So rather than acting like the jilted girlfriend in front of his wife, maybe I could just act like Armaan and I were the closest of friends and nothing more: "We've been friends since college. To this day, he remains one of my closest friends." But she'd probably wonder why he never mentioned my name if we had been so close. Besides, if she were like any woman, traditional or not, she would not welcome the idea of him being that close to any other woman.

Maybe I didn't have to say anything besides just "congratulations." I would smile as sincerely as I could, and I would shake their hands, wishing them the very best. At the least, Armaan would have seen me, and we could have shared one final, albeit brief, moment. Yes, that would be enough. Although it would kill me to do it, I felt I owed myself that.

So I took a deep breath and made my way to the line to congratulate Armaan and his bride. My hands began to shake as I walked towards him. I had to do this. I had to say good-bye and smile at his new wife and wish them the best. What would he say when he saw me? Did he think I would come? Had he even noticed me among the hundreds that were there? As I made my way down the steps of the terrace, Reena appeared out of nowhere, grabbed me by the hand, and dragged me across the entire lawn, past countless guests, until she could find a private spot where we would not be overheard.

"Just where do you think you are you going?" she asked, arms crossed and nostrils flaring.

"What?! I'm getting in line to give them my congratulations!" I said, defensively and turned my attention to the bluff that lay below us. The wind had picked up, pulling some of the loose tendrils out of my up-do. I tucked a stray strand behind my ear.

"Sarai, are you really that masochistic?" When I didn't respond, she continued.

"What were you expecting? Did you think he would take one look at you in your beautiful white wedding *lengha*, decide he couldn't go through with marrying the other girl, and drag you up there and marry you instead?"

"No!" I spouted, crossing my arms defensively. "That's ridiculous!" We stood there in a silent face-off for a few moments.

But Reena wasn't ready to let it go. "Sarai, are you honestly going to stand there and deny that you wore your wedding *lengha*, the very *lengha* you had been saving for years to wear at your own wedding, for no other reason? Why would you waste this beautiful outfit on him, on *his* wedding?"

Reena had a way of piercing right through to the heart of everything I did. And while she was highly opinionated, she rarely judged me. I soon found that I could no longer hold Reena's stare and averted my eyes. "Fine," I relented. "Maybe, maybe not. I don't know, Reena. I just know I had to be here even if it killed me. I had to see this. I had to see him one last time. You're right. I needed to see if he could actually go through it," I said, my hands gesturing towards the *mandap*. "As far as the *lengha* goes, do you honestly think that it would be right for me to wear this to my own wedding now after Armaan?"

Reena shot me a dubious look, and I explained, "From the time I met him, I had imagined wearing this very *lengha* to our wedding. Whether I wore it tonight or not, it was already ruined for my own wedding. It wouldn't be fair to whichever guy I end up marrying. Because the entire time I would be reminded of Armaan and how it should be him instead."

Reena sighed and shook her head sympathetically. "Sarai, why are we even here? I know this is killing you."

I turned around to face the entire wedding scene. The colorful mandap decorated with thousands of flowers. The countless guests mingling in their finest Indian wear and nibbling on gourmet appetizers. *Why were we here?* It was undoubtedly the question of the day. I remember telling her so confidently in the bookstore that I had to be here. But now I was no longer sure why... at least not entirely. Had I expected him to see me in my bridal *lengha* and cancel his wedding because he realized he couldn't go through with it? Maybe. Had I just hoped to see him one last time to see if he were happy or just as miserable as me and was regretting his decision? Maybe.

I did know that part of me needed to see her, and part of me needed to see him. And part of me needed *him* to see *me*—one last image of me to carry for the rest of his life. Eight months ago, I was a sobbing wet, heartbroken fool in a park. And today I looked the best I had ever looked in my life. Yes, part of me most definitely wanted him to see me and hoped he would have some pang of regret where I was concerned. But I knew even then that you can't force that on anyone any more than you can force someone to love you.

I knew with ninety-five percent certainty that Armaan would go through with the wedding. After all, he had already gone through with the engagement in India. If he couldn't risk shaming his family in India, when things had not yet progressed so far, he would not cancel everything at the last minute and shame everyone on the actual wedding day. But I still needed to see everything with my own eyes. Though we had talked on the phone less than a handful of times, I hadn't seen Armaan since the night at the bridge. But as I watched him, I realized he seemed totally fine. More than fine. While I had spent the last eight months pining for him, he had moved on with his life, planning his future with his soon-to-be wife. And as painful as it was to realize that, I'm glad I had seen first-hand that he had obviously moved on. The question remained whether I would be able to move on. I feared my love for him would be an undying torch that I would be carrying to my grave.

✧ ✧ ✧

APPARENTLY, THEY WERE ready to continue to the next part of the ceremony, and the MC asked the guests to take their seats and assured those who were still in line that there would be time, once again, after the ceremony to personally congratulate the couple.

They moved on to the *Mangal Pheras*, the ceremony where the bride and groom circled around the sacred fire four times. I've always been intrigued by that "one" moment where a couple officially becomes husband and wife. I found it fascinating that one minute you're single, and the next minute you're officially married, spiritually and physically bound to this one person for the rest of your life. The precise moment is almost imperceptible. In the traditional, Christian ceremonies, it's the *I Do's* and the signing of the marriage certificate. But with a Hindu wedding, it gets even more complicated; the celebrations last for days, culminating with the last day, which in itself consists of several ceremonies and rituals. Some, like Armaan, consider the engagement just as binding as the wedding, just without the "fringe benefits" that come with being officially married.

When I glanced down at the program and read the brief description of the *Mangal Pheras*, I realized that this, indeed, was the moment that I had been awaiting and dreading. The program described the end of the ritual as when "the bride changes place to the left of the bridegroom as a gesture to signify the change from 'bride' to 'wife.'"

So I watched as they circled the fire four times. Then I watched as they proceeded to the *Saptapadi*, the final seven steps around the fire symbolizing nourishment, strength, prosperity, happiness, progeny, long life, harmony and understanding. With every step they took around the fire, I felt the sharp pain of a knife in my heart being pushed deeper into my soul.

The pain was undoubtedly evident on my face for Reena grabbed my hand, "Sarai, let's go. We don't need to watch this."

Without taking my eyes off them, I shook my head vehemently and said, "No!" I said defiantly. "I have to see this. I need to see this."

Reena's eyebrows wrinkled in frustration, but I stared straightaway in defiance. Finally, she relented. "Okay... okay. We'll stay, okay?" she said, squeezing my hand.

I nodded without even looking at her. I couldn't take my eyes off them... *them*... they were officially a couple. A few months ago she was no one, a stranger. If he had passed her on the street, he wouldn't have even bothered giving her a second look. Of that I was sure. And now she was his wife. Did she have any idea how lucky she was? Was he her dream come true? Or would she have settled for almost anyone her parents would have picked for her? Now she was his wife... *his* wife. And I was just no one. No, not "no one." I was his friend, always his friend. Forever destined to be his friend.

As I watched the final ceremonial observances, Reena excused herself. "On second thought, I can't watch you do this to yourself. I'm going to find Maya and Anjuli and make our way to the car. But take your time, and when you're ready, we'll leave."

After Reena left, I finally began to fully realize why I had come. Contrary to everyone else's opinion, my dress choice and color could not have been more appropriate. For white was truly a versatile, symbolic color choice for this occasion. I had come here, hopeful like a bride, and I would leave here, devastated like a widow. For Armaan's wedding was my sati. As he became another woman's husband, he would, in a sense, be dead to me and with him would die the Sarai who loved and adored him. The carefree Sarai, the hopelessly in love, love-conquers-all Sarai who fell for the larger-than-life, out-of-my-dreams Armaan. For after today, neither of them existed anymore, and my only hope was out of the ashes, a new Sarai would emerge; a stronger, more cautious, and a more resolute Sarai. Yes, just like my dream the night before, the wedding fire had indeed turned into my sati.

So I watched them take their final step around the fire. I watched them throw the celebratory rice. I watched until there was nothing left to do but congratulate the couple. They returned to their seats on the stage beneath the floral *mandap* as the photographer began snapping their final wedding shots.

It was finished. Armaan had made his choice, and there was no turning back for either of us. I walked across the lawn and up the stairs of the terrace, but before I walked through the French doors, I indulged myself with one final glimpse at the most beautiful, enigmatic man I had ever met. As the afternoon turned to dusk, the *mandap*, which had been lit with small overhead lights, came alive in the fading sunlight. A spotlight illuminated Armaan from behind, reminding me of an angel. He looked more serene and content rather than excited and jubilant. While I watched him, his eyes drifted from the priest to his wife to the expansive number of guests that still dotted the lawn and then to the terrace where I stood, a lone figure in silver and white.

For a moment, I could have sworn his eyes seemed to be directed towards me and when he paused, I momentarily held my breath. But his eyes continued to drift randomly, and I exhaled slowly, resting my hand briefly on the terrace door. I once again gathered my resolve and walked through the open foyer, past lingering guests. I then jerked open those magnificent hand-carved front doors with determination and allowed them to close behind me with a thud, a resounding finale to a chapter in my life.

Chapter 13

SINCE I WAS a child, my father repeatedly told me his two dreams were for me to be a doctor and then to marry a doctor, or as he phrased it, to provide him with a *"nice, doctor son."* At nineteen, after a year of being pre-med and utterly miserable, I dashed his first dream. But he didn't let his dream die without a fight. First, he threatened not to pay for my tuition. When I reminded him that I had a full scholarship and that he didn't pay for anything but my books, which I could pay for if they would allow me to get a part-time job, he then threatened to disown me. Fortunately, my mother intervened and convinced him that my decision to not be a doctor was simply not the worst decision I could have made. She reminded him that the Desavanis' son was on drugs and had quit school, and that her co-worker Sri had an unmarried daughter who had gotten pregnant by her boyfriend, a (gasp!) *black* boy. She emphasized the latter not because she herself was prejudiced against anyone non-Indian, but because she knew my dad was and that fact alone would soften his heart and make him realize that I had not betrayed his dreams in the worst possible way. After about three weeks, he came around, during which time I had to endure each encounter as a reminder of the pain I had inflicted upon him as he was truly in mourning. All that he lacked was the Biblical burlap sackcloth to symbolize the extent of his grief. Each time I saw him, he scowled and complained about how any *other* child in India would have given his or her arm or leg to have had the opportunity to become a doctor. "But wouldn't that make walking around the hospital very difficult?" I asked in my most serious and confused voice. He then slapped the palm of his hand against his head in utter frustration and despair. "Don't be over smart, Sarai. You know what I am trying to say. You are lucky. You are throwing away a lifetime opportunity!"

But after dashing his first dream, he was even more determined that his second dream would not die. What amazed me more about my father is after years of threatening me, warning me that I'd better not be hiding a boyfriend or going on any dates, I was then expected from the age of twenty-two to just quickly pick someone to marry. He made it seem as if it were as easy as going to Macy's and picking out a pair of shoes. The reality was there didn't seem to be a lot of available Malayalee Christian guys around my age. Either they were a lot younger, or I had grown up with them and could only see them like a brother, or there was zero chemistry. Plus, added to the fact that I was five-nine and towered over most of them didn't help matters either.

I couldn't help but feel the whole Indian marriage system was hypocritical in some way. All our lives we are forbidden to date. Even in church, the boys are seated separately from the girls. We are expected not to think about them or look at them. Suddenly though, as soon as our parents deem it appropriate, which is typically after completing college, we are to go from not dating anyone to making a lifelong commitment and being intimate with someone we hardly even know. It made no sense! Not when emotions, hormones, and personal dreams and expectations were also involved.

With my twenty-eighth birthday fast approaching, my father's determination to get me married had taken on a new fervor, and I found myself looking for ways to avoid my parents as well as any aunts and uncles who jumped on their bandwagon. Regardless of the occasion or situation, the topic of marriage would invariably become the center topic of discussion. I was amazed at my father's ability to take any topic and turn it into a discussion of marriage and the importance of me getting married soon. We could be talking about the weather and somehow by the third sentence, it would be, "Sarai needs a husband."

This morning was no different. Lizzy Auntie was at our house, along with her husband's cousins, Sandosh Uncle and his wife,

Lilykutty, visiting from New Jersey. I hadn't taken two sips of my morning chai when my dad began asking our guests whether they knew of any eligible young men who were under the age of thirty-three.

I instinctively rolled my eyes, momentarily forgetting that I was sitting directly in front of my father. He immediately frowned. "See this is what I am saying," he said, inclining his head in my direction. "She doesn't take marriage seriously. She thinks it can be done anytime." Lizzy Auntie gravely shook her head in agreement. She had often thought my father was far too lenient with me and she had even voiced her opinion that they should take me to India and arrange my marriage there.

My dad continued, "You young people think you will be young forever. I was twenty-three years old when I was arranged to be married to your mother." He then digressed into the story that my brother and I had heard countless times since we were children. My Lizzy Auntie had gone to school with my mother's older sister, Merci Auntie who told her they were looking for a husband for her sister, Lela. Lizzy Auntie then told her parents, who then went to my mom's parents' home. The families liked each other and arranged the marriage of my parents without even consulting them. My parents didn't even see each other until the engagement day, my father boasted.

My brother glanced at me and sighed shaking his head. He was only twenty-one, but he had been forced to listen to all this incessant talk of marriage since he was fifteen years old. I mouthed an "I'm sorry" and took another bite of my breakfast as I waited for my dad to finish his "how I met your mother" story. Once he finished, he continued his diatribe on marriage, holding his fork as if it were a teaching stick. "There is a time for everything." And then he started with his quoting of the Bible. "A time to die, a time to live, a time to be single, and a time to be married." My dad read out of the SCD version of the Bible (Stubborn, controlling dad version).

"Dad," I said, my fork paused in mid-air. "That is NOT in the Bible."

My dad dismissed my comments with a shake of his head. "I've been telling her since she finished college that she better get serious about marriage. She is getting old, and boys like the young girls. No one wants an old lady." To my horror, my dad continued with his own rendition of various quotes. "You know what they say, why buy the cow when she no longer has milk?"

My brother choked on his juice while I jerked my head towards my mother, my eyes pleading with her to intervene. But she refused to look at me and only stared down at her plate.

Since neither of them would rise to my defense, I spoke up. "The saying is '*Why buy the cow when the milk is for free?*'" I attempted to talk over my brother whose coughing suddenly took center stage with everyone except my father. I again glanced at my mom and aunt for support, but they were both at my brother's side, alternatively patting his back.

Part of me wanted to yell out the truth—that I *had* been dating someone and that we *had* always planned to get married. But while I could usually count on my mom to be my ally, my father could never be told the truth, lest I had a secret death wish. And the last thing I wanted to do was give Lizzy Auntie any more ammunition on me. As much as I longed to shock my father into silence, I knew my confession would only instigate another one of his tirades on my ingratitude and disobedience. I devoured the rest of my food as quickly as I could and excused myself from the table, escaping into the solace of my room.

I lay on the bed, with my arms folded under my head as I absent-mindedly stared at the rotating blades of the ceiling fan. When had life become so complicated? Couldn't they just leave me alone? How can one force love...or marriage? My mind reflexively conjured up my mom's voice. *Don't worry...just pray. God has a plan and a time for everything.*

But hadn't I prayed? Had I not waited on His timing? What more could I do? There were times, like now, when I felt that if God truly did exist, I was praying to the ears of a deaf, uncaring God.

Chapter 14

TWO WEEKS LATER, I joined Reena, Maya, and Anjuli for a girls' night out at the Samba Room. I had just placed my order for a Mojito when I saw all three girls' eyes narrow and hone in on me. "What?" I asked suspiciously.

"When's the last time you were on a date?" Reena asked with her wine glass raised just below the level of her beady eyes, challenging me across the table.

Great, was this an intervention? Had they decided that I had been single too long and that it was time for me to start dating? Rather than take the defensive and admit it had been well over a year since I had gone on a real date, I took the offensive. "But *you're* not dating anyone!" I said, accusingly to Reena.

"Yeah, but *I'm* happy being single. I *want* to be single. *You're* not happy being single, nor do you want to be single."

She was right. I wasn't happy being single, but being single was preferable to dating just anyone. And lately, there seemed to be a lot of just "anyones" out there.

"You're just not giving any guy a chance," insisted Anjuli.

"What?! That's so not true! There's no guy who wants a chance right now, and trust me, there's no one to date! Name one guy." I asked challengingly.

"My brother's friend, John Phillips," said Maya, as if he were some-one I had known and been turning down for a date. Where did that come from? And more importantly, who was he? Reena's and Anjuli's heads were bobbing up and down, as if they had all conferred prior to this and were in agreement.

"Wait, you guys have obviously been discussing this without me," I said, my eyes narrowing suspiciously at each of them. They, in turn, had their best pleading expressions on display. I sighed and surrendered. "Fine. Please, do *teeell* me about this friend of your brother's, John Phillips. Wait, is this your older brother's or younger brother's friend?"

"This is my older brother's friend. John is an engineer and works with my brother at Quantum Engineering." Engineer, okay, my dad would like that, but I hope it didn't mean he had the stereotypical engineering type of personality. "Okay. Go on," I prodded, still quite cynical about this whole setup.

"He went to Notre Dame and played football for them one year before an injury put him out for the rest of his career."

Great, a jock. Somehow I was never the type to go for football players. Nor was I the type they typically went after. I saw the black cloud looming above this setup already.

Then there was the blind date setup with Maya's co-worker, Roy Nair. Maya's co-worker was Malayalee, a very nice guy she assured me, and he was cute. He was very into nutrition and health and was environmentally conscious.

Finally, it was Anjuli's turn. The guy she had in mind for me was a thirty-three year-old doctor named Daniel Ninan. "And how well do you know this guy?" I asked.

She glanced at Reena and then focused on her plate. "Um, well, we kinda met not too long ago." There was something highly suspicious about her vagueness and her inability to look at me while she told me about him. Had she met him randomly at some bar and told him a sob story about me? Or was it even worse than that?

"How did you meet?" I asked again, alerting all of them to my suspicions. She glanced at me and then glanced at Reena, all the while wringing her napkin as if it were a wet washcloth. She reluctantly opened her mouth to answer, but Reena cut her off.

"Fine. I'll tell her. We created a profile for you on Indianmarriages.com, and he was one of the guys who responded whom we felt is worth going out with."

That was a response I hadn't anticipated. I belched out a "*WHAT?!*" Two patrons at the neighboring table turned to look at me, but I ignored them as I attempted to incinerate my three closest friends with my horrified and unflinching stare.

Reena was unbothered by my reaction and repeated herself. "We created a profile on Indianmarriages.com for you..."

"I heard you!" I bit out. I looked down at my salad plate, grabbed my fork, and began stabbing at the lettuce leaves while I attempted to gather my composure. I lowered my voice and in the most indignant tone I could conjure, "I CANNOT, CANNOT believe you guys!"

"We did it for you, Sarai," Anjuli said hesitatingly.

"For me? *For me?* I'm sorry, but I don't recall asking you to do anything like that for me!" I said, trying to control my voice. "Do you think after all this waiting, that's how I want to meet a guy? Through the Internet?! And you guys did it without my permission or knowledge! My profile is out there for the whole world to see! Do you know how embarrassing that is?"

I was livid. I was furious. The Internet? How cold! How unromantic! How embarrassing! How invasive!

"Calm down. A lot of people are doing it now. With everyone's busy schedule, soon this will become *the* way to meet your future spouse! This isn't like those cheesy newspaper dating ads. It's a legitimate way of meeting people of the opposite sex from around the world. No longer are you limited to just the people in your workplace or city. Now you can meet anyone, anywhere! Anjuli is on there..."

"Anjuli, you're on there?" I asked in shock.

She nodded.

"Rekha, Rakesh, Nandini, Jancey, Jim. They're *all* on it," said Anjuli, counting them all on her fingers.

While part of me found comfort in the fact that I wasn't alone out there, I still felt violated. "I don't care who's on there. *I* don't want to be on there!"

Reena ignored me. "Well, here you get a couple of choices. There's Anish. He's a software developer. He grew up in Kuwait. Then there's Jason. He's from New York and works as a nurse. And finally there's Daniel, the guy Anjuli mentioned. He's a doctor, thirty-three years old..." her voice lowered, so I barely heard her mumble "divorced."

I put both my hands over my heart, and in the most sarcastic way, I said, "Awww, what choices! How will I ever choose?" This is what my life had been reduced to—having my *single* friends pity me enough to covertly put up my profile on an Indian marriage website.

"We just want you to meet someone, and we know you won't do anything about it," said Maya.

"What do you expect me to do? Do you guys honestly think I don't want to date? I would, but somehow from the time I met Armaan to the time he broke up with me, every decent available Malayalee male got married."

I continued to stab my salad with my fork. I appreciated their concern, but this time they had taken it too far. My picture and bio were out there for everyone to see, and they were communicating with these guys as if they were me.

"It's not that I don't want to date, it's just that there is no one to date! At school, I am primarily surrounded by female teachers. There are a few male teachers, but most of them are married. Then there are the coaches, either married or missing a few crucial brain cells, and, of course, there are no Indian guys, much less Malayalee Christian guys in the teaching field."

"Exactly. That is why we had to intervene," Anjuli said.

Reena then jumped in. "I want you to promise us you'll go on at least one date with one guy that we each pick for you."

"No!" I said firmly.

"Why not?"

"Because I don't want to go on a blind date! I'm uncomfortable with all of this. You guys had no right to do any of this without my permission. Do you want me to continue with why this is wrong on every level?" I asked, raising an eyebrow to Reena.

Reena stayed quiet for a few moments, no doubt thinking of something I wouldn't be able to say no to. "What do you have to lose?"

"My dignity, my self-respect..." I readily supplied.

And Reena countered with, "Yes, because maintaining your dignity and self-respect are so much more important than opening your mind and your heart and realizing there are more ways of meeting Mr. Right than just your eyes converging across a room at a crowded Indian cultural event."

I inhaled sharply, ready to retort back, but I could think of nothing. I exhaled slowly as I contemplated my options and finally came to the conclusion that she was right. There were different ways to meet Mr. Right, and I shouldn't limit myself.

"One date and you guys will back off?" I asked, pointedly looking at each of them for their promise.

"*One* date with *one* guy that we *each* pick for you," countered Reena.

"What?!" I asked, horrified. "NO!"

"Yes! We're not saying any of these guys are Mr. Right. We just want you to go out and start meeting people again. That's all."

Okay, I was glad they weren't expecting me to pick my husband out of those three guys. I pondered their proposition. *Be open-minded, Sarai.* That was the mantra for the year. "Okay, fine. And then you'll leave me alone? No more setups, no more blind dates. You each get one shot at trying to set me up. Agreed?" I asked, cocking my eyebrow, as I pressed them for their promise.

They briefly exchanged glances, and realizing it was probably the best deal they were going to get out of me, they each raised their glasses to cinch the deal.

I had nothing to lose, I decided, raising my own glass in agreement. Maybe it was time to be open-minded and open-hearted again.

Chapter 15

TWO WEEKS LATER, I met up with all three girls at Lupe's Cantina, a popular Mexican restaurant, to fill them in on my dates. As we sipped on margaritas and nibbled on nachos, I regaled them with the details of dates 1, 2, and 3.

Date #1: John Phillips. Former Notre Dame athlete-turned-Engineer. Handsome guy, tall, broad-shouldered, but from the start of our date, there was just something missing. He was heavily into sports, and I was heavily not into sports, which in and of itself is not necessarily a bad thing, but when all he wants to do is talk about sports, it can be. Our date was, *get this*, at a sports bar, which again, isn't a bad thing. But the deal breaker for me was when I noticed him several times, during our conversations, looking over my head at the television screen at the bar. If this was how he acted on our first date, then what would life with him be like? I envisioned weekends of him sitting on the couch, sitting alone or with buddies, and my sole role was to provide him with a steady supply of buffalo wings, chips, and other popular snacks. It was an image that had no appeal for me. He must have felt the same way about me because after our first date, he never called, and I felt relieved.

Date #2: Roy Nair. Maya's co-worker. Vegetarian Hindu guy. Yep, Apparently, Ms. Maya didn't do her homework. While Roy was a Malayalee, he was also very much a Hindu, maybe not in all ways, but one thing he definitely followed was a strict adherence to vegan living. Our date was at a vegan restaurant, a fact that was initially lost on me.

While I scoured the menu for a meat dish, I made the mistake of mentioning to Roy that I couldn't seem to find one chicken dish. After getting over his horror that I would even consider eating anything that once had a heartbeat, he began the two-hour tirade on the value, health, and morality of being vegetarian. I tried to change the subject, but he seemed hell-bent on converting me to vegetarianism. My only break was when he had to go to the restroom, during which I texted Reena to call me with an "emergency" so I could get out of the date.

Date #3: Daniel Ninan, aka Divorced Doctor from the Internet aka Doctor of Love. While I tried to be open-minded, I knew he was going to be a tough sell to my parents even if, by chance, I really liked him. With his pronounced jawline, he was handsome in an exaggerated cartoonish type of way. Despite his attempts to play up the handsome, doctor role, thirty minutes into the date I was sure I knew why his wife had left him. After ordering appetizers, he immediately expressed his admiration for my tall, thin frame. His philosophy, he told me, was you could never be too rich or too thin. Within the first five minutes of our date, he reached for my hands across the table. While I am not opposed to affection, I prefer to be affectionate with someone I've known for longer than just a few minutes. While I initially admired his confidence, I quickly realized he definitely had the "god complex" when it came to his profession, though he thought he was quite humble about it. He attempted to illustrate this humility to me by telling me how when asked about his profession, he often replies that he's a janitor—even though the person asking probably already knows that he's a doctor. Either way, towards the end of our date, I quickly determined he was one of the cockiest doctors I had ever met. While it was quite obvious he loved the status of being a doctor more than actually helping people, there was one thing he liked more... *himself.* Not once during the date, did he ask me anything, and I mean *anything,* about myself.

By the end of the night, when he realized I wasn't responding to his overtures, he decided to turn his attention to our waitress, a cute, perky twenty-year-old blonde.

"What?!" asked Maya with one hand resting against her chest, almost as if she were trying to calm her heartbeat. "He flirted with the waitress right in front of you?"

"No!" I said, mockingly. "Of course not! That would have been uncouth and unbecoming, even for him!"

The girls looked relieved.

"No, he did it behind my back. When I was walking back from the bathroom, I heard him asking for her number, just before he patted her on her behind as she cleared our table!" I then lifted my margarita glass for an imaginary toast.

As each of them stared back at me dumbfounded, I clinked my glass with each of theirs and then gulped down the remainder of my margarita. "Those, my darlings, are my three dates. The three dates each of *you* set me up with!"

Anjuli reached for my hand across the table and patted it apologetically. "I am so sorry that we did that to you."

I shrugged my shoulders nonchalantly. "Well, I think I should thank you guys. You've just proven what I already suspected. There are no decent, available Indian guys *anywhere*!"

"Hey, what about that speech and drama teacher we ran into at the Art Festival that one time? He was Indian, and he was cute!" said Anjuli.

Maya and Reena both looked at Anjuli skeptically. "Hello! Speech and drama teacher, has a lisp and uses more 'oh, my gosh-es' than a teenager. He probably has more facial products and designer clothes than all of us combined."

Anjuli blinked absently, looking totally oblivious to what they were implying.

Reena rolled her eyes and sighed. "*Hello,* he bats for the other team."

Anjuli shrugged her shoulders. "So? Lots of guys are into clothes and toiletries these days. That doesn't mean he's gay! They even have a word for it," she said, pausing as she searched for the word, "A met-, metro- yes, a *metro*sexual."

"No, Anjuli darling, read my lips. Not metro—homo. *Homo-sexual.*" said Reena. We all burst out laughing.

Frustrated, Anjuli turned to me, "Is he really gay?"

"Honestly, I don't know. No one's 'straight-out' asked him," I said, pausing for effect at my own pun. We all burst out laughing again, and this time even Anjuli couldn't hold back a smile. "But yeah, Anjuli," I said, "The general consensus is that yes, he's gay."

"So where *are* all the cute, intelligent, available, heterosexual Indian guys?" asked Maya. I had asked this same question myself before meeting Armaan when I was twenty-two, and now here I was, along with three other single girls, asking it again six years later.

Anjuli then said something very odd. "Maybe they're all in India."

"*Huh*?!" asked Maya, Reena, and I in unison. I glanced at my glass, wondering if I hadn't just been drinking a little too much and misheard her.

Anjuli spoke softly, "So, I have something to tell you guys, and I don't want you guys to judge me."

We put down our glasses of margarita and gave her our undivided attention. Anjuli's hands were clasped together, resting on her empty plate. Judging from her demeanor, I knew this was serious.

She took a deep breath and looked at each of us pointedly. She took another deep breath and then blurted out, "I'm going to India."

As she waited for our shocked "Whatdayamean's," we waited for the punch line.

"Say something, guys," prompted Anjuli.

"Congratulations that you're going on vacation to India?" ventured Maya.

"No, you goofs! Yes, I'm going to India but not for vacation. I'm going there for an arranged marriage."

Mission accomplished. For about five seconds we were all left with our mouths gaping open in stunned silence as we each tried to process what she had just said. And then at the same time, a flurry of questions catapulted out of each of our gaping mouths: "*What???*" "*How???*" "When did you decide this?" "Are you sure this is what you want?" We also added in: "Are you insane?" "Are you giving up on love?" "Is your family forcing you? That's not legal, you know."

Anjuli held her palms up, fending off our questions. "*Whoa*, guys. One question at a time. Sarai, you first. You look the most shocked."

I cleared my throat self-consciously. I think we were all equally shocked, but I was probably the most curious about how she had arrived at this decision. My parents, at the insistence of Aunt Lizzy, had been bugging me for months about going to India, but I hadn't entertained the idea for more than a brief second and then only to scoff at it. "What made you decide?" I asked.

"Well, for one, my cousin Bini. She married a Malayalee guy raised in Bangalore, and he just arrived a few weeks ago. He's not only handsome, but he's very open-minded. Now get this, his dad is an engineer, so his family had money, and he actually grew up watching MTV. *I* didn't even grow up watching MTV!" she said, jabbing her index finger at herself. "He was telling me about all these old school rock videos I had never even seen."

Okay, so he watched MTV growing up. Obviously, we all needed more than just that to convince us that he was forward-thinking. Since my father and uncles were my only frame of reference for males raised in India, I still had my doubts. "But he probably expects her to have a traditional meal cooked every night..."

She chuckled and said, "No, he likes to cook, so he actually cooks more of the traditional stuff, and she sticks to the basics like spaghetti and macaroni and cheese."

Reena was skeptical. "What about the laundry?"

"They take turns."

"And the dishes?" I asked.

"They take turns."

Then Maya asked, "So do you have a picture? You mentioned that he was good looking."

"Actually, I think I do. Bini was handing out her wedding picture at our last family gathering. I can't remember if I put it in my wallet." Anjuli rummaged through her purse and then smiling, she pulled a small picture of her cousin and the groom. She handed me the picture first. Her cousin wore a traditional white sari with a gold border, and her hair was pulled into a bun. She wore a short, tiered wedding veil with a tiara that reminded me of something from the 1980s. The groom was dressed in a light gray suit and tie, and to my surprise, there was no bushy mustache (as that had been the favored style of every male family member I knew), and I had to agree with Anjuli about him being a handsome guy. His eyebrows were a bit bushy, and he could definitely use the assistance of some hair gel to tame his hair, but he had nice smile. His eyes drooped down, but they seemed kind. The most distinctive feature on him was something most of us didn't expect. He had a long scar on his left cheek that actually gave him an edgy, more dangerous look. I handed the picture to Maya, who immediately began nodding and smiling, giving her full approval, and then she handed the picture to Reena. Reena held the wallet-size picture in her hand for a few seconds. Leaning forward in the chair towards Anjuli, she then asked in the most somber, sincere voice, "So does he have a brother?"

We all busted out laughing. She handed the picture back to Anjuli who tucked it away in her wallet. "See, guys, I told you. There are Malayalee guys our age out there. They just might not be here in the US."

"So when are you going?" Maya asked.

"Next month, and I'll be gone for about five weeks."

"Wow! So you really are going through with this?" I asked.

"Yep, I am. What do I have to lose?" she asked shrugging her shoulders. "Besides, if it doesn't work out, I'll come back here single." We all looked at each other and nodded. It didn't sound so bad, after all. Just another option to consider in the midst of other dwindling options.

Chapter 16

ANJULI LEFT FOR India the following month, and three weeks after she left, we each got an engagement announcement and a wedding invitation addressed from her. Anjuli was getting married, and the wedding was to be in India! I couldn't believe she had really gone through with it.

I laid the invitation on my dresser table and tried to grade some papers, but I couldn't get Anjuli out of my mind. Even if she had found someone, I had expected it to take a while. I figured after meeting him, she would come back home to think about it and get to know him better over the phone at least and then go back to India for the wedding. But within two weeks of meeting him, it was a done deal. As I thought about Anjuli, the reality of my own age came back to me. I had to agree with my dad to a certain extent. I was running out of time. I had always hoped to have been married by my late twenties, or at least, dating the guy I was going to eventually marry. I didn't need my dad to remind me how badly I wanted or needed to get married. There was an internal alarm clock that beeped every day, reminding me of that very thing. Reena was also twenty-eight, but she didn't seem to feel the same pressures of our age. She had two older brothers who were still single and her parents were more worried about them at the moment.

As much as shows like "Sex and the City" promoted the fabulousness of single life, there is an undoubted pressure in our American society to be married—regardless of your ethnicity. And if that weren't enough, according to every fashion magazine, the chances of getting married once you were past your twenties decreased exponentially in direct proportion to the ever increasing chances of getting hit by a bus. The odds were definitely against me. According to the latest article I read in Cosmo, I had two years before *all* the stats rotated out of my favor. Maybe the time to act was now.

Following my heart had only led me to trouble. Perhaps I needed to use more of my brain and less of my heart when making a decision about the right guy. After all, that's what the arranged marriage is all about. Parents screen the guys and determine compatibility and only present the ones who meet with their approval. All I had to do was say "yes" or "no." I no longer had to concern myself with the "what will my parents think?" dilemma. The more I thought about it, the more appealing it sounded to meet a guy and have all your cards on the table. There were no questions like: *Where is this going? What are his intentions? Does he like me enough to want to marry me? Is he just playing with my heart?* All those questions are left at the door. The intention, the goal, is always marriage. I would be left to answer only one question: *was this the person with whom I wanted to spend the rest of my life?*

But my major problem with this entire process was that it seemed to leave out the all important ingredient—the ever elusive, inexplicable, unpredictable phenomenon of chemistry.

But after Anjuli's wedding invitation arrived, I could not shake the feeling that perhaps the reason I hadn't met anyone was maybe because my own Prince Charming was across the ocean. So maybe…

Snap out of it! I commanded myself, horrified at where my thoughts were heading. *What was wrong with me?!* Was I actually contemplating an arranged marriage? Not only that, but one arranged in India? Had I gone mad?!

I fearfully eyed Anjuli's wedding invitation, regarding it like it was some infectious, alien virus slowly taking over my body and mind, causing me to contemplate things I never would have before.

I rose from my bed and quickly stashed the invitation in my dresser drawer, hoping that by somehow hiding it, I could stop the insidious direction my thoughts were taking. As I shut the drawer, I felt a sense of relief. *Crisis averted*, I assured myself.

✧ ✧ ✧

ANJULI RETURNED HOME the following month without her husband, Shibu. It would take a few months, she explained, to file his paperwork and get his visa. In the meantime, they were spending a lot of money on phone cards. The day after she arrived home, Maya, Reena, and I met up with her at her house to get the full scoop on exactly what happened and to see pictures of her engagement and wedding. As she spoke, I watched her closely, wondering if I would see remorse regarding her decision. But as she described meeting Shibu and their conversations, she sounded and acted like a typical girl who had fallen in love. She glowed and smiled like a happy bride-to-be in her engagement and wedding pictures, and the only compromise I could see that she had to make was not being able to wear a wedding dress on her wedding day. Instead, she had to wear a traditional white sari. For me that might have been an issue, but Anjuli didn't seem to regard that as being a sacrifice.

My big question to her was, "How did you know he was the one?"

With the hapless smile of someone in love, she answered with the ever cryptic cliché, "You just know." It was an answer I found to be both frustrating and confusing. What does that mean, *you just know?* I hated when people used that phrase. It was one of the most over-used phrases spoken by people in love, but to those of us who were single and clueless, it was a vague, meaningless phrase.

So what did "*you just know*" really mean? Was it a strong, over-whelming feeling of conviction? Was it the knowledge that there could be no one else in the world for you? Was it the feeling that even if there could be someone else out there, it didn't matter, because this person was enough? I recalled the way Armaan made me feel. With him, I couldn't even think. There was only a sense of feeling, "Baby, if loving you is wrong, I don't wanna be right." I don't know if I "*just knew*" with Armaan, but one thing I did know, I was absolutely crazy about him from day one.

But what if there was some amazing guy there in India, just waiting for me to find him, and here I was being close-minded and stubborn?

And maybe things would work out differently this time because I would have my parents' blessing.

I cringed inwardly as I realized for the second time, Anjuli had me contemplating following her footsteps and going to India! Was I seriously considering going to India to marry someone I would barely know? This wasn't about being open-minded; this was about the desperation of a late twenty-something! There was *no* way I could seriously consider it. Just because it was right for Anjuli didn't mean it was right for me.

Chapter 17

I BLAMED ANJULI, her beautiful wedding pictures, and the way she glowed when she talked about her husband. I indirectly also blamed her cousin, Bini, even though I didn't even know her personally. I blamed all of them for what I did two days later. Like an out-of-body experience, I walked towards the living room like a robot. My mom was napping on the loveseat while my father was sprawled out on his easy chair with the remote control in one hand as he watched the final minutes of the Cowboys and Redskins game.

"Dad?"

"Hmmm…" he mumbled, his eyes glued to the screen.

"So I've been giving it some thought, and I think I would be willing to go to India and give the arranged marriage thing a shot."

My mom's head reared up, and my dad did something he had never done my entire life. He turned off the television set in the middle of a Cowboys game and swiveled his easy chair towards me. His eyebrows drew together in a crumpled "V" as he studied me in silence.

With my shoulders back, and my head slightly raised, I continued. "I'll go, but I just have one condition."

My father crossed his hands over his chest.

"My decision is final. If I don't like a boy, or *any* boy for that matter, I have the right to say no. Neither you nor Aunt Lizzy nor any of the other uncles or aunties can force any marriage on me. It is ultimately my decision."

My father stared at me intensely for a few minutes and then grunted. It wasn't a yes, a nod, or anything that most people would perceive as acquiescence, but it was all I needed. I nodded, essentially sealing the deal. I then ran up the stairs to my room, shutting the door behind me, and crumbled to the floor.

✧   ✧   ✧

IN THE WEEKS that followed, I asked myself one question over and over—*what had I done?* Everyone knew that once you went to India, you were as good as married. No one I knew, male or female, had ever returned from India still single, even if they hadn't initially intended to go there for an arranged marriage. Heck, that's how Armaan had been roped into getting married. Although my dad had threatened to arrange my marriage, I was always sure that love, not utility and not expediency, would be my primary reason to marry.

But how could I expect to find love in India in a matter of weeks? But then again, I had found it with Armaan in a matter of seconds. Well, maybe that was more lust, but my instincts about him were right, and there had been enough there to build love on. So it was possible, right? And if it happened once, it could definitely happen again. If there was any justice in the world, it would most definitely happen again.

At this point in my life, I could count it as an adventure, right? It would just be an experience, a tradition in my culture that I probably would, otherwise, never have considered. And maybe along the way, I could meet the perfect guy for me. Besides, it wouldn't be completely arranged, right? I would have the final say in the matter. As Anjuli had pointed out, I really had nothing to lose.

After I had fully come to terms with my decision, I made my announcement to Reena. To my surprise, she didn't try to talk me out of it. In fact, after she said, "Are you serious?" a couple of times and then followed it up with an expletive, she became very quiet, and then to my complete surprise, she became very supportive. "Hey, I've been sayin' all along that you gotta be open-minded these days!" Maya, too, was supportive. I guess after Anjuli, the idea of me going to India didn't sound so foreign to either of them.

Besides my immediate family and closest of friends, I didn't tell anyone else, especially not Rakesh, Mani, and the rest of the gang. If they knew the real reason I was going to India, they would mostly likely freak out and try to persuade me not to go.

Although I was very cognizant of the fact that I was going to India to possibly find a husband, I was surprised how calm, matter-of-fact, and practical I had become about life and love. So far I hadn't freaked out, not even once. My parents were happy, but I could tell even my mother worried that at the last minute, I would somehow change my mind and refuse to go.

I spent the next few months slowly preparing for my trip. I did everything I needed to ensure that I made the flight. I renewed my passport, and I went to the Indian embassy to get my visa. I even began packing well in advance of my trip, which was not like me at all. Perhaps this was truly meant to be.

Since I was going to be spending at least two months there, there seemed to be so many things I needed, and I found myself making multiple trips to Wal-Mart in the weeks before my trip. Two days before my flight, I made my final pit-stop at Wal-Mart, carrying my two-page shopping list. I bypassed the travel-size toiletry bins and went straight to the full-size toothpastes and other necessities I knew I would need.

Everything was going as planned. I checked off each item as I filled my shopping cart. I bought extra bottles of anti-frizz serum and extra deodorant sticks to distribute to my cousins who viewed deodorants more as a luxury rather than as a necessity. The last two items were nail polish and jewelry, which were both for my cousins. I was quickly getting through my list, drama-free, until I passed the jewelry department and a sparkling one-carat solitaire cased in a glass egg beckoned for a closer look. I had never looked at wedding rings before and part of me felt silly looking at one now since I was still single. But the reality of what lay before me in India seemed to make it justifiable.

An eager salesperson approached me. "Is there a particular ring I could show you, miss?"

I was about to decline but then thought, *why not?*

I selected the princess-cut solitaire mounted on an eternity band. I slowly put it on my ring finger, and I moved my left hand back and forth, watching the light bounce off the ring. I sighed, knowing full well that if I were to get married in India, this, unfortunately, would probably not be the type of ring I would be getting. Engagement rings in India were very different from engagement rings in the US. According to Anjuli, solitaires had caught on in the larger, more metropolitan cities, but Kerala was still not on the fashion edge, and most people there still favored the traditional, plain 22K gold bands, like the one she wore.

As I stared at the ring, I knew it wasn't only the ring I would be giving up, it was the whole proposal. There would be no gourmet dinner, romantic locale, or guy on bended knee asking for my hand in marriage. More than likely, once we met, we'd both be giving our consent to our parents, and then the actual engagement, along with an engagement ring exchange, would take place in a formal, solemn ceremony in front of family and friends.

For so many months, I had made this decision based on reason or logic. I had not indulged my emotions, but for whatever reason, as I stood there in the middle of Wal-Mart, looking at the ring on my finger, the gravity of my decision began to hit me, and the emotions that I suppressed began beating down that wall of denial I had built.

In the midst of all these thoughts, I faintly heard my name being called, "Sarai?"

I turned around and there, standing with a fully stocked shopping cart, was Diandra Kurian. "Dee!" I said, finally breaking that downward mental spiral. I knew Dee from church. We had met at a church singles event a year before. Dee was from Trinidad, but her great-grandparents were all originally from India. Dee was in her late 30s and never married though I could never figure out why. She was intelligent, beautiful, and had a very outgoing personality. The only conclusion I could come to was that perhaps men found her looks and success to be intimidating.

Dee worked as legal counsel for American Airlines and always seemed to be traveling to some exotic location for work. What I envied most about her was that she seemed to just always have it together. Although she wasn't married, she had it all—the cool downtown loft apartment, the nice luxury sports coupe, the designer clothes, the glamorous career, and most of all, she seemed very happy and content with her life.

"I thought that was you," Dee said, smiling. Her eyes dropped down to the ring I was wearing, and she gasped. "Are you getting married?"

I looked down at my hand to the ring and shook my head, my cheeks turning red. I removed the ring and immediately placed it back in its case. "No! No... no... at least not yet. I was just looking. Just being a girl, you know." Then I nervously placed the case back on the jewelry counter.

"Oh," she said, clearly not knowing what to say next. "So, um, what are you up to these days? What are your plans this summer? Taking any trips?"

"Actually, I'm going to India for the entire summer!"

"India? For the entire summer?" she asked, taken aback. "And you're always telling me how jealous you are of my traveling! I only get to take a few days or a week when I travel!"

"Well, my trip isn't exactly a vacation per se. I'll be staying with one of my dad's brothers in his home in Kerala." I hesitated, but then for whatever reason, I admitted, dropping my voice to a whisper. "I'm actually going there because my family wants to look for me..."

"Look for you?" she asked, confused.

My voice dropped even lower, "Yeah, to look for a husband for me."

Dee blinked several times, and then her eyes bulged out. "Wow! Really?!" When I smiled back at her, her eyes then narrowed down on me suspiciously, "Wait, really? You're not just pulling my leg, right?" She searched my face for any sign that would indicate I was kidding.

I nodded, empathizing with her disbelief. Heck, there were times when I didn't believe it either. "Yep! Shocking, huh?"

"Well, it is a little surprising, but not in a bad way. You just caught me off guard that's all. Based on our previous conversations, you didn't strike me as being open to an arranged marriage."

"Yeah, I think I surprised myself."

"So what made you change your mind?"

"The reality that there are absolutely no available guys my age," I said shrugging my shoulders.

Dee laughed and said, "Oh, come now, it's not that bad."

I shot her a dubious look.

"Yeah, actually, you're right. I don't know why I said that," she said thoughtfully. "It *is* that bad. I was just telling my sister that I can't even remember the last date I had, and I don't even have all those cultural restrictions that you have."

"Well, I am going to the motherland that manufactures exactly what my parents want for me. So if I don't find a husband in Kerala, I am truly a lost cause."

Dee laughed and hugged me, wishing me all the best. "Let me know how things work out! And definitely give me a call once you get back in town. If nothing else, it'll be an adventure." She hugged me again, and then she continued on with her shopping.

I glanced back at the ring, which was still sitting on the counter, waiting to be put away. I picked it up and slipped it on my finger again. Had I, Sarai Mathai, for once in her life, made a decision based on reason and logic rather than just pure emotion? I had learned the hard way that following my heart could lead one astray, so maybe it was time to let some of my other faculties lead me to love. After all, what did it matter how I got there? As long as I got to the destination, right? Right, I answered, nodding to my reflection. With new-found optimism, I returned the solitaire to its glass egg case and handed it back to the saleswoman. Breathing deeply, I once again found my inner resolve and continued my shopping.

Chapter 18

THE DAY OF my send-off to India was what I had imagined my wedding day to be like. Uncles, aunts, cousins, and even a few second cousins were all jammed into our house. Everyone was in a jovial mood, and my parents were beaming proudly as if they were taking me to the church to get married rather than just the airport. I guess in their heads, by sending me to India, I was as good as married.

After we checked-in at the ticket counter, I had to wait another three and a half hours with my family at the gate. As I scanned the area for three empty seats, my eyes settled on an adorable little Indian girl who looked to be about three years old. She was standing on the seat between her mother and father and was holding a lollypop in one hand and her mother's lipstick in another as she entertained herself and other on-lookers with a dance. Aware of the stares that her daughter was getting, her mother was trying to coax her to sit properly in her seat, but she seemed to pay no attention and continued her little jig, which consisted of some squats that would have made any aerobics instructor proud and some side sways and head bobs that followed no particular rhythm.

My mom must have noticed me looking at her because she leaned towards me, then smiled, and said, "That was the age you were when you arrived in the US, and you looked a lot like her except your hair was curly and your lips had this natural red color. People often thought I had put lipstick or tinted gloss on your lips."

"I couldn't have been that cute."

"No, I think you were cuter," my mom said lovingly as she stroked my hair. "But I do miss your curly hair. Sarai, why don't you leave your hair curly anymore?"

I smiled and squeezed her hand without answering her question. My eyes then drifted from the dancing toddler to the young mother. Her hands were suspended in mid-air near her daughter's waist. Her hair was dark brown and pulled back into a thick traditional braid that reached her lower back. She was dressed in a traditional *salwar kameez*, a loose tunic top with coordinating pajama-like pants. Like the delicate flower embroidery of her outfit, she, too, seemed delicate. She had small hands and a delicate bone structure. As she watched over her daughter, she wore a broad smile, but when she glanced at her husband, the smile diminished.

Her husband, who was wearing a plain white dress shirt and black slacks, sat on the other side of the little girl, and his eyes were fixated straight ahead. His hair was jet black and thick, and he had a small frame. The nostrils of his sharp nose flared out, and his eyebrows, which were too thick for his face, were pushed together, creating a temporary uni-brow. With the thick, dark mustache that covered most of his facial features, and a serious countenance, he was intimidating, even though his features and body frame were small. In his tightly clenched hands, he was holding a magazine, which he slowly rolled up. He then turned towards his daughter and hit her firmly on the bottom with the rolled up magazine. Then he grabbed her by one arm and tried to pull her down into a sitting position. The child began crying, and the mother picked her up and held her like an infant as she tried to console her. Not once did she say a word to her husband or look his way.

They seemed like two strangers bound by tradition and now by a little girl. I sighed, wondering what I had signed up for by going to India.

As if he could read my thoughts, my dad leaned over, patting my head. "Sarai, don't look so sad. Your mother and I had an arranged marriage, and look how happy we are."

✧   ✧   ✧

AS THE PLANE landed in Mumbai, I smelled the putrid stench of urine and decay that rose from the surrounding slums and penetrated the steel exterior of the plane. The smell got so strong that I lifted the collar of my shirt and used it as a breathing mask. After walking through customs, I found the terminal where my local plane flight to my home state of Kerala would be boarding, and I waited there for five hours. I slumped down into the white plastic space-pod looking chairs and attempted to sleep, but the discomfort of the chairs did not allow me to sit comfortably, much less sleep. As I sat there, I wondered what I would see if I could flash forward to two months from now when I would once again be in this airport on my return flight.

As I sat there, I noticed the airport was getting busier. I stared across the main terminal aisle to the other gate when a handsome man in his full navy-blue pilot uniform walked by. I was admiring him when the sight of three additional good looking, distinguished pilots walked by and distracted me. They were followed by another group and then another. I leaned forward in my chair and glanced down the aisle, noticing there were easily ten to fifteen clusters of remarkably hand-some men. Most were accompanied by young women who were equally tall, attractive, graceful, and almost model-like in matching fitted blazers, pencil skirts, hose, and heels. I glanced at the clock on the wall. It was seven in the morning, and the flight crews were just arriving in time for the morning departures. I watched the pilots conversing with the women in their crew. Some were talking, and some were flirting while others were joking and laughing with their heads thrown back in genuine amusement. All of them looked to be between the ages of twenty-two and twenty-eight years old. I wondered how many flights there were, as there seemed to be no end to the caravan. I just smiled appreciatively, noting that with their bone structure, tall stature, and light coloring, they were probably all North Indian. Who knew there were so many good looking men in India? They all looked more like actors playing pilots and stewardesses.

Surely out of the deluge of all these educated, good looking males, there would have been one close to the qualities I was seeking. As silly as it sounds, I momentarily wished I could have set up my own checkpoint, started taking resumes, and conducting interviews. They were each so clean-cut and handsome and the way they seemed to talk so effortlessly with their female counterparts made them even more appealing. Finding someone who would transition smoothly into American culture was very important to me. But I instinctively knew that while on the surface they each seemed like they were modern and Americanized, once they spoke, their accents would undoubtedly remind me they were raised in India and were probably a lot more traditional than they appeared.

I sighed as I wondered if I would be so lucky to meet any men in Kerala who looked like any of the pilots I had just seen. I sighed and shook my head, knowing that was highly unlikely. I thought of the last time I had visited, and I could not recall seeing anyone who resembled the bone structure, coloring, or demeanor of these polished pilots. But then again, I didn't need a deluge of candidates. I just needed to find one, right?

Chapter 19

I EVENTUALLY BOARDED my plane, and as I passed the cockpit, I couldn't help but smile as I wondered what my own pilot looked like. Was he one of the pilots I had admired?

Once seated, I buckled my seat belt, and before the plane even took off, I unknowingly nodded off, only to wake up an hour and a half later as the pilot announced we would be landing. I looked out my window and through the dispersing, wispy clouds, I could see the beautiful, dense, evergreen jungle of Kerala laid out below me. Rivers snaked along some of the hills and down into the rice paddies, a total contrast to the dust and desert and pollution of western India. Kerala was like a hidden jungle oasis of the South, a sparkling emerald. Palm trees, coconut trees, and countless vegetation covered every square inch of Kerala.

"It's God's own country," Anil, the oldest cousin on my dad's side, had proudly declared to me when I had once visited India as a child. Filled with abundant rivers, hills, and trees, the villages of Kerala retained the raw, untamed beauty that God had initially intended. It was only March, but I could feel the heat and the lack of central air as soon as I walked off the airplane and into the airport. The summers in Kerala are painfully humid and hot, which are only momentarily relieved by the thick, wet rains of the monsoon season.

When I arrived in Cochin, I attempted to speak my native language, Malayalam, as I made my way through the final customs checkpoint, but my tongue refused to cooperate while I stumbled over basic pronunciations. The customs clerk chuckled to himself, his smile revealing an overbite and two missing teeth, as he scribbled notes on his clipboard. He gestured me through the line and to baggage claim.

After gathering my luggage, I made my way to the metal front gates of the arrival area, where people were calling out names and pushing their way to the front of the line for a glimpse of their loved ones. Though he stood towards the back of the chaos, my uncle's posture-perfect frame was clearly visible. He wasn't that tall, but I was sure that his rod-straight posture rendered him an additional two inches of height. My uncle had long retired from the military, but he still retained the stately presence of an officer. He wore a khaki, safari-style shirt with matching slacks, carried his walking cane like a police baton, and walked as if he were marching. His most prominent feature was his mustache. Like most Indian mustaches, it was full and amply covered his upper lip to the point that it almost seemed non-existent. The ends, however, tapered to a perfect symmetrical curl, reminding me of the little maharaja logo on the Air India flight I had just taken from New York to London to Bombay. I glanced around for any sign of my cousins, but I didn't see anyone. Upon seeing me, my uncle walked briskly towards me, placed one hand on my right shoulder, affectionately squeezed my left cheek, and then patted me on the top of my head. Suddenly I was six years old again, and I stood there partially expecting him to pull candy magically out of thin air like he did when I was young. But instead he looked me over and shook his head as he assessed me from head to toe. "You're too skinny, Sarai-mol. No Indian boy will want a girl who looks like a skeleton. I'll have to make sure we fatten you up before marrying you off."

I learned long ago to ignore comments about weight from Indian relatives. You're always either too skinny or too fat in their eyes. And even when they're complaining that you've gained too much weight, they are adding two more scoops of rice to your plate and telling you to eat.

I climbed into the back seat of the cream Ambassador car, which reminded me of the cars from the 1950s. I winced as the scorching heat from the pleather seats stung my hands. We drove quickly through

Cochin, and my uncle kept the window open, resting one arm on the open window, and turned back towards me. The airplane ride would be the last time that I would enjoy central air for the next few months, I realized with a grimace.

"Sarai-mol, you would like some fresh coconut water? Your father told me that you like very much. He said you also want to see Ko-valam." I nodded an emphatic *yes*, and minutes later the driver pulled into the seaside resort town of Kovalam, just outside Cochin. Kovalam was a popular vacationing spot for foreign tourists, and while it resembled other parts of India in its tropical, jungle-like vegetation, to me, it resembled more of the Caribbean islands with its light sandy beach and perfectly placed coconut trees that lined the water's edge. It was probably also one of the few places where you would actually see tourists wearing bikinis in Kerala. But it was only tourists who dared to wear bathing suits. The locals were equally enjoying the beach, splashing in the water. They just did it fully clothed in *saris* and *salwar kameezes* that covered them quite thoroughly from their neck to their ankles. For all their modesty, it was sometimes hard to believe that Kerala is part of the same India where the Kama Sutra originated.

We walked up to a vendor who let us select our own coconut, which was still wrapped in its natural green casing. He whacked off the top to create a small opening, stuck a straw in it, and handed it to me. I said nothing for the next few minutes as I greedily savored its natural sweet deliciousness while I enjoyed the beautiful view of the coastline. Numerous young people were splashing, fully clothed, in the water, and in the distance, I could see small fishing boats casting their nets against the afternoon tide.

I hadn't visited Kovalam since the last time I had visited India with my family. It was hard to believe I was only twenty-two years old then. It was even harder to believe that I was here yet again searching for my husband.

I pulled out my camera and took pictures of the beach, capturing the beautiful palm trees lined up against the coastline. My uncle indulged me, even posing in some of the shots. I tried to get him to smile, but he stood there, unsmiling, at attention, with his handlebar mustache as if he were posing for a formal military portrait. I wish we could have stayed longer so I could capture the beautiful sunset later that day, but my uncle informed me that we had to be on our way, as *Ammachi*, my grandmother, was waiting to see me. We then began the three-hour journey to my father's hometown of Manchikal.

Once we traveled outside of tourist-friendly Kovalam, the true Kerala, in all its untamed rawness and glory, emerged. And although many years had passed since I had last visited, to my amazement, Kerala was still unchanged. Most of it looked just like what I had seen through my airplane window seat: lush, jungle-like greenery everywhere. Occasional billboards dotted the roadways, advertising mostly gold wedding jewelry, Bata shoes, and a few electronic items. We passed through the heart of several small towns, which to me resembled small villages with shanty-like storefronts. Everything was written in the mother tongue of Malayalam, which I couldn't read, but I would occasionally see an English word like *hotel.*

Driving in India reminded me of the same adrenaline rush I had when going on a roller coaster ride. Rickshaws and scooters were everywhere, darting randomly and honking rather than signaling, following traffic rules that only they seemed to know. Das, our driver, narrowly missed hitting several of them and plunged on ahead at the same frenetic speed as if he were just maneuvering a go-cart ride at Dave and Busters. The streets were narrow and more designed for one-way driving. When coming around the curve of a mountain or hill, only honking and quick reflexes separated a common driving experience from becoming a personal tragedy. Das seemed unaffected by my gasps, expertly shifting gears and honking, all the while balancing a cigarette between his lips. My uncle seemed just as unaffected as he enjoyed the fresh air. He turned to me, unphased by the crazy driving while I tightened my grip on the door. I dug my nails into the hand rest of the car door, clinging on for dear life as we hugged the bends and curves of the road. I was positive that the vinyl would retain the imprints of my fingernails long after my car ride was over.

We soon passed the flatlands and reached the hilly areas. Rice paddies were framed by hills that were dotted with coconut trees, rubber trees, and banana trees. In Kerala, one didn't need to find a good backdrop for a picture. You only had to step outside your front door.

It took us three hours to reach my father's hometown village of Manchikal. When the car turned finally slowed and traveled through rusted iron gates that read "Tholanikunnal House," I knew we had arrived home. We were greeted by the same gray stone gates caulked with algae and a loose gravel path interspersed with terracotta colored dirt that I had remembered as a child. I breathed a slow sigh of relief and quickly made the sign of the cross. I wasn't Catholic, but it seemed befitting. Now I understood why India didn't have a need to build amusement parks. A regular ride in a car would be harrowing enough.

Long gone was the two-room cement home where my father had grown up. In its stead was a modest five-bedroom, two-story home that had been slowly remade, room by room, with money my father had sent over the years. My father's youngest brother, appropriately named Babykutty, and his wife, Milly, now lived there with my grandmother, my Ammachi, whom we all affectionately referred to as Manchikal Ammachi. Dressed in a plain white *sari* with the *pallu* tied around her waist, Manchikal Ammachi sat on the wicker chair right next to the main door of the house. It was her signature spot where she could see everything. Every time we visited India, she spent most of her time sitting there.

As I got out of the car, Milly Chechy had rushed to the door carrying a bowl of chopped vegetables. She was only five years older than me, and I often thought of her more as a cousin than an aunt, which was why I called her "Chechy" as it befitted someone who was your older sibling or cousin.

"Milly Chechy!" I exclaimed, running up the stairs. She had married my uncle at eighteen and already had three children. When she set aside the bowl, I noticed her burgeoning stomach. I lightly touched it and teased her in Malayalam, "So do you have any special news to tell me?"

She blushed and used the mixing spoon to playfully hit me. "When are YOU getting married? That is the news everybody is waiting to hear!" she teased, her hands stroking her stomach.

I made my way towards Manchikal Ammachi whose official name was also Sarai—my namesake. I not only shared a name with her, but I could also attribute my thick and often unruly black hair to her. She wore her hair pulled away from her face in a loose bun. Her face, a pincushion of wrinkles, turned up to me. Her left eye was sealed shut while her right eye observed me closely. My father had told me that her left eye had been damaged well before his birth by a stray coal when she was cooking in front of an open flame. But he had also warned me not be fooled as her right eye seemed to have double the sight, and as a child, he hadn't been able to get away with anything.

My father had always been her favorite, and everyone knew it, maybe because he was the first child of hers to leave home. I kneeled to hug her, but she grabbed my face and held it within her palms as she stared at me, searching my face. I wondered if she could see my dad's face in mine. I was often told I resembled my mother, but my nose and eyes, both larger than I would have preferred, were definitely reminiscent of my father. Tears streamed down her cheeks, resting in the crevices of the deep wrinkles lining her face. She gave me her signature kiss, touching her cheek with mine and breathing in deeply as if she could absorb my essence into hers. This was my grandmother, a woman for whom I had deep affection, but in many ways, was still a stranger to me. Her face had always been familiar due to the large picture of her and my grandfather that hung predominantly in my parents' living room, but I had actually only seen her less than a handful of times in person.

Her hand rested on my clavicle as she began telling me that the reason I was still single was that I was too skinny. I laughed, grabbed her hand, and kissed it. She smiled affectionately back at me but then began telling Milly Chechy to bring me food to eat. I sat there for a short while, speaking broken Malayalam with my Ammachi. Her face crinkled into a smile, and I couldn't be sure if my attempts were amusing to her or if she truly could understand me.

I looked around the main family home. It seemed so empty now. I remembered visiting India as a child when all nine of my dad's brothers and sisters still lived in India. A big group of them had piled into a Jeep to pick us up at the airport, unlike today where the only person who showed up was Rajan Uncle. Back then there seemed to be so many kids running around. Most of them had since immigrated to the US with their parents and lived near us, leaving only Babykutty Uncle, Velya Uncle, and Rajan Uncle and their families here in Kerala. Now it seemed that the only kids left at home were Babykutty Uncle and Milly Chechy's three kids, one of whom was fourteen years old and the other two were eight and four. Velya Uncle and Velya Auntie had two "kids," both of whom were married and living and working in Ernakulam, which was about a four-hour car ride away. Rajan Uncle had one son who was in engineering school in New Delhi. Without the presence of my parents and with no cousins around my age to keep me company, this visit to India was certainly going to be very, very different from my previous trips.

When we got to my uncle's house, I quickly showered and changed into a clean set of clothes. I grabbed a book and joined my uncle on the front porch as he smoked his cigar. Within minutes, the fatigue of my journey began kicking in, and the words I tried to focus on began to blur. Just as I began to nod off, my uncle patted me on the knee. "Sleep… go sleep," my uncle said and then flung the nub of his cigar across the porch railing. "You sleep good tonight. We have much to talk tomorrow." Even through the jet lag and haziness of sleep, that statement sounded ominous.

Chapter 20

I WOKE TO the sounds of the rooster crowing the next morning and countless, unseen insects and bugs buzzing, slugging, slithering, and scurrying just outside my window. Being in Kerala was like living in a jungle and on a farm at the same time. With two cows in the backyard, chickens running sporadically across the yard, and a goat that was tied to the mango tree, my uncle had several of the requisite farm animals. But with mango, coconut, palm, and banana trees, along with exotic insects that I didn't even know the names of, the Kerala landscape was undoubtedly tropical and jungle-like.

I thought of my bedroom back home. Once in a while, I would hear the sound of a bird chirping on the tree outside my window, but typically, I was awakened to the blaring sound of my alarm clock or the humming of the air conditioner. But here, I could hear every imaginable sound. As I stretched leisurely in my bed, I noted the tops of the walls had three-inch gaps from the ceiling to the upper walls, which would explain how the outdoor sounds were so pronounced. Though my uncle's house was still considered new at four years old, I noticed the cracks and a faint hint of yellow in the cement. In America, the houses we live in are sealed to the outside elements and closed off to our neighbors. But in India, there seemed to be an openness, where people and insects alike could venture in and out freely to their liking.

I sat upright and stretched again, attempting to shake off the lingering jet lag. It felt so odd to be here without my parents. Without them, I didn't feel quite at ease but more like a formal guest whom everyone had to tiptoe around. For a moment, I began to wonder if I shouldn't have come. But Anjuli's words, "What do you have to lose?" kept echoing in my head. Whether I met my future husband here or not, if nothing, at least I would have a story to tell later on.

Pungent smells of cardamom, turmeric, and ginger began to fill the morning air, and the smells of breakfast were intermingling with the preparations for lunch. I ventured into the kitchen where Lali had already prepared my morning chai. Before I could even ask, she handed it to me in a small juice glass. I eagerly took it and held it close, allowing the steam of the chai to massage my face as I breathed in deeply the familiar smells of cardamom and ginger mixed with black tea leaves.

My Malayalam had indeed become rusty, but apparently Lali knew a little English. "Auntie iz market. Ungle iz thar," she said, pointing towards the front of the house.

"Sarai-mol, you awake?" my uncle called from the front porch. When he saw me, he motioned towards the empty chair next to him. He was holding his tall, skinny chai glass in one hand and the newspaper in the other. He glanced at me and smiled, or what I took to be a smile since his thick mustache hid most of his mouth, and then he returned to reading the newspaper.

As he sat quietly reading, I settled into the wicker chair on the front porch, observing what I assumed to be the daily routines of neighboring residents. A mother hurried by, umbrella in hand, followed by her two young elementary school-aged children who had to skip to keep up with her brisk pace. A group of young teenage girls dressed in the school uniform of white shirts and long blue skirts walked by, holding tightly to their schoolbags while chatting and giggling as they made their way to the bus stop. Countless scooters and rickshaws raced by, beeping at pedestrians as they weaved their way through the busy road. Funny, I thought, the morning scene was so different from home because here mostly everyone walked, waving at neighbors and engaging them in conversation while back at home, everyone raced off in their individual cars, sealed off from everything and everyone. But even in the differences, there was still that "everyman" quality to the scene. Children were still going to school. Parents were still rushing off to work.

Though each of the houses was fenced off by stone or iron gates, I was once again struck by the openness in India to the outside. Front doors were often kept unlocked during the day, a total contrast to home, where everything was sealed airtight, even when we were home. From our cars to our homes, there is so much metal, wood, and material that separates us from our neighbors while here in India—from the rickshaws to the scooters to the way the homes are built—there is such an openness to the outside that even when you're inside, you still feel as if you're outside.

I turned my attention back to my uncle, whom I unnervingly found sitting there, newspaper folded neatly on his lap, observing me keenly as I was observing the road.

Not knowing what to say, I smiled and took another sip of chai. His mustache twitched and he cleared his throat before he began speaking.

"So…" he began, prodding me for conversation.

"So…" I echoed.

"Sarai-mol, tell me what you think of India. Are we so different than your America?"

I continued watching the street as I attempted to describe my thoughts. "Yes, actually, I was thinking of how open everything is here. In America, we often stay in our homes and when we come out, it's to get in our cars to go somewhere else—somewhere else that's also *inside*…"

A "*hmmm*" was all I got from him. I didn't have to look at him to know that he was studying me, dissecting me with his shrewd, military-trained eyes. We continued in silence like that for a few minutes. Then he cleared his throat, a habit I soon came to realize was a precursor to a discussion that I might not find to my liking. "I really surprised that your daddy call me to look for husband for you. I think it is better you find husband in America, no? Why you no like boy from America?"

He seemed to settle deeper into his seat as he awaited my answer. I realized that we only knew each other on a very superficial basis and had never really discussed anything in depth, but I knew he was not just seeking an answer to his question but an understanding into my thought process.

Where would I begin? What should I say? How could I simplify the complications of finding a compatible Indian mate in America? "Because, Uncle, the selection for a nice Malayalee boy from a good family is limited."

His mustache twitched as he asked, "So there are no Indian families in America who have nice boys?"

"None who are available and want to marry me," I answered as truthfully as I could.

"Or none you wanted to marry?" he countered and then took a slow sip of chai.

"I could safely say in some cases, it was mutual, Uncle," I said, not sure if he was sincerely asking or if he was trying to imply something.

"I ask because for you, it is better to find boy in US, no? It might be difficult for you here. Boys raised here are very particular. They want chai in morning. They want chai in afternoon. They want a lot of things that you may think not good because of vemen's bib."

"You mean women's lib," I said, trying not to chuckle at his mispronunciation.

"Yes, vemen's leeb. You correct. It may not be easy for you as you think to marry a boy from Kerala."

This was the second time this morning he mentioned it would be better for me to find someone in the US. Why was he discouraging me now? And if he felt this way, why had he been so enthusiastic when my dad talked to him about my coming here?

"Well, I do know several friends who came to India and got married, and they are happy. My friend, Anjuli, married a boy from Kerala just a few months ago. He studied in Bangalore, and he's very open-minded. In a lot of ways, he's more forward-thinking than the boys I went to school with."

"Well, maybe it is possible. But I think it won't be easy to find boy here like you think. You don't have education."

"*What???* I have a Master's degree!" Had my father forgotten to tell him that I had both my undergrad and master's degrees?!

"Yes, but in teaching," he said, flicking his wrist dismissively. "In India, that means nothing these days."

"I got my degree in Biology *and* English, *and* I not only received my teacher's certification, but I also have my master's degree in curriculum and instruction!" I asserted, crossing my arms across my chest as if I had just proven my point. I had worked very hard in all of my classes, and I was appalled that my uncle spoke of it as if I had taken Basket Weaving 101. Not even Armaan had ever made me feel inferior about my education.

"Don't be defense, I'm just telling you truth. Your father wants doctor for you. Here the doctor wants doctor, and they want big dowry." He looked at me, pausing as he waited for my reaction. Why would my parents have to pay a big dowry? I was taking the guy to the US. My family and I would have to incur plenty of expenses. Wasn't that enough? Then my uncle smiled or what I perceived to be a smile under his thick mustache. Was he just testing me?

He sipped the last of his chai, almost slurping it, as he added, "But you are American. You have a chance because of that."

Great, I thought, my US citizenship would be my ticket to a husband and his ticket to the US.

My face must have reflected my displeasure because my uncle leaned forward, patting my knee. "Don't worry, Sarai-mol. You will still get plenty of proposals." Proposals... how anti-climatic, I thought as I pondered the word used to describe a viable, interested marriage candidate. But I guess the word fit. One family would "propose" their child as a suitable marriage candidate for the other. I knew before coming here that if I were to have an arranged marriage, I would have to let go of my romantic expectations. Gone was the vision of a man on bended knee, declaring his undying love for me. That vision was slowly slipping further and further away. Now my engagement would be an official, solemn ceremony performed in front of family betrothing us to one another and announcing the date of the wedding. But even after the engagement, rather than romantic strolls along the beach or in a park, I would be meeting my future husband, just a few times, under the watchful eye of our parents or relatives. It wouldn't be until after the wedding that I would even be able to get to know my husband on my own and spend any time with him without raising any eyebrows.

I finished my chai, savoring it to the last drop, and crunched on the small crystal pieces of raw sugar that lined the bottom of my small glass.

Chapter 21

LATER THAT AFTERNOON, my uncle took me into town on his scooter. I sat on the back seat side-saddle, which, according to my uncle, was the only way for a female to sit on a scooter. His face had turned almost beet-red when I initially attempted to sit astride on the bike.

We stopped by the outdoor market to pick up some groceries so Lali could make dinner. The grocery store was very similar to an outdoor farmer's market, and while the selection was limited, I was impressed with the freshness of the vegetables and fruits. As my uncle made his purchases, I walked through the bins of display baskets, admiring the variety of vegetables. Health food stores in the States would kill to have such freshly grown, organic food, but here in India, they knew nothing else. Everything was homegrown in someone's backyard. I picked up a thick, juicy tomato with admiration when my uncle caught my eye and shook his head. Out of the corner of my eye, I could see the sales clerk, eyeing me disapprovingly. I gently placed the tomato back in its display bin and continued my admiration without touching anything else. After we made our purchases, the cashier used the previous day's newspaper to wrap up the vegetables and fruits into separate packages, which were then tossed into a wicker tote bag my uncle had pulled out of a storage space in the scooter.

With the packages tucked securely under his arm, my uncle climbed the stairs where a second level of storefronts was housed. We walked past a dentist sign and through a door without a store sign. It was a tiny one-room setup. A tattered maroon curtain hung in one corner and in front of it was a brown, 3-legged stool. In the other corner was a metal desk with an old-fashioned typewriter and three chairs grouped in front of it. A stocky, swarthy man in his mid-forties, wearing a standard white *mundu* and a short sleeve plaid shirt, arose from behind the desk. His droopy eyes lit up, his eyes widened, and he smiled in recognition. "Raj-sar!" he said and extended his hand in a firm handshake. My uncle introduced him as Ramesh.

I smiled and nodded, and out of habit, I extended my hand for a handshake. Ramesh seemed surprised at my gesture and then awkward-ly shook it, holding it loosely and releasing it quickly. His head inclined towards me as I heard him ask my uncle if I was "the girl." *What did that mean?*

My uncle and Ramesh spent a few minutes exchanging pleasantries, and I sat there, wondering why I had agreed to tag along. Ramesh must have realized I was bored, so he pulled out a thick binder and pushed it towards me. I glanced at my uncle, and he nodded for me to open it. A black and white photograph of a twenty-something boy greeted me and under his picture was his full name, birth date, education history, and job experience. As I read on, I realized that the profile also included information on his hometown and family history. My eyes widened as it dawned on me that I was looking at a marriage catalog. Was Ramesh a marriage broker?

I looked to my uncle and then at Ramesh, both of whom watched me with intense interest. Was I supposed to pick my future husband out of this book? I flipped from one page to the next, quickly scanning to see if there was a picture that stood out to me. But had any of them been handsome, I would never have known it. The photographer must have once worked for the prison system. Each picture looked more like black and white mug shots. Each subject had a deadpan, stoic expres-sion, and not one of them was smiling. I recognized the maroon curtain in the backdrop of each picture as being the same one in the office. Based on their expressions, I couldn't help but wonder how many of them had been dragged by their parents to this very office to have their pictures taken. Had they, too, given into society pressures and the constant nagging of their parents?

As I flipped from one page to the next, the faces ranged from baby-faced twenty-somethings to lean, long-faced thirty-somethings. The one common denominator between the pictures seemed to be that the majority of them had mustaches... *thick, bushy* mustaches. Some had thin faces, some wore glasses, some had chubby cheeks... but yes, I realized as I turned yet another page, most of them seemed to have a mustache.

My uncle covertly glanced around the room and lowered his voice as if he were about to divulge top-secret information that he didn't want overheard. "Sarai, this is not common practice. The family tells Ramesh what they want, and he chooses a boy."

"Really?" I asked, wondering why all the profiles had been inserted into a binder if it hadn't been intended for browsing through like a catalog.

As if reading my mind, my uncle responded. "This is for Ramesh to track candidates. But you are so picky so he agreed to let you see it."

"Picky?" I asked. Had my father said something to him? Had he somehow observed something within the past day? "What makes you think I'm picky, Uncle?" I asked, defensively.

My uncle leaned back into his chair. "You are twenty-eight years old and single. A pretty girl, a smart girl. Of course, you are picky. Other-wise, you be married right now."

I couldn't argue with that line of reasoning, so I just shrugged and smiled sheepishly. But what did I have to be apologetic for? After all, this would be the rest of my life, right? I had better be picky!

As I glanced through the pictures, there wasn't one picture that I was particularly drawn to. Maybe if I met them in person, I'd feel differently. Or maybe if they smiled. It was hard to react in the marriage sense to anyone without feeling some initial physical spark.

"You like?" Ramesh asked, when I paused on a page.

"Huh?" I asked, thrown off. I had been thinking to myself, not looking at anyone in particular. My eyes readjusted to the album I was holding, and I found myself staring back at someone with a long, fleshy face and a bad case of frizzy hair.

Ramesh seemed pleased with what he thought was my selection. "Very nice boy... good family. His father is a police chief in Udumbanoor."

My immediate reaction was, "N-n-n-no!" but that would be rude, so I just did the nonchalant, noncommittal shrug of the shoulders I had seen in many Malayalam movies. I flipped to the next page where I was rewarded for my perseverance with a handsome face. I pointed to him and asked my uncle, "What about him?" My uncle shook his head from side-to side in that Indian way that means *yes, it's good*. Ramesh took the binder from me and readjusted his glasses. "No, no good," he said shaking his head gravely. "He just got engaged last week. You came one month ago, he would have been available. Sorry, I forgot to take his profile out."

It figures that I would pick the one unavailable guy out of an entire book of potentials.

My uncle patted me on the shoulder, and tried to reassure me, "Don't worry, they get new peoples every day."

Ramesh bobbed his head up and down quickly, "Yes! New ones we get every day." I looked through a few more unflattering shots of potentials.

As I glanced through the rest of the pages, another thought occurred to me—what if Ramesh passed on a perfectly good candidate, someone I would have considered but, for whatever reason, he didn't think would be a good match? After all, that one picture was proof enough that his taste vastly differed from mine. It was disconcerting to know that someone who barely knew me, much less what I really wanted, would be the person conducting all the screenings for my marriage proposals. He was a relative stranger; yet, he would be the one to hold the key, or in this case, the book to my future.

Chapter 22

MY FIRST "PROPOSAL" arrived during the second week of my visit. Apparently, this proposal hadn't been in the marriage book I had seen, and Ramesh described him as good looking with a "wheatish complexion" and very educated. Despite all my protests, my other two uncles and their wives gathered at Rajan Uncle's house to meet "the boy" and his family. I found it humorous that even though he was in his late twenties and of marriage-age, he was still referred to as "the boy" by my uncles and aunts.

When we heard the horn of a jeep at our front gate, my uncle and aunt went outside to greet our guests while I, eager to get a glimpse of "the boy," peeked through the window of my bedroom. As they piled out of two black Ambassador cars, I cringed when I saw how many members of his family had come. Why was everyone treating this as if it were a done deal rather than just the initial meeting? There must have been eight or nine people. But before I could make anyone out, Lali was there, shooing me away from the window. She reminded me in rapid Malayalam that I was, as my uncle instructed me, to wait in the kitchen. Yes, this was my life, but yet I had to wait in the back, in the façade of domesticity, making the tea. Of course, it was Lali who would actually prepare the tea. I would only have to serve it. But that didn't seem to matter to anyone as long as it *appeared* that I had made it.

I heard the front door open, and I assumed our guests began filing in and taking their seats. I pressed my ear closely against the wall separating the living room and the kitchen, but I could hear nothing but muffled voices through the concrete wall.

I stood there, heart pounding, as I awaited my fate. My brain felt like a mosh pit as countless questions raced and collided in my mind. Would this be the one? Did my future lie right outside through those kitchen doors? I lost my battle on remaining calm and serene and alternately shifted my weight to each leg. When that didn't help, I began pacing back and forth and rubbing my queasy stomach. I anxiously stood there in the kitchen, awaiting my fate, as Lali busied herself with the final preparations. She seemed so unaffected by it all, and her focus remained on her duties of preparing snacks for the guests. Next time I was going to request that Cochemole wait with me. This was too nerve-racking to wait by myself. I was wringing my hands and my *pallu* when, after what seemed like an eternity, my uncle finally appeared at the kitchen door, his expression grave as he nodded and motioned for me to join him and our guests.

Lali quickly handed me the tray of chai, and I followed my uncle into the living room. I placed the tray on the coffee table and handed a cup to each guest. I suppressed my immediate urge to scan the room for my proposal. My patience was soon rewarded. "The boy" sat between his parents, hands resting on his lap as he glanced at me and then quickly turned away, very preoccupied with my uncle's floor tile. He had a full head of hair that was in dire need of hair gel. Behind his thick, gold-rimmed glasses, his eyes were small, and even with glasses, he squinted a lot. His cheeks were full and round and reminded me of someone who was trying to talk when his mouth was still full of food. He had a pronounced chin and, of course, the standard, full and bushy mustache.

His eyes remained averted, and he only gave me a passing glance when he reached for his chai from my tray. There was no light in his eyes, no sign of interest. And with that realization, an instant sadness soon followed. Sadness for my aunt who was eagerly prompting everyone to have seconds and was already treating them as in-laws, sadness for my uncles and aunts who had left work early to gather at the house, and sadness for the boy's entire family who had come to meet a finicky American-born Indian who was still somehow hoping for some semblance of romantic love.

After I served the chai, my uncle motioned for me to sit on one of the empty tan Rattan chairs. I crossed my legs, attempting to look like a proper and refined lady while all I felt was clumsy and awkward. Everyone except my proposal was staring at me. Was I supposed to say something? Had I done something wrong? The boy's father cleared his throat and asked about my education, my parents, directing all of his questions to my uncle. Their facial expressions were so serious at first, assessing me from head to toe, as my uncle talked about my family and my education. I, for the most part, kept my eyes on the floor. When I glanced at my proposal, I noticed he was also staring at the floor. His mother sat next to him, her eyes focused on my crossed legs. I sat up straighter, but based on the look in her eyes, I realized I was committing some sort of faux pas.

Very soon the small talk died down, and my uncle then motioned for me to rise. "Come, Sunny," he said to the boy. "You can both talk here in this room and get to know each other." He brought two of the folding chairs from the kitchen and put it in the spare bedroom next to the living room. "You talk and get to know each other here in private," my uncle said and left the room. I didn't know what the point was because I could see everyone staring at us from the living room.

I looked at Sunny and wondered if he felt even remotely the way I did. I smiled at him, more out of politeness, and he quickly smiled back before staring at the floor. We both said nothing for a few moments. I knew then that I would have to be the one to start the conversation.

"So you study in Bangalore?" I asked, even cocking my head to the side so I could see his face more clearly. Was there any way I could be attracted to him? Could I force it? Was that even possible? Either you were or you weren't, right? Sometimes attraction could grow after you get to know someone. But what if it didn't grow? Then what?

"Yes, at Normandy college," he said, his hands clasped in his lap. He spoke English well, but his accent was strong. He wore a white button down shirt, gray slacks, and brown leather sandals. He glanced up at me when he started talking, but then before his sentence was even finished, he was staring back at the floor.

How different this was compared to when I met Armaan! While we couldn't take our eyes off each other, Sunny would barely look at me. How was I supposed to even consider someone who was so painfully shy that he couldn't even look me in the eye?

"So, um, what do you like to do?" I asked.

He smiled nervously and then responded quickly, "I like computers. Video games. Writing."

Writing? That was a new one. I used to write for the school paper, and I had dabbled in some poetry in college. So maybe we would have something in common. "So what do you write? Fiction? Short stories? Poetry?"

He gave me a confused look. "I told you, no? I write video games."

"Oh, sorry, I thought you meant you liked video games and writing. I didn't know you meant you liked writing video games."

"Yes, I like video game writing," he said. Now I had managed to offend him. I tried to think of something else to talk about, but there seemed to be no point. I already knew how I felt. I soon grew quiet, and our conversation went from slow to a dead stop. I also noticed that just one room away, his family as well as mine were just as quiet, no doubt trying to listen in on our conversation. I began to rise from my chair to return to the living room when he glanced up at me, probably sensing what I was about to do. "So you like to live in America?"

"Yes, I do," I said, staying seated as I wondered if this would be the first and last question.

He just nodded his head, and after some additional awkward seconds, he tried again. "How you like India?"

"Yes, yes, I like India," I said. "It's beautiful..." my voice trailed off. I didn't have any energy to put into this conversation.

He looked at his hands, clearly out of things to say, so I rose from my chair, and he followed as we returned to the living room, taking our original seats. My uncle exchanged a few more minutes of chit-chat with Sunny's family, but soon Sunny's father rose to leave and the rest of the family immediately followed. My uncle and aunt escorted them out while I remained seated, unsure whether it was proper for me to follow them out or whether I was to remain in the house. As he reached the front door, my uncle beckoned me to join them.

As soon as the two cars left the gates, my uncle and aunt rushed to my side, their faces eager and excited. "So…" my uncle began.

Confused, I repeated, "So…" I stared at my uncle, wondering what he was getting at.

"So what you think of the boy?" my uncle asked.

Not wanting to be negative or put him down, I described my thoughts in the most neutral way possible. "Um, he was um, nice, I guess." I said, shrugging my shoulders.

"So your answer is yes?" my uncle said, his eyes widening with joy by the second.

"My answer is yes?! What?" I couldn't believe they even had to ask. I thought it was quite obvious. Surely, they could see that I wasn't interested. Heck, we hadn't spoken more than a few sentences to each other.

Before I could say anything else, the phone rang, and my uncle grabbed it before anyone else could. "Uhmmm… I see…" he said. After a few more seconds, he placed the phone down and joined me and aunt.

"That was Ramesh?" my aunt asked.

My uncle nodded. "Yes, he called to find out what Sarai thought. And to say that the family said yes."

I cringed. I hoped he would have said no, relieving me of both burden and guilt. Surely, he couldn't have liked me either! My uncle turned to me, not saying a word. But I knew what he was thinking: *It's up to you now, Sarai. Do you want to get married or not?*

Everyone's eyes were on me like their own entire future also depended on my answer. I was beginning to hate myself for expecting so much here in India. But was I really being that picky? This guy wasn't even remotely close to what I liked, personality-wise or physically. Marriage was a once-in-a-lifetime decision for me. There would be no turning back. I could not settle for just anyone, especially someone who was that shy and awkward and someone with whom I could barely have a conversation. I had to feel like I was selecting someone I wanted to be with. I glanced at Rajan Uncle, Babykutty Uncle, Velya Uncle, and then at their respective wives. I could see the hope, even the desperation in their eyes for me to say yes. I didn't want to disappoint them. Everyone had gone through so much trouble for me.

My first thought was to bluntly say, "No, and how could any of you expect me to say yes?!" But feeling the pressure of the silence and the pleading in their eyes, I brokenly replied, "I—can't, Uncle. I—I just can't." I visibly saw their shoulders sag in defeat. I felt sick to my stomach, knowing that I was the reason for their disappointment.

They said nothing for a while, all staring at the floor, as they digested my disappointing news. Were they all really that surprised? Did they honestly believe this guy was a good catch and I was letting go of my one chance at marriage? Then my Rajan Uncle spoke to my aunt in rapid Malayalam, almost seeming to forget that while I wasn't entirely fluent, I could still understand most of what he said. Apparently after Ramesh told Sunny's family about me, they called Sunny, and he had traveled home all the way from Bangalore, a nine-hour train-ride, overnight, just to meet me. My uncle then shook his head in dismay and said in Malayalam, "We can't do this to families if she's going to be picky like this. We'll tell Ramesh only to bring local families then."

Now I really felt sick to my stomach. I had no idea he traveled so far overnight, just to meet me. But as bad as I felt, that didn't obligate me to say "yes," did it? I wanted to get married, but not like this. Why did I even have to justify why I didn't like this guy? If this was what it was going to be like each time I met a proposal, I didn't think I could continue. How did I even think that an arranged marriage would work for me? The whole day had taken an emotional toll. If I could have, I would have left right then and there for the airport. I had a strong feeling this arranged marriage process was not going to work for me.

"Uncle," I said, my eyes filling with tears, "I'm sorry. Maybe I was wrong to think I could come here and go through this process. Maybe it's just not for me."

My uncle looked alarmed, realizing that I was on the verge of stopping the whole process entirely. "No sorry, okay?" he said, flicking his wrist in the air, as if to say the whole situation was not a big deal. He lightly patted my head the same way he did with Tipu, their mutt dog. "Don't worry. Your father told us not to force you. It is your choice. We are just showing you boys. If you don't like, it is okay... okay? I will keep showing you boys until you like one."

"But I don't want to inconvenience everyone—"

"What inconvenience?" he asked, shrugging. "I have nothing else to do anyway. I go to work, and I come home. We keep looking, okay? You will find what you like soon."

I nodded, and my aunt stopped in front of me and lifted the edge of the *pallu* of her sari to wipe my tears.

Chapter 23

TWO DAYS LATER another "proposal" arrived at Rajan Uncle's house. This time only Babykutty Uncle and Milly Chechy joined us. And like I requested, my cousin Cochemole, Milly Chechy's fourteen-year-old daughter, kept me company. While the rest of the family greeted our guests, I was once again sequestered in the kitchen until it was time for me to be introduced and serve the chai. But this time, while I paced back and forth in the kitchen, waiting to be called, I was not only waiting to meet my proposal, but I was waiting for a report from Cochemole whom I had sent to do some initial scoping on my behalf.

As soon as she entered the kitchen, I raced to her side excitedly, "So tell me! What do you think?"

She wrung the edge of her *pallu*, her face contorted with confusion. This wasn't her proposal! Why should she be so nervous? "It's okay. Just tell me," I encouraged her. "Is it someone I might like?"

I studied her face for any sign of excitement or displeasure, but her face only seemed burdened with my request. I rested one hand on each shoulder and looked her straight in the eye. "It's okay. I just want you to tell me what you think."

She shrugged her shoulders nonchalantly and hesitantly replied, "He's good."

I again looked for any sign of excitement in her expression or in her eyes, but her face was as neutral as Switzerland.

Good? *Good?* What the heck does that mean? *Good.* It was such a neutral word! But no matter how good "good" was, good was still not great, and I wanted great. "So is he better than the other guy I saw?"

"Better?" she asked, her lips puckered up in confusion again. "Oh, Sarai Chechy, I *dooon't* know. Your taste is so different. He's…" she paused, searching for the right word, "He's… he's good," she said, shrugging her shoulders again, unable and unapologetic for not being able to think of another word.

Exasperated, I realized I would just have to wait to find out. The moments ticked by very, very slowly, and my imagination conjured up various scenarios of how this proposal would work out. But within another ten minutes, my curiosity was sated. Good ended up being okay, and sometimes okay was good enough but not when it came to marriage. Although he didn't resemble Sunny in the slightest, save for the bushy mustache, I had basically the same lack of attraction to his personality and to him.

Chapter 24

I CONCLUDED THAT one of the most nerve-racking aspects of the arranged marriage process for me was just waiting in the kitchen while everyone else had a chance to see and converse with my proposal. The longer I waited, the more the anticipation and nervousness grew, no matter how often or how many times I attempted to wait patiently. Why couldn't I just meet the proposal and his family along with everyone else? Why did I have to be "presented" like I was a sixteen-year-old making her cotillion debut? Besides, if they were guests in our home, wasn't it more courteous if I greeted them along with the rest of our family, rather than making a delayed appearance? It made sense. I knew that bringing it up to my uncle or aunt would have been useless though. My uncle had one view of how a marriage proposal should go, and he was determined to follow that tradition to the letter. It was better to just let him realize that it really wasn't a big deal.

When the third proposal arrived, Rajan Uncle and Auntie once again went outside to greet our guests. Unbeknownst to them, rather than scurrying to the kitchen, I took a seat in my designated wicker chair. Within three minutes, they re-entered the house with our guests in tow. As soon as he saw me seated there in the living room, my uncles' eyes widened in surprise and then narrowed to a stern, reproaching glare. My earlier confidence evaporated. This must have been the same stare he used on his subordinates in the military. I cringed and quickly decided from then on, I could just continue to wait in the kitchen. Besides, what did an additional ten or fifteen minutes of waiting matter? After all, I was going to see my proposal eventually, right?

Proposal Three was Vijay Koshy. He was an accountant, raised in Kottayam. To my relief, unlike the entourage that had accompanied Proposal One and Proposal Two, Vijay came only with his older brother. I couldn't help but note while they were brothers, they looked nothing alike. My proposal was taller, with a thin, long face, and had a full head of hair. The older brother was not only shorter with a round face, but he had a receding hairline that made him look more like the father rather than the older brother.

They exchanged pleasantries with my uncle, talking about their family while my uncle talked about mine. Lali brought out the tea, and when I rose up to serve it, my uncle lifted his hand up, motioning for me to sit back down. My aunt arose, instead, and served us all.

My uncle took a sip and rested the saucer on his thigh. "So Vijay, you work for an accounting firm in Ernakulam?"

To my uncle's and my shock, the brother whom we assumed was the older one answered. "I've been working there for five years now since college."

My uncle looked from one brother to the next and then back again. "I'm sorry... you're Vijay?" he asked, pointing to the shorter, older looking brother. He looked to Ramesh. "Which is the proposal for Sarai?"

Ramesh patted the back of the shorter brother with the receding hairline. "This is Vijay, Sarai's proposal, and this," he said, leaning across Vijay and patting the knee of the other brother, "is Bejay, Vijay's older brother."

"*Ohhh...* okay, sorry, Vijay. My pardon, I thought *you* were the older brother."

My uncle glanced at me and quickly ascertained my response. This time, without even ushering us to another room, he moved an empty chair next to Vijay and motioned for me to sit there. "Why don't you two talk and get to know each other." It wasn't a question.

What?! I balked internally. I thought my uncle would have gotten me out of this somehow! Now I was not only forced to talk to him, but

I had to do it directly in front of everyone! But unless I wanted to come across as rude, I had no choice but to sit there and for a few minutes, feign some marginal interest. Having to talk in front of everyone also put Vijay in an awkward position, and he seemed just as uncomfortable. For a few seconds, neither of us said anything, and we just smiled hesitantly at each other. Finally, after his brother nudged him, he looked at me, and smiled uncomfortably. "Ummm… so you are a teacher?"

I nodded and smiled. "Yes," and immediately took another sip of tea so I wouldn't have to say anything. After a couple of more minutes of stilted conversation, my uncle thanked them for coming and escorted them out.

As soon as they left, my uncle turned to me, his voice stern. "Next time you are to wait in kitchen until I or Auntie come for you, okay?" It wasn't a question, and there was definitely no room for discussion, so I just quickly nodded. Then he added, "At least, you could have stood up when we all walked in. You sat there like a proudy girl. What will they think?"

I had the urge to correct his grammar and say, "You mean proud girl," but I decided not to press my luck.

When Ramesh called fifteen minutes later to say Vijay was interested in proceeding, my uncle slapped his hand on his forehead in frustration and told him in rapid-fire Malayalam that the proposal looked like he was old enough to be my father. Apparently, Ramesh, too, knew it was a long-shot, but he said that Vijay had been very interested in meeting us when Ramesh mentioned that I was an American citizen.

Chapter 25

FTER THE NEXT two proposals, we had become a well-oiled machine. Since this was my first experience with the entire arranged marriage process, I hadn't realized how unusual my case was for Ramesh. The only other time he had such a busy schedule for one marriage candidate was when he had only one weekend to help a computer programmer working in the US on an H-1 Visa find a spouse. The programmer had come home on a two-week vacation and had to pick a wife in two days so they could schedule the engagement for that weekend and the wedding for the weekend after that.

What amazed me was rather than being discouraged with every no, my uncle seemed even more determined to find someone to whom I would say yes. I wondered if the marriage broker had also taken this as a personal challenge because he never seemed to tire of bringing me potentials. With each no, his eyes seemed to fire up with more determination and his jaw appeared more set and purposeful.

Unfortunately for all of us, Proposals Four, Five, Six, Seven, Eight, and Nine soon went the same way as Proposals One, Two, and Three. Finding fault with each potential suitor, I quickly began to feel like a character on the show *Seinfeld*. Although I didn't consider myself an overtly critical person, somehow there always seemed to be something about each proposal that I just couldn't get past.

Most of the time, we had a proposal every few days at our house. One day, however, Ramesh scheduled three proposals, and our worry was that their arrivals or departures would overlap, especially since the heavy afternoon rains had caused major flooding, causing our second proposal to arrive two hours late. But luckily, our third proposal had the same issue and arrived late as well.

Though it may sound like the proposals took up all my time, it was quite the opposite. The entire process, end to end, probably took up two to three hours on any given day. If you add another eight hours I spent sleeping, I was still left with thirteen hours to spare. I found that if I watched a Hindi movie, I could easily kill three additional hours. But I quickly realized that Bollywood movies were probably the worst things for me to watch, as they seemed to reinforce the magical, unrealistic aspects of falling in love, and many of them reminded me of how I felt when I first met Armaan.

For the first few days, all that extra time felt luxurious. Over time, though, I grew bored. Between the scorching heat and the monsoon rains, which started the week after I arrived in Kerala, I was often stuck within the confines of my uncle's home. My aunt worked as a nurse at the local hospital in the next town over, and my uncle owned an electronics store downtown. Downtown Udumbanoor was no more than one long, two-story, worn-down, strip mall setup right off the main road. Even though my uncle owned a small shop there, apparently, the downtown area was still not an acceptable place for a young lady. The only appropriate place seemed to be at home. So with no cousins my age to hang out with and my uncle and aunt at work most of the day, I found myself alone at the house with Lali.

After the first week, I went from restless to insanely bored. Being in Kerala didn't bring the refuge or escape I sought. I thought it would help me forget Armaan and our past. I thought distance was what I needed, but here I was more tormented than ever. I realized that it didn't matter where I was. The torture and the conflict were in my mind. But how does one escape one's own mind? So I gave into the constant temptation (or perhaps addiction) of thinking of Armaan.

In fact the only time I could escape boredom or thoughts of Armaan was when I went for a walk and explored the surrounding rice paddies and hills. Although he was initially reluctant, my uncle finally relented and let me go walking as long as I promised to stay somewhat close to our property. I started by walking in the morning when the air was still cool and temperate. I not only enjoyed getting out of the house, but I soon found my walks to be therapeutic and refreshing. When the weather permitted, I quickly added a late afternoon walk to my daily routine as well. I took different paths each time, but my favorite path was when I followed the road in front of my uncle's home until I passed through to a perfect symmetrical line of rubber trees sitting on a raised slope. The road eventually led to a hill that overlooked my uncle's property as well as neighboring fields, and I climbed its unpaved trail until it led me to its very top, providing me with a beautiful, scenic view of the rice paddies and valley below. I even found a large flat stone to sit on while I surveyed everything below me. This became my signature spot, and I especially enjoyed the view after a heavy afternoon rainfall. A soft mist would often linger around the neighboring coconut-laden hills while the rain made everything even more lush and green. Sitting there on my spot, I could forget Armaan and escape the pressures of the moment and just enjoy the magical beauty that surrounded me.

Chapter 26

A FTER FURTHER COMPLAINTS of boredom, my uncle finally managed to borrow some books for me from a local teacher. I was sitting on the porch, snacking on some fried banana chips and re-reading Dickens' *A Tale of Two Cities*, which I had already read a lifetime ago in high school. The afternoon monsoon winds had picked up, cooling off another unbearably hot day. The phone rang, and assuming it was my uncle checking up on me from the store, I went to the living room to pick it up and was surprised to hear a familiar, feminine voice on the other end.

"Reena?" While her voice was relatively clear, there was enough static on the phone to make me doubt that it was her. That and the fact that I was beginning to really miss her and momentarily wondered if I hadn't just imagined her voice.

"Sarai, is that you?"

"Yes, Reena, it's me! Oh my gosh, have I missed you! How are you?"

"Whatdaya mean 'how am I?' How are YOU? Are you married yet? I haven't heard anything from you, so last week I called your parents, and they assured me you weren't, but I want to hear it from you."

I laughed and in my most assuring voice I told her that I wasn't. "Not even close!" I added. I briefly told her about some of my proposals and how after the first one, I wanted to give up because I felt so guilty for disappointing everyone.

"Man, that's tough. I would not want to be under that kind of pressure. But remember, it's your life. You're the one who has to live with the guy for the rest of your life, so choose wisely. And don't forget, you can still come back single."

"True, but I feel so bad. Everyone is going through so much effort for me. I feel like with every 'no,' I'm just letting everyone down."

"I kind of know what you mean. My mom's sister from New York is trying to fix me up with some guy whose family goes to her church and who just so happens to be in town this weekend. From the way she's talking, you'd think we had already met, fell in love, and were getting married!"

"Really?" I asked, surprised that Reena had even agreed to the set-up.

"I think they're tired of waiting on my brothers, so they've moved on to me. But yeah, I cannot believe I said yes to this, but I figure if you are willing to fly halfway around the world to look for a husband, then I should try to be open-minded, too. I made it clear they should have no expectations, and that my 'no' means an emphatic 'No!'"

"You tell 'em, Reen! So when are you supposed to meet this guy?"

"Tonight."

"WHAT?! You're meeting him tonight?!"

"Yeah, it's really no big deal. It's just a dinner thing at my aunt's house later today. Nothing to get all excited about..."

She didn't sound that excited, so I calmed down. "Okay, well then at least tell me what you know about this guy."

"Yeah, that's the thing about these setups. They don't tell you *any-thing*. Except that he's a 'nice' boy—whatever that means! And oh, wait, he's a doctor about to finish his 2nd year of residency. He comes from a very good family. And yep, that would be it—no physical descriptions, no details on his personality—nothing!"

"Yeah, that's really not that different from my experiences here. I'm usually in the kitchen waiting for my uncle to call me so I can bring in the chai, and that's when I finally see the guy."

"No way! They're making you serve chai?"

"Yep! Apparently, I have to be dressed in a *sari* or *salwar* and wait in the kitchen until they call me into the living room so they can 'present' me to the family. Then I get assessed by the family. I eventually talk to the boy for a few minutes in a semi-private room, and then they leave. Then I have to give them my final response as to whether I want to marry him or not!"

Reena whistled softly. "Oh, Man! I could never go through all that!"

"Well, never say never!" I warned her. "I never thought I'd be doing this either, but here I am."

"Yeah, you're right, but none of this is going to matter when you meet the right guy. It'll be worth it. I just saw Anjuli last week. Her husband arrived a few weeks ago, and she's really happy."

"*Really?!* She is?" I asked, "I'm so happy for her! I hope I'm just as lucky."

"You will be, Sarai. Life couldn't be that cruel now, could it?"

I was afraid to jinx myself so I changed the topic. "So tell me, what's been going on with everyone since I've left?"

"Nothing really. Same old, same old. After Anjuli's husband arrived, they had a reception party for him at a banquet hall, and the whole gang was there: Maya, Mani, and Rakesh—" She suddenly stopped and took a sharp intake of air.

"Are you okay?" She suddenly got quiet, and I realized something must have just happened. "Did you stub your toe or something?"

"Um, yeah, I'm okay," she said clearing her throat. "Uh, yeah, no, I didn't stub my toe. It's just that um, yeah, actually there *is* something that's happened since you left."

"Okay," I said slowly as I waited for her to continue.

"So yeah… I was talking to Rakesh and he mentioned that he saw… um… well um…"

"What?" I asked quietly, gripping the phone even tighter as I braced myself.

"Sarai—"

"Just tell me, Reena. It's okay. Just say it."

"Rakesh ran into Armaan and his wife at the Hindu temple."

"Okay…" I prodded, expecting her to continue as I braced myself for more, but all I could hear was the dull humming static of our connection. Well, that must have been it. They were married. They would make appearances together as husband and wife. Granted, if I had run into them myself, it would no doubt have been painful, but other people running into them didn't seem so bad. I didn't see how it was any big deal until Reena finally added, "She's pregnant."

Those words were like the final nail being hammered in the casket.

"*Oh…*" was all I could manage, feeling as if someone had just punched me in the stomach. I knew that the door to any possible future with Armaan shut on his wedding day. Now the door, along with the rest of the casket, was being lowered deeper into the ground.

"I'm sorry. I shouldn't have said anything. It doesn't matter any-more… I'm sorry," she said, her voice getting softer. "I just thought you'd want to know."

"It's fine," I said, shaking my head dismissively, as if I could also shake the shock out of me as well. "I'm glad you told me. They're married… it was inevitable." I tried to sound nonchalant and mature.

We were both quiet for a moment before a beep sounded. "I think your calling card minutes are up so I had better get going. Thanks for calling… and you better let me know how things go with that guy you're meeting. Maybe he'll be the One."

"Yeah, I highly doubt that, but okay, I'll call you and let you know how things went," she said quietly. Then her voice brightened up as she added, "And you better call me if you meet someone! You have a much higher probability of being engaged in the near future than me."

"I don't know about that, but yeah, of course, I will," I said, my voice devoid of all energy and joy. I paused and then added, "And Reen, thanks for telling me. I'm glad I know."

I hung up the phone and lowered myself onto the living room chair. *Pregnant. She's pregnant.* The words echoed in my mind over and over again, like bullets ricocheting off the deepest hollows of my mind, inflicting more hurt into the ever-festering wound in my heart.

I conjured a mental picture of them, family in tow, at the temple. Armaan had his hand on the back of her waist, gingerly guiding her as she walked. They were all in Indian clothes. She was dressed in a red *lengha*, probably because my last image of her was at the wedding, wearing her orange-red wedding *lengha*. Images of her burgeoning stomach flashed into my mind, torturing me far more than the image of her in her bridal dress.

It was time enough to put away the delusions and the fantasies. I would be lying if I didn't admit that there was a tiny part of me that had been nursing the idea of Armaan regretting his decision and coming back for me. I didn't necessarily believe it, but it didn't stop me from daydreaming about it.

Reena's voice continued to echo in my head. She's pregnant. *She's pregnant.* I was unable to quell the rising anger and jealousy I was feeling. Pregnant already?! I choked on my outrage. "But they just got married!" I sputtered out to the empty living room. Well, they had been married a year now, so I guess it was inevitable, but if she was showing to the point that even Rakesh could tell, then she must have gotten pregnant just a few months after the wedding. As far as I was concerned, it was still too soon. Did she do it on purpose, I wondered, as if to secure her place with him? Did she sense that maybe he really wasn't into the marriage?

Somewhere deep inside I believed he still thought of me. He had to, right? He couldn't just forget me like that, *could he?*

She was going to have *his* baby. I felt nauseous at the thought that their union was now complete. I felt like she was living *my* life. That should be *me* with him. *Me* having his children. *Me* building a life with him. I huddled on the couch, feeling the walls of the house closing in on me. I became overwhelmed with this desperate need to get out of the house. I raced out the front door and down the steps of the porch, startling Lali as she walked up the porch steps and carried the groceries from the market. The daily afternoon drizzle had finally started, and it would soon be a downpour, but I didn't care. I needed to get out of the confining walls, somewhere high and far away from prying eyes, somewhere I could cry and scream without being heard. This time I climbed the hill with a determination and a fervor I didn't know I was capable of. Between the tears, the running, the climbing, and the ever increasing altitude, breathing became very challenging, and my lungs started to burn with the limited amount of oxygen I was getting. I eventually reached my favorite spot. I sat on the smooth, flat rock and drew my knees to my chest as I tried to catch my breath. I sat there overlooking the rice paddies and neighboring hills. The beautiful mist had already started encircling the nearby hills and momentarily calmed me with its breathtaking beauty. But soon the mist temporarily blurred in the distance. When I could no longer suppress my tears, they flowed down my face, mingling with the drops of rain that began falling down on me.

He made babies with her. They were having a family. He broke my heart, so how was it fair that he got to move on so quickly and so completely? Did he ever think of me? Did he ever regret leaving me? Life seemed to happen so easily and naturally for some. But for people like me, here I was in India, almost forcing marriage and still nothing was happening.

As I sat there, huddled on the rock with the rain beating down on me, I cried for the pain I still felt, and I cried for the jealousy I no longer had a right to. But mostly I cried for that silly girl I had been, who was still clinging onto a silly, outdated dream.

Chapter 27

THAT EVENING WAS poker night for my uncle and his friends, and my aunt and Lali had prepared a feast of unhealthy but delicious "manly man" food. No matter what hemisphere you're in, some things never change. "Manly man" food seemed to consist of meat, meat, and more meat and some form of starchy and nutritionally challenged carbs. There were no buffalo wings and pizza, but even Malayalees had their own version of "real man" food with refried dried beef (basically their home-made version of beef jerky), fried pork in a thick curry sauce with steamed yucca.

One of the wives of my uncle's friends hosted the corresponding women's gathering a few houses down the street. My aunt invited me to join her, but I preferred to sulk in my room, still digesting the news Reena had delivered. As I daydreamed about all the possible paths my life could have taken, I eventually fell asleep, and woke well after it had turned dark. My throat was parched, so I made my way to the kitchen to get some water when my uncle spotted me. He and his friends were all gathered in the dining room area, still playing cards. "Saaa*raiii*," he slurred, his arm motioning me clumsily towards him. "Come here. Meet my friends."

I obediently walked to him and stood by his side. He encircled his left arm around my waist and began swinging his right arm in an elaborate introduction. "Friends," he said pausing to make sure everyone was listening. "Friends, this is my daughter!" he exclaimed, as if he was introducing me to each of them for the first time. He took note of the confused, doubtful faces. He lowered his voice, and his eyebrows bunched together as he clarified. "Really, she is not my daughter. She is my brother's daughter." He swung his head towards me and gave me a lopsided smile. His eyes were already glazed over, and he blinked several times as if he were having difficulty seeing my face. How many shots had he had? I noted the four empty bottles of Johnnie Walker that lined the dining room wall near my uncle's chair. As he looked at me, he proudly thumped his palm against his chest and he continued his diatribe. "But while she is here in India, she is my daughter." Raising his shot glass to the group, he proclaimed, "Now let's drink to my daughter!" They all cheered and gulped down another shot of Johnny Walker Black. "Don't tell Auntie," he said, slowly waving his index finger at me, and then he burst into laughter.

I had always seen my uncle act so formal and so composed, and it was really funny to see him inebriated. Observing him with his friends made me feel like I was seeing the Underground India. He poured all of them another round of drinks. "Friends, before my daughter leaves me, she will be married. Let's now drink to her marriage."

I shook my head. Today was not a day of optimism for me. After news of Armaan's expanding family, I felt as pessimistic as ever about my own life.

My uncle turned towards me. "Whyyy you shaking your head?! You will be married, I tell you. I will see you married! It is my dying wish," my uncle declared, holding his drink dramatically in mid-air.

He then grabbed an empty shot glass from the Lazy Susan and poured a drink for me. "You must believe. Now drink with us."

I eyed the seemingly innocent ounce of clear liquid. I had no desire to drink it, but I didn't want to refuse my uncle and unintentionally insult the one person who was just as eager for my marriage as my parents and I were. Or maybe it was the emptiness I felt that was begging to be filled with something more. I'm not sure what made me reach and chug the shot of whiskey. But I did, and I immediately regretted it.

The pain as it went down my throat was like the first time I had sushi and dipped it into the wasabi sauce without first mixing it with the soy sauce. The head rush was excruciating. But this was worse because as someone who rarely drank, the alcohol seemed to have an immediate but lasting effect on me. They say that one drink can diminish your ability to make rational decisions, and I believe it. As painful and as undesirable as that first shot was, I actually agreed to take another… and another… I remembered nothing else from that night, not even how I got back to my room. And for the first time, I forgot Armaan. In fact, I forgot everything, and to be honest, that felt good. I had been doing too much thinking lately, and my head hurt. Some drunken forgetfulness was definitely in order.

At least until the morning when there was hell to pay. I woke up in my room. My skin didn't even feel like my own. My eyes were bloodshot, my throat was parched, and my head felt like it was on a super fast merry-go-round while my body lay paralyzed on the bed. I felt like my head had been pounded by two titanium cymbals. The sheets were sticking to me. The sun seemed extra strong, and the morning sounds of roosters and all those unimaginable animal sounds were like a torturous cacophony. I threw the thin sheet over my head, but in seconds, my skin had acquired a thin layer of sweat.

I very slowly rose from my bed. Using my dresser and then the wall as support, I made my way to the living room. My aunt took one look at me, turned to my uncle with her arms crossed, and gave him the look of death… or what I assumed to be the look of death since I couldn't see very clearly. My uncle responded by moving faster than I had ever seen him move. He caught me just before I collapsed on the floor and helped me lay down on the couch. My aunt ran to the kitchen, returning with a spoonful of thick brown liquid. "Take it Sarai-mol. You feel much better later." I swallowed even though the concoction looked and smelled disgusting. Luckily, though, I didn't taste anything. Perhaps the alcohol had killed a few taste buds along with my brain cells.

"You take rest today. Just watch TV and rest."

But isn't that what I always do? I thought to myself.

She touched my face so gently, but as soon as she got up, she faced Rajan Uncle, hands on her hip. "What will we tell the boy and his family when they come today? It is better you cancel than let someone see her like this."

My uncle looked helplessly at me and knew she was right. I was in no condition to be meeting potential in-laws, but neither was he going to give up an opportunity. "This boy is supposed to be from a very good family. I don't want to cancel. Ramesh thinks he might be a good match for Sarai." He peered at me closely and said, "She'll be fine by this afternoon. Just give her some rest." My aunt glanced at me, shaking her head at Uncle and mumbling something in Malayalam that I couldn't hear, which was surprising because every other sound in the room seemed magnified.

I spent the rest of the day sleeping and lying on the couch like a zombie, which only made me feel more tired. By noon, most of the head-spinning had subsided, but I still had a throbbing headache and felt like I had just run a marathon. The last thing I wanted to do was meet another proposal. I didn't have the strength or energy to go through the motions today. But my uncle was hell-bent on making sure we left no stone unturned.

Chapter 28

DESPITE HOW WRETCHED I still felt, surprisingly, the preparations went like clockwork that evening. When my latest proposal arrived with his family, before my uncle or aunt said a word, I obediently shuffled into the kitchen, waiting to be called.

Lali said nothing as usual and just busied herself making the chai. She was such a simple person, keeping herself busy throughout the day. I wondered what she thought of me with all of my pickiness. Most Indian women didn't keep saying no, and this was what, the tenth or eleventh guy now? I was beginning to lose count. Lali probably thought of me, just as the people in the marketplace thought of me and what most Europeans would think—*American!*

Ten minutes later, rather than my uncle, it was my aunt who came to get me. Probably knowing that my balance would be off, she handed me the tray of snacks and picked up the tray of chai herself. She smiled and her eyes twinkled with hope. "Maybe this time you will like the boy."

But tonight, I wasn't thinking about marriage candidates. My entire focus was on avoiding tripping on my sari and making sure I balanced the tray of banana chips and spicy trail mix. I hadn't given a second thought to what my proposal would be like. There were none of the usual worries, wishes, and wonderings, but that was probably because anything that resembled a true thought or idea hurt my head. Today I just wanted the evening to be done and over with. I only wanted to lie down and wait for the fatigue and head-spinning to stop.

I entered the living room, eyes down, focusing on each step, and carefully set my tray down with meticulous care. Relieved that I had managed to do all of this without stumbling or dropping anything, I sat in my chair and visibly sighed in relief. My uncle loudly cleared his throat, reminding me that I had missed something. I immediately rose from my chair and began serving the chai. As I did, my eyes locked with a pair of brown eyes belonging to a very pleasant looking, a very handsome twenty-something. His eyes crinkled in the corner, and just as my mind registered that he was probably my proposal, he broke into a smile, revealing a dimple on each cheek. I wondered if the Johnnie Walker was still having an effect on me. This proposal was actually cute... very, very cute. He made direct eye contact with me, and he didn't strike me as being socially awkward. In fact, the smile and dimples made him appear downright charming in a very boyish way. I glanced at my aunt, her smile reaching from one ear to the next, clearly very pleased. I then focused my attention back on my proposal. For once, I was actually looking forward to speaking to him. I was more surprised that my aunt realized this as well. Maybe she and my uncle were finally getting it.

As I sat there, I went through the usual interrogation from his family. Yes, my parents are in the US and did not join me on this trip due to their work schedules. Yes, of course, they would come to meet everyone before the marriage. No, I am not the only child; I have a younger brother. Although I had to answer all of their basic questions, I had to remain silent even though there were plenty of things I wanted to ask in turn. But thanks to my uncle and his inquiries, I learned some basic information about my proposal. My proposal's name was Jensin, and he was the only son but had a younger sister who had gotten married the previous year. While he was raised in Kerala, he went to college in Bombay and that was where he also got his MBA. My ears immediately perked up with that tidbit of information. Bombay—or Mumbai, as it is now known as, was a modern city. Knowing he was exposed to a more forward-thinking lifestyle made him even more appealing. I could only hope that he was a little more open-minded than someone who had never left the ultra-conservative boundaries of Kerala.

After the preliminary questioning was over, Rajan Uncle motioned for Jensin and me to move to my cousin's empty room to talk. We both rose from our chairs at the same time, and unlike the other proposals, he paused at the door, motioning me in first and then he followed. A gentleman who believes in opening doors for women. Check.

As we settled into our seats, I didn't know whether I should start talking or wait on him, but he surprised me by not only speaking first but also speaking in flawless English. He still had an accent, but it was slight and not the heavy, staccato-laden accent that my uncle and other older-generations used when they spoke English.

"So how are you liking Kerala? You must be bored, no?" He spoke clearly and articulately, and I felt more comfortable with him than I had with anyone else since arriving in India.

"Honestly," I said, almost playfully. "I *am* a little bored." I lowered my voice like I was telling him a secret. "All I've been doing is watching TV, and when I get bored, I sit out on the porch and watch the rain."

He lowered his voice, too. "Watching TV all day and then watching the rain—you know, that even *sounds* boring!"

I laughed and then raised my right index finger as a reminder, "But hey, if you need to know what's happening in any of the Indian soap operas, let me know. I can fill you in on all of them."

"Oh, no!" he said, hitting his palm against his forehead in mock frustration. "Not you, too! My sister and mother are addicted to those shows! I was begging them to let me watch the latest cricket match, but between the hours of four to eight every evening, I'm forbidden to touch the TV remote while they watch their shows."

We seemed to strike an instant rapport and conversation flowed, but before I knew it, he threw me off guard with his next question. "So why did you come to India to find a husband? A girl like you should easily be able to find a husband in America." I was surprised at his forwardness. Most of my previous proposals never asked me this, just as I never asked them if they were only interested in me for my US Visa.

"A girl like me?" I asked, raising my eyebrow in mock offense.

"Yes, a girl like you. Smart, charming…" he paused and his eyes crinkled in the corners before he added, "and beautiful."

I blushed a few shades of pink. To say "thank you" would have seemed silly, so I said nothing and stared at my hands, which I had clasped together in my lap.

"And how did you decide that I was smart, charming… and beautiful? You don't even know me!" I asked playfully, pausing just as he had. I looked up from my hands to find his eyes on me. His dimples deepened, and I smiled back.

"Part of it is instinct… and part of it is quite obvious," he said. He seemed to revel in the fact that my cheeks had changed color.

"So are your instincts always right?" I asked.

"Actually, yes, they've yet to fail me." He sure didn't talk like a guy raised in India, I thought to myself. Did boys in India flirt? Well, the ones in the Bollywood movies did, but in Kerala? But he hadn't lived in Kerala for a while, I reminded myself.

"So to answer your question, I came to find a nice Indian boy."

"Oh, really, so there are no nice Indian boys in America?" he asked, crossing his arms. That was the same question my uncle had asked me on my second day in India.

"In America there might be, but I haven't met them. Or if I did, it was usually just before I met their wives and kids."

"So are there any nice Indian girls in the US?"

I nodded, knowing he was just teasing me. "There are a few of us left." Crossing my arms across my chest and using the same mocking tone he used on me, I asked, "So now, what's a guy like you want with an American-born Indian girl?"

"A guy like me?"

"Yes, a guy who likes smart, charming, beautiful girls like me. Aren't there any nice, local girls that you could have selected from? Why would you come see a girl who came to India to find a husband?" I asked, challengingly.

"I don't know. Maybe I'm just curious. God works in mysterious ways." *God... hmmm... he mentioned God... that was nice,* I thought. My mom would like him.

"So you don't mind marrying a FOB?" he asked.

My mouth fell open at his use of the word FOB, the acronym for Fresh Off the Boat, a term we American-raised Indians snobbishly bestow on anyone who has recently immigrated to the US.

"As long as he doesn't mind being with an ABCD," I retorted with a smile. ABCD is short for American-Born Confused Desi, and it is the term for Indians raised in America who seem to have lost their cultural identity. "For me, it's more important to find the right guy than focus on which country his passport is issued from."

"So what qualities constitute the right guy for you?" he asked, clearly undeterred by me. *Constitute?* So he was well-spoken and articulate. Check and check.

Suddenly, I felt bold. I was curious to know how his mind worked. Rather than answering his question, I asked one of my own. "So what qualities are you looking for in a girl?"

He seemed a little taken aback with my question but answered, "I like girls in blue saris and girls who wear jasmine in their hair."

I lightly touched the jasmine flowers my aunt had intertwined into my hair. My aunt hoped that any leftover scent of alcohol that might seep through my pores would be diluted by the fresh scent of jasmine.

He was definitely a charmer, especially compared to all the other proposals.

"I would also like someone who can make me chai every morning, who will wash and iron my clothes, and who will have breakfast and dinner ready for me."

"Oh, so no lunch?" I mocked.

"Well, I would like lunch also, but I'm a reasonable man. I just want to make sure she has time to do the rest of her chores."

He said the latter with such a dead-pan expression that I must have look horrified, but then he laughed, revealing white, even teeth. "I'm just kidding. What I'm really looking for is an honest, family-oriented,

God-fearing girl." My mom would definitely like this guy. He had already mentioned God twice.

"So what qualities do you have to offer a girl?"

He smirked at my question. "Hmmm... well, I like to cook..."

"Good because I like to eat..."

He laughed and continued, "So now it's your turn. What qualities are you looking for?"

"I'm looking for someone open-minded yet conservative, someone who helps his wife with the dishes and dinner, and someone who doesn't expect his wife to make chai but rather makes it for her..." I added the latter with a twinkle in my eye.

He cocked an eyebrow over that. "So you're a modern woman, I see."

"I am," I said, raising my chin defiantly. I wasn't going to hide it.

"So do you cook?" He asked.

"Sometimes." I then deflected the question back to him before he could ask me what I knew how to make. "So when did you learn to cook?"

"I learned when I was in school in Bombay. When I first moved there, I lost 10 pounds, and when I came home, my mom made sure I had learned to cook all the basics. The next time I came home I had put on 20 pounds, and then she encouraged me to start skipping meals again." He was funny and articulate, and I could verbally spar with him.

"So would you ever consider living in India?" he asked, extending his arms with a flourish as if he were talking about the room in which we were sitting.

"Live in India? Hmmm... I could definitely visit here at any time, but I'm not sure about living here—"

Before I could finish, my uncle walked in, motioning us to join everyone else in the living room. Our time was up, but I wanted to continue the conversation. I still hadn't completely answered Jensin's last question. I wasn't sure if he was asking that last question out of curiosity or if that was one of his requirements.

When I sat back down, I could sense Jensin's parents' eyes on me. They were smiling broadly, seemingly pleased about something. After a few more pleasantries were exchanged, Jensin's father stood up, announcing they had to leave. As their car made its way out of my uncle's driveway, I stood with my uncle and aunt and waved goodbye. On cue, they both turned to me, and even though I could not see them, I could feel their questioning stares. They were eager for my answer.

I again mentally assessed the handsome man who had stood in front of me just moments ago. Intelligent. Articulate. God-fearing. Good looking. He had many of the qualities I was both physically and mentally attracted to and based on our conversation, if I had met him in different circumstances, I would probably still have been attracted to him. I didn't hear fireworks exploding in the background. I didn't see stars. I didn't feel mushy or goose bumpy… at least not yet. I felt good, happy, and comfortable. I couldn't think of one reason to say no.

So was this the infamous "you just know" feeling? I think most of the time when people say that, they really don't know. They may hope or wish they did, but how does anyone really know until they actually last? Don't as many people say, "I just know," only to find out a few months later how wrong they were?

It wasn't that all-compelling, all-encompassing feeling I got when Armaan was around me, but how realistic was that anyway? So was this enough? I didn't want to say no, but neither was I completely ready to say yes based on one, short meeting. But in India there is no "maybe." There is only, "Yes, I want to marry this person," or "No, I do not."

Finally my uncle spoke up. "Well? What is your answer?"

"Yes," I said, almost in a whisper. Surely it was someone else who said it because it was only then that I knew the answer myself. My uncle turned back to my aunt, shaking his head in dismay.

It took a few milliseconds before my "yes" had fully registered. And when it did, his eyes snapped from my aunt back to me. "Yes?" he repeated.

"Yes!" I repeated this time louder, more confident. My uncle's eyes widened in disbelief, and his mouth gaped open. He looked very happy—as happy as I imagined my parents would feel. I was touched that he cared so much and that he considered it his own personal responsibility to ensure that I would find a husband.

"Yes?" he questioned me, pressing me again to make sure he hadn't misunderstood me. "Yes, you like the boy?"

"Yes, I like the boy!"

"Yes, she likes the boy!" he said, raising his hands in triumph. "Yes, she likes the boy!" I was watching Lali close the gates where their Jeep had just driven through when out of the corner of my eye, I could have sworn I saw my uncle skip.

"I heard her the first time, you daft fool!" my aunt said. She laughed, grabbed my cheeks, and kissed me on the forehead. She, too, seemed relieved. I didn't realize how much of a burden my single status had been for them.

With the baton tucked securely in the crook of his arm, my uncle formally marched up the porch into the house. His chest puffed out proudly, "She likes a boy. I tell you I will find a boy for her, no?"

Like clockwork, fifteen minutes later our phone rang. It was Ramesh calling with their response as well as to find out our answer. I watched my uncle closely, knowing there was still a chance Jensin or his parents hadn't liked me. My uncle grabbed the phone in his bedroom, and my aunt and I followed him. I waited in the doorway. His earlier jubilant spirit seemed to give way to his serious, rational side. His back was to me, and he was "*uh-uh*-ing" and "*ah-ah*-ing." Maybe I was wrong, and Jensin hadn't liked me. I still wasn't sure what to make of his last question. Or worse, maybe his parents didn't like me. All this time that I was doing the rejecting, I never thought about the family or the guy rejecting me, especially if I liked them.

My uncle hung up the phone, and with his back to us, he sat on his bed, shoulders slumped. He turned to us sadly and shook his head. Jensin hadn't liked me. Although he seemed to enjoy talking to me, maybe he didn't like the fact I was so talkative and modern-thinking. Maybe like many Indian men, he, too, just wanted a nice, traditional woman. Leaning with my back against the door frame, I slid down to the floor in defeat. My aunt joined me on the floor, allowing me to rest my head against her as she stroked my hair. We sat there in silence, all of us too tired and defeated to say anything. I glanced at my uncle, knowing his disappointment was second only to mine. My uncle then shot off the bed, both hands raised, and faced me, mustache twitching from ear to ear. "They said yes! They want to proceed!"

My aunt and I looked at each other in disbelief. After feeling so disappointed that another proposal had gone south, I was suddenly so happy that I didn't care that my uncle had just played a prank on me.

My aunt embraced me, and I just stared at the floor in dumbfounded disbelief. "I am getting married," I whispered.

Chapter 29

W E CALLED MY parents right then and there to tell them the ecstatic news even though for them, it was the middle of the night. Despite his sleepiness, I could hear my father's smile in his voice. He sounded energetic as he talked about travel plans. My mom, on the other hand, seemed more concerned about me. "Are you sure this is what you want?" she asked.

I wanted to get married, and Jensin seemed like a good man. It would all work out, *right?* "Yes, mummy, this is what I want," I said, trying to ignore the reality of my decision, which as soon as I thought it, began to weigh on me.

I knew Reena didn't like to be awakened before ten, but I didn't have the patience to wait. Besides, she did say to call her right away.

"Hello…"

"Reen! It's Sarai!"

"Sarai?" Her voice was groggy with sleep.

"Yes, it's Sarai, your best friend."

"Is everything okay?"

"Well, you said to call when I had something to tell you, right?"

"Oh, oooh, my gosh! You're getting married, aren't you?"

"Yeaaaah," I drawled out.

"Reaaaally?"

"Yeeaaah!"

"Reeeeeeeeeeally?" she sang, her voice taking on the high-pitched squeal that most girls are known for and guys hate.

"Yeeeeeeeeeeeeeeaaaaaaaaaaahhh!!!!!!!!!" My pitch matched hers. I peeked out the living room window and saw my uncle cover his ears.

"How do you feel?" Reena asked.

"I feel good. Nice…"

"Happy?"

"Yeah, I guess… yeah, of course, I feel happy! I just don't think it's sunk in yet. It's all happening so fast."

"Excited?!"

Hmmm… that was a word I didn't think of. I was not *not* excited either, so yeah, then I must've been excited, but in a calm, mature way. "Um, yeah… sure…" I actually felt peaceful, but that didn't sound like the right thing to say at a time like this, so I used another nondescript word. "Good," I said, testing the word out. "Yeah, that's the word. I feel good."

"That's good, especially since you've agreed to marry him!" she teased. "Soooo, tell me about him! What's his name? What does he do? What's he like?"

"His name is Jensin, and he's really nice and very handsome. He studied business in Bombay and worked there for many years and just recently moved back home. He has this accent that's not typical Indian, but neither is it completely British—"

"He has a British accent? Now he sounds completely hot!"

"Well, it's not the typical British accent either. He speaks formally with a slight Indian clip, but he seems to be 'with it.'"

"Sarai, I'm so happy for you! And I'm *so* glad you called because I, too, have some news to tell you, too! I was going to give you a call anyway! Okay, so remember that guy I told you about that my mom's sister had in mind for me?"

"Yeaaaah…" I said, beginning to feel a nervous tick in my stomach.

"Well, he came over with his family yesterday."

"Okay," I said, holding my breath for some big news.

"And I've been dying to talk to you, but yeah, they came over, and he's totally cute and really sweet, and we already went out to eat together. Twice."

"Twice?" I asked, surprised. "But if you just met him yesterday, how did you manage to go out twice already."

"Well, he and his family ended up coming over for an early lunch rather than dinner. So after the lunch, he and I left the house to grab some coffee and talk. Then he called me again later that afternoon, saying he wanted to take me out to dinner!" I could hear her smiling from ear to ear through the phone. There was an excitement in her voice that I hadn't heard in years. She sounded different.

And then I felt it. It was like a nervous quiver in my gut. I could literally feel it. It was this inexplicable feeling, a tingling that I could only describe as not a feeling but almost like a "knowing." There was no logical reason for me to feel it, except I did... and strongly. Somehow I knew this was happening. I don't know how or why, but I just knew. I hadn't even met this guy, but I knew he was the one for Reena, and I knew Reena was going to marry him. Funny, that I couldn't seem to have this same gut feeling for myself, but I could for her.

"You're getting married!"

"Whoa, whoa, there, sister, I'm not in India. I don't have to marry a guy after meeting him one time! But he was really nice, and cute, and he seemed interested, and he wants to take me out again tomorrow. He's only in town for the rest of the week, so we're probably going to hang out until he has to go back!"

"And what did your parents think?" I asked.

"They love him. He's a doctor like every parent dreams about. He comes from a nice family, and he speaks perfect Malayalam!"

"Well, don't forget that you're a doctor, too!" I reminded her. "They didn't just hand you that pharmacology diploma. You worked hard for it."

"True, but I'm not an MD!" she said mocking an Indian accent.

"Reena, you know if things work out between the two of you, we're probably going to get married around the same time!"

She spoke, quietly at first, but then with increasing excitement. "Well, you're obviously getting married, but *if* this thing works out, then yeah, I guess you're right." She was quiet for a moment. "Oh, my gosh,

Sarai, you're right! We're both gonna get married! Oh my gosh, oh, my gosh!" Her voice broke off as we simultaneously broke into our synchronous high-pitched squeals.

I glanced at my uncle as he sat on the porch and read the newspaper while he eavesdropped on my conversation. I wanted to inform him that he was holding the newspaper upside down but decided to let him continue his farce. His mustache twitched, indicating that he was smiling and amused with my conversation. But at the sound of our squeals, he winced, and his face puckered unpleasantly as if he were eating a lemon. As our squeals continued and grew even more high-pitched, he looked almost catatonic as he glanced helplessly at my aunt, hoping she could shed light on my girlish outburst. Unphased, she just smiled at me, nodded, shrugged, and went back to her sewing. My uncle straightened his newspaper and shook his head, utterly baffled. I had to stifle a laugh.

"Sarai, wait! You're not going to get married in India like Anjuli did, are you?" she asked. And before I could stop her, she got carried away. "I think my passport expired years ago, so I'd have to renew it. Then I can only hope they give me the time off at work, especially right now since we're short-staffed. Two of our pharmacists are on maternity leave."

"Reena, calm down!" I said. But Reena had brought up a valid point and that was something I hadn't considered. I just assumed the wedding would be in the US, but Jensin seemed the type to be very close to his family. It would be natural for him to want the wedding here. "I hope not, but even if I do, you better believe I'm getting married again in the US in a white wedding dress. But the engagement will probably be here, though."

"So you wouldn't wear a *lengha* anymore?"

"No," I said, momentarily picturing the white *lengha* I wore to Armaan's wedding. "The one *lengha* I would have worn has already been worn. It's time for me to move on to something new."

I heard the warning beep that indicated we had just one minute left in our conversation and Reena said, "Okay, I guess we don't have much time left. Well, call me once you guys start finalizing plans. If by some chance the wedding is in India, I'll, of course, try to come. And as soon as I have any update on my end, I'll give you a call, okay?"

"Reen?

"Yeah?"

"I really miss you. I wish you were here."

"Me, too."

I smiled into the phone. "Okay, bye and try and take some pictures of this guy so I have an idea of what he's like before you guys get too serious."

I lay in bed that night, going over my entire conversation with Reena. Her voice sounded so different than mine. She was so excited, and her voice had that initial, euphoric anticipation that went along with first dating someone while I sounded matter-of-fact, like I had been married for years already. And why couldn't I tell her straight up that I was excited? To be excited you had to anticipate something, and I didn't even have the chance to anticipate anything. There was no buildup. It was basically a done deal. We met. We agreed to get married. And now we were getting married. All that remained was the planning for the wedding preparations, and even that would primarily be decided by my relatives. There was no, "Does he like me?" "Will he ever ask me out?" "Where is this going?" There was no anticipation, no questions. And let's face it, often it is the "in betweens" that lead up to the proposal that make the idea of getting married so exciting. I had come here wanting marriage, but I still longed for the romance, the anticipation, the challenge.

I then began to wonder if the immediate pressure to see Jensin as my husband hadn't killed the natural excitement that would have already been there. Maybe if I weren't over-analyzing it, I would feel some of these things naturally. Yes, that was it. I was just over-thinking everything like I always did. If I could quit being so analytical, these lingering doubts would go away. After all, I didn't question the authenticity of what I felt for Armaan when I felt it. I liked him, and I accepted it. Of course, at the time, I didn't have to make a life-long commitment to him either.

I thought about my mom's reaction. Why wasn't she more excited for me? Isn't this what *she* wanted? What would my brother, Sajan, think? Would he think I was crazy to do this? It was so weird to tell my parents, brother, and Reena that I was getting married. Reena was like the sister I never had, and here I was about to make the most life-changing decision, and neither she nor my family had even been part of the initial discussion nor even met my future husband.

Later that night, veiled by the shadows of night, I thought of Armaan. As much as I willed myself not to think of him, especially now that I had met Jensin, he still managed to creep into my mind. I succumbed to the comparisons. I guess as unfair as it was to Jensin, it was also inevitable in some ways. Armaan had become my six foot measuring stick against which all men were compared. Even if they were physically taller, they all somehow still came up short in my eyes. I groaned realizing how immature I sounded. It was time to put away my childish, romantic fairy tales. Marriage was about being practical, not about having butterflies in your stomach. He was no Armaan, but he was nice, handsome, and educated. It was enough.

Chapter 30

THE NEXT MORNING, my uncle informed me that Jensin's father had called and invited our family to their home the following weekend, but I would not be able to accompany them.

"But *I'm* the one getting married," I protested.

"You already saw the boy. What else is there to see or talk?"

At first I thought he was kidding, but his mustache did not twitch in the slightest. "I'm getting married to this guy, and you expect me to be okay with just seeing him one time? What if he wasn't who I thought he was? Maybe it was the alcohol clouding my judgment. I don't want to base a lifetime's decision on a mere one-hour meeting."

I kept up the nagging and even got my parents involved in trying to convince my uncle that meeting the guy a second time would not violate any of our customs. My uncle reluctantly relented, but he didn't forget to remind me that he was making an exception only because I was American.

Two days later, my uncle dropped me off at my Ammachi's house to spend time with her as well as Milly Chechy and her kids. While I brushed my Ammachi's long, wiry hair, Milly Chechy was cooking in the kitchen. She eventually joined us on the front porch, and brought us some freshly squeezed lemonade. She sat on the chair next to Ammachi and began fanning herself. She turned her head to smile at me while I braided Ammachi's hair, and then she leaned over and patted me on the shoulder before going back into the kitchen to check on her rice and *sambar*. "You be okay," she said.

I paused mid-French braid and looked at her inquisitively. "Whatever do you mean, Chechy?"

"The boy," she said, stopping in mid-stride to turn back to look at me.

"The boy?"

"Jensin."

"Jensin?" I asked laughing. "What about Jensin?"

"Babykutty just told me."

"Babykutty Uncle told you what?" I asked.

"He said the family canceled everything."

"Huh?! They what?! They canceled everything?" What was she talking about? If they had canceled, why didn't Rajan Uncle tell me?

Milly Chechy's eyes widened with the realization that she just told me something that she shouldn't have.

"Where did Babykutty Uncle find that out?"

"Raj Chachan told him."

Why did everyone but me know that Jensin's family had reneged on their proposal?

I called my uncle at his store immediately, furious that I had not been told anything. Wasn't this my life? Why was I the last one finding out about this?

"Calm down, Sarai-mol," he said. His voice was surprisingly calm for someone who was so determined to get me married. "They canceled the invitation to come to the house this weekend, but not everything is lost. They said they just want more time to think."

"Why? How come they get more time to think about it, but I have to make a decision the first day I meet him? I thought you said that was custom?"

He ignored my question and instead asked his own. "Did you tell Jensin that you're not willing to live in India?"

"I can't recall us talking about—oh, wait, I think so," I said. "Yeah, basically, I guess I did. We didn't really talk about it because you had walked in—"

"Oh, Sarai-mol, why would you say that?"

"Uncle, you know I can't live here permanently, but I'm more than willing to visit as often as he'd like."

"Well, the family liked you, but Jensin is his father's only son. He's the only son among all the brothers. He will inherit everything from the family, so they don't want to let him go to US. They want him here."

"Well, *he* wants to go to the US, but if that's how his family felt, why did they come to see me?"

"You really like this boy, Sarai-mol?"

"Yes."

"Then you don't worry. You will marry this boy, okay? You just wait. I will take care of everything. They will call."

Two days later the invitation to visit their home was back on.

Chapter 31

THE SCENT OF fresh jasmine filled the air as Milly Chechy helped me out of the Jeep. Jasmine bushes framed the outer perimeter of the road and led to the gate that encompassed Jensin's home and family estate. The house loomed atop a small hill, sandwiched between two rice paddies. This could possibly be my future home, I realized. It was an off-white color, and darker near the foundation, probably due to the daily ravages of heat and rain. For a family who was reportedly wealthy, the family home was quite modest. The house reminded me of my grandmother—old and weathered, but sturdy and stable.

The ground was moist and wet, almost sticky, and after the heavy afternoon rain, my wooden sandals made indentations everywhere I stepped. We had to climb twenty cement steps to reach the house, and with each step, I cursed the invention of the sari. I was desperately trying to keep it in place while trying to also prevent the hem from grazing the mud. Despite safety pins that kept the front pleats in place, I was well aware that with one tug, it could all come undone. I glanced at Milly Chechy who seemed to take each step in her sari effortlessly and gracefully.

I sighed deeply by the time we had reached the front steps, but a reproachful glance from my aunt reminded me that a lady never makes unnecessary sounds in front of other people, particularly ones that indicate exasperation and frustration. Like my daily morning cup of chai, I must swallow what comes my way and accept it without question.

My heart was racing frantically by the time we reached the top step, reminding me how out of shape I was and doubling my nervousness. Would I still like him? Would he be as handsome as I remembered, or had my hangover hampered my senses?

My curiosity was quickly sated. Jensin stood at the front door next to his father, ready to greet us. Dressed in a gray-striped dress shirt with the sleeves rolled up and the traditional white *mundu*, he struck me as being nothing like the urbane, modern person I had spoken to earlier. Even his hair, which was now in coarse, unruly waves, rather than artfully styled, made me wonder if I had gotten a wrong impression of him.

But no one, including Jensin, seemed alerted to my own disappointment. My uncles and aunts exchanged pleasantries and engaged in chit-chat with his father and two uncles. His mother and sister came from the kitchen bearing trays filled with teacups of fresh-brewed chai and plates overflowing with homemade fried banana chips, jackfruit, and spicy snack mix. I nervously reached for some banana chips at the same time Jensin did, our knuckles brushing against each other. I glanced up and Jensin was smiling a knowing grin. I turned away, embarrassed, as if my uncles had just caught us kissing. When he smiled, I was reminded of the same boyish, yet gentlemanly demeanor that had first charmed me. My nervousness returned, and I once again silently and desperately tried to connect with him, pointedly trying to ignore the effeminate yet typically Indian male way he had of crossing his legs, one knee over the other.

I was eager to talk privately with him. I had so many questions. What had changed? How had it gone from a "yes" to a "no" and now back to a "yes?" I didn't know if he, too, was giving into parental pressures or if he was just fighting for what he wanted.

"Shall we?" Jensin motioned me towards the dining room. I looked at my uncle, and he nodded, giving me permission to follow Jensin while everyone stayed in the living room.

But we didn't stay in the dining room. He walked me through it to a room right off the dining room. I looked around, noting its bareness, its stark walls, much like many of the houses I had seen in India. There was a desk in one corner of the room, cluttered with paper, mail, and books. The bed occupied the other end of the room, and above the bed was a window that provided a view of the backyard. Next to the bed was a matching dresser with an attached mirror. With the exception of a family portrait on the wall close to the door and a cross above the door, there were no other wall adornments or decorations.

"So how do you like our house? It's a simple house, no?"

I wasn't sure what he was getting at, but I replied, "Yes, it is, but often there is beauty in simplicity."

He rewarded my answer with a smile, and I wondered if the question had been a test.

"So what do you think of this area?" I wasn't sure how to answer that question because it looked exactly like the rest of Kerala to me. "We are a simple people, living in a simple house. I want to make sure you understand this. My American cousins come here, and they are so bored."

A simple people, living in a simple house. Well, when he put it that way, it didn't sound all that appealing. But I assured myself that it was just a language barrier. He was just saying they don't live lavishly. I guess he wanted to make sure I wasn't marrying him just for the money. Funny how even in an arranged marriage that would be a concern. I wasn't interested in him because of his family's money, but I began to wonder what he did think I was marrying him for. We were obviously not in love... at least not yet.

"So you won't be bored here?" he asked.

"What do you mean 'will I be bored here?' You mean when we visit?"

"No, I mean when we live here."

"Live here? What?! I can't live here—" Is that why he was giving me the grand tour and asking me if it was too simple for my tastes?

"But your uncle told my father that you're fine with living in India. He said that—"

"He what?!" I sputtered out. What had my uncle promised without first consulting me?

Jensin's eyebrows pushed together in confusion. "So you didn't tell your uncle that you're willing to live in India?"

"NO!" I bellowed, startling Jensin. He obviously wasn't used to a woman being so vocal. I lowered my voice. "No," I repeated. "I told you earlier when we first met; I could visit but to live here... I'm not sure I can do that."

Jensin looked at me for a long moment and then got up from his chair and went to the window, staring out at the view. I waited for him to speak, but he was silent.

Eager to break the silence, I asked him a question. "Jensin, if we were to... proceed with this and we lived in America and you told me that you wanted to go back to India, but I said 'no, I can't leave,' what would you say?"

He turned to look at me and leaned against the wood frame of the window. "I would stay with you."

I nodded, pleased to know he wasn't planning to force me to move to India.

"Now let me ask you that same question, Sarai. What if I insisted that we had to return to India? What would you say?"

I looked him dead in the eye. "I would say, 'I'll visit you.'" His head reared back in surprise. I expected my comment to elicit a chuckle from him, but it didn't. While my original intent was to lighten the mood, I was also being honest, and I was glad to see he took my answer very seriously. "If your plan was to live in India all along, why did you come see a girl from the US? Didn't you expect that the idea was to find someone who wanted to move to the US?"

He shifted to his other leg and partially sat on the edge of the window sill. "I am open to living in the US. I just wanted to be sure you were open to one day living in India. My family is here. It's where I was raised. This is my home."

"Exactly," I said. "That's how I feel about living in the US."

He nodded in understanding, or at least in what I hoped was understanding.

We were interrupted by my uncle who asked us to join everyone in the main room. I guess as far as my uncle was concerned, there was no need for a long discussion.

✧ ✧ ✧

WHEN WE RETURNED to our car later that afternoon, I immediately confronted my uncle. "How could you tell Jensin and his family that I'm okay with living in India? You know I can't stay here."

My uncle didn't flinch. "Sarai-mol, do you think once that boy sees America, he'll be coming back to India? Did your parents come back? Did Lizzy Auntie come back? Everyone talks about coming back, but they never really do. He's young. Once he sees the opportunities there, he won't be coming back except to visit."

"But still, Uncle, you shouldn't have made that kind of promise without talking to me first."

"You like this boy, right?" He peered at me closely.

I nodded.

"Well, I was going to make sure I did everything in my power to make this proposal happen. If I didn't agree to his father's wishes, then they would have stopped the proposal. Do you think I would have allowed that to happen?"

I shook my head and said nothing more.

Chapter 32

WHILE JENSIN'S FAMILY wanted to proceed, they had yet to commit to an actual wedding date. As far as my family was concerned, the sooner, the better. Due to my parents' limited vacation schedule, they, too, were waiting for Jensin's family to determine an engagement and wedding date so they could book their airline tickets. But weddings in India did not require weeks or months of planning. Plans could be made and finalized within days. Apparently, I would have to get married in India in order to expedite Jensin's immigration process, but I was assured by my parents that I could have another wedding in the US once Jensin arrived.

While we waited for Jensin's side to confer on dates, my uncle and aunt took me shopping for my bridal trousseau. Just like with the proposals, my uncle insisted on tradition, which, in this case, meant wearing a white *sari*. I would have fought him on it, but according to Milly Chechy, every local church also insisted that females had to wear traditional *saris* to meet with church regulations. I relented only because I knew I would have another wedding in the US, and I could wear and do what I wanted then. As far as I was concerned, this wedding would only be a legal formality and not my actual wedding.

As I went shopping, I looked through what seemed like hundreds of white wedding *saris*. While the cities of Kottayam and Ernakulam are considered to be the hub of fashion in south Kerala, neither of them held a candle to the upscale boutiques of Bombay and New Delhi. Kerala seemed to retain more of the traditional styles, especially when it came to bridal wear. I saw white *saris* with a gold border. White silk *saris* with a silver border. White jacquard print *saris* with a plain white border. While all these *saris* were beautiful in their own way, it wasn't anything that I hadn't already seen many times over in the photographs of my own parents' or relatives' weddings. Nothing really excited me, and within a few hours, I finally narrowed it down to a very pretty, if somewhat forgettable, white silk *sari* with diamond-like bead-work that encrusted the border and the *pallu* that would hang over and off my left shoulder. It was beautiful, but it lacked that striking element that every bride looks for when selecting the outfit for their wedding day. The camera would not capture the detailing of the material and bead-work. It was, unfortunately, a beauty that could only be appreciated in person. My first instinct was to keep looking at every store until I found something I loved, but when I glanced at my uncle and aunt who were seated on stools, fanning themselves with the latest edition of the newspaper, I knew they would not be able to tolerate another day of shopping. They would expect me to make a decision today. I glanced down at the *sari* again and didn't feel I had much choice but to select it. Once again, "good" seemed to be good enough. I sighed and finally nodded to the eager salesperson.

On the drive home, I began thinking of what I just did. It bothered me more that I somehow seemed okay with the *sari* I had purchased. When had "good" suddenly become good enough? In the past, I wouldn't have stopped until I found something unique and extraordinary, and I wouldn't have allowed reluctant family members or tired shopping companions stop me. But now I didn't have the energy to convince my uncle to let me continue looking. I couldn't help but wonder if my *sari* was just a symptom of something else. Was I settling for anything and everything? Had I given up on dreams and fantasies and just settled for whatever "good" came along? What happened to waiting for the "best?" Or was I just saving myself a lot of heartache by being realistic about life? There was a time in my life that I reached for the moon, believing in nothing less and allowing nothing to stop me. But I was tired of stretching for something outside my reach. Now I was just ready to move on.

I wasn't in love with my outfit any more than I was in love with Jensin. But with nothing else better on the horizon, I knew I would be a fool to let either go. What a contrast to the way I felt about my silvery white *chaniya choli*, which was a direct correlation to the way I felt about Armaan. It now all seemed like a lifetime ago. I sighed deeply, not knowing if I was settling or just being realistic… or if there was even a difference between the two.

Chapter 33

A WEEK LATER, Jensin's family still had not determined an appropriate wedding date. My uncle explained to them that my parents were waiting on the dates before they could book their own tickets and that I needed to leave India in another six weeks to go back to work. But they countered with the fact that two of Jensin's uncles and his grandparents were visiting their other brother in Kuwait and they needed them to come back before making any final decisions.

To my delight and to my uncle's horror, they also insisted that Jensin and I spend time getting to know each other in the meantime. My uncle's answer was an emphatic "NO!" but after multiple heated debates with me and my parents, my uncle finally relented. "This is most improper," he said indignantly, shaking his head, "but since you are from America, I will allow it." He looked at me sternly as he warned, "I would never let my own daughter talk to a boy like this." He then walked away, shaking his head and murmuring, "This is not how we do things."

We had followed tradition thus far. Was it really that unconventional for us to get to know each other by phone just a little better? It's not like we would be having clandestine meetings that would not be chaperoned. It was a phone conversation, for goodness sake!

"But Jensin's family is allowing it…"

"Of course, they are—he's the boy. They have nothing to worry about. You're the girl. It's my job to uphold your honor and reputation."

Although my uncle relented, he had two conditions that he was unwilling to compromise on. There would be no in-person meetings, and there would be only one phone call a day and only when he and my aunt were around. I had expected him to be strict about in-person visits, but I didn't think he would also have to chaperone my phone conversations! But I knew, in his opinion, he was already giving me several concessions, and it would be useless to fight him on it. So every night at seven, Jensin called me on the dot. We talked about everything, from our childhood days to sharing stories of family. He was very curious about life in America, and I found that I was the one who seemed to do more of the talking. He seemed particularly amused whenever I talked about all the faux pas my parents committed out of ignorance when they had first arrived in the US.

And there, from the hours of seven to eight, in front of the ever watchful eyes and listening ears of my uncle and aunt, I slowly got to know my future husband over the course of two weeks while we waited for his family to settle on a wedding date. Initially it was a little awkward to talk openly with Jensin while knowing our conversation was being overheard. I treaded lightly at first, keeping conversation to the most superficial, harmless topics like the weather, the movies I watched, school, etc., but as I got more and more comfortable with Jensin and forgetful of eavesdropping ears, I began sharing some of my more personal memories of my childhood and of growing up in the US. I have to admit that talking to Jensin never quite gave me the butterflies I had hoped for, but I still looked forward to our nightly conversations. Talking to him was like talking to a close friend, and I found myself opening up about my former college life, current life, and Reena as well as my other friends. Finally, we reached that one conversation that every new couple treads with extreme caution—the talk of the exes. Everyone struggles with how much detail should be included. For me, that question went even a step further. Do I say anything at all? This is Kerala, a land of extreme conservatism. I knew to be forthcoming with the fact that I had a previous boyfriend would call into question my character and my reputation. Assumptions would be made. But Jensin had gone to college in Bombay, so he had to be open-minded. Besides, if we were to be married, I didn't want to keep such a big secret from him. But as much as I wanted to be open with him, I decided to wait to tell him until we could talk privately. There were still some things I didn't want my uncle and aunt to know about me. So instead, I regaled him with humorous stories from my college days, culminating with the night we met. "You know," I teased, "you should consider yourself lucky! We almost didn't meet. We almost canceled because I wasn't feeling well."

"You were sick?" he asked.

"No, actually," I said as I tried to stifle my chuckle, "I had a hangover after my uncle's party."

"Hang-over?" he asked.

"Yeah, hangover. You know, when you drink too much the night before and have a headache the next day and the room spins."

He gasped audibly, paused, and then asked, "You drink?"

I cringed when I heard the incredulity in his voice, the slight but distinct tone of censorship and judgment. "Well, sometimes but not really. Just one drink, maybe, if even that."

My uncle had risen from his porch chair and out of the corner of my eye, I saw him hovering near the living room door, staring in my direction. I was still processing Jensin's tone, trying to figure out what he was thinking, and so I ignored the fact my uncle was obviously still listening to every word I said. "I typically only get one drink."

"*Uh yo. . .* kudikyo?" he repeated.

Great, he busted out with the Malayalam. And he added an "uh yo!" This was not good. I looked up at my uncle, who now hovered over me like an oversized umbrella. He shook his head. I was digging myself deeper and deeper into a hole.

"You drink, don't you?" I asked in a feeble but desperate attempt to deflect the attention off of me.

"No, I don't drink."

"At all?"

"No."

"Never?"

"Never."

"But you lived in Bombay. Didn't you go out with your friends to restaurants and clubs?"

"Restaurants to eat food. Not to drink and never to a club."

"Never?!" I asked.

"Never."

"Ever?"

"Not even to go dancing?"

"You dance, too, Sarai?" This time he did nothing to hide his disapproval. I closed my eyes momentarily as I winced.

I didn't know how to answer him and felt like a deer caught in headlights. I had totally overestimated Jensin's open-mindedness. But he had lived in Bombay! They have clubs in Bombay! I assumed that if he went to college in Bombay, he did what most college kids do.

"Sarai?" he repeated "Have you danced with boys?"

Have I danced with boys? Technically the answer was "yes," but I knew by admitting that, he would assume the worst, which in my case, wasn't even close to the truth.

"Sarai? Are you there?"

"Um, yes, but my uncle is talking to me. Hold on."

My uncle stood directly in front of me, shaking his head. He mouthed, "Hang up the phone."

"Jensin, I have to go. I'll call you later—"

I hung up the phone tenuously and looked up at my uncle who was glowering at me. His hands were placed firmly on his hips, his eyes bulged out, and a vein near his temple seemed to tick ominously at me like a bomb that was about to go off. I cowered into my chair, bracing myself.

"What were you thinking, Sarai?" My uncle's voice snapped, like a whip cracking the air. "Do you know what kind of impression that boy now has of you?"

"But I explained that I barely drink—"

My uncle raised his hands to stop me from continuing. "There is no explaining this, Sarai. Proper ladies do not admit to drinking even if they have the occasional wine. Your auntie drinks, but you think she tell anybody that?"

"So what do you want me to do? Lie to my future husband when he asks me a question?"

"He's not your husband yet, Sarai," my uncle said, wagging his index finger at me. "You would do good to remember that. We have to be careful until then. No engagement date has been set. No wedding date has been set. And they've already changed their mind once."

"So when do I tell him the truth? After the wedding when he has even more reason to think I lied to him? Or should I wait a few years to spring the truth on him? Or better yet, let me never tell him the truth!"

It was bad enough that Jensin's family would now think that I was some wild-child but who knew what my own relatives would now think of me. I hated feeling like I had something to hide or be ashamed of, and I hated being judged unfairly. "Uncle, I was never a wild teenager. I've never done drugs. I had my first drink in college, and until the other night, I have never been drunk a day in my life. I didn't even want to drink that night! You basically obligated me."

"I know, Sarai-mol. I regret that, but Jensin doesn't know that. All he knows is that his future wife *from America* was drunk the day he and his family came to see her. Why would you even tell him that?"

My uncle was right. What was Jensin thinking of me now? In seconds I had managed to feed into my future husband's worst fears about marrying a girl from America. Our conversation probably only reinforced all the worst things he had heard about Indian girls raised in the US, complete with all the stereotypes—she drinks, she gets drunk, and she goes to clubs and dances with men. For a guy raised very conservatively, I was probably the equivalent of taking home a tattooed, beer-drinking, biker chick home to his parents. But how had he taken two innocent comments and interpreted them in the worst possible way?

Who knew what he was thinking now! I was so annoyed that I had to cut short our conversation because my uncle had been standing there telling me to get off the phone like I was a teenager. If he hadn't been breathing down my back, I could have finished the conversation with Jensin and explained myself better.

"Sarai, don't worry. I believe you. You are my brother's daughter, and I know my brother would never allow you to behave badly," my uncle said, resting his hand on my shoulder. "But let me ask you—what will the boy's family think of you now?"

I looked helplessly at my aunt, but she continued working on her cross stitch, not even glancing up at me. She was staying out of it, I realized, and allowing my uncle to handle the situation.

It wasn't a big deal, I tried to convince myself. I would just explain myself and everything would be fine. Jensin struck me as being a fair-minded guy. Hopefully he wouldn't jump to too many conclusions between today and tomorrow.

The next evening couldn't come any faster. This time rather than waiting for him to call, I rapidly dialed the numbers to Jensin's phone. My uncle was already seated on his usual chair watching me and made no move to even act like he was busy doing anything but eavesdropping.

"Did you think about our conversation last night?" I asked, wishing the telephone cord was long enough so I could have the conversation somewhere privately.

"Yes," he replied in a tight, clipped voice.

"Oh." I said as I began looping my fingers through the spiral cord. "And what exactly were you thinking?"

"I was thinking that maybe my uncles were right—our cultures and background are more different than I first thought."

Oh, no! My uncle was right. He was having doubts about us! "Jensin, I think I might have given you a wrong impression of me. I'm not some party girl. My parents raised me very strictly. But I don't want to lie to you either. I did go out once in a while in college, but to this day, I can honestly say that I never did anything that I should be ashamed of. I rarely drink, and when I do, it's typically no more than one drink." I then tried to explain how I was upset the day before his family came over and how my uncle threw the get-together with some of his buddies and how they were all drinking and how I basically felt obligated to drink when my uncle insisted upon it.

"But how often did you go to clubs with your friends?"

"Maybe once or twice a month, but when I did, I barely had one drink," I said, no longer sure what I should be saying.

"So you're not going every day?" he asked.

"Every day?!" Is that what he thought of me? He had to be kidding. "Where would I have time to go out every day? I don't have time to go even once a week and or even once a month sometimes!"

Finally his voice warmed up, and I swore that I could almost hear a smile in his voice. "Oh, I thought you were going to these places every day. Now I can say I am very relieved. I told my father that you are not like all the other American girls."

"You told your father?" *O.M.G. How could he tell his father that?* If Jensin had such an issue with it, how would his father react? Were we still in the third grade that he had to immediately go run and tell his father everything I told him in confidence?

He seemed taken aback with my question. "Of course! I tell my parents everything," he said, sounding surprised that I would even ask that question.

I was tempted to tell him what I really thought, but I curbed it. "I just don't want them to get the wrong impression of me, that's all," I said. Great, now I had to worry about damage control with them as well.

"I will explain to them. They will understand."

I doubt it, I thought to myself.

The next day the afternoon monsoon rains were especially harsh. Power lines, including phone lines, were down, and according to the news, thousands of homes and streets were flooded. Fortunately, my uncle's home was built on an incline so we weren't affected by the flooding. Unfortunately, none of the phone lines were working, so I wasn't able to talk to Jensin until four days later. At seven o'clock on the dot, I waited by the phone, eager to talk to him. By seven fifteen, there was still no call. I checked my watch and the battery-operated clock in my uncle's bedroom to make sure I had the correct time. Finally, by seven thirty, I dialed the numbers to his home phone.

"Hello?" said a familiar voice.

"Jensin, it's Sarai."

There was a slight hesitation and then the person on the other line said, "Jensin is not here," and hung up.

That was weird. I must have misdialed, but I could have sworn that was Jensin's voice. I redialed his number, and this time a deeper, gruffer, unfamiliar voice answered the phone.

"Hello, may I talk to Jensin?"

"Jensin not here." Did he mean that Jensin was not there or that there was no Jensin who lived at that residence?

Before I could ask anything else, he hung up. I glanced at the doorway where my uncle stood with his arms crossed and eyebrows bunched together.

"No Jensin?" he asked.

"No, they said he wasn't there, but I could have sworn the first time I called that he was the one who answered the phone."

My uncle said nothing at first, weighing what he overheard with what I had just told him. "Okay, we will wait until tomorrow. If he don't call, I will call and talk to his father."

"Okay," I said quietly, shaking my head. I had no idea what to make of the whole situation. Had it been Jensin who answered the first time I called? I could have sworn it sounded like him, but I couldn't imagine him lying like that. I could have misdialed. But then why would he say Jensin wasn't there? I guess I would have to wait another day to find out.

Chapter 34

B
UT I WOULDN'T have to wait until the next evening to find out what had happened. My uncle surprised us by coming home for lunch the next day. My aunt was at work, so it was just my uncle and me at the dining room table. Lali placed a platter of freshly made chapattis and beef curry on the table and returned to the kitchen to get the rest of the food. My uncle always had plenty to talk about, but this morning and now at lunch, there seemed to be an awkward silence between us. As we waited on Lali, I sat with my hands on my lap and stared out the dining room window. My uncle then began clearing his throat, and I internally cringed, knowing he was about to say something I didn't want to hear. He was probably going to lecture me about my conversation with Jensin again or maybe he was going to—

"They called everything off." Although his voice sounded so matter-of-fact, I could see a hint of sympathy in his eyes.

"What?!" I sputtered out. "What do you mean?"

"I called Jensin's father this morning from my store. They no longer want to proceed. They cancelled."

"They cancelled?" I repeated. What could they have possibly cancelled? We hadn't booked anything yet. No dates had been set. No venues or vendors had been selected. What my uncle meant was they had cancelled me. They no longer wanted me as their daughter-in-law. I felt like my forehead had been stamped with a red, CANCELLED stamp.

I shook my head. I had spoken to Jensin. Everything was fine. He *said* everything was fine. I knew what this was about. It was that neither he nor his family could get past the fact that I had admitted to drinking.

My uncle looked at me gravely. "Sarai-mol, they don't want to proceed, and this time I couldn't change their mind. You best forget this boy."

I shook my head, utterly confused. "I just don't get it. He said everything was fine." I looked at my uncle helplessly. "Uncle, he said he understood—"

"Maybe everything fine with Jensin but not with his family. His father said the family decided you two were not a good match. He said he has only one son, and he and his brothers don't want him to go to the US. They don't think he will come back."

"Is that the reason they gave for cancelling the proposal? They didn't bring up anything else as being the reason?"

"That's what he said. But who knows," he said, shrugging his shoulders as he tore off a piece of chapatti and dipped it into the beef curry. "Only they know the reason."

Was it really the "living in India vs. living in America" issue? Or was it the fact that I had admitted to drinking and going out? Was it really over? Just like that? No "good-bye" and no "I'm sorry, this is not going to work." Maybe the family just needed some time again. I could tell Jensin honestly really liked me. Was he just going to let his family decide his entire fate and ignore how he felt? Could he let me go like that?

"Uncle, maybe you can talk to him again."

"Sarai-mol, you don't think I tried? I spent one hour on the phone with Jensin's father. They like you, but that is their only son. They want him here in India with them."

"But how can they decide that now? I thought you said by the second meeting, everything is set. We had the second meeting weeks ago."

"Yes, that is true. Typically after the second meeting, we decide on the engagement and wedding, but they didn't want a date right away. They must have had doubts then, too. What can we do now?" he asked. He peered at me from the top of his bifocals and shrugged his shoulders dismissively. "This isn't a love marriage. It's an arranged marriage. These things happen. Sometime things just don't work out," he said as he shrugged his shoulders.

These things happen. Yeah, only to me, it seemed. Everyone else who came to India managed to find a great guy and get married. But I somehow managed to find the one guy in all of India whose family had no interest in letting their son live in the US.

"You just forget him. There will be someone better," my uncle said. I wondered if he really believed that, but his focus now seemed to be on his food, which he was devouring like it was his last meal. Although the beef curry looked delicious, I had lost my appetite. My uncle glanced at me and then at my plate. "You eat. Why starve yourself over a silly boy?"

Why indeed? Except he wasn't a silly boy. He was going to be my husband, or so I had thought. I may not have been in love, and my heart may not have felt as if it had been fractured into a million pieces, but the feeling of rejection still stung. In some ways, I felt like I was going through a breakup all over again, but this time there was not even a final goodbye.

Chapter 35

I CALLED REENA later that day to give her the latest update, and like I expected, she was furious. Even before I finished giving her all the details, she began her tirade: "What's he expecting? Someone who just stays home all day and doesn't do anything but study and listen to their parents? Did you tell him that was your first time EVER getting drunk? Did you tell him how *I* had to drag you to clubs in college?" It was nice to hear her indignant, angry tone on the phone, especially after listening to everyone else's nonchalant attitude. These things happen indeed!

"Not necessarily in those words, Reen, but yeah, I basically tried to tell him that I'm not really like that."

"I can't believe it!" she said, her voice sounding angrier. "I didn't know these things happened in India. I thought once you agreed, it was a done deal."

"So did I," I said sighing. "So did I. But my uncle warned me. He didn't like the idea of us talking, especially when no definite dates were set. I guess he had a feeling they were on the fence about it."

"Well, Sarai, maybe it's for the best. You really didn't want an arranged marriage anyway, right? You only did it because you thought it was your last hope."

"Yeah, I guess," I said, looking out the window.

"Sarai, just because it worked for Anjuli doesn't mean it's right for you. Now look at me. I wasn't even looking, and somehow the right one came along. Jensin just wasn't the one for you. If he was, it would have worked out."

"I know. You're so right. I should be relieved. And I think part of me is, but then part of me feels very sad. Reen, everyone, *everyone* is moving on with their lives. I feel so left behind."

"You're not 'behind.' Everyone just has their own time. You have a job you love, you have great friends, ahem," she said clearing her throat, as if to say *like me*, "who love you, and except for the marriage issue, I'd say you're living a very fulfilling life. I think that makes you light-years ahead of a lot of people in this world."

I sighed deeply. "Then why don't I feel happy?"

"That, Sarai, is a question only you can answer."

Reena was wrong. That wasn't a question I could answer. I thought the answer was finding the right guy to settle down with, but ever since I had agreed to marry Jensin, even I began to wonder if just being married would be enough, and that was before everything fell apart. "So let's quit talking about me. Tell me about you and Sanjay. So you think he's the right guy, huh?"

At the mention of his name, I heard her smiling through the phone. "Sarai, he's wonderful! He's so sweet and thoughtful," she said, giddily. I had never heard Reena like this. This guy was turning my girl into a girly-girl. *My* Reena was actually swooning over a guy. She had entered the world of the helplessly, hopelessly in love.

"He's been calling me every day. Depending on his schedule, we talk anywhere from one to two hours a night. The other night he was on-call and so sleepy, but he still wanted to talk to me because that was the first time he was free all day. And he sent me flowers yesterday!"

"That's wonderful, Reen!" I couldn't begrudge my friend any happiness with my petty jealousy. She definitely deserved the royal treatment and then some. But neither could I help wondering, "Why not me, too, God?"

"So when are you coming home?" Reena asked.

"I'm flying out in two weeks on Monday afternoon. I have a layover in Amsterdam, so if all goes well, I should be there by Wednesday afternoon. You know, before I came to India, I was so eager to leave home and take a break from my usual routine. Now I'm so eager to get back to it!"

"Well, *I'm* eager to get you back home, but I know what you mean," she said wistfully. "There is something comforting about having something you can depend on." Reena was thinking of her man again. I was going to have to get used to this new side of Reena. She never sounded like this before, not even with her ex, Liju. She had found someone who not only smoothed out her prickly spots, but someone who made her a better person.

Chapter 36

THE NEXT DAY we were gathered around the table eating dinner at the main house, and Rajan Uncle, Velya Uncle, and Babykutty Uncle were in a heated discussion about the latest state elections. Some guy named Anish Cherian had been re-elected, and Rajan Uncle was not happy about it. Since I had nothing to contribute to the conversation and was perfectly content to be lost in my own thoughts, I was a little more quiet than usual. Mistaking my quietness for unhappiness, Babykutty Uncle repeatedly attempted to engage me in conversation. I answered his questions as succinctly as I could and then went back to eating. Finally he gave up and mumbled in Malayalam that I was obviously still upset about Jensin.

Velya Uncle looked at me thoughtfully. "*Are* you still upset about that Jensin?"

I shrugged my shoulders in that same vague way that my relatives were so fond of.

Babykutty Uncle then slapped my back playfully and ruffled my hair. "Don't worry. Be happy!" He started laughing as if he had just cited the cleverest saying. Then he scooped another handful of rice and formed it into a little ball before popping it into his mouth. "You best forget Jensin. They'll be other Jensins."

I waited for someone to jump in on my behalf, perhaps reprimand my uncle for his insensitive words or, at the least, offer me some words of encouragement or sympathy, but they all continued eating their food without pause. I looked at Rajan Uncle, and he, too, seemed so oblivious to how I was feeling. Milly Chechy threw me a sympathetic glance, but she was more focused on making sure everyone was eating another serving of her rice and chicken curry.

In fact, no one seemed privy to my pain and disappointment. I had agreed to marry this guy, for God's sake! I had agreed to spend the rest of my life with him. Did they not realize that it hadn't been an easy decision for me? I had spent time getting to know this guy. I had bought my wedding trousseau with him in mind... and now they just expected me to get over it like... like he was some common cold?

They didn't get it, and after that "they'll be other Jensins" comment, I realized they never would. I could not pick my future husband out of an assembly line of proposals. I had picked someone I liked and could see myself with. I may not have fallen in love, but I had still grown attached. In my mind, with every conversation we had, knowing that this was going to be my future husband, I began weaving a life with him and allowed myself to get attached. And now, just as swiftly, they wanted me to forget him and to just pick someone else? I just couldn't do it. I was done. I was not some robot they could program to say "yes" to a lifetime commitment with a stranger and then just as swiftly, follow their insistence to just forget that person the minute things didn't work out.

"She's her father's daughter, no?" declared Babykutty Uncle to Rajan Uncle and Velya Uncle. He continued in Malayalam. "If he didn't agree to an arranged marriage, then how did anyone expect her to have one?"

The spoon fell out of my hand and onto my plate as my head reared up. I stared dumbfounded at Babykutty Uncle. Maybe it was the alcohol that made Babykutty Uncle so loose-lipped, or maybe they had forgotten that while my understanding of Malayalam wasn't perfect, I often understood much more than they realized. Finally I found my voice. "Did my parents not have an arranged marriage?" I asked in disbelief. Babykutty Uncle paused in mid-gulp and glanced wide-eyed at Velya Uncle who was shaking his head. Neither of them responded to my question.

I then looked at Rajan Uncle who seemed oblivious to everything but the food on his plate. "Rajan Uncle, did my parents not have an arranged marriage?"

No response.

"Rajan Uncle," I repeated firmly, refusing to let the matter drop.

Rajan Uncle finally looked up at me with an annoyed expression. "Yes?"

I repeated my question.

Without flinching, he looked at me straight in the eye. "They had an arranged marriage," he stated with a deadpan expression before once again putting another handful of food into his mouth.

I glanced at Milly Chechy who was clearing out some of the dishes from the table. When I caught her eye, she smiled at me. Frustrated at my uncles' reticence, I gave her a questioning look. She then quickly averted her eyes, furtively gathering the empty dishes from the table, and then hurried back to the kitchen.

As my three uncles got up from the table and made their way to the front porch to enjoy their after-dinner drinks, I glanced thoughtfully at the empty alcove leading to the kitchen. I grabbed my empty plate and cup and disappeared into the alcove after Milly Chechy. Twenty minutes later, I rejoined my uncles on the front porch. As they sat back on their porch chairs enjoying their Johnnie Walker on the rocks and cigarettes, they looked relaxed and content, acting as if life couldn't be sweeter. Feeling that same sense of contentment, I, too, settled into an empty chair with a satisfied smile on my face.

❖　❖　❖

I HAD ONLY two weeks left on my trip, but despite my protests, my uncle was still determined to get me married. Ramesh brought one proposal after another, but I had completely lost my energy and open-mindedness. I was like a vapid doll. I smiled courteously and nodded my head when appropriate, but other than that, I had nothing much to say. Soon my uncle tired of my lack of cooperation, and the proposals finally stopped.

With just a few days left before my return to the US, I decided to spend as much time with my Ammachi and cousins as possible. I wondered when I'd be visiting India again, but after everything I had just gone through during the past few weeks, I had no interest in visiting for a long, long time. In fact, as far as I was concerned, I would not step foot in India again until I was married. I couldn't imagine going through the arranged marriage process again, at least not here in India. It may have worked for many, but not for me. I had come to India at an age where marriage was not only certain, it was inevitable. And only I could manage to go back single.

Somewhere in the back of my mind, I was expecting that last-minute phone call from Jensin's family, telling me they had changed their minds again. But did I really want someone who vacillated so often on whether he wanted to marry me? I wasn't even sure I would take him back. But I never had the chance to find out because they never called, and a week later I boarded the plane as single as I had arrived.

Chapter 37

WHEN I ARRIVED back in the US, it was without fanfare. Unlike the grand sendoff I had been given by all my relatives, it was only my father who picked me up. I trudged the final steps down the long hallway from my gate towards baggage claim and caught a glimpse of his outline just beyond the security checkpoint. He stood there, eyes downcast, as if he were awaiting the final member of some defeated, disgraced sports team to disembark. When he saw me, he shuffled towards me and planted a perfunctory kiss on my cheek. As we waited at baggage claim, I glanced at him, wanting to say something, maybe even an "I'm sorry," but exactly what was I apologizing about? Was it my fault that at the last minute Jensin had succumbed to family pressure? Should I be remorseful for being honest with my soon-to-be-husband? Should I apologize for not being able to compromise on what I was looking for? But in the end, I said nothing, and my dad's eyes remained focused on the conveyor belt as he waited on my last piece of luggage.

The drive home was relatively quiet with my father only asking me some brief questions about our families and their welfare. I, too, was reluctant to speak and gave as brief of a response as possible.

As we drove through the entry gates of our neighborhood, I gasped in delight, noting the changing color of the leaves. It was Fall! I had forgotten how beautiful the colors could be. Red. Orange. Amber. Gold. And every shade in between. It was so different from Kerala where everything was beautiful but green. I rolled down my window and breathed in the hearty, musky smell of the autumn air. The afternoon air already had a slight chilliness, but I welcomed it whole-heartedly, grateful for something besides the humidity and heat I had endured for the past two months.

When we got home, one of the first things I did was call Reena. She sounded just as excited to see me and promised she would be right over. I changed into a long-sleeve jersey and jeans. I ran my finger against the dresser, feeling the smooth polished wood. No dust. No bugs mysteriously appearing in my chai if I were to set it down and walk away. It was so good to be home again!

I wanted to unpack my clothes and shower, but I couldn't shake the restlessness in me that begged to be calmed with a leisurely walk outside. I had only been gone two months, but it felt like much longer. For some reason, the drive home brought back so many memories, and suddenly I felt youthful and alive again. Perhaps it was the changing leaves and the accompanying memories of youth and happier times. Or perhaps it was just being home again after a long time away. Whatever it was, the outdoors beckoned, and I was eager to indulge the nostalgia that had been awakened in me with an afternoon stroll. I abandoned my unpacked suitcases in my bedroom and grabbed a light jacket. As I made my way to the front door and walked past the living room, I observed my dad who had plopped himself down on his oversized brown leather recliner and was flipping through channels until he settled on CNN Headline News. The living room curtains were drawn, giving the room a dark, overcast feel, no doubt reflecting his own depressive mood. My Aunt Lizzy would no doubt blame me, saying I had done this to her brother, that he was depressed because of me and my refusal to get married. I paused, wanting to go to him and comfort him, perhaps even bond with him. I wanted to remind him that I wasn't much different from him when he was my age. I wanted to reassure him that I would be fine, that somehow everything would work out. And I wanted to tell him he no longer had to pretend, that I *knew*. But somehow seeing him sit there, frowning to himself, as he watched the news, I knew unless I were to tell him that I was getting married, nothing else would change his mood or disposition. Whatever I had to say would only fall on deaf ears. Maybe someday, when I was married, I could tell him that I knew. But for now, I'd let him continue the farce. I sighed, glancing at my father one last time, before I walked outside.

The beautiful fall foliage that surrounded our yard and neighborhood instantly lifted my spirits. The burnished leaves smelled of a warm campfire, and I breathed in the scent like a cup of steaming hot chocolate. When had I fallen in love with Fall? As a child, it was always summer I craved. But as an adult, Fall had become the favored season. With its golden autumn beauty, it was the cool respite after a torturously hot summer. It evoked wonderful memories of youth and marked the beginning of a new school year, the start of football season, pep rallies, bonfires, homecoming, school dances, and it heralded the festive holiday season from Halloween to Thanksgiving.

I glanced at each neighboring house where I had driven by or walked by countless times. Long, long ago, it was a busy street filled with neighborhoods kids throwing leaves at each other. But we had all grown up, and now our street was a quiet street filled only with memories. As I stood on the exposed roots of the oak tree in my front yard surveying everything around me, I knew this was where I, too, had my roots.

I was drowning in memories of my childhood when the revving sound of a car engine broke the silence. A forest green Ford Explorer soon came into view, and I recognized the familiar shape of corkscrew curls in the driver's seat. Reena half-hazardly parked her car on the curb of our driveway and jumped out. We ran towards each other like silly teenagers and hugged. She pulled away first and scrutinized me. "You look the same!" she finally concluded.

"I went there to look for a husband, silly, not to get plastic surgery!" I exclaimed. That was when I noticed Reena was dressed up. Reena never wore a dress unless it was for a special occasion, and she wore make-up even less often. I whistled and asked, "You look nice! Where are you going all dressed up? Got a hot date?"

But rather than answering my question, she splayed out her left hand so I could see the two carat solitaire that sparkled back at me. I gasped and looked up at her.

She nodded. "He proposed!"

"What?!" I grabbed her left hand and pulled it towards me for a closer look. It was a two-carat, cushion-cut diamond solitaire, and it sat perched on a smooth platinum band. I looked back at Reena, her face paused in anticipation of my comments. "It's gorgeous, Reen!" I said and then we broke off into one of our high-shrieking squeals and hugged again.

I can honestly say I was truly happy for her, but as I hugged her, my smile waned, and I closed my eyes momentarily, feeling a sudden sense of loss. Though I had only been gone two months, I had already missed so much.

"When?" I asked.

"Monday night. I had called your uncle's house, but your aunt said you had left for the airport earlier. I figured I'd just wait to tell you in person anyway."

"So tell me everything!" I commanded.

He had surprised her by flying in on Saturday night and was staying through the week. Apparently, her whole family was in on it. Her cousins had her convinced they were going out, so she was dressed up, and at six that evening, the doorbell rang, and there he was. He whisked her off to the Spindletop, which was a revolving restaurant in the middle of downtown. Against the beautiful, night-time view of the city, they dined on Surf and Turf and wine. Afterwards, a carriage ride awaited them, and they went for a romantic ride through downtown and Central. When they reached the Waterford Hotel fountains, he dropped on one knee and proposed.

She was now engaged to a guy I had never even met, I realized. Just as I was digesting this, Reena continued. "We're planning the wedding for the February after next. He'll then have three more months to finish up his residency, and he's already gotten two job offers to work in Manhattan once he's done and we're—"

"Manhattan? He'll have a job in Manhattan? But then that means you're moving to—"

Looking like a child who had just been caught with her hand in the cookie jar, she then quickly averted her eyes.

"Manhattan—" she finished off for me. "Yeah…"

"You're moving?" I repeated, completely thrown off. For some reason, it never occurred to me that one day we may no longer live in the same town. I somehow assumed we'd all still stay somewhere close. "So how do you feel about moving?" I asked.

"Actually I'm really excited. You know I've always wanted to live in New York City. Remember how I almost took a job out there years ago, and my parents freaked out!"

"Yeah, and your parents weren't the only ones who freaked out with the idea of you moving," I said sheepishly, recalling how I begged and bribed her to stay in town.

"But that's still a year and a half away! We have plenty of time to hang out and do stuff before then!"

"Yeah, but it'll be here before we know it!"

The disappointment must have been obvious on my face because she quickly added, "I'm still torn about moving so far away. Obviously, I'm going to miss you and my family. But part of me is actually looking forward to something different. I've been here my whole life. I feel like I'm ready for something new," she said, her eyes sparkling with anticipation. Then her voice calmed down and she somberly added, "But I do want to come back though. I can't imagine this being a permanent move and starting a family there." A family. She was already thinking of a family. I breathed in deep, steadying myself. She didn't need me to be sad or overly sentimental right now. She needed me to be happy for her, and that's what I intended to do.

Reena launched into full detail about Sanjay, about their dates, their conversations, their future plans. Unlike India, we didn't have to worry about our phone card running out of minutes or my uncle or aunt eavesdropping. As we walked through the neighborhood with the cool brisk breeze of fall and the smell of fallen leaves beneath our heels, I lost myself in reliving those adolescent years when we just walked and talked for hours. As she filled me in on what I had missed, we eventually made our way through our neighborhood and arrived at Central. We made our way towards the swing set and sat on two empty swings. During moments like this, I often felt nothing had really changed, but, of course, rather than Reena telling me about her crush on Scott Ericson or Liju Thomas, she was now telling me about the man she was about to marry.

There was a part of me that wished I could have cherished those times more, but back then, all we wanted to do was grow up so we could start living our lives. Little did we know that we were already living it. I remember us sitting on the steps of our school as we dreamed and planned our future adult lives. I smiled at our naïveté for believing life would fall into place just as we had planned. How I wish life could have been so simple.

When the afternoon sun began to fade and the air dropped a few more degrees, Reena glanced at her watch, and exclaimed, "Oh my gosh—I gotta get going. I have dinner with Sanjay and his uncle and aunt tonight." She looked at me thoughtfully and smiled, "You wouldn't want to join us, by any chance, would you?"

I still hadn't showered, and I knew once I did, all I would want to do was curl up in my bed and catch up on some serious sleep. "I still have some jet lag. I think I'm just gonna hang at home and get organized. Besides, I want to look my best when I meet my best friend's fiancé."

"Oh, he already knows how you look. I showed him our family photo albums and since you're in half of all our pictures, he's basically seen you from the time I've known you."

My eyes widened, and I covered my mouth in horror as I began thinking of some awkward stages I went through as a kid. "Oh, no you didn't!"

"Sho' did!" she said laughing and patted me on the back in mock comfort. "But don't worry. I also showed him some recent pictures, and he said you were very, very pretty! He even said he wants to set you up with his best friend who is apparently quite the catch!"

I groaned, waving my hands in protest in front of me. "No more setups for a while. I don't think I want to see another 'proposal' for a very, very long time!"

"Well, he claims his best friend is a really great guy—and he's good looking, and all the ladies seem to fall for him at first sight, but there's plenty of time for that later. Will you be up for lunch or dinner tomorrow? I really, really want you to meet Sanjay soon!"

I nodded an eager "yes." I most definitely wanted to meet the man who not only stole the heart of my best friend but was also moving her hundreds of miles away from me.

We made our way back home, and as she pulled out of the driveway in her Explorer, she waved enthusiastically. I smiled and returned her wave. I felt a bittersweet twinge shoot up my spine. So much for being back home and back to the way things used to be. Everything seemed to be changing around me while my life stood still. A new chapter of Reena's life was going to begin for both of us; hers with her new husband, and mine without my best friend of twenty-something years. I felt the pricking of tears at the back of my eyes, and my throat was constricted, but I continued to smile, trying to be just as happy as I would have expected her to be for me. I found it so ironic that I was the one who went half-way across the world, looking for a husband, yet she managed to stay right where she was, and it somehow came to her. I still couldn't believe my best friend was engaged. I shouldn't have been surprised, though. I knew when she told me about their first date that he was the one. I heard it in her voice, and I knew that while she hadn't fully realized it at that time, she had known on some level as well.

After she left, I felt the urge to walk back to Central, but dusk was settling in, so I went back into the house. I glanced at the photo frame sitting on my desk in my bedroom. It was a collage photo frame of five pictures Reena had given me a couple of years ago, each one capturing a momentous occasion in both of our lives. The first one was of us in elementary school in our Girl Scout uniforms, posing in front of the tree that our troop had just planted in honor of Arbor Day. The second was at my thirteenth birthday party. We had posed in front of my birthday cake. I had both hands on my hips while she had one arm thrown across my shoulder, and we both had huge smiles on our faces, showing off our new colored wire braces. The third picture was of the day we both passed our driver's license test at the DMV. She wore her Def Leopard t-shirt, and I wore my Madonna "True Blue" t-shirt. Our metal smiles and bespectacled eyes were filled with excitement as we held up our temporary licenses. The last picture was of our high school graduation. We were holding our diplomas in one hand and hugging each other with the other. The final frame wasn't a picture but something Reena wrote, "To many more wonderful memories together!" Reena wasn't overly sentimental, but she knew I was and that made this one gift the best gift she had ever given me.

I wasn't just mourning Reena. I was mourning what I once was. Not feeling in control of my life now made life seem even more fragile. In our youth, we had been so excited about the future, our 20s, and the possibilities ahead. We had never thought about our 30s, though. It was something too far beyond the stretch of our imagination. But in just a few short weeks, I would be turning twenty-nine. The naïve bubble of denial we had encased ourselves in for so long was dangerously close to popping.

Chapter 38

A WEEK AFTER I returned from my trip to India, my mom's brother Babu Uncle, his wife, Gracie Auntie, and their teenage daughter Anu visited us from Philadelphia. As was customary, we took them around to visit the home of each local family member as well as distant cousins. After two days of shuffling from house to house, our final stop was the home of Babu Uncle's Air Force buddy whom he hadn't seen in twelve years. Just like when we were young, my brother and I were forced to tag along.

We had not been there less than twenty minutes when, in the midst of chit-chatting about their Air Force days, my uncle asked his friend, "So do you know of any young, handsome boy for my niece?" His friend paused, looking at me more closely as he rummaged through his memory. My brother shot me a wary, sympathetic look, and then hung his head low and shook it. "Don't worry little brother," I said, under my breath, just loud enough for him to hear. "Soon enough it'll be your turn."

He grimaced, knowing I wasn't kidding.

After a few seconds, my uncle's friend said, "Well, there is this one boy—KC George's son. He is 31 years old—"

"What's his name?" my uncle asked immediately, his eyes lighting up.

"His name is Amit. He is an engineer from MIT and now working on his MBA," answered his friend.

With those few words, my father's body suddenly sat upright, and his eyes and body were more alert, reminding me of a tiger about to pounce on his next victim.

"Do he and his family live close? Maybe you can invite them over or maybe we can stop by?" my uncle asked, not even looking at me.

I gasped and looked to my brother, shaking my head in disgust. To inquire about a boy was bad enough, but now he was pushing an in-person meeting? And tonight? He had to be kidding. Did anyone even think to ask whether I was interested? Did anyone even care what I thought? Whether it was born out of love or worry, their continuous desperation for me only made me feel pathetic. After my experience with Rajan Uncle in India, I probably should have been more under-standing, but rather than feeling touched at the intervention, I felt angry at being treated like some poor, pathetic old maid whose very existence depended on her getting married. Hadn't I given it my all? Most of my friends went to India, kicking and screaming while I went there willing and open-minded. Didn't going through all that count for anything? I wanted to yell out, "Maybe it is time for all of us to accept the obvious! It is clearly not working out for me. Maybe I am truly meant to be alone." But like the good little girl they had raised me to be, I said nothing since we were in the company of guests. I kept my anger and outrage in check as they continued to discuss me as if I weren't sitting directly in front of them.

My uncle's friend made two quick phone calls, and unfortunately for me, plans were made for us to drop by the home of this Amit and his family under the pretense of some family or neighborly connection back in India. Of course, for all intents and purposes, the family would think this was a friendly visit and have no idea that my family was there in hopes to ensnare their son for me.

I silently shuffled into my uncle's Camry, feeling like I was about to be a sacrificed virgin maiden. If I thought my protests would have been heard, I would have said something, but I knew it would fall on unbending ears. I just couldn't believe my favorite uncle was doing this to me. As he reversed the car, I saw him finally looking at me through the rear view mirror, but I quickly averted my eyes outside. "You have to let us try to help you, Sarai-mol. We just want you to be happy," he said. His eyes pleaded with me to understand. His apology just fueled my anger. Had my dad put him up to it?

We arrived at the house ten minutes later, and my uncle and his friend got out to ring the door bell. The door opened and out walked someone wearing a thin white undershirt and khaki cargo shorts. That was definitely no uncle. Although I could not make out the face because the trees were blocking my view, I appreciatively noted the broad shoulders that tapered to a well-defined chest and torso. His well shaped calves indicated someone who spent more than a couple of hours a week in the gym. He was also undoubtedly tall as his entire frame seemed to encompass a good portion of the doorway entry.

My cousin, Anu, was also peering through the passenger's window and turned to me with a knowing smile. I smiled back and shrugged my shoulders. Well, maybe this wouldn't be too bad. I unsuccessfully tried to hide my pleased grin and waited in anticipation. Soon an older looking man in a striped gray dress shirt and dark navy slacks joined the younger one at the door. I assumed the older one was the father and the younger one was none other than Amit to whom I would be betrothed to by the end of the evening if my uncle and dad had any say in the matter.

Father and son both shook hands with my uncle and his Air Force buddy, and my uncle then motioned toward our two cars. Father and son peered through the evening darkness and after seeing us in the car, they both waved.

I hoped and prayed that my uncle hadn't told either of them the real reason we were there. But I was sure he hadn't. Otherwise, like me, Amit would have probably been frowning rather than smiling and welcoming us.

My uncle then motioned to us to get out of the cars, and one-by-one, we shuffled into the house, taking our shoes off at the front door. We walked through the foyer and made our way to the living room. As we did, my eyes connected with Amit who was watching me with a very curious but somber expression. I smiled, and he smiled back.

We seated ourselves on their living room sofas, and Amit excused himself as he went into his parents' bedroom, which was right off the main hallway. My dad, mom, uncle, and aunt sat on the main sofa while my brother, cousin, and I sat on the love seat. The house, in many ways, reminded me of ours: the traditional wood paneling, the bookcases filled with trophies, books, and endless knickknacks from trips to India.

From the living room, I could see into the parents' master bedroom, where Amit was making a phone call. His shoulders were broad and tapered nicely to his hips, and I admired the way he seemed to fill out his khaki shorts. His thighs, or what I could see of them, and his calves were well defined. He obviously played sports and/or worked out.

When he returned to the living room, he addressed my uncle, my uncle's friend, and my parents, letting them know his mom wouldn't be arriving from work for another thirty minutes, but in the meantime, he could make everyone some chai.

"You make chai?" my uncle asked, impressed.

Amit's father responded, "He makes the best chai! Better than his mother and sisters!" Then he put his palms together as if he were wishing everyone *namaste* and begged, "But please don't tell them I said that!" We all burst out laughing.

Amit then looked at us. "Do you guys want chai or would you prefer coke or juice?"

My brother looked at me and shrugged. I glanced at Anu, and she nodded. "Well, we have to try this famous chai, so three more then," I said teasingly.

He grinned sheepishly and went into the kitchen. Twenty minutes later, he brought in a tray filled with steaming cups of chai and served one to each of us. How ironic, I thought, that here I was with my family at the boy's house and this time, he was the one making the chai and serving it! I chuckled to myself as I wondered if Rajan Uncle would be shaking his head in disgust at the role-reversal if he had been here.

As we waited for our chai to cool down, Amit pulled up another chair and sat next to my brother. There was nothing specifically striking about his appearance. His eyes were typical brown and were average in their shape. His hair seemed to have that typical, coarse, frizzy Malayalee texture that I knew could defy even the strongest gel. He sported a goatee, which gave him a slightly edgy look. He had a nice smile and straight, even, white teeth. In a thin t-shirt, his chest and arms were clearly well defined. He wasn't overly built either and seemed to find that happy medium in being fit.

As he and Sajan talked, I chatted with Anu, but I noticed that he occasionally glanced at me, each glance lasting a little longer, and occasionally it was accompanied with the slightest of smiles. Each time he looked at me, I noted that there was something interestingly intense about his gaze, not in a romantic sense, but more like a focused, curious stare—as if he were peering at me through a microscope. Was it possible that he knew why we were here? I squirmed self-consciously in my seat.

I was obviously nervous around him, but I wasn't entirely sure why. While he wasn't particularly good looking, there was something distinctive and indefinably appealing about him. He had an aloofness that seemed to draw me in; not to mention, he seemed mature, polite, and a gentleman. I wasn't sure how many guys would offer to make chai for anyone, much less make chai for eight guests he was meeting for the first time. What girl wouldn't like a guy who wasn't afraid to get his hands dirty in the kitchen?

On the drive home, I couldn't help but wonder if this was why things hadn't worked out in India. Perhaps my trip to India hadn't been meaningless. Maybe all of that was to lead me here to this moment and make me more receptive to Amit.

I had no idea what the next steps would be or even if there would be anything more after this initial meeting. I was just glad that this wasn't India and there would be no final decisions based on one or two meetings.

Chapter 39

THE NEXT MORNING I called Reena to tell her about the unexpected turn of events from the night before. She, too, was curious about this reserved, yet intense guy who was around our age whom we had never heard of or met. "I wonder if Rakesh or Mani might know him," she said.

"No! I don't want Mani or Rakesh knowing about this."

"Okay, then maybe my brothers have heard of him… or wait, my cousin Ruby goes to his church. But don't worry," she said, sensing my hesitation, "I won't let on why I'm asking. I'll think of something credible without implicating you." An hour later, she called back.

"So what did you find out?" I asked.

Her voice sounded enthusiastic. "Good things… good things. Actually neither of my brothers has heard of him, but my cousin knows him."

"Really? Do tell!"

"Well, at first when I said his name, she couldn't place him. Apparently he goes by Anthony, so Amit must be his family nickname. It clicked for my cousin when I said he had two sisters, both of whom were engineers as well."

"So what did she think?"

"She said he's a really nice guy, but he's really quiet. Very intelligent. Went to MIT for engineering. But other than saying 'hi' and 'bye' to him at church, they really don't talk much. He's very close to his sisters and actually helped put the younger one through school after his dad got laid off from work."

"Really?" I said, very impressed with his willingness to help his family.

"And oh, yeah, apparently, he's really into working out."

"Oh, I figured out that one all by myself," I said and smiled as I recalled the image of his fit frame in the thin t-shirt and khakis.

I wondered if anything would really come of this situation, but luckily, I didn't have to wait long because even from hundreds of miles away, my Babu Uncle was still pushing the issue along. Apparently, he had already called the family and "proposed" me for their son. The family expressed interest. But since they had already met our family, Amit's father suggested that before the families meet again, Amit and I exchange email and phone numbers and get to know each other on our own first.

A few days later I got an email in my inbox from Amit. It was just three short lines: "Hi, this is Amit George. We met when your family visited our house a few weeks ago. Hope you're doing well. Just dropping a line to confirm this is your email address." In the signature line of the email was his official name, Anthony George.

I wrote back, and he responded within the hour. We went back and forth through email for several days with our conversation slowly progressing from basic pleasantries to the latest movies to our jobs to basic likes/dislikes. I learned he was working as an engineer for Halliburton and that he was a chocolate connoisseur. By Thursday of that week, he suggested we meet up for lunch on that Saturday. Reena came over early Saturday morning to help me select something to wear. "Jeans. Definitely jeans. You need to look casual, like you're not trying. And you want to look cute and fashionable, but again," she said as she braced me by the shoulders, "you don't want to look like you're trying."

We finally settled on a spaghetti-strap babydoll top with a sheer antique wrap. "Feminine and fashionable," Reena said, as she gave the wrap one finishing tug and leaned back and surveyed her handiwork. "Perfect! You are now officially date-ready."

Date?! Was it a date? I thought of it more like meeting a friend for lunch. But we weren't friends. And he had invited me out. So I guess it really was a date. Suddenly acknowledging that it was a date only heightened my nervousness. This time I wouldn't be able to hide behind my family. It would be just him and me. Me and him. By ourselves. Alone. I breathed in deeply, imagining the date. Would it go anywhere? Would we have chemistry? Okay, stop, I told myself, don't jinx it yet. He's just a friend. No, I reminded myself, he's a stranger, but the flutter in my stomach told me I was hoping for much more.

I thanked Reena for helping me get ready and was on my way. I arrived at the restaurant and found him already waiting at a table. As I approached, he immediately got up and held my seat out for me. He's chivalrous, I thought with a smile, as I mentally checked off that characteristic from my list.

After placing our drink orders, we both browsed the menu. I peeked a look at him. He had shaven off the goatee he had when I first met him, and his clean-shaven face made him look like he was twenty-three rather than thirty-one. His eyes, however, retained that same sense of serenity and maturity that I had initially been drawn to. As we looked over the menus, neither of us said anything, though we glanced and smiled at each other intermittently.

"Do you know what you're going to order?" I asked, hoping to break the initial awkwardness.

"Actually, I do," he said, closing the menu and placing it next to his plate. "My favorite is chicken panang, and somehow I always end up ordering that even though I always tell myself I should try something new."

Panang? He loved panang? I loved panang! I put a mental checkmark next to our food/restaurant compatibility.

"When I like something," he continued, "I stick with it." He said it in an odd, serious way that made me think he wasn't just talking about the food. "Some people may consider that boring, but I like to know what I'm getting."

"I know what you mean. I love chicken panang, too, and the one time I didn't order it was when I decided to go with the beef panang."

My attempt at humor elicited a grin from him. "But since you're ordering the chicken panang, I'll be daring and order something completely different like Pad Thai. If you don't mind, we can share so we can have the best of both worlds." He chuckled and nodded.

After placing our orders, I asked him about his job. We then moved onto people we knew in common, a topic of conversation we had already started in our emails, and then to our college days. I was listening to him talk about his economics class when my eyes drifted to two tables away and a familiar face came into view. "Lisa!" I squealed, much too loudly, I realized, noting that I seemed to have startled Amit to the point that he had almost lost his grip on his Thai iced tea.

Lisa was an old friend from college. We had both served on the newspaper staff, and we had been in the same teaching program. I vaguely remembered running into her at an alumni event a few years ago, but since then, we hadn't kept in touch.

She saw me at the same time and immediately approached our table. We didn't talk long, just enough to exchange numbers, email addresses, and catch up on the basics. She was married, but as of yet, no kids, and was teaching in a nearby school district. I introduced her to Amit, describing him as a "friend" and Lisa arched her eyebrow and smiled, a gesture not unnoticed by Amit. We hugged, squealed, and promised to stay in touch.

"Sorry about that. I hadn't seen her in years!" I said, as I once again settled into my seat.

"I figured something like that. You're very… outgoing," he observed. I noted the pause and tried to figure out what that meant. Although he didn't say it negatively, I had the slightest feeling that he didn't view it as favorable either. But opposites attract, right? He was probably just taken aback by my enthusiasm, which had been heightened because of our date. But hopefully, he was drawn to my outgoingness, just as I was drawn to his reticence.

We talked about friends. About our families. Our siblings. Being Indian. About our favorite TV shows. Our favorite books. He read a lot, including books that I had only read because they had been assigned reading in school. As our date wore on, I completely forgot that we were being set up by our families, and I was just able to enjoy getting to know him.

Although our personalities were quite opposite, I found that we had a lot in common, from our conservative outlooks on religion to politics. He made me feel completely at ease, and he seemed to be just as comfortable with me. I had initially thought he came across as a little standoffish, but now I better understood him as just being reserved. Like most reserved people, once he felt comfortable with someone, he seemed to open up much more. In a lot of ways, he was like most guys I knew. He loved watching and playing sports. He hated shopping and considered it a complete waste of time. As odd as it sounds, he actually reminded me of an onion, with multiple, endless layers. Perhaps it was the way he spoke or carried himself, but there was something aloof about him, something almost untouchable, as if I would be peeling the layers for years to come. I always liked a good mystery, and he was definitely interesting.

We were stuffed after lunch, but ordered coffee so we could linger longer. Then we had seconds of coffee. Three hours had passed from the time we were seated for lunch, and we still weren't ready to end our lunch date. But we finally took the hint from our waiter, paid our bill, and left.

Once we were outside, we lingered near the entrance of the restaurant. I wasn't totally ready for our date to end, but I thanked him for lunch and prepared to go my own way. Before I could say anything else, though, he suggested we walk around the promenade and browse through some of the shops.

I was happy that he didn't want our date to end either, but I cocked an eyebrow and teasingly alluded to one of his biggest dislikes, "You know this might be construed as shopping, right?"

He laughed, "Yeah, you're right. It would be shopping, but as long as you promise not to try on any clothes, I'll be okay."

As we walked, I could see him giving me a long side-ways once-over. His next question completely caught me off guard. "So what's your timetable?"

"My timetable?" I asked.

"Yeah, I assume your parents have you on some timetable. What age do you have to be married? Have kids? Etcetera…"

I started laughing. "I think I'm 'overdue' on everything they had planned for me. If it had been up to my parents, my wedding would have been the day after my college graduation, and nine months and one day later, I would have popped out my first child! They've given up on me for the most part. So now I just operate on my own timetable."

"So what is *your* timetable then?"

"My timetable?" I asked, not sure how forthcoming I should be, especially knowing I was fully capable of scaring him off. "To be honest, I wasn't expecting to be single at this age, but life happens, so I'm just rolling with it. When it happens, it happens. I'm just hoping it happens in the next couple of years." Was that vague and non-threatening enough of an answer?

"So you're not on this super rush to get married?" he asked, looking at me as if he wasn't quite sure whether to believe me or not. "Well, you're the first Indian girl I've been set up with who isn't on a mission to get the ring within three months or less!"

"Well, don't get me wrong. I would like to be married, preferably sooner than later. I always assumed I would be married by thirty, but since I'm turning thirty in two weeks, that's obviously not going to happen."

He laughed, "Unless you go to India or something!"

I laughed nervously. "Yeah, unless I go to India or something…" No need to tell him about India, at least not yet. There would be plenty of time for that conversation later.

"So have you been set up with a lot of Indian girls?" I asked.

"I don't know how you'd define 'a lot,' but yeah, my parents have tried to push the issue a number of times. They learned, though, to back off and leave it up to me."

I don't know how he did it exactly, but even though he answered my questions, he remained very vague and elusive. Guys weren't known for being open, I know, but this one was less forthcoming than most guys I knew. If I'd known him longer or felt more comfortable, I would have definitely drilled him for more details, but I backed off since it was our first date. I knew this conversation was reaching its course, so I changed the subject.

"So tell me about your sisters," I prompted. "Are you close to them? Did you ever feel left out with two girls in the house?"

"I'm close to both of them, but I think the older one and I are probably closer. Our personalities gel a little more. She's more reserved and quiet. The younger one is much more outgoing and brash."

"Brash?" I asked. That was an interesting word choice. "In what sense?"

He looked at me oddly at first, like he was surprised I would ask him to explain, but then he did. "Yeah, she doesn't always think things through before making decisions. She bases a lot of her decisions on her 'feelings' rather than doing what's practical."

I laughed, and he looked at me curiously when I said, "She sounds like a normal female to me!"

He thought about what he said and chuckled. "Yeah, I guess those traits could be construed as being stereotypically female."

After browsing through some of the shops at the Promenade, we stopped at one of the cafés and grabbed some dessert. I got a tiramisu, and he, in keeping with his chocolate addiction, got a slice of Death by Chocolate. I glanced at my watch and my eyes widened in shock.

"Are you okay? Am I keeping you from something?" he asked.

"No, no, not at all. I just can't believe the time," I responded, as I checked my watch again, even blinking a few times to make sure I was seeing correctly. "It's six!"

"Oh, really?" he asked calmly. He didn't seem surprised in the least, but then again, he didn't strike me as the type of guy to react to too much anyway. "I guess time flies when you're having fun."

I smiled and stirred my latte again. So he was having fun, was he? We lingered another twenty minutes and though we were both a little reluctant to call it a night, we did.

He walked me to my car, opened the door for me after I unlocked it, and then held it open while I got in the driver's seat. "I had a really nice time," he said and then he broke out into one of his rare smiles. "Call me, email me… we should definitely do this again."

I nodded and then offered to drive him to his car. "I'm just two cars down," he said. Then he shut the door and waved as I drove away with the biggest smile on my face. It was refreshing to be able to talk to someone who was a true potential, but the added bonus was that I didn't have any of the pressures to make any type of decision right away.

Later that night, I called Reena, Anjuli, and Maya who were all on pins and needles waiting for an update. The girls were so happy for me and patiently listened as I went into excruciating detail, retelling every conversation verbatim and analyzing every gesture.

I wrapped up the details with, "And he said to call or email, that we should definitely do this again!"

"Sarai!" Reena said shrieking. "That is greeeeeeeat news! Maybe if all goes well, mine won't be the only wedding we'll be planning in the coming months!" We both knew it was way too early to jump to marriage talk, but it was a nice feeling to know that the possibility, no matter how remote, was still there.

Chapter 40

I APPROACHED THE coming week with renewed energy and excitement. My birthday was near, and I was finally talking to someone with true potential. The timing couldn't have been better; otherwise, I'm sure I would have been depressed. The day did seem to be a little brighter, and I felt happier than I had been in a long time. He didn't call or write that day or the next day, but I didn't worry, knowing how busy he was with school. I knew he was heading toward his session finals, so I didn't worry when he didn't call the following two days either. He might have also felt embarrassed at having so clearly expressed his interest that he probably wanted to give it a few days so he wouldn't seem too eager.

A few days of no phone calls soon turned into a week, and then I began to worry. Doubt crept in, but I kept going back to our date, which had been a five-hour lunch that culminated with a, "Call me, email me… we should definitely do this again!" He had said it with a loopy smile on his face. He was definitely interested. There was no doubt in my mind that we had a great time and that he wanted to stay in touch. But then why wasn't he calling? Something must have happened. I briefly entertained the worst, picturing a number of possibilities, from him lying in a hospital bed to something less melodramatic, like him losing my number or my email.

The obvious crossed my mind, too—that he just wasn't interested. But I wasn't in high school anymore. I didn't mistake the interest. No guy would stay on a five-hour lunch date unless he was clearly interested. No guy would clearly say, "call me… email me…" and then not be interested. I was telling this very thing to Reena, Anjuli, and Maya a few days later when we met up to celebrate my birthday early since Reena would be out of town on my actual birthday. We were at Mango's, having dinner al fresco, and enjoying a live band.

"I'm with you, Sarai. It sounds like he was definitely interested," Anjuli said, as she nibbled on our appetizer of fried calamari.

"Yeah, but if he was interested, then why hasn't he called?" Reena was unconvinced. She always felt that women read far too much into what guys didn't do. "I'll tell you what he's doing," she said, "He's not calling. And if he's not calling, he's not interested. Actions speak louder than words."

"But initially you thought he was interested in me, too!" I spat defensively.

"True, but that was before he didn't call. And if he *is* interested in you and just not calling, you don't want a guy like that anyway."

Although I didn't know why he wasn't calling, I was pretty sure he wasn't the type to be playing games, so I ruled out that possibility.

As the girls debated on whether Amit was interested, I kept going back to the last words he had said. *Call me… email me…* The words hit me like a stampede of brides at a Waters and Waters trunk sale. *Call me… email me…* Wait a minute. He had put it in *my* court! No wonder he wasn't calling. He was waiting on *me* to call *him*! How could I be so stupid?

I wondered if perhaps he, too, wasn't somewhere wondering why I wasn't calling. Maybe at this very moment he was with his guy friends, huddled together at some local pub or sports bar, talking to his friends about why I wasn't calling him. I imagined him, tie loosely around his neck, hair disheveled, eyes blood shot as he stared into his drink, shaking his head. "I don't get it guys. I told her clearly call me… email me… why hasn't she? Why does the guy always have to do all the work? Hadn't I been obvious enough? Can't she leave me with a shred of self-esteem?" His friends tried to console him by buying another beer and advised him to just "fo' getta' 'bout it" and then assured him "it's her loss anyway."

The girls laughed at my imagined scenario and all of them, except for Reena, were in consensus that I should make the next move since he had so clearly put it in my court. Maya lifted her glass, "Here's to Sarai and Amit."

We laughed, raising our cocktail glasses in response. Over the glass rims, my eyes met Reena's. She wasn't shaking her head or frowning, but I sensed her disapproval just the same.

Chapter 41

EVEN THOUGH SHE was no longer my biggest Amit champion, it was Reena who was with me when I made the call the next day.

We were at my house sitting on my bed and staring at my phone. I was on one side. Reena on the other. The phone sat between us. It was a pink, Barbie princess phone, a gift from Reena for my ninth birthday.

Reena was shaking her head. "I cannot believe you still have this phone! Don't you want something a little less, I don't know... Barbie-ish?"

"Hey I've had this phone for almost twenty years. It's served me well," I said, as I gingerly touched its smooth surface like a beloved antique. The press numbers were a little bit worn, but I had taken excellent care of my phone. It was now one of those quirky, sentimental items I just couldn't part with. "And," I added defiantly, "I think it's cute. It's like one of those collectibles that could be worth money down the road."

"Okay, fine," Reena said, rolling her eyes, "Now call Amit. Let's get this over with so we can all move on."

I had lingering last-minute doubts as I prepared to dial. "Maybe I've been reading way too much into it, and he just got busy and just hadn't had a chance to call." I placed the receiver back on the phone and got off my bed, pacing as I once again went over all the possibilities of what could have happened since our five-hour lunch date. "Or maybe he lost my number."

"But he has your email."

"But he could have lost that, too!"

"Yeah, but unless he deleted your emails after reading them, he would still have a copy of your email address. And if he planned on talking to you, he most definitely would not have deleted your emails."

I was still not convinced and knew there had to be some legitimate reason for him not contacting me. "Or God forbid, something horrible could have happened in his family, some real tragedy that would have prevented him from calling me back."

Reena sighed, shaking her head. "Okay, we're never going to find out unless you call him, so call him!"

"So you *do* think I should call him?"

"No."

"But you just said—"

"I know what I just said, but I'm a firm believer in that if it's meant to be, it'll just happen. But I know you're obviously not going to be fine with letting it go. So call him!" she said, holding out the receiver.

"But what if..."

"I don't want to hear it! Call him and find out!" Reena said and began dialing the number I had scribbled on the notepad next to my bed. She held out the phone again.

I looked at it like it was a used Kleenex.

"It's too late. The phone is ringing," she said with an evil smile.

I reluctantly took the phone and cringed as I listened to each ring. The voicemail eventually kicked in, and I left a message, trying to sound very casual and nonchalant. "Hey, it's Sarai. I haven't talked to you in a few days. Hope you're doing well. Give me a call when you get the chance." Then I hung up and immediately buried my head in my pillow. "Do you think I sounded desperate?" I asked Reena. Then I involuntarily shuddered, thinking of the message I just left and all the possible things I should have said instead.

Thirty-five minutes later, my phone rang. I looked at Reena, and she looked at me. I glanced down at my phone, and then at the separate caller ID display box next to it. Yep, it was his name and number. I nodded to signal to Reena that she should pick up the extension while I picked up the main phone.

"Hello?" I answered, trying to sound playful and nonchalant.

"Hey Sarai, it's Amit."

"Heeeey, stranger! How's it going?"

"Good. And you?" His voice sounded strangely distant, almost flat as if devoid of emotion. Was he tired or had I just called at a bad time?

"Good," I said, waiting for him to jump-start the conversation. He just needed me to take the initiative.

"Cool."

"Very cool," I said, not knowing how to respond. Reena glared at me for my silly response. I shrugged back at her.

"Yeah, I saw that you had called. I was just returning your call," he said.

"Um, yeah, I was just calling. I hadn't talked to you in a while."

"Yeah, just studying for finals."

I waited for him to ask what I'd been up to, but he didn't. "Cool, um, yeah, I've been very busy, too. We're getting ready for the new school year. I had a couple of teacher in-services," I said, trying to think of something interesting to say, looking even to Reena for a suggestion. She just widened her eyes at me helplessly and shoo-ed me on with her free hand.

"Cool," he repeated again. He wasn't making this easy for me at all! He wasn't saying anything to keep the conversation going, and it left me with the feeling that I was almost bothering him.

"So what's new?" I asked. That was a question he couldn't answer with just one word or one sentence.

"Um, nothing really. Just the same old, same old," he said and was quiet again. Well, at least I was right. He did need more than one word and more than one sentence to answer my question. I waited for him to ask me something or say something more, but it was just complete silence. I felt like I was talking to a brick wall.

"Okay, well, I just wanted to say hello and see what you're up to..." My voice trailed off in one final attempt to get him to say something.

"Okay, thanks," was all he said, indicating the conversation was definitely over.

"All right, good luck with the studying."

"Thanks."

"Okay, bye."

"Bye."

I hung up the phone and stared at the receiver, not quite believing what just happened. Then I looked at Reena, who had also put down her receiver. "That was weird, don't you think?" I asked.

She just nodded, waiting for me to start the inevitable discussion and analysis. But I was curious to know what she thought.

"So what do you think that was about?" I asked, hoping she wouldn't jump immediately to an "I told you so…"

"Maybe you caught him at a bad time," she said encouragingly.

"Yeah, that might have been it," I said, but when I looked at her, she didn't seem to believe her own words. She looked at me sadly and maybe with a bit of pity.

I could guess what she was thinking, but I had to hear it from her. "Okay, just say it."

"Sarai—" she said, hesitantly. "Sarai, I don't think he's interested."

Ouch! I said to myself. But like a masochist, I couldn't seem to get enough, so I prodded her on. "What makes you think that?"

"He obviously didn't lose your number; otherwise, he would have said so, and he would've been happy that you called. He hasn't emailed you, and unless he deleted your emails, he would have had that to keep in touch with you."

When I didn't say anything, she continued, lowering her voice, perhaps to soften the blow of her next words, "And he didn't sound excited to talk to you. He didn't even make an effort to keep the conversation going."

I sighed, feeling utterly defeated. Was this never going to work out for me? "I just don't get it, Reen. If he wasn't interested, why did our lunch date last till dinner time? At this point in my life, I know when a guy is interested. Everything he did on our date indicated he was interested. He was attentive, he was talkative… and in the end, he basically admitted to being interested. He said he had a great time. *He* was the one who suggested we continue being in touch. Even *you* thought he was interested," I pointed out.

"I know, you're right, but there's a big difference in what a guy says and what he does. Actions speak louder than words. Isn't that the adage of all relationships? How many times has a guy told a girl he would call her and he didn't? Even worse, how many girls have slept with a guy, believing that he cared, only to find out that he didn't?"

Reena hit the nail on the head. So basically I had gotten the insincere brush-off, and like every girl who gets that brush-off, I was in denial even though the truth was staring me right in the face. How could I have been that stupid? Just days ago, I was on top of the mountain, and now I felt like I was standing on quicksand with my self-esteem sinking lower and lower. As much as I wanted to find excuses, I knew Reena was right. I swallowed that bitter pill of truth as if it were bile making its way down my throat.

"Sarai, I just don't want you to set yourself up for more disappointment. Bottom line is if he is interested, he'd be calling you and making plans with you."

"Okay, yeah, I got it," I said, holding my hand for her to stop. My ego could only handle so much truth. This time, rather than just feeling let down, I felt embarrassed. I wore my shame like a scarlet letter, except in my case, I had a big ole "D" for Desperate. "So what do I do now?"

"There is nothing you can do. If he's interested, he'll call you. Like I said before, if it's meant to be, it'll happen. You just have to let it go for now."

Let it go? *Let it go?* Why did I always have to be the one who had to let it go? And where had letting go gotten me? I was alone and single at twenty-nine! I would soon be eligible for the spinster adopt-a-cat club. I couldn't help but feel annoyed at her cliché advice. Of course, it was so easy for Reena to say that! *She* was getting married. *She* no longer had to worry about the rapidly diminishing pool of candidates.

Chapter 42

PERHAPS THIS WHOLE situation with Amit wouldn't have bothered me so much if my twenty-ninth birthday hadn't come on the heels of it. Reena had just left for New York that morning to visit Sanjay, so I felt even more alone. I was in no mood to celebrate another year of getting older. I spent most of the day at home lounging in my room. I received calls from old college girlfriends and even a few old high school girlfriends. Most of them were dating or married and knew that I wasn't, so after the initial pleasantries were exchanged, I got the inevitable question that is asked of every girl who is not married: "So are you talking to someone?"

Because I didn't want to sound like absolutely nothing was going on in my life and because it was still on my mind, I relayed my story of Amit. I started from the beginning when my family had unexpectedly dropped by his parents' home to our first and only date, culminating with our last phone conversation. Everyone was at a loss. They all said that they, too, were just as thrown off by our date and our last phone conversation. It didn't add up because based on our first date, they all agreed, he was clearly interested.

While I initially welcomed the sympathy, as I re-told my story over and over again, I realized how pathetic and lame I sounded. I was clinging onto something that wasn't even real. Amit had never even been a friend, much less a boyfriend. At least when I mourned Armaan, we had dated for several years. I hadn't gone on more than one date with Amit, and I was acting like he had broken up with me after a long-term relationship.

In the back of my mind, I did question whether it was Amit I mourned or what he represented to me at the time—the last available, seemingly compatible, educated Malayalee Christian guy in my orbit.

I used my self-pity like a wool blanket, allowing it to comfort and warm me, and all the while it scratched at my pride and self-esteem. For me, there was something about turning twenty-nine that was more traumatic than turning thirty. And it was probably the realization that if I hadn't met anyone yet, then there was a greater chance that I would probably still be single when I turned thirty. And by age thirty, the statistics were no longer on my side. Not only were my insurance premiums increasing, but according to the latest stats, so was the bitter probability that I had a higher chance of getting bitten by a shark or getting eaten by an alligator than finding a husband.

But as I felt sorry for myself, I realized how pitiful I was acting on the one day when I should be celebrating my life. Next year, yes, *next year*, I promised myself, would be different. I would celebrate my birthday, no matter what. Whether I was single, dating someone, or married, I would celebrate it with my friends in a big way. And it wouldn't be some lame, generic 30th birthday party. It would be somewhere really cool… maybe I could start the new decade with a trip somewhere amazing like Spain or Italy. I called the girls, and they sounded just as excited and promised to join me on my 30th birthday trip.

Chapter 43

SANJAY CAME INTO town the following weekend, and we decided to meet up at O'Hara's on Saturday night for dinner and drinks. Unbeknownst to Reena, I, along with the help of Maya and Anjuli, decided to throw them a surprise engagement party so the rest of our old college friends could meet Sanjay before the wedding. As requested, everyone showed up at least thirty minutes before Reena and Sanjay were scheduled to appear, everyone except Rakesh and Mani who were, as always, late.

When Reena and Sanjay made their appearance, we greeted them with loud applause and cheers. We had reserved two long tables in a semi-private room, and we had decorated it with balloons, streamers, and table confetti. I had enlarged a picture of them and framed it. It sat on an easel in the corner of the room and guests were able to sign the mat as a keepsake for the couple. As we took our seats next to each other, Reena whispered a "thank you" to me, but I was quick to acknowledge that Anjuli and Maya had also helped.

I was looking at the menu trying to decide on my main entrée when Reena nudged me with a surprised look. She motioned toward the front doors. Walking toward us were Rakesh and Mani with their respective dates. Mani was with a girl I had never met before, but Rakesh was walking with Tejal! They walked closely together, and his hand rested on the small of her back. I raised my eyebrows at Reena and she shrugged. Under her breath she mumbled, "I have no idea." There was that small chance Rakesh may have just given Tejal a ride and they were just coming as friends, but then again, maybe not.

It was nice to see everyone together again with the added bonus of their significant others. When was the last time all of us had been together in one room? Feeling nostalgic, I dug through my memory, and the only time I could remember was after our last final exams during our senior year. After two weeks of intense cramming, sleeplessness, and overeating, we had all crammed into two cars and drove down to Houston, where U2 was in concert at the Compaq Center. Knowing this was our last night together before we all graduated and started going our own ways, none of us were in the mood to sleep. So after the concert we picked up some Taco Bell and McDonalds and headed to Galveston Beach where we devoured our late night snack. We had laid out blankets, tarp, and whatever else we could find in the trunks of the cars. We ate, joked, laughed, threw sand at each other, and attempted to play beach volleyball in the dark. But as the first rays of sunlight cracked through the dark gray horizon, we quieted down, settling down next to each other on the sand. There was something calming about the sound of steady crashing waves. It soothed us like a lullaby, and as the sun rose and broke the horizon and spread its rays over the still, gray waters of Galveston and onto us, illuminating our faces in its golden glow, we were all gripped by the gravity of the moment. We looked at each other, and without saying a single word, we each knew we were all thinking the same thing—an era was ending. As excited and hopeful as we were about our future, the life that had bound us so close together was now splintering us into various directions. We knew our lives and our friendships were going to change dramatically, and while we had every intention to stay close, we knew that might not always be the case. Fortunately, for the most part, we had all managed to stay in touch, although not all of us were as close as we once were.

As I affectionately remembered those good ole days, I felt a strange nostalgic tugging of time pulling at my heart again, leaving me bereft and sad and wondering how time had gotten away from us so quickly. I sipped my glass of White Zinfandel, and as the warmth of the wine penetrated me, time seemed to slow down. I leaned back into my chair and enjoyed the jazz music. In moments like these, I was happy to settle into the background, like an unseen, omniscient narrator in a novel, the ever-present, ever-observant voice that just seems to be more in tune to the moment. As I observed my friends around the table, I felt like I was watching a movie in slow motion. I noticed Rakesh's arm around Tejal and how she leaned into his partial embrace. Her genuine glow of happiness, those private exchanges that seemed to convey strong sentiment… they were obviously more than just casually dating. With Sanjay's arm firmly around her waist, Reena was showing her engagement ring to Maya and Anjuli who were gushing over the two carat wonder even though they had already seen it. Maya's boyfriend, a classmate from her doctorate program, and Anjuli's husband were chatting while Mani and his date seemed to be lost in their own world. Everyone seemed too content with the obviousness of the moment to be pulled into the undercurrent that seemed to be pulling at me.

As I watched them mingle, I began to hear it again—that slow ticking of time. It was ever so subtle, ever so stealth, but it was there, lurking, continuing its steady, rhythmic chant. Somehow I seemed to be the only one to hear it. Not only did I hear it, but also my heart seemed to beat in sync with it. As I sat there watching everyone immersed in conversation, I realized that while the changes in each of us were subtle, they were still there. For the most part, thanks to genetics, adulthood had seemingly eluded most of us throughout our 20s with many of us still looking younger than we actually were. But our once youthful, unmarried faces now crinkled in the corner when we smiled and laugh lines were subtly appearing around our mouths and remaining, even when we were no longer smiling or laughing. As I glanced at each member of our group, I realized time had indeed caught up with us all. There was no mistaking it any longer—we were adults. It was still hard to believe that these polished professionals, ranging from doctors to pharmacists to engineers, were the same goofy, awkward 18 and 19 year-olds I had met during freshman orientation.

It was when Tejal lifted a glass of wine to take a sip that I finally noticed the large round diamond sparkler on her left ring finger. My gaze immediately flew to Rakesh. His eyes were already on me, as if he were waiting with bated breath for my reaction. I smiled slowly and mouthed a "congratulations." He smiled back slowly and mouthed a "thank you."

Before I could wonder if they were keeping their engagement under wraps, Rakesh tapped his wine glass with his dinner fork and stood up. "Everyone, I'd like your attention please. I have an announcement," he said, reaching for Tejal's hand. She blushed as he pulled her up to stand next to him. "Tejal and I," he began and turned to her look at her with adoration, "we are engaged." The table erupted into applause.

I smiled, but internally I was struggling to digest it all. Rakesh and Tejal engaged? When had this happened? *How* had this happened? I recalled her leading him away at Armaan's wedding, trying to save me from Rakesh's obnoxiousness. That was over two years ago! Had they been dating since then? Tejal had called me for my birthday, but she hadn't mentioned one word of Rakesh. I had no idea they were talking, much less that they were engaged.

Tejal looked genuinely happy and had the non-stop smile of a radiant bride-to-be. I glanced around the table and again noted how everyone else had a significant other while I was the only one who was alone. I had been in the minority for a while, but Reena and Rakesh had always been there to keep me company. I had never felt alone with them around, but for some reason, it was the knowledge that even Rakesh had found someone that distressed me the most. Part of me expected him to be the confirmed bachelor... or at least until I had gotten married.

The cloud of nostalgia quickly mushroomed into an atomic cloud of emotional chaos that was threatening to overwhelm me. Maybe it was the wine or the sight of everyone together that was making me overly emotional. I excused myself to go to the bathroom where I braced one hand on either side of the sink, fighting back tears. At times, that feeling of being left behind made me feel confused, lost, and helpless, but never more than that moment as I realized *all* my friends were moving forward in their lives while mine was at an absolute standstill.

I'm not sure how I did it, but I gathered my resolve and returned to the group. Determined not to ruin this night for Reena, I pasted a steadfast, unwavering smile on my face and spent the remainder of the night laughing, talking, and mingling. I made sure I had not one moment to myself and my thoughts. But the night inevitably ended, and as I drove home alone, my thoughts returned, and with them, a dark shadow fell over me again, pressing down on me, making me feel as if I couldn't breathe. For all of my resoluteness to be happy and to wear my singleness like a badge of honor, the tears of pain and hopelessness spilled down my face as I drove, further impeding my ability to drive in the rain.

Once again I tried to make sense of my life. I quickly glanced up at the dark sky, silently pleading for an answer, but again, nothing answered me but the pounding sound of rain beating on the windshield of my car.

Chapter 44

WHILE IT WAS still a difficult and emotionally challenging year, in retrospect, my twenty-ninth year was probably one of my most empowering years. As the saying goes, what doesn't kill you makes you stronger. On the personal front, nothing major or minor happened. Life just was, continuing its ever steady march onward. On the career front, however, things were falling into place better than anything I could have planned. I was attending one of our bi-annual teacher in-service meetings when the principal approached me about slowly transitioning into administration, specifically in planning the school curriculum, which is what I had specialized in for my master's degree. He was still giving me the option of teaching two classes as well. Even my parents were thrilled with me for once because this career move would result in the doubling of my salary. While the year didn't yield everything I wanted, it was still relatively a good year, and I felt very happy. Well, alright, maybe not *that* happy, but I was okay, and I hadn't been okay in a long time. I worked. I went out with my friends. School kept me busy. Friends and family kept me social. The year began with little to no expectations, and it passed along the same way.

What did surprise me was while I knew my father had been visibly disappointed when things hadn't worked out with Amit, my new-found attitude seemed to bother him even more. The line that had always divided us soon formed into a chasm of silence. He didn't want me to be okay with being single, I realized. He wanted me to be miserable, hoping that the misery alone would force me to pick someone, *anyone.*

My mom had often been my greatest ally in the past, but now she seemed more than a little horrified when she realized I no longer felt the urgent, desperate need for marriage. Ironically, my mom was the one who always seemed to put all her faith in God. She had half of India praying for my future spouse. But for all her faith, if it was really all up to God, then why was she worrying?

What my parents didn't understand was that I hadn't accepted my single status as much as I resigned myself to it like a very reluctant martyr. They just mistook my veneer of contentment for true happiness.

My father continued to nag me about marriage. There were times when I could dismiss it, but some days, his nagging grew exponentially worse. One night after dinner, he even brought up the idea of my going to India again. By then, I had reached my breaking point.

"You've got to be kidding!" I retorted as I helped my mom clear the plates from the dining room table and load the dishwasher. "I will not go to India again for an arranged marriage. Besides, why are you always forcing an arranged marriage on me when you and mom didn't even have an arranged marriage?"

My dad looked at my mom. "What nonsense is your daughter talking?"

My hands flew to my mouth as I realized what I had just said. This wasn't how I had planned to bring up what I had learned in India about my own parents' marriage, but there was no turning back now. Besides, I was furious and feeling a little spiteful regarding my dad's hypocrisy. "I'm talking about how you and mom had a love marriage, Dad!"

Sajan's and my father's eyes both widened in shock. "Love marriage?" my father asked disgustedly, as if I had just accused him of some heinous crime. "We had an arranged marriage! Merci Auntie told Lizzy Auntie about her younger sister—your mom. Then Lizzy Auntie told my parents, and my family went to your mother's home—"

"Dad," I said raising my hand to stop him. I was furious that he couldn't admit the truth to me even when I told him I knew. He had been feeding my brother and me this same fictional story for years. I was beginning to realize that on some level, he believed his own lies.

"I already know that nothing you told us of your wedding was true. Sajan," I said, taking a seat next to my younger brother at the table, "you should know that mom and dad defied mom's parents' wishes for her to marry an accountant they had selected for her, and then mom and dad traveled to New Delhi and eloped. *That* is why they only have a couple of pictures of their wedding day, and that is why both sets of our grandparents and relatives are missing from those pictures."

My father's bushy eyebrows pulled together, and his face turned beet red, which I didn't think was possible for someone with his dark complexion. "I don't know who is telling you stories, but you don't know anything! Were you there? I tell you—my parents saw your mother. They liked her and arranged—"

"Okay, Dad, if by arranged marriage, you mean, you defied mom's parents and *arranged* to marry mom without any of your family being at your wedding, then okay, you had an arranged marriage."

He shot a furtive glance to my mother whose eyes were downcast. I calmly got up from the table and walked towards my room. I closed the door just as my father, once again, slammed his closed fists against the kitchen table and thundered out, "We had an arranged marriage, I tell you!"

Chapter 45

AFTER REENA GOT engaged, she and Sanjay decided to hold off on the wedding until he had almost completed his residency. So with her wedding nineteen months away at the time of her engagement, Reena had spent the first few months basking in her engagement glow, blissfully unaware that she should have been selecting her wedding dress, selecting a reception venue, and finalizing other countless details. Then one day she was talking to one of her co-workers who had just gotten married. Apparently, wedding venues were often booked as early as a year in advance, and even after finding the perfect bridal wedding dress, it could take several months before it arrived. She called me in a panic that night. As her maid of honor, I assured her that a year was still plenty of time to plan a nice wedding and that I would help her every step of the way. Of course, little did I know what that promise would entail.

✧ ✧ ✧

THE FIRST THREE weekends of wedding dress shopping were exhausting but still fun. We had initially been overwhelmed and in awe of the variety of choices and the sheer beauty of the dresses. However, as we went from one bridal store to the next, I quickly concluded that Reena's goal was not to just find The Dress but to try on every dress within a two hundred and fifty mile radius of her home.

With still a year left to plan for her wedding, Reena was taking full advantage of the time to explore every possible option for every possible wedding day decision. Even after she found something she really liked, she wanted to see if there were additional options for her or even better prices. For the fourth weekend of dress shopping, Reena made an appointment with one of the most exclusive wedding dress boutiques in the city. They were appointment-only, and unfortunately for me, the only appointment they had available was at eight in the morning. I kept hitting the snooze button that day, so when Reena called to tell me she was on her way, I was still in bed. I raced into the bathroom to brush my teeth and after struggling to style my hair, I realized I had no option but to tie my hair in a pony tail. I was looking through my closet for something to wear when I heard the honk of Reena's horn outside. I eyed sweats lying on the foot of my bed and then at the wrinkled khakis in my hand and then at the clothes hamper overflowing with laundry that I hadn't done for the past two weeks. I closed my eyes and made a quick decision, and then changed as quickly as I could. I raced down the stairs and out the door, and basically collapsed into Reena's SUV. She greeted me with a smile and a cheery disposition, and gave me a once-over as she playfully shook her head at my t-shirt and sweats. She handed me a caramel macchiato, which I greedily sipped. I immediately winced when I scalded my tongue and rested the cup on my knee as I impatiently waited for it to cool.

Despite it being an early Saturday morning, the parking lot was already filled. As we pulled into our spot, a graceful woman in her mid-forties, dressed in a cream suit with her hair tied in an elegant chignon, unlocked the door and greeted customers as they entered the store. I self-consciously tugged at my t-shirt. I felt seriously under-dressed. I followed Reena in, but was immediately stopped.

"I'm sorry, ma'am, but we don't allow beverages and food of any sort in our boutique." I started to protest, but before I could say a word, she interjected, "I'm sorry. We make no exceptions when it comes to our dresses."

I was contemplating how rude it would be if I drank my coffee outside when, before I could even process what was happening, she boldly took the coffee from my hands and dropped it into the waste-basket at the front of the store. I winced helplessly, as my perfectly good caramel macchiato disappeared in the black plastic abyss of the trashcan.

Between the shock and the lack of caffeine in my system, I found myself too dumbfounded to speak. I turned from the perfectly coiffed woman to Reena, hoping she had a smart-ass retort for the woman. But Reena was paying no attention. Her attention was focused on the displays of designer dresses before her. She had discovered bridal heaven. I closed my eyes and prayed she would find her dress today because I wasn't sure I was up to another weekend of wedding dress shopping.

While she walked in a trance towards a couture Vera Wang dress, I shuffled myself to the nearest plush velvet chair and collapsed into it. Luckily, I didn't have to get up from that comfortable spot since the store had a personal bridal assistant who gave Reena a tour and then helped her pick dresses to try on. Before she disappeared behind a thick, maroon velvet curtain, she turned back to me with a radiant smile.

Fifteen minutes later she emerged wearing a body-hugging, strapless mermaid Vera Wang dress. The silk shantung fitted dress was stunning, but I knew she'd never buy it as it was far too sophisticated and sexy by Indian standards. I gave her a thumbs up on the dress, but reminded her that her family would never allow it. She glanced at the price tag and made a face. "Well, it doesn't matter. It's $12,580!"

She struck a few poses in front of the mirror and then laughed as she once again disappeared. My stomach rumbled, and I touched my stomach as if I could calm it. I glanced at my watch again and sighed, realizing it was going to be a very long day.

Over the next two and a half hours, Reena tried on five more dresses: two were over her budget, two looked like something out of the eighties, and one was just... *no*. Throughout this tedious show, I'd taken to flipping through the wedding magazines strewn about the seating area. I was reading an article on how to buy a wedding ring in the midst of trying to calm my belligerent stomach when Reena stepped out in a ball gown dress with a fitted lace top and a very, very poufy skirt that came with layers of tulle. The skirt had a metal hoop, but even without the hoop, the skirt was entirely too big for Reena's small frame. She looked like she was drowning in the dress.

"What do you think of this?" she said, obviously pleased with her selection. "It's like something out of Gone with the Wind," she said, coquettishly batting her eyelashes at me. By this point, her up-do had come undone and pieces of hair were sticking in various directions, including straight up. Her eyeliner had smeared, and the only part of her lipstick that remained was the red lip liner. I personally thought she looked more like she was going to a Halloween party as a Southern belle than as the bride to her own wedding.

As my stomach once again protested to the lack of food in my system, I sarcastically quipped, "Actually you look more like Scarlett O'Hara on crack."

Rather than laughing as I half-expected her to, Reena glared at me and turned on her heels to look at herself in the mirror. She smoothed down her hair and wiped off the remainder of the lipstick. She glared back at me through the mirror, turned, and marched right back into her dressing room with the bridal assistant following quickly behind her… just like a southern belle would have done. If I'd had a hat, I would have tipped it off in her direction.

I glanced at my watch. It was almost eleven. I couldn't believe it! I had expected that finding the dress would be challenging, but not as hard as she was making it. For someone who had never really given thought to her wedding, Reena ended up being one of the pickiest brides who ever walked the earth. Even when she found something she really liked, she had to see more options before making a final decision, just in case there was something better out there. Were all her decisions going to be like this? After the dresses, we had to select invitations. Then it would be the bridesmaid dresses, the flowers, the DJ, the wedding favors, the table linens, the menu… and on and on. I wasn't sure I'd survive the madness!

When Reena emerged from the dressing room in her regular clothes, I internally sighed with relief, grabbed my purse, and shot up from my chair. "So are we going to grab something to eat now?" I asked eagerly.

Reena brusquely brushed past me and bit out, "I'm not going to be able to go. I'll drop you at home."

I waited until we were in the parking lot before I grabbed her by the arm and turned her toward me. "Are you angry at me?" I couldn't believe she was annoyed! Was I not the one who had to forgo sleep and food so she could indulge herself in her narcissistic bridal fantasies? And after skipping breakfast and spending hours with her at the bridal salon, now we weren't even going to lunch?

She said nothing as she pulled away from me and unlocked the car door. We both climbed in and before she started the engine, she rested her arms on the steering wheel and took a deep breath as if trying to steady herself before talking. She opened her mouth and turned toward me, but still avoided looking at me. Then she mumbled, "Never mind."

"Okay, obviously you have something to say, so you might as well just say it!" I bit out, my own irritation rising at her selfishness. Why would she be so upset with me? Hadn't I woken up at the crack of dawn on the one day I could have slept in? Hadn't I given up breakfast and then been forced to throw away my untouched coffee so she could play dress up? Hadn't I sat there bored out of my mind while she decided to try on every fashion faux pas imaginable? What more did she want from me?

She braced both hands on the steering wheel and without looking at me, said, "I cannot believe you acted like that!"

"What are you talking about?" I asked, my own voice rising.

"I'm talking about how you acted in there. You didn't help me pick out any of my dresses or help me try them on. Then you just sat in your little chair, bored out of your mind, making it obvious how bored you felt, and you judged me like you were some fashion expert dissecting celebrities at the Oscars. I figured as my best friend, you'd want to share in my joy, which is why I invited you to tag along. Rather than share in my joy, you'd rather me share in your misery."

"I have been sharing in your joy! I've been non-stop sharing in your joy for months now! I'm so sharing in your joy that I am about to drown in all of your joy!" I said, arms flailing. I should have stopped, but I blamed my hunger and exhaustion for my frustration and my inability to censor my next few words. "What I didn't expect is for you to turn into an obsessive/compulsive, selfish, materialistic, narcissistic Bridezilla! All you've talked about for the past few months is the wedding! The wedding this, the wedding that! There's more to life than just your damn wedding! And for the past FOUR weekends I have done nothing but go from one bridal store to another with you. You've tried on some great dresses and at prices you can afford, but that wasn't good enough. So instead, you take us to a high-end boutique and you try on something that's just totally out of your budget or something that's just hideous. Just pick something already!" I felt winded after my diatribe. Even my stomach grumbles quieted, no doubt shirking from my anger.

"Well, I think three *months* of listening to my wedding planning is a hell of a lot easier than taking almost three *years* of your rantings! Poor Armaan, I miss Armaan, how could Armaan leave me, will I ever find someone like Armaan… for God's sake, move on, because he sure has!"

My face reddened, and I flinched. Reena had never slapped me, but her words were as painful as if she had. Without a word and without realizing what I was doing, I opened the car door and just walked out, slamming the door after me. I had no idea where I was going, but I knew I couldn't stay in the car without worse things coming out of my mouth.

After a few seconds, I heard the car start and pull away. There was no begging me back into the car, no following me to see if I'd be okay. Reena simply drove away.

I don't remember ever having fought with Reena. Sure, as best friends, we had occasionally irritated or snapped at each other, but we had never had a full-fledged, all-out fight, nor did I recall ever having intentionally said a word to hurt her feelings. My stomach made one last feeble gurgle. Of course, now that I could finally eat, I had completely lost my appetite.

I called my brother, and he picked me up. "What happened?" he asked. He then glanced around, "And where's Reena? I thought you came here with her?"

"Don't ask!" I said as I got into the car. During the drive home, I replayed the events of the morning, and I got angrier.

But as the drive wore on, I recalled my comments, and guilt began to slowly seep in. Every bride wants to be beautiful, and Reena, despite her tough, tomboyish demeanor, was still a girl. I couldn't blame her for wanting to try on dresses. Heck, I'd want to do the same.

I think part of me, though, was genuinely thrown off by Reena's behavior. She was always a no-nonsense, low-key type of person. If it weren't for her traditional family, she would be the type to elope or have a no-fuss beach wedding. I, on the other hand, was always the one who was over-the-top romantic.

As happy as I was for her, it still wasn't easy watching someone who never seemed to care for a wedding suddenly become overly obsessed and detailed, just like I would have been. Reena was wrong. I *was* glad to share in her joy. But I could only share so much. I was still struggling with my own life, and there were times when I felt like she totally forgot about me and my feelings. At times, it just didn't seem fair.

As all these thoughts ran through my head, I gasped. Oh my gosh! I was jealous. I, Sarai Mathai, was jealous of my best friend. Me. Someone who had always prided herself on being a loyal, unselfish friend, *especially* towards Reena. Part of me protested that I *was* happy for my friend and that I had been very supportive until today. But it was still jealousy. I felt horrible. I was a horrible friend. There was no doubting it. Because she had always downplayed the part of being a bride, I think part of me felt as if I were somehow more worthy of it. But seeing Reena the past few weeks was proof that she wanted the wedding and all its hoopla just as badly as I always had.

Either way, this was Reena's moment, and I had ruined it for her. So later that night I called but got her voicemail. I left a long, weepy apology, explaining that I really hadn't meant any of the sarcastic remarks and how hunger, fatigue, and even a little bit of jealousy had gotten the best of me.

Thirty minutes later my phone rang. "Hey," she said. Her voice lacked her usual sarcastic inflections, so I was not able to completely gauge her mood. Was she still annoyed or had she forgiven me? She had called me back so that accounted for something.

"Hey!" I said, trying to sound like my normal self. "Did you get my voicemail?"

"I did, and Sarai, it's fine. I'm sorry, too. I know I've been monopolizing all your weekends and free time. I really do appreciate you coming with me everywhere. I just want my wedding to be perfect, and I really value your opinion. You have such good taste, and you seem to know all about planning a wedding while I'm clueless."

"That's because I've been reading wedding books and magazines since college, and I've been planning a wedding in my head even before I met Armaan," I said in an attempt to lighten the situation and comfort her. "I want to be there for you, and I really am so happy for you, but lately, the wedding is all we ever talk about. You know what I'm going through. It's still hard for me."

"Yeah, I realized that after I thought about what you said."

I groaned. "Please don't take what I said to heart. I was just tired and hungry. I really don't mind going with you to places and helping you. It's just that's all we do any more."

"I know, I know. If the situation were reversed, I would have been more irritated than you were. I was never a big fan of weddings until it was time to plan mine, so I get it."

I was as uncomfortable with talking about our fight as I was with the actual fight, and I was eager to move on. "So we're cool then?" I asked.

"We're cool!" she said, her voice returning to the tone I knew so well.

Chapter 46

AND TRUE TO her word, we were cool. Reena still invited me to accompany her on her wedding planning errands, but she was more careful to balance out our time and conversations with other topics. She also brought along snacks and made sure I was well fed during all our outings.

As summer approached, I was consumed with thoughts of where the girls and I should go to celebrate my thirtieth birthday. It was fast approaching, and so far no plans had been made. Not one of them had brought it up, and I worried that it wouldn't occur to them until it was too late to plan anything. While I was not the type to say, "Hey guys, my birthday is coming up, let's do something... hint, hint," I was beginning to realize that if I didn't plan it myself, nothing would ever happen, especially since recently everyone was so busy and preoccupied with their own lives.

After giving it considerable thought, I narrowed it down to two options. One was to do a comprehensive tour of Italy. Italy would definitely be an amazing way to commemorate the beginning of a new phase in my life. After all, it was the birthplace of the Renaissance—a time of artistic and intellectual rebirth. Perhaps, I, too, would experience my own renaissance while I was there. Yes, the more I thought of it, it seemed very fitting that I have my own "rebirth" in Italy.

The second option was to go sight-seeing across the most popular places in Europe, including Italy, France, and Spain. How cool would it be to see all those countries in one trip! But because we only had a week's time, that meant we'd be limited to visiting only a few of the cities in each country.

I called a few travel agents and did some research to get an idea of the costs as well as a basic itinerary so I could present it to the girls at our next get-together.

We all met up at Pappadeaux a few days later, and after we ordered our drinks, I handed each of them a manila folder with a preliminary budget and itinerary as well as various vacation package options.

"What's this?" asked Maya.

"Now you guys remember the pact we made last year on my birthday, right?"

The girls glanced at each other and then back at me, shaking their heads.

"Come on, guys, you remember. Reena was out of town, neither of you could celebrate with me, so we didn't do anything. Then to make matters worse, things totally fell apart with Amit right around that time. *And* we had promised that this year we would do something really cool for my thirtieth—like going on a European trip."

The girls exchanged looks again and this time with a more worried expression. "Anyways, so I've done all the research, and all we need to do is come to a consensus about where we want to go and what our budget should be."

The girls opened their folders, but without even looking at it, Anjuli glanced nervously at the other girls before speaking. "Um, Sarai, I don't think I can go on a trip like that without my husband."

I gave her a blank stare, not completely understanding what she was getting at. Wasn't she the one who was always telling us how cool and open-minded he was for a guy raised in India? And while she felt guilty about it, wasn't he the one always pushing her to continue her girls' night out with us?

She continued, "Meeting up with you guys for dinner or a night on the town is one thing, but I don't think he would be okay with me taking a week-long trip overseas..."

I looked at Maya, and the apology was already in her eyes. Her folder was open, but she had barely glanced at its contents. "I have summer classes this year, so there's no way I can make it. I *have* to complete my thesis by the fall and defend it so I can graduate in December." She reached out to touch my hand, and said, "I'd much prefer to go on this trip with you though."

I turned to Reena, my last hope. Her eyes were on the budget I had outlined. "Three thousand dollars?" she asked as she glanced down the list of expenses I listed. "And that doesn't include food and spending money."

"Well, we are talking about going overseas," I reminded her. "We can eat on a budget and, of course, the spending money is totally dependent on how much you want to spend."

Reena looked at me, holding the budget sheet in her hand and shaking her head. "Sarai, I can't afford this right now with the wedding. My dad just told me that I had to help cover the expenses of some of his family flying in from India. I would love to go to celebrate with you, but there's no way right now. I'm working over-time as it is to cover everything."

"Oh. Okay. No worries," I said as the smile disappeared from my face. I gathered up the folders, careful to keep my eyes averted as I unsuccessfully tried to hide my disappointment. "It's just a birthday. We can do something else..." My feelings were hurt, but I shouldn't have been surprised. I was beginning to see a glimpse of my future. Everyone had their own lives now, and I couldn't depend on my girlfriends like I did when we were in college and all still single. I was on my own. Besides, who was I kidding—Europe for my thirtieth? It now seemed silly to even think that had been a remote possibility.

"Can we do something more local?" suggested Anjuli.

"Like what?" I asked, trying to keep my voice as monotone as possible to hide my irritation. We were always doing something local.

"Like going out for dinner—"

I narrowed my eyes at her. "Like what we're doing tonight?" I asked. Surely, she had to be kidding. I did not want my thirtieth birthday to feel like one of our regular monthly get-togethers.

"No, no, it would be much more special," she declared.

"Really? How?" I asked, putting her on the spot. I knew I was being a little difficult, but I couldn't help it. It was my thirtieth birthday, and I could already see that I was going to be alone again. At the moment, I felt entitled to be a little difficult.

"We could go to one of those fancy downtown gourmet restaurants."

Pappadeaux wasn't the crème de la crème of all restaurants, but it was definitely one of the nicer restaurants in town, and it wasn't completely overpriced.

"Don't get me wrong. I love a good meal as much as the next person, but that's not what I was waiting all year, *all my life*, to do for my thirtieth."

As I drove home that night, I was irritated that they had completely forgotten last year's pact or that when they had made the pact, they had taken it very lightly and had no intention of honoring it.

I had a flashback to the year before and how I basically just sat in my room, talking about Amit as I tried to make sense out of the whole situation. At the mere memory of last year, I shook my head vehemently, refusing to celebrate my thirtieth like that. I had vowed to myself last year that I would celebrate no matter what, and I intended to do that one way or another, even if it meant celebrating alone.

Maybe Anjuli was right, and I could still plan something local. I still didn't want to just go out for dinner, and I wasn't necessarily in the mood for a party either. Even if I wanted a party, I realized with dismay, I would probably have to throw it for myself anyway.

I couldn't go to Europe alone, could I? As soon as I asked myself the question, I realized how silly it sounded. Besides going to India, I had never taken any trip by myself, especially to another country or another continent. I was too big of a chicken to undertake a trip like that alone. So then maybe I could plan a domestic trip for the weekend so the girls could join me, maybe like New York. Although it was domestic, there was still so much to do and see. The only time I had visited New York before was with my family, and all we did was visit the typical landmarks like the Empire State Building, the Statue of Liberty, and Ellis Island. The rest of our time was spent within the confines of the four walls of my uncle's home. So if the girls were game, we could catch a Broadway show in Times Square, bargain shop in Chinatown, upscale shop in Soho, grab coffee in Greenwich Village, and more. The more I thought about it, the more I felt like New York could be a nice alternative since Europe was no longer an option. I guess I would just have to settle for my "renaissance" experience in Little Italy… or in one of the countless exhibits in The Guggenheim or The Met.

Chapter 47

L ATER THAT WEEK, I went to the mall and was shopping at Macy's when I ran into Dee. Although we had chit-chatted briefly in passing, we hadn't really had the chance to talk since I had run into her at Wal-Mart right before my trip to India. Working out of the LA office, she had been out of town most of the year and used her weekends to fly back and forth. We were talking about our summer plans when she told me about her next trip.

"Rome?" I repeated with envy. "You're always going to the most amazing places for work!"

"For work?" she asked, adamantly shaking her head. "No, Rome is definitely not for work. I'm going on vacation. Working for an airline has its perks. I get two free vouchers every year to go anywhere I want. A few months ago I went to Egypt, and now I thought a nice Italian holiday in early July would be nice."

"I am so jealous. I would kill to travel the way you do. I was planning on going to Italy for my big 3-0 until the other day."

"Really? You were planning on going to Italy this summer?" she asked curiously. "So what happened the other day?"

I first told her about last year's pitiful birthday and the pact with my friends. Then I told her about all the research I had done and how I had put together a folder of information, complete with possible itineraries and budgets and how they, one by one, had declined.

"Why?" she asked. "Who would turn down a trip to Europe, especially Italy?"

"Spouses, school, and tight budgets seemed to be the dominant excuses."

"So now *none* of your friends are going?"

"Nope, not to Italy, at least. So I came up with a plan to do something more domestic, like New York, but I haven't spoken to them about it yet," I said.

"So when is your birthday?" she asked as if mulling something over in her head.

"August 10."

"August, hmm… yeah, I could probably postpone my trip until then."

"Excuse me?" I wasn't quite sure what she was getting at. She wanted to come with us to New York?

"Well, you still want to go to Italy for your thirtieth, right?" she asked.

"Yeah…" I said hesitantly.

"Then come with me! I can change my reservations. I was planning on going to Italy in July, but I could postpone it for the following month—"

"What?! Are you serious?!" Was she serious? Oh my gosh, please be serious. Oh, God, *pleeeease* let her be serious. Despite my excitement, I didn't want to act entirely selfish. "I couldn't ask you to do that. I'm sure you've already made plans and booked your hotel room."

"Really, it's fine!" she said, laughing at my shocked expression. "Otherwise, I'll be traveling alone, too! My sister usually accompanies me on my trips, but now that she's pregnant, I'm on my own. Besides, it would be fun! Consider it a birthday present from me! And I could get you discount fares as my flying companion!"

"REALLY?! You're serious?!" I asked, even more dumbstruck. Was this really happening? This was like a dream. I was so sure I had to be dreaming this! These types of things didn't happen, did they? I couldn't have planned this better myself. Italy! I was going to Italy!

As much as I would be grateful to see Rome, for someone untraveled like me, it would be a tragedy to be so close to other famous Italian cities and never see them for myself. It wouldn't hurt to ask. "Would you consider adding Venice to our itinerary?"

"I've never been to Venice either." Her head tilted to the side, and she once again started mulling. "Venice would be nice, and since we're definitely going to Rome, we might as well add Florence!"

"*Really?*" I squealed and hugged her.

"Really!"

I drove home in a hypnotic state, unable to believe I might be going to Europe after all! That night, I felt the way I used to as a kid, when I would start counting the days down for my birthday or for Christmas. For the first time in a long time, I began to feel that maybe God hadn't completely forgotten about me.

Chapter 48

SINCE DEE WAS the more seasoned traveler, she made all the travel arrangements. After discussing various itineraries, we opted to join a tour group to maximize the number of places we would be visiting. Plus, it would be easier as they would be coordinating all the travel between the cities, the tours, all the accommodations, and even some of the meals.

For the next two months, I floated on air. I hadn't been this excited in years! June and July passed surprisingly quickly, and a few days before my trip, Reena came over to my house to hang out with me as I packed. "I am going to Italy!" I said, looking at my reflection as I tried on various outfits for the trip. I reveled in the fact that I would not be spending my birthday as I feared, locked in my room, alone, pitying myself, retelling my pathetic life to friends who would be calling me that day. Nor would I be at some lame dinner or at a cliché party that I would probably have to throw for myself. Instead, I would be spending my birthday exactly as I dreamed—touring beautiful museums and cathedrals and nibbling on fine Italian pasta, followed by devouring authentic tiramisu by the slice!

I turned to Reena, who was sitting on my bed, arms crossed, in a glum mood. "I am going to ITALY!"

She glared at me. "I know, I know. Quit rubbing it in or I'll... *I'll...*"

"You'll what?" I challenged.

"I'll..." she looked around the room, desperately trying to think of something to threaten me with. Then she looked at me, a smile breaking across her face.

I cocked my eyebrow at her.

"I'll drag you to another weekend of trying on wedding dresses!" Reena exclaimed.

Oh, she was good. "But you've already picked your dress!" I reminded her.

She paused momentarily. "But the bridal store won't know that!" She narrowed her eyes back at me, waiting for my retort.

I clenched my jaw, about to admit defeat, and then I slowly smiled. "I would just tell them that you're a crazed, single woman who is obsessed with wedding dresses and weddings and loves to try on dresses just for the heck of it even though you don't have a boyfriend in sight, much less a fiancé!"

"You wouldn't..."

"Wouldn't I?" I asked, crossing my arms across my chest.

"Fine! I give up!" she said, throwing up her arms in defeat. Her face turned from a mock frown to a wistful smile. "Now what am I going to do without you for almost two weeks?"

"I don't know, but I'm going to Italy!" I said with my arms raised in victory.

"I'm so jealous! I would love to be able to go!" Reena said as she curled out her lower lip in a pout.

"Well, you can still change your mind and join us!" I said in a light sing-song voice as I folded more clothes and placed them in my suitcase.

"Yeah, but then how am I going to pay for my roses? Do you know just because I'm getting married in February, I have to pay a premium price because they are not in season and because it's close enough to Valentine's Day when prices are the most expensive? Whoever heard of such a thing? Don't they have greenhouses for that kind of thing? It's not like they're going into the fields to pick them! Roses have to be one of the most popular flowers. They should have them ready to be plucked by the millions all year long."

"Well, have you thought about going with a flower that is in season then?"

"It's my wedding! I have to use roses!"

"Well, in times like this you have to look at the bright side then!" I said somberly, placing a comforting hand on her shoulder.

"And that would be?" she asked, her face upturned towards me as she awaited my words of encouragement.

"I don't know, but I'm going to ITALY!"

Reena took the sweater she was attempting to fold, rolled it into a ball, and threw it at me.

Chapter 49

TWO DAYS LATER Reena dropped Dee and me off at the airport. We took a connecting flight to New York and then a direct flight from there to Rome. After arriving at the airport in Rome, Dee and I caught an express train into the city. We arrived at our hotel and checked in. In our room was a welcome basket and note from our tour guide, letting us know that the official "meet and greet" for our tour group would be at 7:30 that evening in one of the banquet rooms in the lobby restaurant. I glanced at my watch. It was only 10:30am, so Dee and I decided to spend the rest of the day on our own, exploring the city. We procured a subway map from the front desk. The subway system was surprisingly easy to follow with an A (Red) line and B (Blue) line that crossed each other at the Termini railway stop. We caught the B line, which took us straight to the Coliseum.

As soon as I got off the subway, I rushed up the stairwell onto the sidewalk next to the street, and I twirled around, trying to take it all in. I was in ITALY! I was actually here! Then just as suddenly, I stopped in mid-twirl and my mouth fell open. Right across the street, I encountered the Coliseum. I say "encountered" because it was right there in the open, not shrouded in some corridor or corner of a museum, but right there where it has been for centuries. I blinked several times, questioning the veracity of what I was seeing. With the sunlight seeping through its hollow windows, illuminating them, I felt as if I were looking at a hologram. I closed my mouth, swallowing my astonishment as I once again digested the reality of being in Italy. At first glance, the exterior of the structure seemed untouched, but as I made my way around it, I could visibly see the ravages of time and Mother Nature. I was so caught up in its significance, I had to remind myself not to confuse it with beauty, that it was more infamous than famous, and that it was the site of brutality for the sake of sport. But its historical significance was undeniable—I was walking where gladiators, emperors, and noblemen had walked centuries ago.

We waited in line for a tour so we could see the interior. We both purchased the recorded headset guided tour that provided more of the history. As we walked around, the deterioration was more evident. Eroded, jagged stone stood in the place where senators and spectators once sat, and supporting metal beams were being used internally to keep things intact. A wooden walkway had been suspended over the former arena floor.

After our self-guided tour, we walked a few blocks to grab lunch at a local eatery. As we walked, I kept turning back, unable to believe this was the same Coliseum I had seen in pictures for as long as I could remember. It would definitely take a few days for it to sink in that I was actually here.

We took the subway again and spent part of the day exploring the Piazza di Spagna also known as the Spanish Steps. We walked down the steps and through the streets to the nearby exclusive boutiques where leather shoes cost just as much, if not more, than the full-priced designer shoes at Macy's and Nordstrom's. After more than an hour of walking and realizing we wouldn't be getting any bargain shopping deals, Dee suggested we take a tour of the catacombs on our own since that excursion was not included in our tour. We still had a couple of hours before we were due back at the hotel, so I agreed.

We visited the Catacombs of Domitilla, which had underground burial caves and corridors spread over about ten and a half miles. They were not only the oldest of Rome's underground caves, but the only ones that still retained the bones of the deceased. We descended into the catacombs through a subterranean basilica. Most of the burial sites were dug into the wall, right into the stone, in rectangular shapes, and, to my relief, all the ones I saw were empty. As we were guided through the narrow, dimly lit labyrinth, I continuously calmed myself by glancing at Dee who didn't seem the least bit phased how dark, creepy, or claustrophobic the subterranean tour felt.

Once we were back on the surface, I closed my eyes, breathed in the fresh air, and stretched, extending my hands without fear of touching anything that I shouldn't be touching. "Sarai!" Dee grabbed my extended hand and pulled me close to her.

"What's wrong?" I asked, suddenly wide-eyed and worried.

"That's an Indian boy!" she exclaimed.

"Huh?" I asked, thoroughly confused. I was expecting a more dramatic answer like she had spotted a fire or a spider was hovering too close to me. Somehow her urgency made me believe that there had to be more to it than just an Indian boy who happened to be standing in the vicinity. I followed the direction she pointed, and through the cypress trees, I recognized the familiar drape of a sari. And next to her stood one young Indian female and three Indian males, one of them was clearly her husband while the others towered above her.

"Oh, yeah, you're right." It just looked like a family traveling together and enjoying the scenic beauty of Rome. I still failed to see what her point was.

"We should go up to them and introduce ourselves!" she said eagerly. I paused, waiting for her to say she was kidding, but she didn't. She seemed eager, excited, and very, very serious. I knew where her mind was headed.

"Um, that's okay, Dee, let's not."

"Why not? You're always talking about meeting a nice, Indian boy. Now here's your chance."

"First of all, how do we know he's a *nice* Indian boy? Second, what am I supposed to say, Dee? 'Hi, I'm Sarai, and this is my friend Diandra, and we couldn't help but notice you had a son of marrying age.'"

Dee bit her lower lip and pondered what I said. "You have a point. That does come across as a bit desperate. Well, you don't have to say anything. I could though," she offered, sincerely trying to be helpful.

One minute I was thankful that she was so caring, and the next minute I was mortified as she winked at me and then began walking towards the family. I froze, temporarily in denial of what she was going to do. Finally, I found my voice, "Dee, pleeeeeeease, don't," I pleaded, calling after her, but it was too late.

My first instinct was to hide. I could see the guy she had in mind for me was tall and broad shouldered. I caught a glimpse of his profile and saw that in some ways, he did have some of the typical features of most Malayalee men I knew—thick, wavy hair, dark, deep-set eyes, a slightly round face that still seemed to retain some of the soft plumpness of youth. Although I had to admit, with the goatee he was sporting, he had a more edgy, modern look that I found appealing. I wasn't necessarily interested in this guy, but I momentarily entertained the thought of how romantic it would be to return to the US and introduce my family and friends to a Malayalee man I had met in the catacombs of Rome. Yes, it would be a story to top all others. A story for the books. My inner optimist said, "How romantic," while my inner pessimist sarcastically countered with, "Yeah, like that is gonna happen."

I watched as Dee chatted with the mother and father as the two sons and daughter surrounded her and listened in. She pointed to me occasionally, and the entire family turned to me and then smiled and waved. I made a concerted effort to avoid looking at the older son while I waved in response. I prayed Dee was being as subtle as possible and not saying anything that would warrant immediate murder and/or suicide. Our bus arrived, and as we boarded, Dee continued to chat with the mother and younger brother. There was standing room only in the bus, and I remained towards the front and looked out the window, taking in the scenic drive in an attempt to numb the embarrassment I felt as I listened to Dee converse with the younger brother. She transitioned from chit-chat to not-so-subtle inquiries about his older brother and his marital status and availability. I was sure my cheeks were burning red even though I did my best to tune her out.

As I stood facing the window, I glanced to the back of the bus. On the very last row stood the handsome Indian guy Dee was working so hard to set me up with. He stood facing forward and was looking straight at me, his eyes dark and unreadable, and his expression seriously intense. I smiled stiffly and then focused my attention back to the scene outside my window. I doubted he could hear Dee talking to his younger brother, but the paranoid side of me still worried that somehow he knew what Dee was up to.

I could partially see Dee through the reflection of the glass window and was doing my best to ignore her conversation, but I then heard her choking out the words, "Twenty-two? Your brother is only twenty-two?" In the reflection, I saw her head whip towards me, looking to see if I heard, but I pretended to act like I didn't. While I hadn't necessarily expected things to go anywhere, I had to admit that I, too, was surprised at his age. He looked to be no younger than twenty-eight. At twenty-two, he was way too young for me, and to my relief, Dee also arrived at that same conclusion and finally let the matter drop.

Two stops later, he and his family disembarked. I glanced at the back of the bus and just before his head disappeared beneath the rail, he glanced at me, his eyes dark and unreadable. I smiled slightly to myself, partly amused and partly embarrassed by the failed setup although I highly doubted he had overheard Dee's conversation. Glancing out the window, I noticed he stood outside facing the bus, scanning it until he found my specific window and then continued with his unflinching, unreadable stare. Now that I knew his age, I found the stare more curious than unnerving. Just another ship passing through the night, I thought as I internally sighed to myself.

As the bus heaved around the corner, I tightened my grip on the overhead hand latch. I turned to glare at Dee. She smiled at me sheepishly and shrugged her shoulders as if to say, "Well, at least I tried." A few more passengers got off at the next stop, and I was able to settle into an empty seat. I assured myself that despite the embarrassment, I, at least, had an interesting story to take home with me. But as the bus took us back to our hotel, it was the image of his intense, scrutinizing stare that still lingered.

Chapter 50

B Y THE TIME we reached our hotel again, we only had an hour to freshen up before meeting the rest of the tour group. Dee and I rushed to get ready. Dee settled on a pink sweater tank with a matching cardigan and beige slacks while I wore my dressy dark-rinse jeans and paired it with a sheer beige top with ruffled edging and a neutral tank underneath. We made our way down to the lobby, then to the hotel restaurant, where we were led to a private meeting room that had been set up with chafing dishes and a wine/champagne bar. We were greeted by our tour guide, Portia, a thirty-something, petite brunette with spunky, short hair and an even spunkier personality. The tour group consisted of thirty other people, all of whom were couples, with the exception of one family of four with two teenage daughters. To my surprise, Dee and I were the only single women there. The other two women in the group, I quickly ascertained, were a couple them-selves, but then I wondered if anyone thought that of Dee and me. After dinner and some mingling, Portia went over our coming week's itinerary and the "house rules" and then encouraged us to get to know our "family" for the next week.

Everyone seemed very friendly and after mingling briefly with most everyone there, I found myself drawn to one particular couple, the Harrisons. They were in their early sixties, celebrating their thirty-fifth wedding anniversary. Mrs. Harrison had battled cancer just over a year before and was in remission. Apparently, this trip was something they had dreamed of doing when they were just newlyweds. They had been college sweethearts but were never able to have children. As Mr. Harrison told the story of how he almost lost his wife to cancer, his eyes became misty and his left hand shakily clasped hers. He had donated his own bone marrow to save her life. She intertwined her arm with his and affectionately gave him a side squeeze. As I watched them, I couldn't help but feel as if I were seeing love in one of its purest forms. What encouraged me even more was despite their age and despite how long they had been together, the Harrisons seemed more madly in love than some of the newlywed couples on our tour.

The next day we explored the Roman Forum, the Pantheon, and the Trevi Fountains. I recognized many of the historic sites from the Renaissance Art History class I had taken during my junior year in college. As I thought about it, I realized I probably still had the textbook somewhere on my bookshelf and made a mental note to look for it once I got home.

By that evening, the novelty of being in Italy had begun to wear off. I no longer had the phrase "I can't believe I'm in Italy," ringing in my head like an obsessive tune. I was still happy and excited about being on the trip, but somehow, maybe due to my encroaching birthday, the old thoughts and worries re-emerged.

Would it be shocking or even too pathetic to admit that in one of the most historical, most romantic, most beautiful countries in the world, I thought of Armaan? What was it about Italy that seemed to bring to the surface all the longings and dreams that I had worked so hard to suppress? With every historic spot we visited, all I could think of was how amazing this experience would be if I could share it with someone special. Italy just beckoned to be explored and experienced in the company of a beloved.

But as much as I longed for Armaan, I finally began to realize that it was not the Armaan whom I had once dated that I now craved. Somehow, without really knowing when, he had morphed from being my former boyfriend to a symbol of someone who was more of an idea, a dream. It was not Armaan, my boyfriend, but Armaan, the larger than life, perfect Bollywood hero. Like when I first saw him, I once again reduced him to an ideal that I had erected in my head, except now he had evolved: he was still single, a Christian, and someone my parents would happily approve of. And he was out there, still waiting for me to run into him.

At dinner that night, with the exception of Dee, the two teenage girls, and me, everyone was on the dance floor. As I sipped my port wine, I glanced at Dee, who was smiling as she watched everyone dance. How did she do it, I wondered? For as long as I had known Dee, she had been single. Had she ever seriously dated anyone? Was there some long-distance relationship or just some long-lost love that was holding her back from moving forward with someone else?

As I observed her, I couldn't help but envy her. She didn't have that same forlorn expression that had been etched on my face for the past few years. She just seemed content. I had moments of contentment, but I had to admit that sometimes it was a daily struggle. Although I was celebrating being thirty in Italy, I didn't desire marriage any less than before. When I was able to stay busy and not think about it, it seemed much easier. But here in Italy, as in India, I had plenty of time to reflect on my life.

"So how do you do it?" I asked.

"How do I do what?"

"How do you have such peace about not being married?"

She gave my question some thought before answering, "I have peace because there is nothing I can do about it. If all I wanted was marriage, I could easily get married. But being married isn't the end goal—it's more about being with that right person. I should know…"

"What do you mean?" I asked.

"I mean that I should know because I was married before, Sarai. I was married for an entire two months, and then I filed to have my marriage annulled."

My mouth fell open. When I saw her look away in embarrassment, I caught myself, but it was too late. It really wasn't that big of a deal that she had been married. It was more that I just never knew.

"Yep, it's not something I am very proud of, which is why most people don't know that about me. But I didn't get out of the marriage because I was bored or didn't love him. I would have probably put up with a lot of things, but he was abusive, very abusive." As Dee spoke, her voice grew quieter, and she looked away into the distance. I knew she was reliving those days in her mind. "The hitting started on my wedding night. By the fourth week, he had hit me so hard at one point, I went unconscious."

I gasped unintentionally, just before my hand flew to cover my mouth.

"Yeah, exactly," she said still not looking at me. "When I think back on it, it seems like a different life, like someone else's life." She paused and shook her head, "It sounds shocking even to me."

I looked at her profile. There was a pronounced femininity to Dee, but there also seemed to be a strength to her that I had noticed from the first time we met. I had no idea she had been through so much. She just always seemed so put together that I couldn't even imagine her being in that type of vulnerable situation.

"So," she continued. "I had a choice to make—stay married or stay alive. I would have left him immediately because I don't believe a man should ever touch a woman like that. But I kept thinking of my family and how disappointed and especially how embarrassed they would be. But finally I couldn't take it anymore, and I left."

Her eyes focused back on me. She blinked several times and then smiled wryly, almost fatigued. Wherever she had gone in her mind, she was back now. "After that, life hasn't seemed so bad."

"I'm so sorry, Dee. I had no idea," I said as I reached out for her hand at some attempt at sympathy.

She looked down at my hand as it covered hers and then back up at me, her eyes filled not with sadness but hope. "It was then that I learned that happiness can be a choice and not to always let it be a reaction."

"When did you become so wise?" I asked, amazed that the experience had not left her embittered but still somehow hopeful, if not about love, then at least about life.

"When I realized life wasn't perfect, and it doesn't always go the way you plan and wish it to. But that life could still be amazing. It was up to me. I could cry about what happened or didn't happen to me. Or

I could forge on ahead. As cliché as it sounds, it really is about looking on the brighter side of life."

She shrugged her shoulders in that nonchalant, elegant way of hers before continuing, "But now I am living my life to its fullest. I have a life that affords me the money and freedom to travel, and I'm happy. It's not the life I may have dreamed for myself when I was seven years old and reading fairy tales with prince charming and happily-ever-after endings, but it's still amazing. I get to do what other people can only dream of, and I'm grateful."

"I want to feel that way, but how?" I asked.

She reached out for my hand and gave it an encouraging squeeze. "I think I realized everyone has a different path and a different story, and I quit comparing my life to others and just lived mine."

"But don't you ever feel like you've been left behind?" I asked.

She grimaced before continuing. "Actually when I'm around friends with their babies and families, yeah, I do. The irony is they're always telling me how envious they are of the life I lead. They love their kids, but they never have time for themselves anymore. They miss getting a full night of sleep. They would love to travel the way I do. They miss the days when they could do whatever they wanted, whenever they wanted. And here, I have more free time than I know what to do with. I think it's a case of the grass is greener on the other side."

Was perfect happiness an illusion for all of us then? We all seem to spend most of our lives trying to attain it in one form or another, whether it was through another person, money, or personal success. Sometimes the more we chase it, the more it alludes us, like a mirage in the desert.

Chapter 51

THE NEXT DAY was spent touring Vatican City, which included the Sistine Chapel, St. Peter's Square and Basilica, and the Vatican museums. We arrived there at 8 am, but we still had to stand in a long line of eager tourists. When we finally entered the chapel, I was not disappointed. All the Bible stories I had been told as a child were so richly detailed in the wall frescoes by all the Renaissance greats from Perugino, Botticelli, and Rosselli and in each frame of Michelangelo's ceiling frescoes. When I realized some of the possible physical challenges Michelangelo faced in painting the ceiling, my awe increased exponentially.

As Portia was explaining the political climate during the building of the Sistine Chapel, a door opened from the side wall, and an archbishop in all his ecclesiastical glory walked through, nodding to us quickly as he went about his business. The door remained open for only seconds, but I quickly glanced in, curious to see a glimpse of the inner sanctum of the papal offices.

We left the Sistine Chapel through a side exit and were led to a stairwell that eventually led to the front of St. Peter's Basilica. As beautiful as the Sistine Chapel was, nothing prepared me for St. Peter's Basilica. Its sheer enormity was a testament of its grandeur. As I stood there waiting in the queue to enter the front of the church, I had to dip my head back to take it all in. My camera was set on wide-screen mode, but even then, I was still not able to capture the entire front façade of the church in a single frame.

The inside of St. Peter's was no less awe-inspiring. As I entered, I followed the right aisle, which was immediately to the right of the entrance and ended up in front of Michelangelo's *Pietà*, the sculpture of Mary, the mother of Jesus, cradling Jesus in her lap after His crucifixion. I initially stood there like all the other tourists, admiring yet another one of Michelangelo's great works. But as I stood there, I soon became transfixed, and for the first time, my mind was not on the artistic significance of the sculpture but the actual portrayal of the two figures. Whenever I thought of Jesus, it was in the form of His divinity. But now seeing him like this, so vulnerable, so in pain, I was confronted with his humanity.

For the past few years, I had pushed God to the back recesses of my mind. I wouldn't say I forgot Him as much as I felt He had forgotten me. But as I stood in front of the *Pieta*, all my questions and doubts faded, and I was reminded that God in the form of Jesus not only cared for me, but He had paid the ultimate price—His life for mine. In His human form, he, too, had felt pain, physical and emotional. Like us, He, too, had struggled. Like us, He had an earthly mother who grieved for Him—a mother who no doubt did not fully comprehend the purpose of His suffering and who could have understandably questioned the "why" of it all. Yet He went through all of that for me... for all of *us*.

We were instructed to move around St. Peter's quietly as Mass would be held in the next half hour. Although I was raised in a Protestant church, there was something about the formality of a Catholic mass that always seemed to bring grandeur to the faith. As I approached the area around the altar where everyone stood, I wondered if this was what heaven would be like with its ornate, gold gilding and hallowed halls that belied centuries of pomp and circumstance. The priest with his ornate robes led the litany, and the choir reminded me of a host of angels singing. At first, I was just an observer, but soon the litany seemed to echo not only in the hall, but I almost heard it from within. Ever so slowly, it penetrated the barricade I had built around my heart. For so long, I had felt abandoned by God, wondering at times if He cared, and at desperate times, whether He even existed. But at that moment, for the first time in a long, long time, I felt something larger and more meaningful... something, some*one* beyond me. God had been silent for so long in my life that at that moment I decided that if God were going to speak to me, this would be it. Right here in one of the oldest, most hallowed, most revered churches of all time. So while I waited for God's voice, I listened to the angelic singing of the choir, losing myself in the beauty and rhythm of the music, carrying me off like the waves of an ocean. And then I began to feel it, the undeniable presence of grandeur and majesty.

Feeling so small against the physical manifestation of my faith, I once again realized that there was something beyond me and my pain. And even if my own life were in disarray, there was a comfort in knowing God was still God. I waited breathlessly for the spiritual revelation that I knew I was about to encounter. I closed my eyes and waited. I felt that tingling feeling in my hands as I waited with suspended breath, and soon it traveled through me like the impending waves of an orgasm that promised to overtake and overwhelm me. I instinctively reached for it, but like the unpredictable tide of the ocean, it waned suddenly and retreated, taking with it those waves of spiritual enlightenment and revelation that I urgently yearned for. I opened unfulfilled eyes only to realize mass had ended, and everyone around me was leaving. I remained where I stood, closing my eyes again, eager to recapture and fulfill that moment. But the moment had passed, and as I stood there alone, my eyes closed in front of the altar, all I could hear was the empty echo of retreating footsteps against the marble floor.

Chapter 52

AFTER WE LEFT Rome, we made our way to Verona and stopped at the Leaning Tower of Pisa. I, along with countless other tourists, posed with arms thrust forward, giving the optical illusion that yes, in my non-super-human, tourist garb, I could somehow hope to straighten the leaning tower of Pisa. Along with a teacup in the shape of the leaning tower, I also purchased a few miniature Leaning Tower replicas to give as gifts.

We then followed up the trail to Verona, where I tried to imagine whether the Verona of today was anything like the Verona that inspired the setting for Shakespeare's Romeo and Juliet. I was not disappointed. Thanks to its uneven, cobblestone streets and small vintage shops, it certainly permeated the quaint, small village-like atmosphere I had imagined in the play. As a tribute to Shakespeare's play, a statue of Juliet was erected in a courtyard facing a small balcony. As I watched, tourists not only posed with Juliet, but placed their hand on her exposed right breast, which was rumored to bring good luck. Many of the shops displayed beautifully intricate masquerade masks, but I held back on making any purchases as I was advised that Venice was actually the best place to buy them.

✧ ✧ ✧

WE ARRIVED IN Venice by evening and checked into our hotel. Early the next day our tour group went to St. Mark's Square where Portia gave us a tour of St. Mark's Basilica and the Doge's Palace. It was only when we were walking through the Doge's Palace that I suddenly remembered that it was my dreaded thirtieth birthday! Funny how I had been thinking non-stop about turning thirty for months, yet on the actual day, I forgot it, at least initially.

I still had mixed feelings about it though. Even if this had not been a desired birthday, it was still my birthday and a significant one at that. I looked around, and there was really no one with whom I could share my important news. I wasn't the type to tell a group of relative strangers that today was my birthday because I felt like I was obligating them to wish me a "happy birthday" out of courtesy. Not to mention, it seemed childish. I wondered if Dee remembered, but she hadn't said anything that morning, so she had probably forgotten, which was just as well. I was in Italy, I chastised myself. That was a small tradeoff for not receiving any birthday wishes from anyone.

Just before lunch, Portia announced we had the option of joining her on a gondola ride. Since everyone in our group was getting in line for the ride, I, too, stood in line, but just as it was my turn to step onto the gondola, I changed my mind and stepped out of line.

"You are coming?" asked the gondolier, arm already outstretched, ready to assist me.

I had always imagined riding in a gondola down the canals of Venice all the while being romantically serenaded in the moonlight by an amour. But there was no amour and there was no moonlight. Instead, it was a group of fellow tourists, most of whom I barely knew. Somehow by getting in that gondola, I felt as if I were giving up on a dream. A gondola ride, especially your first, was for lovers, not friends, and especially not for strangers. It was like going to your first opera with your girls' scout troop or your sorority sisters rather than in a red ballroom dress on the arm of Richard Gere like Julia Roberts in *Pretty Woman*. It wasn't just the gondola ride I wanted. It was the entire fantasy. So I shook my head and let them know I would wait for them at the piazza.

I knew Dee was giving me a questioning look, but I avoided looking at her.

While my group went on their gondola ride, I explored some of the shops bordering the canals and browsed through some of the Murano jewelry as I selected gifts for Reena and the girls. When the group returned, we all lunched together at a local café. After devouring our sandwiches and pizza, the waiter brought out a large sheet of tiramisu with candles lighted. I had watched as he approached our table, but it wasn't until he set it in front of me and my tour group broke out into the "Happy birthday" song, that I realized it was a birthday cake for me. I sat there sheepishly, basking in my warm, slightly embarrassed birthday glow as they sang to me. I glanced at Dee who winked and smiled. "Make a wish!" she called out just when I had leaned over to blow out my candles. I paused, offering up a prayerful, silent wish from the bottom of my heart. I was so touched that Dee had remembered. Once it was over, I leaned over to Dee to say thank you. That simple gesture of cake and birthday wishes lifted my spirits. I guess no matter how old we are, most of us still have a desire to feel special on our birthday—even amongst relative strangers.

For the rest of the afternoon, we were free to explore Venice on our own. Dee and I spent the afternoon purposely getting lost and wandering around unknown streets as we attempted to experience the "real" Venice and not just the area where all the tourists seemed to typically be.

By that evening, we made our way back to St. Mark's Square and had dinner and drinks on the piazza. We watched the sun as it descended on the horizon. Countless pigeons scoured the plaza and looked for food, but as I watched them, I could see Dee looking at me thoughtfully. "Is everything okay?"

"Yes, everything is great," I said with as much enthusiasm as I could muster. "I'm in Italy—I don't think it gets much more amazing than that."

"Really? Then why did you look so sad most of the day?"

"Did I?" I asked, not realizing I had been that obvious. I dropped my fake smile and noticed that my shoulders immediately drooped as well. "Honestly, I don't know. Maybe it's because as positive as I've tried to be about turning thirty, in the end it's still really hard, and I find myself still feeling frustrated about my life."

"You know that even though to you, your life may not seem perfect or ideal, many people would look at your life and be like, 'You got to go to Italy?!' But you're looking at it and saying, 'But yeah, I went alone.' Do you realize traveling is an unrealized dream for most people? The closest they'll ever get to Italy is in a textbook, a tour book, or the Internet. You're here. You're *HERE*," she said again, her arms outstretched as if she were trying to encompass all of Italy within her reach. "So enjoy it."

"You're right, you're right," I said as I lowered my head. "I know that in my head, I just wish…" my voice trailed off.

"You just wish…" she asked, prodding me along.

"I just wish…" I said lightly touching the lace tablecloth edging. "I just wish I had someone to share all of this with."

"There is nothing wrong with you wanting that. Everyone wants that. I want that. But what you have to realize is even if you don't have that, you can still enjoy things. You can still be happy."

"Yeah, I guess," I said, unconvinced.

"Well, I can tell you that until the cows come home, but until you realize that yourself and truly internalize it, you're never going to be happy, Sarai."

She was right, and I knew it. Yet, I couldn't seem to help the way I was feeling.

"I've been watching you, and after we arrived in Rome, you were so happy. But by the second and especially by the third day, something changed. You weren't only sad, but I began to wonder if you weren't just going through the motions rather than really enjoying being here. Don't ruin this trip for yourself. You don't know when and even if you'll ever come again."

As I drank my peach Bellini and thought about what Dee had just said, I watched the gondolas drift by against the beautiful sunset of the Venetian coast. I was in Venice! How many of my friends could say that?

And just as I knew she would eventually, she finally did ask me, "Why didn't you go on the gondola ride?"

I turned away because I knew my answer would seem silly to her. "I wanted to. I did, but I had always dreamed of taking a ride with someone special, not with a group of other tourists I barely know."

She leaned forward, trying to look into my face, but I kept my face down, hoping the fading light of evening would hide what my hair couldn't. "I know it wasn't the moonlit, romantic serenade that you had hoped, but now you lost out on your chance to say that you went on a gondola ride in Italy. Just because something isn't exactly the way you pictured it, doesn't mean you can't experience it in a different way. Be careful because while you're waiting for everything to go the way you planned, it's not only going to be a gondola ride you passed up, but it might also be your entire life. Be open to experiences, even if it's not the way you may have initially envisioned it. Who knows, it might even be better!"

She was so right. As amazing as being in Italy was, I was allowing a self-imposed deadline to get in the way of my experiencing what could otherwise be an unforgettable, once-in-a-lifetime trip. I thought about what she said and how I had spent the last few years so focused on my single status, that I basically "wished" my twenties away, waiting and hoping for that moment when I would be happy and fulfilled again, believing it was only possible through a relationship and marriage. Now here I was, already in my thirties. Would I wish away my thirties, too? I felt Dee was at that point in her life where she had muddled through the pain and had gotten to a point where she was still hopeful to have someone in her life but content and happy even if it didn't happen.

"I want to move on with my life, but how?" Dee must have thought I was asking her a rhetorical question and gave me a sympathetic smile, only to then look away.

I reached out for her hand again, drawing her attention back to me and said, "No, really, how?" I really wanted to know. I knew I had been in a rut for the last few years, trying with all my might to climb out of it, but I honestly did not know how to anymore.

This time she looked at me thoughtfully. She grabbed my hands, stood up, and pulled me up with her. Curious, I complied. She whispered something very quickly into the ear of a nearby waiter who nodded and smiled. We walked in silence for a few minutes. I followed her as she walked slowly and deliberately. Then she glanced at me, "You move forward by taking one step at a time. Some steps are slower than others and some seem easy. Occasionally you'll take a step back," she said as she paused mid-stride. "But don't get hung up on that. Keep moving forward, one step at a time, and one day you'll look back and see that you're no longer where you once were." She held me by the shoulders and slowly turned me around to show me our former seats. "You'll see how far you've come." The sun had already set, so the exterior of the café was now just a distant glittering of lights and on our table rested our empty wine glasses and dinner napkins, the sole reminder that was where we had been sitting.

"And you'll see how much you have to look forward to," she said, as she nudged me to turn around again. The Venetian waters of the Grand Canal were spread out before me, glittering under the light of a full moon, full of promise and mystery. It was a gorgeous, unforgettable view as we stood there in silence and allowed the cool breeze of the ocean to flow through our hair and caress our faces.

Chapter 53

U NDOUBTEDLY, VENICE WAS a beacon for lovers. In the dusk hours, they all seemed to emerge from their lovers' nests and occupy every inch of St. Mark's Square. The evening grew cooler as I watched couples snuggle together.

After we made our way back to our table, like a masochist, I began watching this one couple who were seated just a table away from us. He held both of her hands with one of his and used his other hand to caress her arms sensuously. She sat there, languishing in his adoring gaze. The waiter arrived to serve them and then poured the remainder of the wine into their goblets. As he removed the bottle and the ice bucket from their table, I caught the eye of someone who was seated at the table on the other side of the couple—someone who had been apparently watching me as I watched the young couple. With his dark hair, deep-set dark eyes, and olive skin tone, I quickly deduced he was probably Italian. He was dressed in a fitted suit, which probably meant he wasn't a tourist. He smiled at me slowly, transforming his face from one of chiseled hardness to one of boyish charm. He then raised his glass in a toast. Startled by his gesture, I looked behind me to make sure he didn't mean it for someone else. But all the other patrons were busy, engaged in conversation, with someone else. I turned back to the gentleman again, wondering if I hadn't just imagined it all, but he was busily talking to a waiter. The waiter nodded to whatever he was being told and then left the table. The stranger leaned back into his chair, one arm resting on the chair arm, and the other resting on the table. He twirled his wine glass slowly between his index finger and thumb as he once again made eye contact with me. His gaze was hypnotic and sensual. Armaan was the only guy who had ever looked at me like that. My mouth went dry, and my cheeks burned red.

I smiled shyly and looked away. A lady never stares, right? Or was the phrase a gentleman never stares? Well, whatever it was, I somehow found the strength to look away, even though that really was the last thing I wanted to do. It had been a long time since I had been the object of such an intense stare. I briefly thought about the Indian boy at the catacombs, but somehow with him only being twenty-two, that just didn't seem to count.

The waiter set another glass of white wine in front of Dee and a second glass of Bellini in front of me. "But I didn't order that," I protested.

The waiter smiled, inclining his head in the direction of the stranger. "Yes, it's from the gentleman at the other table. He noticed both your glasses were empty and asked me to bring another glass for each of the beautiful ladies."

I smiled at our admirer. He once again raised his glass in a toast. I looked at Dee, and she shrugged. So we both raised our glasses in response.

He took a few sips of champagne and then to my surprise, got up from his chair and slowly made his way towards our table. I panicked, not quite believing this was happening. Flirting across two tables was one thing, but now this guy was headed for my table! I, Sarai Mathai, never flirted with a perfect stranger, especially in a foreign country. I began to feel light-headed, not sure if it was the second glass of the Bellini or my nervousness.

I must have had the look of panic. Dee lightly patted my clenched fists and said, "You're going to be fine. I'm here—"

I cut her off immediately. "But—"

"There is no 'but.' *Carpe diem*, remember?"

"But what if he's a serial killer?" I asked.

She looked at me as if I had lost my mind. "He is not a serial killer. Besides, if he's going to kill you, he'll have to kill both of us because I'm not leaving you alone."

"Promise?!" I asked her, my eyes pleading.

"Promise," she said, winking at me. Her voice softened to a whisper because our admirer was standing in front of our table.

"*Mi scusi*, but do you mind if I join you two beautiful ladies?" Though he was talking to both of us, his eyes were on me. He spoke English well, but he also had a strong Italian accent. We both looked up at him, craning our necks just to see him clearly. He was at least six-three and appeared to be in his early to mid thirties. His suit was well tailored and fit his frame like it was custom-made. Under the jacket, he wore an open-collared, striped blue dress shirt. Standing up close to us, he resembled an Armani or Calvin Klein model, but he was more distinguished looking and striking. His face had more of a hardness stamped on it as if it were chiseled from smooth rock, and the lines of his face, from his high cheekbones to his jaw line, were sharp and angular.

Since I seemed to have lost my voice, Dee introduced us. "Hi, I'm Diandra, and this is my friend, Sarai."

He nodded at Dee and then focused on me. "Sarai," he drolled out softly, almost whispering it. "That is a beautiful name, simple, elegant, and unique. I would have expected nothing less than that for such a beautiful woman." I lost myself in his accent.

He took my hand and kissed it softly, all the while looking into my eyes. On a less attractive man, it would have been a cheesy, unwelcomed gesture. On a less polished man, it would have come across as a sleazy come-on. But with him, all I could feel was flattered, and I blushed a couple of shades of pink, which is actually a feat, considering my naturally tanned skin.

"And your name is…" Dee asked. Ah, yes, good question. He had to have another name besides Señor Handsome.

"I am Arman."

I stared at him blankly, feeling like I had the wind knocked out of me. "Excuse me?" I choked out. Was this some cruel joke?

He seemed amused with my wide-eyed reaction. "Actually, my name is Armani Di Francescantonio," he paused giving us time to absorb his name. "But when I say 'Armani' people always say, 'like the designer?' So a long time ago, I decided to go by just Arman."

But, of course, I wasn't thinking of Giorgio Armani.

"And how is it that you beautiful ladies are here alone on a beautiful night like tonight?" His eyes were again on me as if he were expecting me to answer, but all I could do was smile nervously. I was too caught off guard to think.

Clearing her throat, Dee glanced at me and spoke on our behalf. "Well, we're vacationing here in Italy and just enjoying the sights on our own. And you? How is it that you're alone on a beautiful night like this?" Yes, that was a good question. How was a man who looked like him, alone... ever?

"I'm in Venice on a business trip."

"Really?" Dee asked. "We took you for a local."

"You did? No, I am actually from Rome. I just thought I would enjoy a nice drink on the piazza before heading to my hotel room."

"Really? We were actually just in Rome a few days ago, and we'll be heading back in a few days before we fly out again."

"And how did you like Rome?" he asked, looking at me.

I nodded and finally found my voice. "It was beautiful. Just as I expected it to be."

"Rome is beautiful, but I have to say that Venice is one of the most unique and romantic cities in the world. And as such, it is not to be experienced alone. And since both of you are here alone, I must insist you let me be your tour guide."

I looked at Dee for guidance, not knowing how to politely refuse his generous offer. Friendly or not, he was still a stranger.

Dee smiled sweetly, "Thank you, signore, but we are not actually alone. We are part of a tour group."

"Ahhhh, I see," he said as he mulled over Dee's response. He swished his glass of wine slowly and then took a sip. "Well, it would be my honor to be your tour guide, but I understand. Two women. A foreign country. A stranger offering to take you for a tour..." He shrugged eloquently and then continued, "I don't blame you for refusing me."

"Well, I'm glad you understand, signore," Dee responded.

He inclined his head toward her. "But of course."

"Well, even if you can't give us the tour, maybe you could tell us what, outside the guided tours, that you would recommend?"

"Have you been to the San Polo neighborhood?"

We both shook our head.

"Just cross the Rialto Bridge, and it will take you there. In the morning you can walk right into the food market along the Grand Canal. San Polo is also where Venice's master mask makers can be found. There is the Scuola Grande di San Rocco where you can see beautiful, spiritual paintings by Jacopo Tintoretto covering its ceilings and walls. Dee immediately pulled out a piece of paper and a pen and quickly jotted some quick notes.

Arman paused to give Dee some time to get it all down and then continued. "And, if you still have some time, you must visit Ca' Rezzonico for its view of 18th-century Venetian life. Inside are paintings by all the greats, a complete apothecary, rooms exploring women's life in noble families, and a ballroom that stretches from one side of the grand palazzo to the other."

"Wow! Thank you, I don't know if we can fit all of those places in before we leave back for Rome, but we'll certainly try!" I exclaimed.

I noticed many members of our tour group were getting up from their tables and gathering to head back to the hotel. "Well, thank you, signore, for the drink and for the names of all those places to visit, but you must excuse us as it is getting late and we have to be getting back to our hotel." As we gathered our purses, Arman rose from his seat and helped us from our chairs.

"It was nice to meet you, Mr. Arman Di Francescantonio," I said, hoping I didn't butcher his name. I extended my hand for a handshake, but he looked at it awkwardly as if he didn't know what to do with it. He then took my hand and turned it so he could kiss the back of it. Then my heart stopped as he gently pulled me close and kissed both sides of my cheek. He then did the same with Dee who seemed completely at ease with his gesture. I had forgotten that it was the European custom of greeting.

"It was an honor, signoras. I hope I have the pleasure of running into both of you beautiful women again." He flashed a smile that melted both of us.

He inclined his head towards me, and part of me wished that we didn't have to go back to our hotel just yet. I smiled in return and walked away with Dee. She gave me a long sideways glance, accompanied with a knowing smile. I returned her look with a wistful smile of my own, sighing as I waved good-by to yet another ship passing through the night.

Chapter 54

THE NEXT DAY our tour group toured one of the oldest Murano glass-producing factories in Venice, and we had the chance to observe an artisan shaping and creating a vase. Later we walked through St. Mark's Square where the morning tide flooded the streets. We had to walk on long tables that were specifically put out for pedestrians. I later gasped in surprise to see that a couple of feet of water had also entered the church, but this was obviously a common occurrence because no one else seemed troubled by it.

We browsed the local stores and shops where I purchased my own set of Murano glassware. The weather was unseasonably beautiful. We were warned about the August heat, but while it was sunny, there was still a light, cool breeze, which only added to my elated mood. I felt vastly different that day than the days before. I felt freer and more carefree than I had in a long time. My birthday had come and gone, and along with it, those chaotic, contradicting emotions that seemed to be commonplace with getting older. The day had passed, and I was still intact. My hair had not grayed overnight nor had a web of wrinkles appeared out of nowhere. There was comfort in knowing that while I was older, I didn't necessarily look older. I knew I probably wouldn't feel that way every day in the coming years, but for today, rather than feeling pathetic and alone, I felt empowered and independent.

I browsed through some of the outdoor displays of the souvenir stores, looking for unique gifts when I glanced across the canal directly in front of the stores. There were clusters of small stores on the other side as well and nestled between them was a small café where, to my surprise, I spotted a familiar face sipping coffee and reading the local paper. It was none other than Mr. Arman Di Frances-something. He was dressed in slacks and a nice white dress shirt, sitting with his legs crossed effeminately, though there was nothing effeminate about him. I debated whether to go up to him or yell out a "hello" from across the canal when he looked up from his paper and spotted me. He broke out into a smile and motioned me over. I later blamed that empowered, carefree mood I was still in, but without even giving it a second thought, I held up my index finger, asking him to wait as I made my way to Dee to tell her that I was joining him for coffee.

"Do you want me to join you?" she asked, concerned.

It was mid-morning and there were endless crowds of people walking and shopping. I felt quite safe, not to mention, my gut told me this guy was safe. There was something about him that oozed gentlemanly decorum.

"No," I said, "I should be fine. But do join us once you're done shopping."

I walked down another block where there was a stone bridge connecting one side to the other. After crossing to the other side, I walked back up to the coffee shop. Arman had already pulled up another chair and stood next to it, holding it out for me to be seated.

A waiter approached and handed me a menu. He took my initial order of cappuccino. Although I was still full from breakfast and had no intention of ordering anything, I browsed through the menu anyway, trying to distract myself from the enigmatic man who sat across from me. What had gotten into me today? I was usually not one to be so bold. I looked over the top of my menu. He sat there, patiently waiting for me to acknowledge him. *Smile, Sarai, smile*, I reminded myself. I just needed to start off with a smile, followed by some light, casual chit-chat.

"So what are you doing here at a café in the middle of the morning? Didn't you say you were here on business?" I asked with a teasing smile as I set my menu down. I braced my elbows on the table and leaned forward. "Shouldn't you be in some business meeting or something?"

"Ah! But that's the beauty of owning one's own business. I can do what I like, when I like," he said with a flourish of his hands and then leaned back into his chair.

"I see. So what *exactly* do you do?"

He chuckled and leaned forward to whisper, "I am an architect."

"Really?" I asked with more surprise than I was actually feeling. I moved my arms so the waiter could set my coffee and sugar in front of me.

He looked at me curiously. "What did you think I did for a living?" he asked with his head cocked to one side.

I opened up three packets of sugar and added them to my coffee. "I don't know actually," I said as I stirred my coffee. My carefree mood had returned in full-force, and I found myself acting more flirtatious than I normally would with someone I had only met briefly for the second time. "Maybe you're a part of the Italian mafia and you are here 'taking care of business' or... *maybe* you're an Italian actor here on location for a movie."

He laughed heartily. "So you thought I was either part of the mafia or an actor? Now I understand why you and your friend were afraid to have me be your tour guide! You were afraid I'd kill you with a gun or bore you to death with my ego."

I glanced around, leaned forward in my chair, and then lowered my voice. "Well, actually, what I really thought was that you were one of those Italian men who prey on the innocent, unsuspecting, American female tourists."

That response seemed to surprise him. I think part of him suspected that I wasn't entirely joking. His eyes narrowed down on me as he leaned back into his chair again and crossed his arms across his chest. "And what would I prey on them for?"

"For money, of course!" I said. "You have expensive taste. You wear designer clothes, live a nice lifestyle, and you don't seem to have to work during the middle of the day. You could use your charm to woo some rich, lonely, old woman, and then before she knows it, she's spending every spare dime on you."

"So are you a rich, lonely, old woman then?" he asked, raising his left eyebrow at me.

"Ah… but last night, you decided to totally change your strategy and go for the poor, lonely, young woman!"

"And how is that working out for me?"

"Definitely a bad move," I said, shaking my head in sham disappointment. "Old woman or young woman, either one is fine, but definitely stick with someone with money. Otherwise, you'll find that you might actually have to get a real day job, and it would be a shame to have to give up your free time and your mid-morning coffee."

That brought a chuckle out of him. "You are an interesting, imaginative person, Ms. Sarai Mathai."

He remembered my name! Well, I had remembered his name, too… or at least part of his name. Of course, it was easy since it was the same name as my ex.

"So are you one of those men, Mr. Arman Di Frances…?" I asked coyly.

"Francescantonio," he readily supplied, obviously used to people forgetting or butchering his name. "Am I one of which kind of men?"

"Are you one of those Italian men who prey on the innocent, unsuspecting young American female tourists?"

His lips curved into a knee-weakening smile. "Well, that all depends," he asked, "Are you innocent and unsuspecting?"

I gave out a hearty laugh, "Touché!" I slowly sipped on my coffee, assessing Mr. Di Francescantonio.

"So last night we met for the first time, and now we meet again the very next day," I said, my eyes narrowing at him playfully. "Are you sure you aren't following me?"

His elbows rested on the arms of his chair, and his two index fingers connected to form a steeple. "Well, I was seated here well before I spotted you, so maybe it is *you* who is following *me*."

"Hmmm… interesting theory, but I'm with my tour group," I said as I gestured across the canal. "So if I were following you, I would have had to drag them along. But if you, sir, are part of the Italian mafia, then you would have used your sources to find out that our tour group would have been around in this area, and you conveniently placed yourself here, knowing that we would probably run into each other."

"You should work for Scotland Yard! You have the most imaginative conspiracy theories!"

"Please, don't get me started! I have plenty of theories about you," I said with a twinkle in my eye.

"Well, you must stay and tell me about all these theories," he said. "I am quite interested to know all these other lives I could be leading."

"So, can I ask you a question from one stranger to another?"

He leaned forward again, and his hand lightly brushed my arm that was resting on the table. "I would hope you still wouldn't consider me a stranger, but yes, please ask me your question."

My heart slammed into my chest, and I momentarily looked away to gather my composure. "Out of curiosity, why did you come up to me the other night?" I asked. I looked at him directly, curious to hear his answer but just as curious to see his reaction to my question.

His eyes softened as he looked at me thoughtfully. "After a long day of business meetings," he said, with a small smile, alluding to my earlier comment, "I went to St. Mark's to relax with a nice glass of wine and to people-watch, and you caught my eye. I know you think I am just— how do you Americans say—'buttering you up.' But you know you are..." his voice trailed off and then he looked away, averting his head to the point where I could only see his side profile.

I cocked my head to one side inquisitively, trying to see his face more clearly. "I know I am what?"

He turned back to me, looking me squarely in the eye. His light gray eyes glittered in the mid-morning sun and his voice softened to a whisper as he said, "*Bellisima*,"

Beautiful. He called me beautiful. A small shiver ran down my spine.

The wind picked up, bringing a cool breeze to an already beautiful sunny, temperate day. I was in Venice, sipping a cappuccino at a café that overlooked a picturesque canal where flower boxes containing bright pink, yellow, and red flowers decorated the window sills of small businesses and home windows. This, I realized, was exactly how I had always imagined Venice. The hot Italian man sitting across from me telling me I was beautiful was just an unexpected, added bonus.

"I saw you and then your eyes. Your eyes were so sad. Like a puppy dog."

"So you had to come rescue me, like a puppy from the pound."

"Maybe I am your prince, your knight in armor!"

"You mean my knight in shining armor?" I asked teasingly. I playfully mulled it over. "Or perhaps, you're one of those chivalrous footmen dressed in their fine livery who turn back into a rat at the end of the night?"

I'm not sure if he understood my joke because he ignored my playful barb at him and instead, reached out to move a lock of hair the wind had strewn across my face. Startled by his boldness and familiarity towards me, I was afraid to move. "When I first saw you, you reminded me of our southern Italian women with your dark black hair and caramel skin. But your eyes were so exotic, so full, so expressive and so sad. I knew," he said as he cupped his hand for added meaning.

"You knew what?" I asked with bated breath.

He took another sip of coffee and then rested his cup on the saucer. "I knew you were looking for love and sad because you didn't have it."

I leaned back into my chair. "Oh really? That is quite presumptuous of you," I said, as I unsuccessfully hid my annoyance. Was I really that transparent or was he just trying to use his romantic charm so I would let down my guard? "Well, that answers my question," I said, trying to lighten the mood. The conversation had gotten a little too personal and intimate for my taste.

"What question?"

"Whether you're just one of those Italian playboys who preys on unsuspecting American tourists."

"Really?!" he said, almost imitating my indignant tone. "So I went from Italian mafia to actor to now playboy? I don't know if I'm gaining or losing esteem in your sight!"

As much as I tried not to, I thought about it and laughed. "I guess I'm not sure either."

I spent a little more time trading barbs with Arman before we were joined by Dee who had a couple of shopping bags in tow.

"Please join us. Have a seat," Arman invited with a flourish of his hands.

"Thank you, but we really have to get going. We are supposed to meet our tour group for a tour of Burano."

"Ah, yes, the famous island of Venetian lace."

"Have you been?" I asked. That was a dumb question, I thought to myself as soon as I had said it.

"A long, long time ago. You will enjoy it. It's a very small island with colorful homes. Just be careful to make sure the lace you're buying is authentic Venetian lace. They actually also sell lace from China, but you can probably buy that cheaper in America."

Good to know. Mr. Arman Di Francescantonio was full of good ideas and tips.

Before I could gather my belongings, he rose and stood next to my chair. He extended his hand to assist me, but this time I felt even more self-conscious as he kissed both sides of my face. I smiled and said, "Well, it was nice running into you again."

Instead of nodding and saying good-bye, Arman continued to hold my hand as he asked, "So rather than waiting to see if we have another accidental run-in, why don't we plan it instead?"

I looked at him curiously, not quite sure what he was getting at.

"Would you do me the honor of joining me for dinner tonight?"

I looked at Dee, not wanting to abandon her for the night. She was looking away, trying to give us a little privacy. Sensing the quietness, she looked back at us to find us both staring at her as we waited on her approval. "Oh! No... I mean yes, please go... enjoy dinner with Arman. A couple of people from our tour group were talking about getting some dinner together, so I'll be fine."

"You're sure?" I asked.

She nodded.

I walked away with Dee to join our tour group, and I couldn't resist one last look back. Arman was still watching us and winked.

Chapter 55

THE ISLAND OF Burano was a forty minute boat ride away from Venice. The sky was overcast, and a strong wind was blowing. Luckily, it didn't rain so we were still able to enjoy exploring the little island.

As Arman had described, Burano was a small island filled with quaint homes situated on canals, just like Venice. The homes, however, were painted in various, vibrant colors, ranging from tangerine to sky blue to Pepto-Bismol pink. We made our way through the various lace-making shops and stopped at one in particular where an elderly woman was trying to sell her own home-made creations. I purchased some cream lace placemats for my mom and made some other small purchases for a few of my aunts.

We got back to our hotel just in time to change for dinner. After a quick shower, I spent the next forty-five minutes getting ready. I slipped on a halter top, maxi dress with a brown and pink paisley print and wore my hair in long, loose curls. As I was slipping on a pair of high heeled sandals, Dee emerged from the bathroom in a towel and was wrapping another towel around her hair like a turban when she paused in mid-stride and gave me a once-over, followed by a low whistle.

I chuckled and stood up as I did a slow turn to model my dress. "What do you think?" I asked.

"I think you look beautiful!" she said, her hands on her hips. "Now I'm not sure if I do want you to go to dinner alone. Arman is going to take one good look at you and decide to kidnap you after all."

"Well, don't worry! Since he's still technically a stranger, I insisted we stay in the vicinity of St. Mark's Square for dinner."

"He seems like a gentleman, so you'll be fine. You're going to have a great time!"

"I think so, too."

Arman picked me up from the hotel at seven on the dot. He was dressed in a fitted, gray crewneck sweater with a dark blazer and matching slacks. As soon as he saw me, his smile widened as he appreciatively assessed me from head to toe. "How beautiful you look!" He pulled me close and kissed me on one side of my cheek and then the other. I breathed in the light clean scent of his cologne.

He took me to St. Mark's Square, and for a minute, I thought he was going to take me to the same restaurant where we had first met, but we walked past it. I followed him until he began to descend some steps near a canal. When I paused mid-stride, he turned around and extended his hand to help me down the narrow steps, but I evaded his hands, my eyebrows wrinkled with question. He gestured past the hip-level stone stairway wall, and there, to my utter delight, was an awaiting gondola, complete with a gondolier who was wearing the signature white and black-striped shirt, a straw hat with a red scarf, and black slacks with a red sash tied around the waist.

Arman held my hand and led me down the stairs. He then helped me board the gondola, and we soon settled into a plush, red velvet cushioned loveseat. The gondola had a typical black exterior, but the entire edging of the boat had elaborate gold painted flourishes, particularly its helm, making it appear very luxurious and new. With only canal lampposts and our gondola lantern lighting our way, we glided quietly through the foggy night. As I listened to the rustling of the parting waters, I felt like I was caught up in some faraway dream. The fog thickened, and I was reminded of the scene from *Phantom of the Opera* where the Phantom takes Christine into his shadowy lair. I surreptitiously glanced at Arman. Despite his dark good looks and hard lines, there was nothing about him that hinted of danger or raised my suspicions.

By day, Venice was beautiful, but by night, it was breathtaking and magical. We were both quiet as we traveled through the canals of Venice, as if we were both afraid to break the spell of the moment. Arman rested his arm behind me. At first I sat upright, but as the minutes passed, I relaxed and began leaning back into my cushioned seat, further into the crook of his arm. The damp, night air was cool, so I welcomed the warmth that seemed to emanate from his suited framed. Now *this* was a gondola ride, I thought to myself.

Twenty minutes later, the gondola stopped in front of a small, intimate restaurant called Ciò è l'Amore.

To my surprise, it wasn't the typical, fancy, five-star restaurant I had expected. Instead, it reminded me of a quaint, out-of-the-way place that only the locals would probably know about. The restaurant resembled a tiny cottage with both indoor and outdoor seating. With two menus in tow, the hostess guided us through the restaurant to the back, which opened up to a small, garden area. Tiny white lights twinkled throughout the trees. There was something very cozy and enchanting about the ambiance. It was as if we were dining in a small cottage in some forgotten fairy tale.

Our waiter appeared and poured us both a glass of Pinot Grigio. Arman and I first shared a small plate of stuffed mushrooms and calamari. At his suggestion, I ordered a plate of Shrimp Fra Diavolo for my main course. As soon as I had my first bite, my eyes flew to Arman. He smiled knowingly, obviously anticipating my reaction.

"Oh, my gosh! What is this sauce?! It's amazing!"

"I know," he said with a slow, lazy smile. "This place makes some of the best pasta I've ever had in my life." He glanced over his shoulder and then leaned closer to me, "Just don't tell my mama'! I always tell her that hers is the best."

"Well, bring her here, and she'll agree with you!" I said, devouring the pasta like it was my last meal on earth. Eating this food was like a religious experience. With every bite, I shamelessly gave off a soft moan or whimper or closed my eyes in utter ecstasy as I savored the sauce. I soon found myself using my hands more than my fork. Even the garlic bread tasted divine, and I kept tearing off pieces to dip into my pasta sauce. I was so absorbed in my dish that when I finally looked up to see how Arman was enjoying his food, I was surprised to find he had stopped and was staring at my mouth.

I immediately grabbed my napkin, assuming from the way I had been eating, pasta sauce was probably all over the corners of my mouth. "No, no, no! *Perdonami!* I'm sorry for staring. It's just that I've never seen someone eat their meal so sensually before. It's nice to see a woman enjoy her food. I never understand how women can only order a salad and be satisfied with that."

"Yeah, I'm definitely not a salad girl," I said as I took another bite and closed my eyes in ecstasy.

"So tomorrow you leave for Rome." I wasn't sure if that was a statement or a question.

"Yes," I said. "Tomorrow is Rome, and the day after that is back to the States."

"Since you didn't allow me to give you a tour of Venice, then I must insist that you give me a couple of hours to take you and your friend around Rome." Thinking of how amazing this night had turned out, I immediately nodded.

"So when will you come again?" he asked as he poured me another glass of wine.

"Honestly, I don't know. I'd love to visit Italy again soon, but realistically, it maybe not for a while."

That answer didn't seem to sit well with him at all, and he immediately frowned. "Then don't go."

"Don't go?" I repeated, surprised at his forwardness. I leaned back in my chair and sipped my wine as I briefly pondered his suggestion. To live in Italy would be amazing, but there were so many practical things to consider. "Where would I live? What would I do if I stayed?" I asked him.

"Do nothing," he said and then his smile deepened mischievously, "And do everything—live, travel, eat," his eyes darkened as they focused on my lips again, "and most of all, love." He didn't say "make love," but I knew exactly what he meant.

I laughed nervously, "You'd like that wouldn't you?"

He nodded slowly, "Very much so…" He took another slow sip of wine, keeping his eyes on me all the while.

I must have turned a thousand shades of red. Arman chuckled, clearly enjoying the effect he was having on me. Arman didn't ask me to stay again, and neither did I ask if he wanted me to. It was almost as if we both silently agreed to enjoy what we had for the moment. For the first time in my life, I didn't feel a need to define a relationship, nor did I need the relationship to define me. The whole night felt like a dream, and, for once, I was content to enjoy it for the moment, accepting romance in whatever form it came, without the need to dissect it or the expectation of "forever."

After we finished our dinner, we drank more wine, ate tiramisu, and topped it off with an amaretto coffee. As we dined, a Spanish guitar player approached us. The wine was already making me drowsy, but the combination of music, wine, a heavenly meal, and a decadent dessert proved to be too heady a combination for my inexperienced soul, and I found myself slowly being lulled further into a dream-like trance. During our gondola ride back, I settled comfortably into the crook of Arman's arm as it rested on the top of the loveseat, just above my shoulders. I wanted to close my eyes, but I was afraid that I would open them only to find that I had indeed been dreaming.

By the time we arrived back at the hotel, it was one in the morning. Arman assisted me out of the car and ushered me through the lobby, up the elevator, and safely to the doorstep of my hotel room. "Thank you for a perfect evening," I replied, unable to suppress my loopy smile.

"*Il piacere è tutto mio*," he said as he tucked a stray lock of hair behind my ear. "I was saying, 'The pleasure is all mine.'"

He lightly caressed my check with the back of his hand, looked me deep in the eyes, and then down at my lips. I held my breath and kept my focus on the hotel door behind him as I awaited the inevitable kiss, but instead, he sighed and took my hotel key card. After opening the door for me, he turned around to leave. But before I walked through the door, I said, "And thank you for being the perfect gentleman." I then walked up to him and kissed him lightly on the cheek, a gesture that startled him.

The next morning I woke to find Dee lying sideways on her bed, facing me with her head propped up by her left hand as she waited for me to wake up. She had a knowing smile on her face. "Soooo… don't keep me in suspense. How was the date?"

The memory of last night immediately put a smile on my face.

As hard as I tried to only give her a brief overview, I inevitably went into every detail of the evening from the dreamlike gondola ride to the decadent dinner to my parting kiss on his cheek. Dee listened with a delighted smile on her face the entire time.

"Wow! I knew you'd have a great time, but I even have to say that I am impressed!" she said as she swung her feet off her bed and moved toward the dresser. Two dozen red roses stood there, symmetrically arranged in a beautiful glass bowl. "These roses, along with that," she said, pointing to the other dresser where a tray of breakfast items were waiting, "arrived this morning while you were sleeping." She picked a small envelope and handed it to me. "And this came with the flowers."

The note read, *I would be honored if you would join me for coffee at 10:30am in the hotel lobby. Arman.*

It was like the night had extended into the morning. I grabbed a rose, holding it close to me as I inhaled its sweet fragrance. I glanced at the clock next to my bed. It was almost 9:30, so I quickly enjoyed the breakfast and then showered and dressed. I donned a simple white sundress and tied my hair back with a short scarf. I quickly packed and headed to the café downstairs.

When I arrived at the hotel lobby, Arman was already in the café waiting for me and sipping on an espresso. A steaming cup of cappuccino was sitting in front of an empty chair next to him. As I walked towards his table, he glanced up, grinning. He rose from his chair to greet me, kissing me on either cheek. At this point, it was a gesture I was getting used to, although I wasn't sure if I still wanted that to be the standard greeting for everyone I met.

"*Buongiorno!*"

"*Buongiorno!*" I responded.

As we sat down, he started to say something but then shook his head.

"What?" I asked.

"You look so beautiful, so fresh. Like a rose."

"Well, I can't be more beautiful than the vase of roses I received this morning." I reached out to grab his hand and gave it a squeeze. "They are beautiful, and it was a very generous gesture as was the delicious breakfast."

"Sarai, thank you for joining me this morning."

I looked at him, perplexed. "Thank me? I haven't done anything. No, thank *you* for breakfast, for the flowers, for last night's dinner, for the gondola ride, for—"

He chuckled. "Stop. Please," he said, with a dismissive flick of his wrist. "It was nothing."

"Nothing? No, I've done nothing. You've been extremely generous with your time. Italy should be proud. I'm leaving Italy with an excellent opinion of her people. I think I should be the one thanking you for everything you did for me… and unlike most males, you didn't have any expectations, which was very refreshing."

"I don't know if I can say that is completely true. Being with you pleases me, so I don't know if I am really as unselfish as you think I am."

In the past, I would have had a witty comeback, but now all I could do was bask in the glow of his compliments.

"So when are you leaving for Rome? Our group is leaving at noon. Dee and I are excited to see Rome through your eyes! I was telling her about the amazing gondola ride and—"

Before I could continue, he cut me off. "Sarai," he said hesitatingly as he reached out for my hand. "That is why I asked you to join me for coffee…" He lowered his voice. "Unfortunately, I will have to remain in Venice longer. I will not be returning to Rome until a few days from now, so I am unable to show you Rome as I had hoped."

I blinked a couple of times and looked down at my hands. "Oh!" I said, trying to hide my disappointment. "So this is good-bye then."

"I hope it is not *arivederci*, but I believe the French have a saying...
au revoir."

Until we meet again.

Not that he had ever given me a reason to doubt him, but I
couldn't help but wonder if this weren't an excuse in some way.
Perhaps since I was leaving Italy, he decided not to waste his time and
was looking for a way to end things quicker. But why didn't he just
follow Amit's example and just pretend our date never happened? I
hadn't expected the flowers, the breakfast, or even the formal good-bye
from him.

I pulled my hand from under his, and he quickly interjected, "My
client requested some changes to the design of the executive offices for
his company, and I have to finish them by this evening, so I can present
it to them tomorrow morning."

I smiled and nodded. "No worries. I understand." I said, doing my
best to sound as light-hearted as possible.

He looked at me thoughtfully, and as the seconds ticked by, he said
nothing.

What did he want me to do? Was he wanting me to protest? Well, I
wasn't like all the other clingy women in the world. If he said he had
other things to do, well, okay then. I was fine with that.

"I really would have liked to take you around Rome," he repeated.

"I know, but work comes first," I replied stiffly.

Well, it was going to end soon enough anyway, so it might as well
end sooner than later. So why did I feel so let down? How quickly I had
gotten used to his attentiveness and grand gestures!

"You will call me if you come to Rome again?" he asked, as he
handed me a business card. "This has all my information whenever you
want to reach me. My email, my cell phone number, my work number,
and my fax number."

He glanced at his watch, his eyebrows curled, and he looked at me
apologetically. "I must go now, bella. I have a meeting at noon with my
client." He watched me tuck his card into my wallet as we both got up
from our chairs.

I walked him to the hotel lobby doors where the doorman was holding open the door of an awaiting limo. Before walking away, he looked at me for a few long moments, his eyes momentarily resting on my lips. He bent down to kiss me on each side of my cheek and whispered, "Don't make me wait too long."

He climbed into the limo but craned his neck out the window. I held up my hand in good-bye, and he waved back with a wistful look in his eyes.

It wasn't until later that it hit me that he hadn't asked me for any of my contact information. He was leaving it up to me to make the next move, I realized.

An hour later, we boarded our tour bus, leaving Venice for Rome. I stared out the window, sighing deeply as I took in my last view of the beautiful Grand Canal. The gondoliers and fishermen were in the distance, their boats bobbing up and down in the shimmering sea under a bright noon sun.

Chapter 56

WE ARRIVED BACK in Rome by early evening and spent our last night with our fellow tourists, dining at a local trattoria. The next day, Dee and I spent some final hours shopping and then caught our early evening flight back to the States.

When I arrived home, I showered and began to unpack my suitcase and put away my clothes and souvenirs. I was placing a miniature Leaning Tower of Pisa on my bookshelf when I spotted the textbook I had thought about when I was in Rome. It was the same textbook I had used for my Renaissance Art History class in college.

I pulled the heavy book from the shelf and began browsing through it, recalling how it was surprisingly one of the more challenging classes I had taken in college. The class was taught by three professors, each of whom specialized in art, music, and architecture. While the idea of traveling through Europe had always sounded appealing, this class was where I had initially fallen in love with Italy. I flipped through the pages and smiled as I immediately recognized the sculptures, paintings, buildings, and artifacts I had seen in person only days before. Mid-way through the book, a small index card fell out, landing at my feet. I bent down to pick it and recognized some notes scribbled in my handwriting. An old "To Do" list was on one side, and the other side contained some personal goals I had set for the new year. While most of the goals were short-term goals, such as working out and graduating *summa cum laude*, the first goal I had written was one I had obviously given myself some extra time to achieve—*visit Italy before turning 30*. I reached deep into the recesses of my mind, trying to recall writing these goals and more so, trying to remember what I felt when I was writing them. I couldn't recall either, and all I had was the familiar cursive slant of my handwriting to confirm this index card had even been mine.

A small shiver coursed through my body as I began to realize that my trip to Italy had been more than just happenstance. I considered all the factors that led me to take this trip to Italy—from each of my girlfriends being unavailable to celebrate my birthday to even the year before where I spent my birthday holed up in my bedroom mourning Amit. I then recalled how a seemingly chance run-in with Dee led us to eventually plan the trip to Italy together. But Dee asking me to join her in Italy had not been just chance, luck, or fortune but truly one that had been divinely designed.

Closing the textbook, I hugged it and held it against my chest as I felt an inexplicable peace overwhelm me. And it was at that moment I didn't feel quite so left behind. I realized that I shouldn't mourn the "what ifs" in my life. For the first time, they, too, had meaning, rather than feeling like lost opportunities or random, erroneous choices on my part. Like pieces of a puzzle, my past suddenly clicked into place.

I had long tried to makes sense of my relationship with Armaan but to no avail. But now I knew... I finally understood why he had been in my life although we didn't end up together. Had I never gone to India, I would have wondered what or who could have awaited me there. But I now knew that neither of them was for me. I could move on and continue with my life, living it without regrets, believing that I was still destined for happiness. I may have taken some detours, but I had not lost my way. In the end, I would still arrive at my destination, right on time.

And there was the epiphany I had been seeking. It wasn't in the hallowed halls of St. Peter's Basilica or the Sistine Chapel or even on the romantic canals of Venice. Instead, it was there, in my childhood bedroom—a realization that yes, my life, once seemingly only filled with detours and dead-ends, was actually right on course... and had been all along.

Chapter 57

O NCE I GOT back into the groove of my life, I was able to approach everything, from my job to my personal life to the chaos of Reena's wedding planning, with renewed energy rather than merely out of feelings of duty and obligation.

We were at my house, vegetating on my living room couch and snacking on some pretzels and sliced apples, which was Reena's feeble but final attempt to lose a couple of more pounds before her wedding.

"So do you at least have a picture of him?" she asked after I piqued her curiosity with my story about Arman in Italy.

"Actually, no I don't." Why hadn't I taken a picture? I guess it wasn't something that had occurred to me at the time. But I didn't need a picture to remember Arman. It was an experience I would never forget as well as something for me alone.

"Are you going to contact him?" she asked as she reached across the cushioned ottoman for another apple slice.

"Honestly, I don't know. We just left it open."

"How weird that they shared very similar names and even resembled each other!"

"Tell me about it! I wouldn't say they looked alike or anything, but there was something I couldn't quite put my finger on that reminded me of the other." I grew quiet for a moment. "I wonder if I'll ever see Arman again..."

"Armaan? You mean your ex?"

"No, no. I mean Italian Arman."

"Oh."

"I wonder how Arman would react if I were to write him. Do you think he's completely forgotten about me by now?"

"Your ex-Armaan?"

"No," I said, shaking my head. "Italian Arman."

"Oh…" she said as took another apple slice and mulled over my question. "I doubt it. It's only been a week. He put it in your court, so he's probably more worried about *you* forgetting *him*."

"Yeah, I guess. You know, now that I think about it, Reen, since I got back from Italy, I've hardly thought about Armaan at all. I guess I'm finally getting over him."

"Italian Arman?"

"No, my ex-Armaan."

"Oh…" Reena said as she massaged her temples. "Okay, now I'm getting a headache trying to figure out which one you're talking about."

I laughed out loud. "Yeah, it is a little confusing, isn't it?!"

Reena looked at me thoughtfully, and her eyes narrowed.

"What?"

"What would you think if I told you that I found someone who meets everything on that silly list you made years ago?"

I looked at her blankly. "I already found someone who met my list and things didn't work out, remember?"

"Are you talking about your ex-Armaan or Italian Arman?"

"My ex-Armaan, of course!"

"Okay then, does your ex-Armaan have hazel eyes?"

"What?! No."

"Was he Christian?"

"No."

"Was he Malayalee?"

"No."

"Then he wasn't everything on your list."

"True, but he made me feel like throwing my list away and creating one that described him instead."

"Now let's try this again. What would you think if I told you I found someone who meets *everything* on your list?"

"Then I would think you are a miracle worker!" I said, half-joking.

"Hmmm, well start thinking I'm a miracle worker then!"

"So you're telling me you found a Malayalee Christian guy with hazel eyes?"

Reena nodded her head.

"Well don't keep me in suspense! Who is this guy? And how is he still single?"

Reena's lips curved into a mischievous smile. "It's Sanjay's best friend. The one I mentioned to you before—"

Before she could even finish, I cut her off, "No-no-no!" I said emphatically.

Reena was taken aback. "And why not?"

"If he's Sanjay's best friend, then that means he'll be a groomsman, maybe even his best man."

"Yeah, so?"

"Well, hell*ooo*... your wedding! What if things don't work out? Then I have to see him at your wedding! Do you know how awkward that'll be?!"

"Oh, come on! You don't know anything about this guy. You haven't seen him, and now you're not even going to give this a chance because things might not work out? Heck, you went all the way to India for marriage, and now you won't even give a great guy right here a chance?"

I didn't respond, and Reena could see I was determined. "Okay, fine. I'll drop it for now. Besides, you'll see him at the wedding and realize what you're passing up!"

Chapter 58

S OON REENA'S WEDDING planning again took over every spare moment of my life, but I was able to give of myself and my time in a way that I hadn't been able to before. I even found myself enjoying all the planning, if for no other reason than it was all for my best friend. The months flew by, and slowly but surely, one by one, we tackled all the remaining things left on her to-do list.

If the months and weeks before Reena's wedding were hectic, the day before her wedding was even more so. After all that time we spent, I thought surely we had everything taken care of, but there still seemed to be an infinite amount of details that needed to be addressed. I glanced at my tattered checklist. *Pick up bridal bouquet.* Check. *Give the final music CD to the DJ.* Check. *Stop by the church and make sure the printed programs arrived.* Check.

I glanced at my watch. The only thing left, I realized, was to get dressed and make it to the church on time for the rehearsal.

When I arrived at the church, most of the bridal party was already there. Besides Maya, Anjuli, and me, the other five bridesmaids were Reena's cousins, all of whom were either in high school or college— very girly, very giggly, and very much on the prowl. They openly flirted with the groomsmen, who were enjoying the unabashed attention.

"Did we ever act like that?" I asked, amused by their brazen behavior. As I observed them, I began to feel like a jaded, judgmental thirty-year-old auntie.

"God, I hope not!" Reena said, rolling her eyes. "If we did, then we deserved to be shot."

"Who's that guy?" asked Maya, pointing to someone who had just walked in the church foyer. He looked to be around six feet tall and broad shouldered, something even the blazer he wore couldn't hide. He had that tanned Malayalee skin, but even from a distance, I couldn't help but notice his eyes, which under the dim, yellow church lights, seemed to sparkle.

Reena followed the direction of our gaze and smiled. "That is Sanjay's friend, Ryan," she said, elbowing me.

"Ryan?" asked Maya. "Is he Indian?"

"Yep!" answered Reena with a grin. "He's 100% Malayalee!"

"Malayalee? Really? With those eyes? And his name is Ryan? That's not a very Malayalee name! What's his real name?"

"Actually, his real name is Ryan. Apparently, his mom was a big fan of that old soap opera, *Ryan's Hope*."

"Is he wearing contacts? His eyes are definitely not just regular brown." Anjuli commented with a dreamy smile. Reena cleared her throat loudly, and Anjuli immediately snapped out of her trance. "What?! Just because I'm married doesn't mean I'm blind!"

"*Uh huh*. And for the record, no, he has natural hazel eyes," Reena said as she pointedly looked at me. "Sanjay said it runs on his mom's side."

"*Niiice*," said Maya, not taking her eyes off him. I found myself feeling annoyed that this guy could reduce my girlfriends to a puddle of drooling teenagers. Was no one immune to a pretty face and nice pair of eyes?

Reena watched me and waited for me to say something. "So, what do you think? You're the only one who hasn't said anything. He was the one I spoke to you about."

I looked at her blankly.

"The best friend, the one I told you whom Sanjay and I wanted to set you up with…"

"Oh, *that's* the guy you two have been raving about," I said, turning my head in the direction of the foyer to give him a second look. Well, I

could definitely see why Sanjay had described him as "quite the catch."
He was not only a doctor, a fact that would happily resonate with every
Indian parent, but he also met all the generic criteria that qualified him
as being very good looking—he was tall, built, good bone structure, and
had a very nice smile.

I inclined my head towards Reena's cousins who seemed to have
suddenly forgotten about the other groomsmen and who were now all
focusing on Sanjay's best friend. "Well, you have your work cut out for
you, Reena. I doubt he'll even notice me. Two of your cousins are all
over him!" I said, amused with the girls' fickleness. Poor groomsmen.
Reena frowned when she saw her cousins, Suni and Subi, openly cooing
over him. Reena crossed her arms and shook her head. "Not to worry.
According to Sanjay, he's used to girls acting like that and typically it
turns him off when they act so aggressive."

I didn't want to burst Reena's bubble, but I wasn't worried. I had
no interest in him, and I had serious doubts as to whether I would be
his type. He was entirely too good looking and too suave for my taste.
With that amused smirk on his face, I highly suspected he knew it, and
that, in and of itself, was enough to turn me off. He was undoubtedly
used to girls hitting on him, and I had no patience for guys with big
egos. They were typically too narcissistic and too selfish for my taste.
Plus, at thirty, I was too old and too unwilling to spend my time
reforming a former playboy, no matter how cute, charming, and nice
my best friend and her fiancé purported him to be.

Before we started the wedding rehearsal, everyone was asked to
gather near the altar as the wedding coordinator went over the program
and order of the ceremony. We were paired off with the groomsmen
with whom we'd be walking down the aisle. I, of course, as the maid of
honor, got paired with Ryan, the best man. As we were introduced, he
inclined his head towards me, smiled, and then extended his hand. "Hi!
It's nice to meet you!"

To my dismay, his eyes were more beautiful up close. And they
were set off by his tanned skin. Was Reena sure that they weren't
contacts? If they weren't, then he was the first Malayalee guy I had ever
met who didn't have the standard dark brown/black eyes. He smiled

again. Great, he had perfect teeth, too, I realized, that enhanced his already perfect smile. No doubt he was waiting for me to melt and become all giddy like most girls would have done. Well, I was not like most girls, so I smiled politely in return, extended my hand for a handshake as I said hello, and then I immediately excused myself as I made my way to the wedding coordinator to discuss some final details regarding the wedding.

But before I could approach the wedding coordinator, Reena followed me and pulled me aside. When she was sure we could not be overheard, she loudly whispered, "Why did you do that?"

"Why did I do what?"

"Why did you act so dismissive? He was trying to talk to you, and you just walked away!"

"First of all, a simple smile and 'hi, nice to meet you' is not trying to talk to me. Second, I did say hello and then politely excused myself so I could discuss some last minute details with *your* wedding coordinator regarding *your* wedding, which is tomorrow, might I add. I'm not sure how you can call that being dismissive!"

"I know you, Sarai. I know when you're being defensive, and God knows you have every right to be leery of this setup, but please trust me on this one and just give it a chance. I wouldn't be trying to set you guys up if I didn't think you guys would be compatible."

"Reena, you know these setups never work out for me, and you forcing us to communicate isn't going to make him fall for me, or for that matter, me for him. It'll just make both of us run the other way. Besides," I added, using a mocking, mimicking tone, "if it's meant to be, it'll happen." I recited a line that Reena had often used on me.

She recognized it and gritted her teeth in frustration. "Fine! You're right! If it's meant to be, it'll happen. However," she added, wagging her finger at me. "You have to be open to it. Remember that you can't act dismissive or the guy will think he doesn't have a chance with you." And with that said, she turned on her heel and walked back to the main rehearsal area.

"Was I acting dismissive?" I asked myself as I took my place at the end of the bridal processional line. Maybe. But it wasn't intentional, at least not entirely. From the moment she introduced me, I decided I didn't care whether Ryan showed any interest in me or not. For me, it was more imperative that I not be categorized with all the younger bridesmaids who were practically swooning at him. I had swooned over my share of cute guys, and I would swoon no more, especially at my own expense. So perhaps in an effort to distance myself from the girly behavior of the rest of the bridesmaids, I found myself being unintentionally dismissive. I found it annoying that he seemed so sure of himself, but perhaps I was more annoyed with myself and the fact that I did find him so darn good looking.

Chapter 59

REENA'S WEDDING WAS scheduled for 10 am, and we were all strictly instructed by Reena to be at her house, dressed, with hair and makeup done, by 8 am. I calculated that if I needed to be ready by then, I could sleep in that morning, at least until 6 am. At 4 am, a frantic Reena called, begging me to help her cousin Joby re-do the slideshow for the reception. Apparently his computer had crashed, and he had lost everything, including all of the pictures Reena and Sanjay had scanned for their wedding. I quickly showered and raced over to Reena's where Joby and I spent the next 2½ hours recreating the slideshow and setting it to music. I then raced to the hairdresser to get my hair done in an up-do, rushed back home to put on my bridesmaid dress and makeup, and then rushed to Reena's house to make her 8 am deadline. Maya and Anjuli still hadn't arrived, but all her cousins had taken over the second floor of the house and were getting their makeup and hair done. They had also slowly infiltrated Reena's room, which was now a mess as shoes, purses, bridesmaid's bouquets, and makeup seemed to occupy every square inch.

Reena, I was told, was in her parents' master bedroom getting the final touches on her hair and makeup. I walked into the room to check on her. I shut the door behind me, turned, and froze. My hands flew to my mouth as I stifled a gasp. Reena was sitting in front of the window. The curtains were open, and the light filtered in. Reena pursed her lips as the makeup artist applied the final touches of her lipstick. When the bedroom door clicked, Reena heard it and turned to me with the most beautiful smile. Her curly hair was pulled back into a loose chignon, secured with diamond pins at the nape of her neck, and soft curly tendrils framed her face. With the light softly filtering in through the sheer curtain liner, the scene had a subdued, natural, sepia-like quality to it. Her skin had a dewy glow and looked flawless. I had never seen Reena look more beautiful. I softly shut my eyes like a photographer's camera shutter, determined to remember that moment forever.

"What do you think?" she asked, her eyes shining.

"I think you look amazing… undoubtedly the most beautiful bride!"

"You're just saying that!" she accused.

"Well, in this case, I actually mean it! You look gorgeous! Wait until Sanjay sees you!"

"Promise?"

"I pinky swear it!" I said, emphatically, and pulled her into a hug, being careful not to smudge her makeup or mine. The makeup artist left the room to assist the other bridesmaids, but before I could say anything else to Reena, her eyebrows wrinkled with worry and her mind immediately went into Bridezilla mode. "Did you see the church? Does everything look okay? How are the flowers? Were the programs delivered to the church?"

"Everything is perfect. All your planning and attention to detail have paid off. The flowers are gorgeous. The programs are in a box, waiting for the ushers to distribute them," I assured her as I handed her the bridal bouquet filled with hot pink and white calla lilies. She inhaled sharply and stared at the bouquet for a few seconds.

"They're beautiful," she said, gingerly taking it from my hands as if the flowers were made of fragile bone china.

"They are, and so are you. I told you everything is going to be fine," I replied in the most reassuring tone I could muster. "Now save the tears for the wedding ceremony!" I gently commanded, holding up a tissue for her.

She looked back at her reflection, holding the tissue loose in her hand. "Sarai, I can't believe it. I'm getting married. *Me…*"

"I know," I said, walking to stand next to her as she faced the full-length mirror. I looked at our reflection, not quite believing we were here. I remembered standing here in front of this very mirror when we had tried on dresses for our eighth grade dance and then later for our senior prom and then even later for our many college banquets and balls. But now here we stood, all grown up. "I can't believe it either. I feel like just yesterday I was in India and you were telling me about this guy coming to your house, and now here we are!"

She glanced at me through the reflection. "You know your day is coming, too. I can feel it. Don't ask me how, but I just know it."

"Oh, great! Are you going to be one of those brides who, now that she's married, is determined to marry everyone else off as well?" I teased.

Reena's wedding was the beginning of a new stage of life for both of us. For Reena, it was the beginning of her life as a married woman, and for me, it was the beginning of my new and improved life as a single, *fabulous* young woman... one who would no longer be defined only by her marital status.

The bridesmaids rode with Reena in a white limo to the church. While Reena, Anjuli, Maya, and I just sat back enjoying the moment, Reena's cousins were crowded over one shared hand-held compact as they primped and prodded themselves into perfection. I glanced over their heads and winked at Reena who was rolling her eyes at their vanity. I was a little more sympathetic, knowing that there was a time when I would have done the same thing. I smiled to myself, finally enjoying one of the perks of getting older.

Twenty minutes later, the limo pulled in front of a large white church with the requisite traditional large steeple and a front exterior flagged by four thick Georgian columns reminiscent of a southern plantation. When we arrived, we were quickly ushered into the bridal dressing suite, away from prying eyes as we awaited the ceremony to begin. And then at 10 am on the dot, we were all taken to the front of the church aisle, awaiting the cue of the processional music.

"Do I look okay?" Reena asked again, her eyebrows wrinkled with worry as she awaited my response. I smiled, knowing the word "beautiful" didn't quite capture it. She beamed radiance. For this moment, she was the sun, radiating pure and unadulterated joy. I stood there—as I've always stood there, by her side, where I've always been, and where I'd always be. Her eyes were pools of hope, excitement and nervousness. I smiled back, reassuring her that she looked wonderful and that she would be unbelievably happy.

As each bridesmaid walked down the aisle, my nervousness for Reena increased. When the wedding coordinator prompted me for my turn, I gave Reena's hand a quick squeeze and said, "I'll meet you at the end of aisle, Mrs. Chacko." She looked momentarily startled by my use of her soon-to-be last name.

I made my way down the aisle, and my own breath caught in my throat. The interior of the church was an explosion of spring. White, hot pink, and soft pink calla lilies accented with hydrangeas, baby's breath, and champagne colored roses filled two large vases at the altar. A cream runner decorated the aisle and was flagged by soft and hot pink rose petals on both sides while every pew was accented with an elaborate candelabrum intertwined with hot pink and white roses. With a year and a half of planning, there was no detail that had missed Reena's eyes.

I walked down the aisle in awe, continually reminding myself to keep my eyes forward as the wedding coordinator had instructed us. Just as we had rehearsed, Ryan met me at the seventh pew from the front and walked me up the steps to my designated spot right next to where Reena would soon be standing. As he released my elbow, he whispered, "You look gorgeous." Startled, I said nothing and just stared after him as he took his place on the steps of the altar next to Sanjay. Before I could make anything else out of it, the bridal processional song began, and everyone rose to their feet. The double white doors of the church swung wide open, and Reena stood next to her father in all her bridal glory.

Reena walked down the aisle, and everyone's eyes were planted on her as they admired how beautiful she looked in her *Eve of Milday* Chantilly lace dress. The cap sleeve dress tastefully conformed to her silhouette and gracefully curved into a mermaid flare at the tip. I shifted my gaze to Sanjay, whose face revealed a kaleidoscope of emotion, from amazement to adoration to excited nervousness. I have always secretly enjoyed watching the groom as he sees his bride for the first time. Thinking that everyone is looking at the bride, their facial expressions are often unguarded and vulnerable. And Sanjay's face, to my delight, did not disappoint. With his eyes dead-set on Reena, he was looking every bit the smitten groom. I could see the tenderness and love in his eyes and felt assured that my friend would be well taken care of. As I wiped a tear, my eyes encountered Ryan's gaze.

I wondered how long he had been staring at me when he smiled sympathetically and mouthed, "I'm sorry." I returned his smile but quickly looked away. Suddenly, I stood straighter, and nodded in haughty deference as I both acknowledged and dismissed him with a curt, almost imperceptible nod. Guys don't cry at weddings, so to him I was probably just another silly, overly emotional girl. Suddenly I felt like a cliché, the eternal bridesmaid, overcome with emotion, crying at her best friend's wedding. Was she crying tears of joy for her friend or crying, wondering when, if ever, it would be her turn?

Well, I didn't care what he thought. *I* was the one who took care of Reena after her breakup, just as she was the one to take care of me after mine. *I* knew how long and painful the road had been to get here, and *I* had walked every step of that long road right along with her. I had every right to stand here and cry if I wanted.

I glanced at Ryan whose eyes were focused on the groom. So what did *guys* think of at weddings, especially at the wedding of a close friend? I doubted very seriously that they were harboring any similar sentiments of dreams come true and happily-ever-afters. I smiled as I realized that my sentimental "maid of honor" musings would probably send Ryan hurling. No doubt he was more than likely wondering if beer and liquor would be served at the reception and wondering who would be his new wing man during nights out on the town.

As I listened to my own thoughts, I began wondering if maybe I was being a little hard on him. When had I become so pessimistic about men? Or was I actually being realistic for once?

I glanced at Ryan again and had to admit, he was very easy on the eyes. With his Caesar haircut, chiseled features, and light hazel eyes, he was a striking contrast to the other groomsmen and stood head and shoulders above them, figuratively and literally. No doubt the tongues of many of Reena's female wedding guests were wagging and wondering who he was as they plotted how to get his attention. If I were being completely honest with myself, I had to admit that he was probably not only the best looking guy at the wedding but the best looking guy I had seen since Armaan. But I was no longer twenty-two years old, and it now took a lot more than just a pretty face to get my attention and keep it. Nevertheless, I assured myself, I could still admire him without being interested, right? After all, Anjuli was married and happy, and even she couldn't seem to take her eyes off of him.

Not only did Ryan have nice, striking eyes, but he also had thick eyelashes that most girls can only attain with the help of fake eyelashes and mascara. His lips, too, were nicely shaped, I decided. I was admiring their fullness and their sensual curve when I saw the edges of his smile twitch into the slightest of smirks. My eyes flew back to his eyes, and sure enough, he had caught me staring. Great. Wonderful. Not only was I one of those weepy bridesmaids, but he also had sufficient reason to categorize me right with along with Reena's teeny-bopper cousins who were drooling over his good looks.

Much to my chagrin, even after I realized that I was staring at him, I still hadn't managed to look away. So I forced myself to avert my eyes and willed my attention back to the pastor who was delivering the preamble to the vows.

The "I Do's" are a powerful promise to God, and as Reena pledged her love for Sanjay... *for better and for worse, in sickness and in health, for richer and for poorer...* her eyes began brimming with tears. The weight of the words took their toll on me as well, and my eyes began misting against my will. I had probably heard those vows nearly a hundred times over the course of my life, but listening to my best friend repeat them brought a whole new poignancy to the promises, especially when I heard Reena's voice crack with emotion as she repeated them.

After the ceremony, the bridal party took pictures at the altar with Reena and Sanjay, and then we made our way to the reception hall. Reena and Sanjay followed all the traditional observances, including the cutting of the cake and the first dance. I surprisingly got through my maid of honor speech without spilling too many tears.

By the end of the afternoon, the petticoat of my sari was digging into my waist, and my three-inch strappy heels were beginning to take their toll on my feet. Soon all I could think about was getting into a comfortable pair of sweatpants and sneakers. I found myself craving one of those nice, long leisurely walks, especially after such an emotionally and physically taxing day, and following that up with a long, hot bubble bath.

Towards the end of the reception, I escaped to the bathroom to do some last minute touch-ups and re-adjusted my sari, which, to my dismay, was slowly unraveling. When I returned, all the bridesmaids had scattered from the table. Anjuli and Maya were with their significant others while the rest of the bridesmaids were clustered around the groomsmen near the dance floor. I spotted Reena and Sanjay across the hall, making their way to every table, greeting their guests as an official couple. I felt a momentary pang. Reena was always the one person I could count on to keep me company, no matter where we were.

I glanced around the hall, searching for any sign of my parents or my brother, but I hadn't seen them since the wedding ceremony. No doubt watching their daughter's best friend get married while their own daughter remained single was not easy for them, especially when it was probably followed by countless questions from their friends about my marital status.

"You okay?" asked an unfamiliar deep voice. Out of the corner of my eye, I caught sight of shiny black patent dress shoes and black pants and immediately recognized it as belonging to a groomsman.

"Yes, I'm fine." I said, quickly trying to blink away tears. I glanced up to find that it was none other than Ryan. His eyebrows were furrowed, and his lips were pursed as he watched me thoughtfully. I threw him a half-hearted smile and immediately averted my gaze, but I knew it was pointless. I was sure he had already seen my tears.

I waited for the inevitable, "What's wrong?" but instead he looked out into the reception hall and took a slow sip of his drink. "Beautiful wedding, isn't it?"

I breathed a sigh of relief, grateful he didn't press the issue. I nodded and joined him in watching guests milling and socializing through the banquet hall.

"Sanjay said you really helped Reena plan this wedding and that she couldn't have done it without you."

I shrugged. "Well, I kept her company as she made all the final decisions. Sometimes we just need someone to confirm what we already know."

He nodded. "And that was a great speech, by the way." I could feel his gaze on me as if he were waiting for me to look at him. When I did, he held up his drink in a toast.

"Thank you, but it was so easy to say so many great things about Reena. The real challenge was keeping the speech under five minutes."

"It's obvious you guys are very close."

"Yeah, we've been best friends for over twenty-five years!"

"Twenty-five years," he repeated, followed by a low whistle. "Wow. That's quite a history. Sanjay and I have been best friends for about fifteen years. I can imagine how you feel with Reena moving. I'd feel the same way if I had to deal with my best friend not only getting married, but moving across the country."

I looked up at him thoughtfully. Did he really understand or was he just trying to be nice?

He cleared his throat. "So you'll be coming to visit Reena, I'm sure…" He took another sip of his drink and although I wasn't facing him, I could see him intermittently glancing at me. "You know, I live near Sanjay, I'd love to show you around New York. I could even—"

Before he could finish, he was interrupted by Reena's Aunt Mini, who didn't even acknowledge him. "Sarai-mol!" she said, her arms splayed out in greeting. She pulled me into an embrace, and then pulled back, holding my arms out like a ragdoll as she looked me over. "Sarai, you look so beautiful! You know how many aunties are asking me about you for their son?" She then leaned in closely and added, "I told them all you were si*iii*ngle," she said in a sing-song voice. "Your parents may be getting some phone calls soon!"

"Mini Auntie, I'd like you to meet Ryan, Sanjay's best friend." Mini Auntie glanced to the left of me, smiled broadly, then swayed her head from left to right slowly in a hearty approval. All I could do was chuckle at her lack of subtlety.

"And Ryan," I said, wrapping one arm around Mini Auntie's shoulder, "This is Reena's mother's sister. But she's like my own auntie," I declared as I rested my head affectionately on her shoulder.

Mini Auntie then pulled away to grab both of my cheeks and squeeze. "Sarai, I tell you, is like my own daughter. I've known her since she was this big," she said, palm down, as she motioned towards her knees. She regarded him for a moment, her face very serious as she said dead-pan, "She is a good girl, a very good girl."

Ryan chuckled and winked at me, "I'm sure she is."

"Sarai," she said grabbing both my hands with hers, "I wanted to ask you something..." She glanced warily at Ryan before continuing.

Ryan bowed his head and stepped aside discreetly.

"Sarai," she began again and grabbed my hands, clasping them in hers. "I may have a boy for you." She then paused, her eyes in the direction of where Ryan stood and her expression soured.

I turned to glance at Ryan to see what he had done to displease her so quickly, but it wasn't what he had done but rather what was being done to him.

While she had been talking to me, two college-age girls had taken the opportunity to approach Ryan and pull him towards the dance floor. He looked at me helplessly as they literally dragged him to the dance floor. He mouthed something to me that I couldn't decipher, but I just smiled back and then turned my attention back to Mini Auntie who was watching the scene with a pronounced frown.

"Girls, these days... no shame at all," Mini Auntie said shaking her head, her frown deepening. Focusing her attention back on me, she quickly replaced her frown with a broad smile.

"But don't worry. I have this boy for you. He is very nice, handsome, but not too good looking like that boy," she said motioning in

Ryan's direction. "But too good looking is not too good either. He's the son of a friend of mine from nursing school. He is an engineer studying in Bangalore." As soon as she mentioned he was living overseas, I tuned out. She began listing off each of his credentials as if she were reading a resume. I smiled and nodded, doing my best to look interested while all I could think about was planning my escape before I was accosted by additional well-intentioned, self-appointed matchmaking aunties.

When she finished, she squeezed my hands in both of her hands and asked eagerly, "So what do you think? I can give you his number, and you can call him."

I blinked in response. I shouldn't have been caught off guard with her forwardness, especially since she, no doubt like all aunties, clearly saw the expiration date that seemed to hover over my head like a halo. Instead of a clever response, I responded honestly, "I don't think so, Mini Auntie, but thank you."

She said nothing and blinked back at me in surprise as if I had just rejected her own son as a proposal. My instincts kicked in as I sought to do damage control, "M-m-maybe you can talk to my parents about it, Mini Auntie. I wouldn't want to do anything without their approval first."

She shook her head from side to side, and her mouth broke into a very pleased smile. She lightly caressed my cheek and gestured towards the girls on the dance floor. "Sarai, those girls can learn from you. More parents would be lucky to have a daughter like you. Yes, you are right," she added, nodding emphatically. "I will speak to your parents then and let them decide."

I cringed internally and prayed my parents had already left the wedding. I quickly excused myself before Mini Auntie had the bright idea to drag me with her as she looked for them.

I glanced at the dance floor and shook my head in sympathy. Poor Ryan was imprisoned in the middle of a circle of twenty-something girls. Most guys would have been flattered if they had been dragged off by cute college-age girls, but he moved stiffly and almost unwillingly, and his facial expression resembled a puppy dog begging to be rescued from the pound. The girls, on the other hand, seemed to be having a blast dancing with him and were completely oblivious of his reluctance.

He caught me staring in his direction, and suddenly his strained smile transformed into a wide grin. He motioned me towards the dance floor, but before I could even think about what I wanted to do, I was accosted by two more aunties—Anamma Auntie and Marykutty Auntie from church.

"Oh, Sarai-mol, you look so pretty! I just saw your mother, and I told her you were the prettiest bridesmaid." Marykutty Auntie then leaned in towards me and made an attempt to whisper, but somehow her voice still carried the same loud volume and projection. "Mole, she looked so sad. I told her not to worry, that you will be next."

She lightly grabbed my chin between her thumb and index finger and shook it, reducing me to five years old again. "Mole, don't keep your mother waiting too long. She wants to have grandchildren, too, you know." She coyly glanced around and leaned in even closer, whispering loudly. "You know, if you have someone, even if he's not Malayalee, you should tell them. Or you can tell one of us and we'll talk to your parents. They just want you married at this point." She looked at me, her eyes wide with expectation as if she were really waiting for me to make a sudden confession.

I chuckled, partly in surprise at her forwardness, but mostly in annoyance. "Auntie, I assure you there is no one. Now if you'll both excuse me, I have to get home and get back to studying." I had learned long ago that when aunties and uncles bombard you with personal questions, you deflect their questions and then excuse yourself, preferably with something that has to do with studying for a school exam. No auntie or uncle wanted to interfere with any of our "studies." Unfortunately, the latter often left them perplexed since they knew I was no longer in school. But that moment of confused stupor was all I needed to make my getaway.

Despite the pleading glances Ryan was directing towards me, I made the decision, then and there, to make my big escape. The petticoat of my sari was still digging into my waist, and I was ready to shed myself of it. So in the pretense of going to the bathroom, I took a detour and found a discreet side exit out of the reception hall.

But the unseasonal sunny weather had disappeared in the midst of a cold front that must have blown in earlier that afternoon. The afternoon had a light gray, dismal mood to it. But somehow it beckoned me still.

By the time I arrived at home, my parents had already changed out of their wedding clothes and were sitting comfortably around the living room fireplace. If my parents had been questioned about my marital status, to my relief, neither of them said a word to me about it.

I changed quickly into some jeans and a sweater and grabbed a windbreaker. "You're going into the cold?" my mom asked, her forehead crinkled with worry. "Stay inside where it's warm. It's supposed to get colder by evening."

"Don't worry, mom, I won't be gone long. I just want to get some fresh air." I stopped by her chair and kissed her scrunched up eyebrows. As I walked towards the front door, the phone rang. I was tempted to keep walking but when I glanced at my mom, she was sitting comfortably in her recliner with a book in hand and a chenille blanket across her lap. I looked longingly outside and sighed as I picked up the cordless phone.

"Hey! There you are!" said Reena, "Why'd you leave without saying good-bye?"

"My heels and sari were killing me, Reen. I just had to come home and change. Sorry."

"Well, are you coming back?! Everyone is on the dance floor!"

"Honestly, Reen, I'm exhausted. I've been up since four this morning, remember?"

"Okay, okay, I know. I understand. But you're missing out! A particular groomsman was looking for you and hoping to get in a dance with you. He is going to be disappointed to learn that you've already left."

"Oh, really," I mumbled as I looked longingly through the living room window.

"So yeah, apparently Ryan couldn't stop talking about you to Sanjay."

"Oh, okay," I replied. The wind had picked up, and I could feel the cold through the window. Yeah, my windbreaker would definitely not be enough. I made a mental note to grab one of my heavier coats just in case it got colder during my walk.

Reena sighed helplessly. "So okay, okay, fine, you've twisted my arm, so I'll tell you what he said. But first, you have to promise me not to breathe a word of this—Sanjay asked me not to say a word, so do NOT tell him I told you—but how could he think I wouldn't tell you?! Anyways, apparently Ryan told Sanjay he thought you were beautiful, *and* he said," Reena's voice dropped to a whisper, "and I quote, 'that he is going to marry you!'"

Or maybe another sweater under the windbreaker would suffice. After all, I would be walking, so I might get hot with all of those layers. "Oh, really?" I asked. I glanced at the sneakers I was wearing and wondered if I should put on my winter boots.

Apparently, I wasn't giving Reena the reaction she had hoped and her exasperated voice pierced my thoughts. "Sarai! Did you hear what I said? What is wrong with you? Are you even paying attention to me?"

"What?" I asked and then absently repeated her words, "Marry... he wants to marry me." I was caught off guard by my own repeated words. "*Marry me?* Who wants to marry me?"

"Ah, ha! I knew it! So you weren't paying attention! Ryan said he wanted to marry you!"

"Ryan?"

"Ryan, the best man, remember? The guy with the hazel eyes who fits your Dream Man list, but for some asinine reason, you won't give him the time of day."

"Actually, I did talk to him," I stated.

"You did?! *Really?!* When?! What did you talk about? Tell me everything!"

"There's not much to tell. We were just chit-chatting during the reception. He seems like a nice guy."

"He IS a nice guy, Sarai. A really nice guy, and I think there's serious potential with him. I wouldn't set you up with him otherwise. Not to mention, your dad is going to be happy."

"Really? And why is that?"

"Hell*ooo,* he's a doctor. Your father will finally get the 'nice, doctor son' he's always wanted."

I chuckled. At this point, I think my dad would have been happy if I would just agree to marry anyone, as long as he was, of course, Christian and Indian. But Reena was right. He would be thrilled. It had been so long since my dad had been happy with me that all I could recall from the last few years were his lectures, reprimands, scowls, and grunts.

"So what do you think? What do you feel?" Reena asked, excitedly.

What did I feel? Should I be honest and tell her beyond finding him very good looking, I felt absolutely nothing? But based on her excitement, I didn't think that was something Reena wanted to hear. So I used the most non-descript word I could think of: "Uhhh, *good,* I guess. I feel good," pondering the word and remembering how I once hated its vagueness. "Yeah good is probably the best word to describe it, I think."

My lack of enthusiasm was lost on Reena, who was already too busy planning my wedding. "Sarai! Oh, my gosh—isn't this perfect?! If things work out between you two, that means you, too, might have to move to New York! And they're best friends, and we're best friends. Two best friends marrying two other best friends! We don't have to worry about our spouses liking each other! We couldn't have planned it any better!"

I could only laugh at Reena's extreme optimism. "Whoa, there cowgirl, you need to slow it down." Love looked good on her. It had softened her rough, pessimistic edges and added a more romantic, if slightly unrealistic, layer to her personality. If I weren't the focus of her new-found optimism, I would have appreciated it even more.

"So can I give him your number?"

I sighed dramatically and relented, knowing full well it would be futile to resist. "Yes, you can give him my number."

"Good because I was going to give it to him anyway!"

I laughed and replied, "I wouldn't have expected anything less."

She was quiet for a moment and when she spoke, her voice brimmed with anticipation. "Can you feel it, Sarai? This is going to happen!" she asked.

I was busy staring longingly out the window, and I absent-mindedly responded, "No, not really." Reena sighed audibly, sounding like a tire that was losing all its air. Before I deflated all her optimism, I quickly added, "At least not yet."

"Just give it a chance, Sarai. That's all I'm asking. I can't explain it. I just have this feeling. Even Sanjay said he's never seen him like this before. He typically has girls beating down his door, but he is very taken with you. And while I was upset that you initially blew him off, I think it's actually the best thing you could have done."

"I wasn't blowing him off!" I protested. "I wasn't doing anything!"

"Well, whatever you did or didn't do, it worked! Do you know how many people were asking me about him? And despite all the other pretty girls at my wedding, the only one he seemed to have eyes for was you!"

So he was taken with me? How could he have been taken with me so quickly? We barely had a few words of conversation.

"You're different," Reena observed.

"Really? How so?" I asked curiously. I felt different, so I guess I probably came across different.

"A year ago, you would have been all over this, and now you could almost care less."

A year ago, Ryan would have definitely been on my radar. I had caught him staring at me more than a few times, but I learned long ago not to pay attention to a silly boy's stares, much less listen to what a boy says, even when he explicitly tells you to call him or email him.

"I wouldn't say that I could care less," I said, recalling the last time we had jumped to conclusions with Amit and how quickly things had fallen apart. I had learned to quit trying to predict life. I would take life one day at a time, allowing it to unveil itself to me. I was open, and that's the most I could promise. Besides God, who really knew what the future held?

"I'm going to give him your number, okay? Just promise me you'll give this a chance."

I hesitated, feeling that I was at the allegorical fork in the road. Experience could have easily made me bitter and closed off. I hadn't given up hope by any means, but I no longer wanted another contrived setup. I thought of Italian Arman and how things just flowed naturally with him. It wasn't awkward or forced, and it was refreshing to see that a guy could not only find me attractive but also take the initiative with me all on his own, without being prompted by his family or mine.

Reena was waiting for my promise, and I knew that an "I guess" would not be good enough. Well, it was her wedding day, and I couldn't let Reena down on her wedding day.

"I promise," I assured her, as I simultaneously made a promise to myself.

Finally satisfied that I was committed to keeping up my end of the bargain, Reena let me get off the phone. I hung up the phone and quickly ran into my room to grab a thicker coat and a wool scarf. I wrapped the scarf around my neck and tucked it securely in my coat as I made my way to Central.

Chapter 60
The Chrysalis

THE SKY IS pallid and grey, a befitting backdrop to an otherwise barren, dead landscape. The cold, dreary weather permeates the atmosphere, sending a deep chill through me despite the layers of clothing. When I arrive at Central, I see that it is completely empty. Dry, brittle twigs and branches snap beneath my feet as I walk the well-worn path, past the swings of my childhood, refusing to veer off to the left or to the right, walking past the bridge of my youth. With eyes focused, I march on, refusing to be pulled back into the web of self-pity that had entangled me for so long. I march on forward, eager to see something new. The landscape, once thriving and full of life, now looks naked, stripped of its golden, autumn beauty, which lays crumbled and gray like ashes beneath thin spiny limbs. But even in the desolate bareness of the trees, there is an arresting beauty. A beauty in its nakedness. A sereneness in its very stillness.

For a moment, it feels as if time has stopped. There is no wind, not even the slightest breeze. I have been here hundreds of times since childhood, and yet here I am, now a thirty-year-old adult, feeling like I am seeing it all for the very first time. It is almost as if my vision had blurred through the years, dulling my perception, and without realizing it, I have been looking at everything askew. Now everything seems so crisp, clear, and bright again, and I could finally see what I had once been blind to. During the winter, everything had always seemed so dead, but I finally understand that to make room for the new, the old had to be shed. This time, amongst all the barren, bare branches, I could see beauty. The beauty of what once was and what would be once again.

I breathe in the chilly air, the acrid coldness pinching my nostrils like a sneeze. As I survey my surroundings, I look around the familiar terrain. Was it over a year and a half ago that I had come back from India and walked here with Reena as she told me about her engagement? And was it only the year before that when Armaan broke the news of his own engagement? Like the rings of a tree, each of these events marks a significant year in my life. And now another year has come and gone. And soon enough, this moment, too, would be a distant memory. I could suddenly feel time ticking again. It is as palpable as my heartbeat. I can feel the grainy sands of time slipping through my fingers. As much as I want to curl my palm into a fist, it is inevitably slipping through my fingers. I have only one choice, I realize. To embrace it. To embrace this life—*my* life. Because Life is happening—with or without me. There was already so much wasted time spent on wishing, wanting, waiting… when life was all around me, ready to be experienced and enjoyed.

Our lives are like this forest. Seasons of beginnings and endings, marking both life and beauty as well as desolation and emptiness, all leading us to where we are, where we are meant to be.

I dig my hands deeper into my pockets in a futile attempt for warmth and march on, eager to explore parts of the forest that I had never seen. It seems to go on for miles, but how far had I ever gotten? Something had always stopped me from exploring—busyness, laziness, fear. I always said that I wanted to explore, but somehow I never had the time. But now the trail lies before me, a seemingly never-ending road of possibility stretches before me, winding and twisting, leading me, and now Life has simultaneously presented me all the time, the interest, and opportunity. As I walk, some markers are initially familiar, but soon enough, I am on unfamiliar ground.

I haven't even gotten farther than a mile when I come upon it—there amongst the brittle, dead, seemingly barren branches—one little leafling pushing through the lifeless tree bark. A bud. Alone in its dark green, fragile glory, it dares to breach its tiny blade through. It is a reminder that yes, change is on its way and what was once barren would bear life once again. One small bud. Of Hope. Of Life. I smile at the reminder.

With outstretched arms, I lift my head to the waning sun and twirl around slowly and then faster, faster—for after the winter, the spring surely comes, and with it, I, too, am reborn.

The ~~End~~ Beginning

Reading Group Discussion Questions

1. In the first part of the novel, Sarai describes initially meeting Armaan in terms of a romantic Bollywood movie. She also references several Bollywood movies, movie stars, and later even likens their break-up to a tragic, romantic Bollywood film. How do these references reflect Sarai's initial attitudes towards love and romance?

2. Why do you think Sarai has such a hard time getting over Armaan?

3. Although she admits Armaan does not meet several of the more important qualities on "The List," why is he so perfect in Sarai's eyes?

4. Do you think Sarai's description of Armaan is a realistic depiction or more of an idealization?

5. The novel opens with Sarai dreaming of getting married while the following chapters liken her to a bride getting dressed for her wedding. Were you surprised to discover that Sarai is not attending her own wedding to Armaan but rather Armaan's wedding to another woman?

6. Why do you think the author intentionally presents the opening chapters to lead you to believe she was getting dressed for her own wedding?

7. Do you think Sarai is truly open-minded about an arranged marriage when she agrees to go to India?

8. Do you think Sarai is settling when she agrees to marry Jensin?

9. After agreeing to marry Jensin, why does Sarai then compare him to Armaan?

10. Why do you think Jensin's family withdraws their marriage proposal?

11. Do you find it ironic that while Sarai flies across the world to look for a husband, Reena ends up meeting her future husband staying right where she is? Why do you think that is?

12. Do you think Sarai's trip to India was a wasted effort? Why or why not?

13. Why do you think Amit never calls Sarai even though he seems interested in her and prolongs their date by a couple of hours?

14. Do you think Amit's response, or lack thereof, has a lasting effect on Sarai?

15. Why is Sarai is so insistent to celebrate her 30th birthday overseas?

16. As she attends mass in St. Peter's Basilica, she seems to be seeking answers from God regarding her life. She can feel His presence, but just as she almost reaches enlightenment, it seems to evade her. Why do you think Sarai is so eager to have this epiphany in Italy?

17. Why is it almost more meaningful that Sarai has her epiphany in her childhood bedroom, after her trip, rather than the hallowed halls of the Sistine Chapel or St. Peter's Basilica?

18. What is Sarai's epiphany?

19. What realization does she come to regarding Armaan's role in her life and her trip to India?

20. Why does Sarai coyly evade Italian Arman's suggestion that she consider staying in Italy?

21. Why is Sarai's father so insistent that he and Sarai's mother had an arranged marriage, even though Sarai confronts him with the truth?

22. If Sarai's parents did indeed have a love marriage, why do you think her father is not more open-minded and understanding towards Sarai wanting to wait and marry for love?

23. Although Sarai has no romantic interest in Rakesh, why is she so visibly upset when she learns he is engaged?

24. Why isn't Sarai more interested in Ryan even though, as Reena pointed out, he clearly fits each and every quality on "The List"?

25. How has Sarai's attitude towards love and life shifted by the end of the novel? What do you think contributed most to that shift?

26. Do you think Sarai ends up with Ryan or do you think she'll contact Italian Arman?

27. Why do you think the author is intentionally vague about Sarai's future?

28. Why are only the first and last chapters of the novel named and what is the significance of those titles?

29. How is the theme of rebirth depicted throughout the novel?

30. Why is the entire novel relayed in past tense while the last chapter is in present tense? What was the author trying to convey with that shift?

About the Author

Like many first-generation Indians, Bindu started college as a pre-med student but eventually diverted from that traditional, well-worn path and pursued her love of books and writing. She graduated *Summa Cum Laude* with a Bachelor of Science degree (courtesy of all those pre-med classes) and double majors in English and Mass Media, along with a host of accolades, including the President's Award and Omicron Delta Kappa (ODK). She later pursued a master's degree in English, but her strong writing and people skills, along with the fervent desire for food, shelter, and clothing, eventually led her towards a very non-literary career path in the software industry. But it was in the midst of the daily 8 to 5 grind where she reconnected with her early love of writing and eventually completed her first novel, *The Chrysalis*, along with *38 Candles*, a personal memoir that describes the rediscovery of her dream to write a novel and her journey to publication.

Although Bindu currently lives in sunny South Florida, she is still known to say "y'all" with a strong Southern drawl, a dead giveaway of her early Texas roots. An avid chai and coffee connoisseur, she loves discovering new coffee houses and browsing in bookstores. She is currently working on her next novel, *Almost Paradise: Book 1 of The Garden of Eden*, a serialized Young Adult (YA) novel.

Coming Soon...

Almost Paradise

Book I of *The Garden of Eden*

Chapter 1
Déjà Vu

S HE WAS DREAMING, Eden assured herself, as she clenched the red crushed velvet seat of the carriage. It was a feeble attempt to steady herself as the carriage rocked and swayed, thrusting her from one end of the plush bench seat to the other. Using one hand to secure herself, she used the other to shove aside the matching velvet curtain that draped over the carriage windows as she attempted to gain her bearings. Dusk had already descended but the moon was full, casting an eerie silver glow, only to merge and disappear amongst the dark shadows of the trees that surrounded them to the left. Déjà Vu. *But where was she this time?* She moved to the right window, pushing it open, and peered out, only to freeze, as her heart skipped a few beats. She was in a carriage, she realized, traveling at break-neck speed. As she craned her neck out the window, she could see the carriage was being pulled by horses as they raced uphill at breakneck speed, racing up a jagged, stony mountainside. She looked even further ahead and could see the carriage was headed towards a precipice that then dropped off into a black abyss. Her heart rate immediately quickened. She knew she would have only a limited amount of time to slow the horses down. If they continued at this speed, she doubted they could stop in time and the carriage, along with the horses, would be catapulted right past the precipice towards the same dark abyss that shouldered the road. But how could she stop them? She looked down worriedly at the sound of the wheels as they crunched, wavered, and wobbled over the various rocks that comprised the makeshift road. The wooden wheels of the carriage looked perilously close to becoming unhinged as they turned frenetically up the rocky road, just inches away for mountain's edge.

She pulled herself back into the carriage and closed her eyes. *Think!* she pleaded with herself. And as if she didn't have enough to worry about, out of the corner of her eye, she caught the flutter of something fly past her window. Once again, she peered out the window and saw two large bats flying in perfect speed with the carriage. *Where did they come from?* She glanced behind the carriage and saw an entire swarm of them, heading right towards the carriage! And then as if on cue, in the distance, she could also faintly hear the howling of wolves. It all felt a little too familiar. Daresay, even a bit contrived...perhaps something more out of Bram's Stroker's Dracula or The Wolfman rather than a scene out of her own life. So maybe she *was* dreaming then?! She closed her eyes tightly and then opened them. Nothing had changed. *Wake up!* she begged herself as her desperation built. The precipice was getting closer, but even if she could get them to suddenly stop, she would then have to contend with the bats that were chasing her and the carriage. She clenched her fists again and lowered her eyes, prepared to will herself to wake up. It was then she caught sight of what she was wearing. She was dressed in a long-sleeve grey dress with a fitted, corseted top and a voluminous skirt. She *was* dreaming, she reassured herself and closed her eyes briefly in relief. In the first place, she did not own any outfit that even remotely resembled the Victorian-era. Second, she wouldn't be caught dead, much less alive, in any voluminous dress that restricted her ability to breathe or move freely. There was only so much she was willing to sacrifice for fashion.

Once she established that she was dreaming, she was then hit with that distinct feeling of déjà vu. It was a faint feeling at first but then gained strength with every passing second. The more she thought about it, the more convinced she was that this had all happened before. Then like reading a script, she began to recall the scene more clearly. It was most definitely a dream, she assured herself. The scene was all too familiar. She *had* been here before.

But if this were déjà vu, she postulated, then that meant that if she were to look outside, on top of the carriage, she would see her father at the helm, dressed in Victorian footman garb as he guided the horses through the night. As she thought it, she pushed aside the glass, despite her fear of the bats, and peaked around to the upper front of the carriage, and sure enough there was the familiar robust shape of her father, holding the reigns of the four horses.

And if this were déjà vu, her older sister would be resting in the carriage with her, quietly in the corner. As soon as Eden pulled herself back through the window, there was her sister, sitting across from her, eyes closed and chest moving gently as she slept the sleep of the innocent.

So if this was one of those déjà vu dreams, then what happened next? *Think*, she urged herself, *think*, but her mind was blank. All she could hear was the beat of her own heart as it beat in rhythm with the steady, pounding sound of the horse hooves as they continued to rush along the rugged Transylvanian-like terrain, pulling the carriage along in a mad dash.

And then it hit her. If this was a dream, she could fly, right? Yes, one could always fly, especially in one's own dreams. She would fly herself out of this predicament. So she began flapping her arms. Up and down. First slowly and then rapidly. But nothing happened. She tried again, faster this time, but by then, it was too late. She heard the horses neigh as they continued to gallop past the final feet of land, straight past the precipice and into the air. For a few brief seconds, their furious leg movements kept the wagon raised in the air but then gravity took over, sucking everything down into a vacuum-like vortex.

As she fell, she could see the bats, just outside the window, their thin, black semi-transparent wings grazing the glass as they descended upon the carriage, following it like vultures ready to feed on whatever was left of the soon-to-be wreckage. And just as she braced her body for the inevitable crash, without understanding how it was even possible, she felt herself being pulled from the carriage. Then like an out-of-body experience, she watched the carriage tumble down the mountaintop just moments before it splintered into a thousand pieces at the base of the mountain.

For a moment, she thought maybe her attempt to fly actually worked. But she soon felt strong secure arms lifting and carrying her away, far away from the scene of the accident and far away from the bats that eagerly swarmed the wreckage like flies on a rotting carcass.

Her head throbbed as her face rested against something that reminded her of cold metal. She opened her eyes, realizing her guess hadn't been that far off. She looked up, eager to see the face of this hero who had just rescued her from death. But his face, too, was covered with the same metal armor that covered the rest of his body. Her very own Knight in Shining Armor! There were so many questions that clouded her mind. *Who are you? Where did you come from? What about my family?* But before she could even begin her tirade of questions, he removed his helmet, and all her questions drowned at the back of her throat. She couldn't even remember to breathe as she stared at the most mesmerizing, ice blue eyes that were looking back at her, concern in their eyes, as they eagerly searched her face to ensure she was unhurt. His face was perfectly symmetrical face, with soft angles, giving him a slightly boyish appearance. His skin was smooth like marble and almost poreless, contrasting with the jet blackness of his hair. A small lock of hair strayed onto his forehead, making him appear even more boyish. As she made her way back to staring at his eyes again, which shimmered iridescently in the light, all Eden could think was that he was the most beautiful man she had ever seen in her life.

He moved quickly and effortlessly, almost gracefully as if gliding through the air. When she did look down, she saw his feet did not touch the ground. She wanted to ask him how he had managed to fly because she somehow couldn't even though it had been her own dream. She wanted to ask him so many things, but her head ached and throbbed. And before she could ask even one question, her surroundings began spinning and then reeling as seconds later, she lost consciousness.

Eden's body convulsed and then jerked awake from her dream to find herself exactly where she had been before she had fallen asleep 20 minutes earlier—in the back seat of her parents' Buick LaSabre. She, her father, and her older sister Elizabeth—Liz, as she preferred to be called—continued the trek home from a week of touring college campuses in California. As reality came rushing back to her, her heart still pounded from the excitement of her vivid dream. Déjà vu indeed! No wonder it had seemed so familiar. This was the sixth time in a row that she had had the same dream. The same dream and to her dismay, the same ending. Despite her efforts to change it in her dream, it always ended with the carriage, along with her father and sister, falling into the unknown abyss. And somehow, each time, by some miracle or mishap she survived while they hadn't. But this time her miracle was in the form of a beautiful stranger decked in shining armor. She smiled at the memory of his face and a delicious shiver went up her spine as she recalled his blue eyes as they looked at her.

But, she reminded herself, it was only a dream. No, she corrected herself, except for the knight, it was a nightmare, albeit a beautiful nightmare. Regardless, though, she was safe now. Seated in the back seat of her parents' silver blue sedan, she and her family were all safe from crazy, out of control horses, dangerous cliffs, bats, vampires, werewolves, and whatever other creatures awaited her during her sleep.

Her older sister slept soundly in the front seat, passenger side, and Eden's father drove their car and maneuvered it expertly as it sped around the narrow road that wrapped around the perilous mountainside of California's Pacific Coast highway. They, minus her mom and younger sister Hannah, had spent the weekend checking out Stanford University and were slowly making their way down California Highway 1 to Los Angeles to check out the UCLA campus. Liz had been accepted into both universities and wanted to visit both schools before making her final decision.

After forgetting her own iPhone, Eden borrowed her father's anti-quated iPod and was listening to his special mix of 70s and 80s music that he had grown up on. Journey, REO Speedwagon, Jefferson Starship, Survivor. She had to admit that the music wasn't half bad and was humming and tapping her fingers in rhythm to the "Eye of the Tiger" when she glanced at the front seat and caught her father looking at her through the rear-view mirror with a questioning look. He gave her a thumbs up and then a thumbs down to ask if she liked the music.

She smiled and nodded her head, and he immediately responded with a broad, toothy grin. Eden chuckled to herself, knowing her dad was loving the fact that she thought his music was cool. Unlike her sister who detested anything that wasn't current and "in style," Eden often had a tendency to prefer the quirky or unusual, which was why she probably shared a special bond with her father. She sighed and went back to staring at the breathtaking view of the water.

An hour later, though, she grew bored and removed her headphones, opting to let them drape around her neck, and edged closer to the passenger's back side window to stare out at the vast ocean that lurked just a stone's throw away. Dusk, her favorite time of the day, had descended, but to her dismay, it was rapidly surrendering to night. Eden briefly lowered the window and rested her hands on the window. Closing her eyes, she allowed the cool Pacific evening to caress her face as the strong wind whipped her hair into a frenzy mess. She smiled as she listened to the crashing of the waves, reminding her of childhoods on Port St. Lucie beach, where her Aunt Beth and Uncle Lou lived. For as long as she could remember, she had always been entranced by the sound of crashing waves, the steady rhythmic patterns had a soothing effect on her, lulling her to close her eyes.

An unexpected blast of cold wind caused Eden's eyes to shoot open. She shivered involuntarily. The wind had suddenly taken on a more frigid feel. She lowered her view to the ocean below. These ocean waves were nothing like her memories of childhood. These waves were menacing and wild as they crashed with unapologetic force into the jagged rocks at the base of the mountain. As she stared at the white foamy chaos beneath her, she was struck by how only a few inches seemed to separate their car from the edge of the road, which was also the edge of the mountain. Just a few inches and their car, too, would be a crashing heap piled against those jagged rocks.

Succumbing once again to her fear of heights, Eden breathed in deep and edged her way back to the driver's side. She wiped her sweaty palms against her jeans and folded her arms across her chest, trying to soothe away the goosebumps and raised hairs on her arms. She tried to forget that just inches separated their car from disaster and attempted to turn her attention to the other side of the road. But it was too late. Night had descended, and the tall magnificent redwood trees that had dotted the left side of the road only moments before were now almost indiscernible. In the dimly lit night sky, they, too, had taken on an almost menacing quality, their shadows casting eerie shapes, preying on old but not forgotten childhood fears.

And then as she continued to look outside, those shadows were quickly replaced with utter darkness. It was as though a black fog had stealthily enveloped their car, encasing them like a tomb. Even the headlights on their car were unable to penetrate the thick fog and were functionally useless. Eden looked back in her seat to see if any cars drove behind them, but they were completely alone on the road. Except for the dim lights on the dashboard of the car, they were basically in darkness. She glanced at her father's reflection through the rear-view mirror. His eyebrows were furrowed together and his eyes were erratically moving left to right and back as he struggled to navigate the car through the fog. He gripped the steering wheel so tightly that his hands looked almost white rather than their usual weathered tan color. Eden glanced up at the sky, but even the full moon that had filled the night sky with light only minutes before was now imperceptible through this dark fog. She attempted to peer out the window again and this time she got a whiff of a burnt, acrid stench. Not quite like sulfur but something even harsher. Once she smelled it, the scent seemed to permeate the air. It seared through her nostrils, burning through each nerve ending from the inside of her nose to deep inside her lungs.

Finally her eyes caught the indistinct shape of something, almost a movement, just outside the side of their car. She jerked around in her seat but there was no sign of another car behind them. She peered closer, blinking, then squinting her eyes, trying her best to make something out. Finally, her eyes adjusted to the darkness and she was finally able to make out the curved, feathered shape of a wing. A very large wing. Was it a bird… maybe an eagle or even a vulture? Whatever it was, it was huge, and it had a tremendously large wing span. She leaned closer to the window when suddenly the outline of blood red eyes peered right back at her. She opened her mouth to unleash a blood-curling scream, just as she felt a thud against the car, sending the car off the road and to the very edge of the mountain. Her father swerved to the left but another thud caused the car to skid to the right again. Before she could scream again, she knew her father had lost control of their car. The car spun off the road, over the rocks that formed a fragile barrier, and then veered off the mountain. It momentarily suspended in air, only to come crashing down with an uncontrollable speed into the same rabid, foamy waters and jagged rocks Eden had feared just minutes earlier.

Déjà vu indeed.

But this time, it was no dream, and unlike her dream, no beautiful, dark-haired knight decked out in shining armor appeared at the final minute to save her.